NIGHTBREAKER

COCO MA

VIKING

VIKING

An imprint of Penguin Random House LLC, New York

First published in the United States of America by Viking, an imprint of Penguin Random House LLC, 2023

Visit us online at PenguinRandomHouse.com.

Library of Congress Cataloging-in-Publication Data is available.

ISBN 9780593621462

1st Printing

Printed in the United States of America

LSCH

Design by Anabeth Bostrup

Text set in Garamond MT Std

To Holly Root and Holly Black.
You make the stars seem within reach.

FIFTEEN YEARS AGO

MANHATTAN, NEW YORK

7:05 a.m.

It begins with a rumble.

A crowd waits at the yellow stripe marking the edge of the abyss.

Disgruntled businesspeople. Overworked laborers. Miserable parents still two cups of coffee away from being truly awake, their equally miserable school-bound spawn clinging to their legs like lint.

To them, it's just another day.

Then, their ears perk up. The distant screech of metal on metal has never sounded so sweet. Even before the train careens into the station and heaves to a stop, they surge forward. Of course, there's another train coming in two minutes, but they're hell-bent on boarding *this* one, no matter the cost.

It will be a bloodbath.

The doors slide open. Before the mob can pile onto the train, a girl darts out. Her backpack is slung over one shoulder, and a pair of shoes—her racing spikes—dangle from a clip attached to the handle. Her twist braids bounce as she gusts through the gaps in the crowdlike wind through the trees.

She can't be late. Not today.

She hurdles over the turnstile. She imagines a cheering crowd, brilliant white stadium lights, the brick-red rubber track beneath her feet. Taking the steps two at a time, she sprints up the stairs leading to the street. Halfway to the top, she feels it.

That first rumble.

It passes through the soles of her sneakers as she emerges street level, all the way up her spine to the base of her skull. The hairs on her arms stand on end. It might've just been from the vibrations of the trains thundering through the tunnels far below, or maybe an earthquake—unlikely in New York, but isn't anything possible here?

Yet her instincts tell her that this is different.

She casts an anxious glance at the people flocking past. No one else seems to notice. And when she catches a glimpse of the time displayed on her phone screen above a photo of her with her little cousin, she swears and continues across the intersection.

Before she can take another step, another rumble rolls through the city. As if Manhattan itself is shuddering. This time, it's loud enough to make the people falter, the traffic waver.

BOOM.

One second she's crossing the intersection, the next she's lying flat on her back, deaf to all but the high-pitched whine in her ears. She blinks. People are getting out of their cars in slow motion. What is she still doing in the middle of the street? *I must be blocking the traffic*, she thinks dully. *I have to get out of their way.*

She picks herself off the gritty asphalt, her ears still ringing, an apology on her lips. Everyone is pointing, shouting—at her? No. She turns around and looks to the sky. She blinks again and again, trying to make sense of the images her eyes are feeding to her brain.

In the distance, colossal, dirty white clouds billow out of the ground, like a volcano erupting in the heart of a concrete jungle. The fog swells upward, thick and viscous and opaque, engulfing all the surrounding buildings in an instant. It spills across the rooftops, devouring even the tallest of skyscrapers.

BOOM! BOOM! BOOM!

Explosion after explosion rocks Manhattan to the core. Dozens of white plumes surge into the sky from the Financial District all the way to Harlem.

The people panic. They stampede straight toward her.

Nauseous with fear, she flees, swept up by the tide. A man crashes into her from behind. She lurches as he grabs on to her backpack to keep from falling. Her racing spikes rip free, and the man topples to the ground. Still running, she glances back, but the masses have already engulfed him.

The wail of police sirens gets tangled with the screams, the chaos. When an ambulance slows down to load an unconscious woman into the back, the fog catches up. The siren chokes off. The red-and-blue emergency lights snuff out like a candle flame.

No one is going to save anyone.

She darts onto a side street, holding her phone to her ear, her hand trembling so hard that she almost drops it. It rings on and on. Heart sinking, she realizes she's called an empty apartment—Dad's already on his shift at the hospital, and Mom is attending the United Nations General Assembly on the East Side. She hits the only other number she has on speed dial.

"Please, please." She pants, hiding behind the corner of a building. Alone. With each empty ring, she feels her hope shrivel to a husk. Then—

"Jiě jie?" answers a young child, her voice like light breaking through the clouds. *"Are you coming over today to play?"*

She opens her mouth to reply and immediately bursts into tears.

"*Is that your cousin on the phone?*" another voice asks in the background, over the familiar *chop-chop-chop* of a knife on a bamboo cutting board and the crackling sizzle of vegetables in the pan. "*Is she okay?*"

"*Are you okay, jiě jie?*"

The ground beneath her feet quakes.

She manages to gasp out three last words into the phone.

"Don't . . . go . . . outside."

Up ahead, a bright orange steam chimney with fluorescent white stripes rises out of the intersection. A ubiquitous fixture of Manhattan, bordering on iconic.

It blows up.

The force of the blast sends her flying. Her phone wrenches from her grip as steam gushes out of the earth. Blistering heat sears every inch of her exposed skin. The stretch of asphalt she stood upon seconds ago fractures and collapses inward. The gaping crater it leaves in its wake sucks in traffic lights, street signs, and New Yorkers alike. Twenty, thirty, forty people gone. Consumed, just like that.

She is glad she cannot hear the screams.

The clouds of steam tumble down toward her like an avalanche of fog, blanketing the street in an impenetrable haze. Everything it touches seems to disappear within, even the light. *Especially* the light. The fog circles around her, swirling and nebulous, almost hypnotic.

She's the last one standing. But she has nowhere left to run.

The fog closes in, filling her lungs—

And Manhattan goes dark.

TODAY

CHAPTER ONE

These days, the only time I have to kill monsters is after school.

It's also the only time I can do it unnoticed. So that's how I've ended up here, lying spread-eagle in the middle of the subway tracks, bleeding out in the darkness with no hope of backup.

I can still see the remains of the shortcake I brought to bait the Deathling out of the corner of my eye, the pretty white frosting and jellied strawberries splattered along the grimy rails like a smashed-in skull.

I try to stay perfectly still as the Deathling sniffs at me. It reeks of sewage and sulfur and piss. The sound of its labored breathing grows louder and louder until its snuffling wet lips brush against my ear. It takes every ounce of control to stop myself from cringing away from those endless rows of teeth.

Since we were children, the rules when it comes to Deathlings have been drilled into our brains.

The first: *When curfew bells begin to sound, it's time for all to be homebound.*

The second: *Don't eat sweets below the streets.*

And finally: *Never let yourself be caught.*

Simple as that. Three rules of survival that any kindergartner could recite to you. Three rules I *could* have followed. Maybe today will be the day I finally learn my lesson.

My grip tightens on the gun clenched in my fist as I wait for my chance. I've only got one nitro-novae bullet left. I can't waste it.

I can only imagine how exasperated Maura will be if I survive to tell her this tale. My older sister's voice fills my head: *How in the name of Lady Liberty do you always get yourself into these messes, mèi mei?*

✳

It all started this afternoon. I stuff my *Inhuman Anatomy IV* textbook into my locker and exchange it for my skateboard and my gun. I tuck the weapon into the inner chest pocket of my blazer right as the bell rings and students flood the hallways of Financial District Preparatory.

I barely beat the rush to the elevators. My ears pop as we descend.

22 . . . 21 . . . 20 . . .

At 1, the burnished gold doors open to the school's lobby with a *ding*, where a burly security guard sits behind the desk. "Have a safe nightfall," he bids each of us as we scurry out.

I weave down Rector Street through rush-hour traffic on my board, veering recklessly between bright yellow taxicabs and buses crammed with people. Their windows reflect the overcast sky, pale gray with wisps of clouds and smog. Slews of bicyclists clog the gaps between each lane, each space barely the width of their handlebars. With the subways shut down, the perpetual war over parking spots, and constant traffic gridlock, most people would choose death by side-view mirror any day.

I make it to the shops in one piece. The owner of the local bakery hovers by the entrance, her weary eyes grimly supervising a construction crew installing a new steel storefront gate lined with spikes. The previous one lies discarded to the side, so severely dented and mottled with teeth marks that it would sooner be showcased at the MoMA than successfully fortify a window. I duck inside, inhaling the sweet aroma of freshly baked cakes and pastries. If only it were less irresistible, maybe the storefront gate wouldn't have needed a replacement.

"Didn't think you'd make it," says the lady at the till, handing a large white box secured with ribbon over the counter to me. I'm the only customer left. "We were just about to burn it."

Before I can reply, a dissonant *CLANG! CLANG! CLAAAANG!* shatters the air.

Something shifts. Like a sudden icy chill sweeping the streets, everyone flurries into motion. The cashier tucks a leftover croissant into my hand and ushers me out onto the sidewalk, where the construction crew hastily tightens the final screw, throws their gear into a gray van, and screeches off. Around me, the city hunkers down, doors locking, shades shuttering, windows going dark.

I should hurry back to my dorm, too. To safety.

But I have something to take care of.

Picking up speed, I skate back to Rector Street, the box cradled in my arms. As I swerve around the corner, I almost crash directly into a pair of enforcers. One of them hollers after me.

"Stop right there!"

Reluctantly, I skid to a halt.

They wear identical dark green uniforms. The taller of the pair pushes a cart on wheels while the other brandishes a shovel at my face. One sniff of the overwhelmingly pungent smell of coffee beans wafting from the cart makes me wrinkle my nose.

"Where do you think you're going?" the one with the shovel demands. "Don't you hear the bells?"

I widen my eyes as if just noticing the warning trills echoing throughout the whole of Manhattan. "Oh my gosh, I'm so sorry. It's just that I left my textbook in my locker—"

"You'll have to wait until tomorrow to retrieve it. You simply can't be out and about this close to curfew."

"You're right. I just *really* need it, I've got the final exam next week—"

"Hold on." Their eyes narrow on my chest, exactly where my gun is hidden.

My heart races. I thought I'd hidden it well enough, but—

"You go to a Prep League school?"

Relief gushes through me. They must have been staring at the crest embroidered across the front of my blazer pocket. I jerk my thumb to the doors down the street. "Yep, FD Prep. Right over there."

"You training to be in the Syndicate?"

I straighten. "Yessir."

The enforcer nods with approval, and a little envy, too. "Keep it up. Lord knows we need more of you in the force."

"Hope we'll see you get to compete in the Tournament, eh?" jokes the enforcer with the shovel, elbowing his partner with amusement.

"Well, actually—" I begin.

A tormented moan drifts out of the sewer grate behind them. The enforcers whip around, batons drawn, the color draining from their faces. Despite the chill down my own spine, I merely roll my eyes and use the opportunity to slip away.

Besides the enforcers, the sidewalks are totally deserted. Void of life. No traffic roars up Battery Place. No more cars crawl along Greenwich Street. The streetlights flicker from green to yellow to red, directing nothing and no one, but they, too, will soon go dark.

Rector Station is but a relic. The lampposts, the dark green railing, even the station placards are nothing but remnants from a past known only to the people who still remember this city for what it once was—like me. And those who fight to restore it. To put an end to the nights reigned by terror and scarlet-stained streets.

Like the Syndicate.

An aggressive barricade streaked with graffiti greets me at the top of the stairs. I duck underneath it without hesitation and head toward the steel doors sealing away the underground from civilization.

WARNING! CERTAIN DEATH AHEAD! TRESPASSING FORBIDDEN!

Even without the bold black letters screaming in your face, no one in their right mind would actually ever try to break through these doors. No offense, but if a Deathling can't break through them, neither can you.

I flip open the keypad and punch in a series of twelve digits. It flashes red. I frown and try again.

No luck.

From above, I hear the rattle of wheels against concrete and the voices of the same enforcers. I punch in the code again, but it still doesn't work.

"You've got to be shitting me," I hiss.

They're closing in. If they catch me . . .

Frantically, I punch in a totally different code. *Come on, come on, please work—*

The keypad flashes green, and the door slides open. I tumble forward. As soon as the door shuts behind me, I slump against it, breathing hard. Something patters against the other side. I hear the enforcer plunging his shovel into the cart, tossing shovelfuls of my least-favorite Deathling repellent down the stairs as if filling a grave.

I push myself onto my feet. The ceiling lights sputter, gleaming sickly white against the glazed tiles. DOWNTOWN. TO SOUTH FERRY. I run my fingers along the cold railing as I skim down the stairs, my footfalls hushed. Like a clammy fist, the air settles against my skin, cool but muggy. Rector is one of the smaller stations near the southern tip of Manhattan, past the final express stop, so only two tracks run through the station for the local trains: one uptown, one downtown.

At the turnstile, I place the glossy white box on my skateboard and give it a nudge. It rolls under the bars. None of the turnstiles are operational, so I brace my hands on the scanners on either side of me and vault myself over. There's no one at the booth to stop me.

With my gun in one hand and the box in the other, I step onto my board and cruise down the subway platform. My rubber wheels roll silently along the smooth floor tiles, carving a fresh trail through the blanket of dust.

Halfway down the platform, broken overhead lights plunge the station into darkness.

I dangle my right foot over the side of my board until the bottom of my boot grazes the floor. I come to a stop right where the shadows begin to flirt with the dwindling light.

I allow myself a moment to stand at the edge of the bright yellow DO NOT CROSS strip. To remember the warm draft gusting my face as the trains careened through the tunnel. The din of the crowd, of millions of New Yorkers and tourists alike teeming along the platforms. The loudening roar of that metal beast, reverberating in my bones. The strap of Maura's backpack clenched in my small fist as she covered my ears with her hands, barely muffling the earsplitting shriek of wheels sparking against the rails.

Stand clear of the closing doors, please.

But the last time anyone rode the subway was fifteen years ago. Before the Vanishing.

With a sigh, I prop my skateboard against the wall. I jump off the edge of the platform, landing in a crouch on the filthy tracks. I take care to avoid the pools of foul brown muck, as well as the third rail—the strip of steel running between the tracks that used to conduct electricity to the subway cars. The Transit Authority cranks up the amperage during the day to double what the trains used to run on—more than enough to fry me to a crisp. Or, more importantly, fry the Deathlings that roam the underbelly of New York City.

Carefully, I set down my precious cargo and pull the ribbon. As it tugs free, the box falls open, revealing a freshly baked strawberry shortcake. With surgical precision, I place the cake between the electrified rail and the track closest to me. Half in light, half in shadow. I check to make sure I didn't get any frosting on my fingers. Then I boost myself back onto the platform and jog over to my stakeout spot—a barricade of three hulking, city-issued black trash cans that I pushed together last week.

Hunkering down, I triple-check my gun magazine. N.N. bullets are *very* hard to come by, and I used half the cartridge the day before yesterday. Specially manufactured by Syndicate weaponsmiths, a single bullet could make all the difference in the face of a hungry Deathling.

Now, the first thing to know about Deathlings is that they *will* eat you. But only at nightfall, when they come out to hunt after the sun's gone down.

The second thing to know about Deathlings is to start running as soon as you smell their signature rotten-egg scent, because by the time one of them is close enough for you to see, rotten eggs will be the last thing you ever smell.

The third thing to know about Deathlings is that they *love* sweets. Anything sweet, really. Belgian waffles. Churros. Banana pudding. However, I've learned that there's nothing a Deathling loves more than cake.

As the saying goes, *Where cake dwells, here be Deathlings.* Or something like that.

I keep my eyes glued on the pitch-black void at the end of the subway tunnel. Count the seconds between every breath, forcing my pulse steady and calm. Not even five minutes have passed when, sure enough, that unmistakable stench wafts into the air. My nose scrunches, but otherwise I remain stone-still.

Like a vulture to a stinking carcass, the Deathling arrives.

CHAPTER TWO

Every Deathling may be unique, but all are born from the same mother of nightmares.

Some prowl through the deepest recesses of the underground, memorizing their victims' screams whenever they emerge to hunt. Through vents and manholes, their haunting singsong cries float into the city above, even during the day.

Some are shapeshifters, sifting through your mind and plucking out the faces of your loved ones to wear themselves. With these stolen masks they show up at your doorstep. The rookies smile through the peephole as if they are late to a party. The clever ones cry.

And then there are some so lethal that they earned a name all to themselves.

I tense as a shadow slinks out of the subway tunnel. The crown of barbed horns tips me off first. Then the sinewy, fur-covered torso, the spine gnarled as some abomination tearing free from the grave. I hear the scrape of its talons against the tracks, like the rasp of rusted iron on steel. Seven on each side, dangling from brawny, elongated arms that drag behind as it prowls nearer.

Finally, its snout parts the veil of darkness. Sniffing. Twitching. Scenting the bait. Coal-black eyes rove the seemingly empty station before fixating on the perfect little shortcake mere feet away. Its teeth spill out of its enormous jaws. Rows and rows of razor fangs, glinting like pearls in the light.

A *nightfang*.

Except . . . something's different. The head is too small and the legs too squat. It takes me a few more seconds of staring to realize why.

It's a nightfang *pup*.

I've never seen anything but a few theoretical sketches of unfledged Deathlings in class, much less a pup in real life. Curiosity burns inside me. I straighten out of my crouch slowly, so as not to startle the pup. The gloom makes it too difficult to see it clearly from afar. I inch closer. It scarfs down bite after bite, oblivious to my presence, its bristly black tail sweeping the air. When my toe brushes the yellow line verging the platform, it freezes—and I freeze, too. A few moments pass. My heartbeat thunders against my rib cage. Then the tension in its small frame relaxes, and it resumes gorging itself on cake.

I creep a little closer, trying to commit every detail of it to memory. I wish I could have brought Zaza here to draw it, but besides the looming threat of getting one's head ripped off, trespassing underground is illegal enough to result in both me and my best friend being expelled. Definitely not the best idea right before the final exam that will determine the rest of our lives.

I know I should capture it. Hand it over to the Syndicate. *For the betterment of all Manhattan.* Then I envision a circle of scientists bent over the pup's dissected body, poking and picking at its tiny organs, and my stomach squirms.

There's no harm in taking a closer look, I convince myself. If it tries to attack, I won't hesitate to neutralize it.

I ease onto my butt and scoot to the very edge of the platform before dropping onto the tracks. The pup tenses again. It lifts its head from the cake, its snout coated in frosting.

A jolt of familiarity runs through me as its shiny black eyes meet mine. They remind me of tapioca pearls, but it's more than that.

We stay like that for a few more seconds, our gazes locked.

At last, the pup's head tilts to the side. Tentatively, I raise my hand. It shakes the frosting from its fur, just like a wet dog, and begins padding over to me. A memory flits unbidden to the surface of my mind.

I swallow hard and banish it.

The pup bends its head. In a daze, I squat lower to give it a scratch, balancing my gun atop my knee. A thought hits me—could I be the Deathling whisperer?

No, I'm just being absurd. Acting docile doesn't make this thing any less murderous. Then again, like a lion cub that hasn't yet learned to make a meal out of anything that moves, the pup doesn't display any of the behaviors of a fully fledged nightfang. In a way, it's almost . . . *cute*.

Something clatters up ahead. The pup's ears flatten. It skitters back into the safety of the shadows, hackles raised, baring its teeth at the impenetrable darkness of the tunnel.

A menacing growl rips through the air. The overwhelming stench of rotten eggs hits me like a truck. In a heartbeat, I rise to full height and cock my weapon. At FD Prep, we spend years training to expect anything and everything in the field.

Yet nothing can prepare me for the *mammoth* Deathling that explodes out of the shadows.

Bang! Bang bang! Bang!

My bullets punch through the chest of the biggest nightfang I've ever laid eyes on. Each should be a textbook kill shot. Instead, with a bellow of agony, it barrels on. It leaps into the air, talons extended and snarling with fury, and slams into my chest.

My blazer rips. I barely register the pain raking across my skin. I snarl and yank the Deathling down with me, trying to twist midair so it takes the brunt of the impact. But it's five times the size of any opponent I've ever sparred with at school. The back of my skull cracks against the ground. My vision goes white. Blood drips from my nose and floods my mouth.

Aim for the soft spots, Coach Lee would roar at my opponents every time I pinned them to the mats. The throat, the eyes, the belly, between the ribs if you can get to the heart. N.N. bullets can't kill a person, but even one should be enough to melt through a Deathling's hide and trigger an explosion designed to disintegrate them from the inside out. At least, that's what the Syndicate tells us.

And the Syndicate never lies.

Trapped beneath the nightfang's talons, I force myself to let the fight drain out of my body. To let my limbs go completely slack. With the adrenaline pumping through my system, it's a struggle. Every instinct screams at me to get up and fight, but I know my chances are next to none.

The Deathling pauses at my sudden stillness. When it nudges my face, I'm all too aware of the menacing fangs poised mere millimeters from my eyeballs. I suck in a slow stream of air through my teeth and inch my gun closer to its chest. I might only have one bullet left, but from this close range, that's all I need. As long as I don't gag from the smell, maybe I can still make it out of here alive after all.

Then, echoing from afar, I hear the sharp *click click* of approaching oxfords.

A threatening growl rises in the Deathling's throat. Its talons dig into my stomach. A grunt of pain escapes my lips. The nightfang's jaws latch on to my collar. Saliva dribbles onto my blouse, soaking my school necktie.

Fear surges through me as it starts dragging me deeper into the shadows.

"Get yourself back on the damn platform!" a voice behind me shouts in an unmistakable English accent.

I curse silently. *Roland.* Getting eaten by a Deathling doesn't sound so bad anymore.

Like a human thundercloud, the star protégé maverick of Master Sasha glides toward me in a swirling black trench coat. Electricity leaps up and down the wicked staff brandished in his fist.

Just as Roland sends a zap into the nightfang's haunches, I slam my elbow backward into the beast's muzzle. Its jaws loosen enough for it to let out a roar—and for me to rip free of its clutches. I haul my ass onto the platform and yell, "Third rail!"

"Don't tell me how to do my job, you insufferable whelk," the maverick retorts while the nightfang sizes him up, hesitating only at the menacing crackle of his electric rod.

I bite my tongue. I don't even know what a whelk is.

Roland takes aim. The nightfang rears up on its hind legs and lunges for us at bullet speed. My heart stutters. If it manages to clear the platform, it's over for both of us. With its focus on Roland, I finally get my chance. I home in on its left eye—the clearest possible shot straight through its skull.

I pull the trigger.

With a scream of agony, the blinded nightfang stumbles into the platform edge—giving Roland the perfect opening to blast a long bolt of electricity from his staff. One end lassos around its neck. The other end connects with the third rail.

The subway tunnel erupts with scorching heat. I fling my arms up to shield my eyes from the blaze of hellish yellow. Sparks jump. Smoke billows. The Deathling's dying shrieks drill into my ears, louder than any subway train. I cover my nose with my blazer. I almost prefer the scent of sewage to burning flesh.

And then everything goes silent.

Roland coughs and waves a hand in front of his face to dispel the lingering smoke. "Spectacular, that was," he says in a very self-congratulatory sort of way. "Another flawless rescue on my equally flawless record."

My nostrils flare. As usual, he smells of coffee. His blue eyes are watery and bloodshot. Probably due to sleep deprivation, but personally I hope it's from crying. "The nightfang would have made it over the platform and mauled us both to death if I hadn't taken it down," I point out.

He inhales sharply and turns on me. His gaze flickers from the blood crusting my chin to my ripped uniform, then the unidentifiable brown sludge oozing down my knees. He sheaths his staff and says, tone dripping with disdain, "Come again?"

"You can't just—"

He lifts a warning finger in my face. "Given this situation and your current position, I would tread *very* carefully if I were you. Now put that stolen gun away."

I don't. I know he's going to report me either way. "It's borrowed, not stolen."

"Oh, the same way you *borrowed* the key code to the station?"

I grit my teeth. But before I can come up with a witty retort, my attention snags on the sheaf of papers sticking out of Roland's back pocket. "Wait. Is that—?"

"Randel's Map? Indeed it is." He smirks and pulls it out. My fingers drift toward it, but he yanks it out of my reach. "Get your filthy rat hands away from my Artifact!"

Now it's my turn to scoff. "*Your* Artifact? It belongs to the Archives."

"As if you'd know anything about the Archives."

"Please. Every New Yorker and their poodle knows about the Archives. It *is* protected by the Syndicate's most illustrious establishment of scholars, after all."

He laughs. "Those arrogant dorks?" As if he's one to talk. "Do you even know what I do? Who I am?"

I shrug. "Scholars are equally important as strikers. You need the Artifacts to fight Deathlings. I wouldn't trust you, let alone the Syndicate, to guard them. So many of New York's most significant historical and cultural objects under one roof, that kind of power falling into the wrong hands . . . you know how it goes."

"Well, aren't you quite the little expert?" he jeers.

No, I want to say. *My dad was.* However, the last thing I need is to feed him enough details for him to piece together my identity. "Can I see the map?"

"No."

I muster up my most angelic smile. "Pretty please?"

He raises an eyebrow and asks, "Why should I?"

Smile still locked in place, I take a deep breath. The Archivists keep the Artifacts under military-grade security, locked away from the public eye, so there are people out there who would kill for the opportunity to see a real Artifact. Including me. Of course, he knows all this, which makes what I'm about to say all the more nauseating.

"Well," I begin slowly. *Eyes on the prize*, I tell myself. "I heard that only the *best* and most *brilliant* of mavs are allowed to borrow the map from the Archives. Is that true?" I bat my eyelashes at him for good measure.

Roland eats it up like the pompous prick that he is. "Fine. I can let you take a quick look. But no touching, you're covered in filth."

"I like to call it the lifeblood of New York City."

He rolls his eyes and unfolds the map. A soft, ethereal glow washes forth, warming my cheeks like sunlight. I peer closer. A condensed, ghostly version of Randel's grid system plan of Manhattan—the *original* plan, drawn up almost a century before the foundations for the city's first skyscrapers were even laid—spreads across the faded parchment. Meanwhile, *today's* Manhattan traces overtop it in molten gold ink, dividing the city into ten sections, each a different district. Harlem crowns the city in the north. Right beneath it, the Upper West and East Sides like wings to Central Park. They make up the three largest Syndicate jurisdictions. Then below Central Park lie Midtown, Chelsea, Flatiron, Soho, the Lower East Side, and Tribeca, combining smaller districts from before the Vanishing, for unity's sake but mostly less for paperwork . . . Last but certainly not least, all the way down south, the Financial District—where we are.

The map looks exactly as fantastical as it does in my textbooks, but for the first time I can actually see the dark green clustered dots of enforcers moving methodically up and down the grid, searching for curfew breakers before dusk descends . . . and the bloodbath begins.

"It's beautiful," I murmur.

He sighs. "I can use it to track whoever I want, so I suppose it's useful enough."

"Useful *enough*? Do you not realize what you're—"

"Don't bore me. Mavericks like me, we control whichever Artifact *we* want, not the other way around. You could only dream about what I'm capable of."

"We'll see about that in two weeks."

Roland snorts. "The Tournament? *You*? Rei . . ." He makes a face. "Whatever-your-last-name-is, the next maverick of Manhattan? Don't make me laugh."

I don't deign to respond. I'm still sorry he even knows my first name, which I made the mistake of giving to him back before I was acquainted with his truly unfortunate excuse for a personality. He has no clue how many afternoons I've spent training myself in secret, or how many Deathlings I've killed on my own. And that's the way I'd like to keep it.

I point at the angry red X flashing at the bottom left corner of the map. "That's me, isn't it?"

"Ah, yes, which reminds me of why I was sent to track you down again in the first place." Roland snaps the map closed and tucks it back into his pocket with a haughty smile. I swallow my envy. "It appears that all your illegal subterranean escapades have caught the attention of one of the masters."

"Master Sasha?" I say, a little too hopefully.

He makes a face that I can't quite discern. "You wish. No, your presence has been commanded tomorrow afternoon at Upper West Side Manor . . . by Master Minyi."

I cuss so violently that Roland actually draws his staff.

"What?" he demands, poised to strike.

"Nothing." With a heavy exhale, I turn my back on the maverick and grab my skateboard. I shoot a mournful glance at the nightfang's steaming carcass before limping toward the station exit. "I was just wishing that you'd let the Deathling drag me away after all."

CHAPTER THREE

It's a miserable trek back to my dorm. The air bleeds with the flagrant stink of coffee. A pair of enforcers hurry down the sidewalks with another pushcart. At every doorstep and ground-level windowsill, they toss fresh shovelfuls of dark brown, roasted coffee beans like rock salt on icy roads. The beasts can't stand the smell—though to be fair, at this point neither can I.

Against both of our wishes, Roland tails me all the way home. His shoes click obnoxiously against the cobblestones of the Financial District. A chill creeps over me as we turn onto Wall Street and pass into the shadows of the brooding stone buildings blocking out the last of the sun's warmth. I wish I could admire them in the fading light, but after the Vanishing, sunsets only serve as a countdown—a reminder of our vulnerability to darkness and everything that lurks within.

"Unnerving, isn't it?" Roland wonders aloud, waving a hand toward Wall Street Plaza. Above looms the New York Stock Exchange with its imposing Corinthian columns. Eleven ivory sculptures nestle in the triangular pediment overhead. In the center is a woman wearing billowing robes and a winged cap, surrounded by other toiling, mostly naked figures: a man gazing out behind the wheel of a ship; a woman wielding a distaff for spinning flax and wool; another man straining beneath the sack borne upon his back. They're meant to represent the "work of humans," but the darkness reduces their majesty to indistinguishable gray lumps.

"What?"

"Walking through an empty New York City."

I don't respond. I don't need to. He's right. It's unreal. It's impossible.

And it's all because of the Deathlings.

The Vanishing came first, of course. An eruption from beneath the streets that cloaked the city in a fog as impenetrable as the mystery of its cause. I remember the anxious murmurings of my parents along with the incessant hum of TV reporters on the news filling our apartment, the lockdown and the warnings not to venture outside. The fear that the fog would never lift, that everything we knew would be lost forever. Then, seven days later, the fog disappeared along with the people it had stolen away. On the surface the city seemed unchanged, and even mourning the lost couldn't completely subdue the relief of being free again. Of breathing fresh air after days of being trapped inside, sometimes without food or medicine or hope of rescue.

In honor of the lost, the church bells rang for days end in ceaseless, anguished solidarity. My parents wore even more black than usual. Withering bouquets piled up on every street corner, cloying the air with their sweet scent of grief and decay.

Everyone thought that we'd outlived the worst of it. That eventually, life could go back to normal.

In reality, the true horrors had only just begun.

"Have you ever thought about leaving this place?"

My head snaps up. At first I wonder if Roland's taking a dig at me, but then I notice the odd, pensive glaze to his eyes.

"It's the same charade," he mumbles as if I'm not even there. "Everyone else pretends everything's fine. They go to work, meet friends, raise families. Clinging to the semblance of normalcy. They're all raving mad."

"What are they supposed to do instead?" I say. "Cower in their apartments? Pick a human sacrifice once every full moon to stave off the Deathlings?"

"Maybe."

I think of the stories I've heard of the earliest nightfalls, when the only pieces of evidence of the brutal carnage to see the light of day were the pools of dried blood streaking the cement and the rare survivor lucky enough to make it to dawn with only half of their limbs gnawed to a pulp. Wrapping my arms around myself to suppress a shiver, I quicken my pace.

"But would you?" Roland prompts, hurrying after me. "Leave, I mean."

Even after the first confirmed slaughters, some people refused to abandon their lives here, determined to wait out the danger. Some didn't have anywhere else to go. But the rest fled in droves. They figured that the Vanishing was a Manhattan problem, and therefore so were the monsters.

That is, until the bloodbath in Boston. In Denver. The massacre in San Francisco, nearly three thousand miles away.

Then a pipe explosion in St. Louis led to the discovery of a Deathling nest that experts traced all the way back to New York. Specifically, the island of Manhattan. Turns out that Deathlings were indeed our problem after all.

The news came the next morning. I couldn't understand at first when my parents tried to explain the indefinite ban on all intercity travel—and not just because of how young I was. No one in or out of Manhattan, no exceptions.

It was unfathomable.

But if Deathlings could steal faces and voices, how else could they trick us? And how would anyone know any better until it was too late?

Of course, the ban wasn't enough to keep at bay the crowds desperate to escape. So the military brought in the barricades, and when that still didn't work, the president met with world leaders in an internationally broadcasted emergency session. From the living room sofa, my parents and I listened in helpless silence as authorities from around the globe unanimously decided that there was no choice but to destroy every bridge and tunnel leading out of Manhattan. To blow our physical connection with the outside world to rubble.

Bridges can be rebuilt, they said. *But lost lives cannot be reborn.*

"This is my city," I say finally. "It may not always be kind, but it's ours. We're New Yorkers. We always find a way to live on, no matter what it takes."

His mouth tightens. "I'm not one of you."

The shadow of George Washington's enormous statue erected atop the steps of Federal Hall swallows us. We cross beneath the first president's hard bronze gaze in strained silence. With the statue's stern expression and billowing coat, one hand held out as if to cast a spell, he towers over the plaza like a master from another time.

The Vanishing might have brought death and despair upon our heads, but at least the Syndicate gave us something—and someone— to believe in.

We stop in front of a glass entrance sandwiched between a high-end jewelry boutique and a smoothie bar. I ring the buzzer and belatedly attempt to straighten out my wrecked uniform, torn where the Deathling's talons sliced my chest. I'm almost tempted to ask Roland to borrow his maverick's coat to cover up the worst of it, but I bet he'd sooner see me electrocuted by the third rail than give it up.

The door swings open. "*Rei Reynolds!* Haven't you a lick of shame?" thunders the dean.

At six and a half feet, Dean Abigail's broad frame fills up the entrance to the dormitories like a matronly roadblock. In her cement-gray blouse and pencil skirt, she certainly looks the part, too. Her gargoyle's glare pins me from above, magnified by the glasses perched on her hooked nose.

Roland snickers.

The Dean's glare locks onto the maverick. "*You*," she snaps. "Don't you have a job to do?"

His nostrils flare. "Ma'am—"

"Don't you *ma'am* me, young man. Come along, Miss Reynolds!"

"Yes, Dean Abigail!" I duck my head, face hot, and step into the foyer as she marches away. Roland watches me, his thin lips pressing into an even thinner line. I clear my throat. "Good nightfall."

Just as the door's about to close, Roland jams his foot in it. "Seriously? Not even a bloody thank-you for saving your lousy arse?" His tone is so snide that each word feels like a slap to the face. Especially after that introspective nonsense he was spouting earlier.

My fists clench. I have to remind myself that Roland is a maverick—a title that wasn't just handed to him. He fought for it during the Tournament. As the highest order of command within the Syndicate besides the anonymous and elusive Board of Directors, the Masters of Manhattan—and their protégés, the mavericks—are the city's first line of defense against the darkness. They are our heroes.

If only this one wasn't such a *dick*.

"Why did you want to become a maverick?" I ask suddenly.

Roland leans against the doorjamb. "Money. Power. Respect. Free drinks at the bar. Et cetera."

At least he's honest about it.

"Do you remember the motto of the Syndicate?"

He makes a face, as if he can't believe I have the gall to question him. "Of course I do. *Rise Above the Rest.*"

"My teachers say we have to be faster. Stronger. Smarter. Better than the rest of society, just to get a shot at being chosen by the Syndicate." I jut my chin up at him. "But do you know what I just realized? People only ever rise for two reasons: to serve those who look up to them, or to look down on those they serve. Which kind are you?"

There's nothing more gratifying than seeing Roland turn redder than a brick. "You infuriating little—"

"*Miss Reynolds!*" the Dean shouts from the elevator lobby.

Hiding my smile, I sketch a graceful bow to the maverick. "I'm afraid that's my cue. My most sincere thanks to you for saving my lousy *arse.*"

He's still gaping when I let the door slam in his face.

"What do you have to say for yourself, young lady?" the Dean demands once the elevator doors slide shut. "Running around with barely fifteen minutes to spare until nightfall? And what in the name of liberty happened to your uniform?"

"On an errand for my aunt as usual, ma'am." I fix my gaze straight ahead. Fifteen minutes is plenty enough for me. And I don't need her reminder—I've missed curfew once in my entire life, and no price I pay will ever bring back what I lost that night.

"And that maverick?"

"I bumped into him on my way back. He insisted on escorting me home."

"How kind," the Dean mutters. Internally, she's waging war. On one hand, she's responsible for keeping all the boarding students—including me—safe. On the other hand, we both know that she doesn't get paid *nearly* enough to deal with all my bullshit. But more than anything, she's powerless against my aunt's authority. At least, that's what I'd like her to keep thinking.

By the time the elevator dings again and the doors slide open, her fury has already simmered down to resignation. She ushers me into the warmly lit hallway. "I assume that your preparations for the final exam are going smoothly?"

"I haven't started."

The Dean's eyebrows shoot past her hairline. "Miss Reynolds—"

"I'm joking, ma'am."

She exhales. "I wish you'd take this a little more seriously, Miss Reynolds. Need I remind you that the only way to qualify for the Tournament is—"

"To rank first," I cut in, my voice as flat as her sense of humor. "Yes, I'm painfully aware. But thanks anyway."

The door at the end of the hallway flings wide open. Out bursts a girl in a paint-splattered smock, her dark brown hair spilling over her shoulder in waves and a steaming mug of coffee sloshing dangerously in one hand. A yellow thumbprint smudges her round, dimpled cheek.

"There you are," says Zaza. "I was just about to start rehearsing your eulogy."

"Please, Miss Alvarez," the Dean implores weakly. "Rei's safety is no laughing matter."

My best friend only takes a sip from her mug and grins. "Neither is training thirteen-year-olds to kill flesh-devouring monsters with electric sticks."

I slap a hand across my mouth to stifle a horrified cackle. The Dean's face goes utterly slack.

At that exact moment, the curfew bells outside waver. A new sound begins. A siren. A howling, harrowing siren, cutting through the air like a blade, climbing higher and higher until the glass windowpanes in our dorm rattle in protest.

"Oh my," Zaza stage-whispers. "Only five minutes until nightfall."

The Dean stands frozen for a moment. Then she snaps into motion, shoving us into our dorm. "Good evening, girls," she snarls before pulling the door shut with a bang.

The second Zaza locks it, I sag against the wall, pressing my fingers against the warm slick of my wounds. "Ah."

Zaza's eyes widen. She sets her mug aside, scrambles over, and slides one arm around me to hold me up. I slump into her. She smells of rose-petal body lotion, acrylics, and inevitably, coffee. It may be the only liquid I've ever seen her drink. "Dios santo, Rei. What happened this time?"

"Got maimed by a nightfang," I mutter. "Help me to the windowsill, will you?"

Without further question, my dormmate manhandles me into the kitchen. We shuffle past her half-finished easel and splay of paint tubes and brushes amid takeout boxes on the marble counter, then into my bedroom.

Striker-themed memorabilia of all shapes and sizes dominates every empty space: posters of my favorite masters and mavericks over the years; collectible action figures positioned in mid-battle; all of Master Sasha's signed autobiographies, multiple icy stares piercing me from their front covers, their pages worn thin from years of devoted reading; and old newspaper clippings regaling the Striker Division's greatest victories.

Zaza dumps me onto my bed just in time for the wail of the siren to choke off. I scoot as close as I can to the window and peel off my blazer. She helps me loosen my tie and unbutton my shirt to reveal the claw marks tearing down my shoulders and torso. My nose wrinkles at the black pus oozing from the wounds.

Zaza's hazel eyes glint, an ever-shifting nebula of green, brown, and blue. "Oh, boy. I'm going to need some samples of that." Her socks slide on the hardwood as she dashes out of my room. "Don't heal too quickly!" she calls over her shoulder.

"Thanks for the overwhelming concern," I grumble before slumping into the pillows, but I don't really mind. Though our studies have set us down in opposite divisions within the Syndicate—strikers and scholars—we still think the same way. Much like hunting Deathlings in real life, opportunities to acquire and analyze fresh Deathling samples as a student are rare. It would be a spectacular waste *not* to take advantage of the situation. And Zaza's much too brilliant for that.

The melodious clink of glass from Zaza's room fills the silence as I perch my elbows on the windowsill and let out a sigh. I stare at the fiery reflection of my ruby-red hair in the glass panes, touching the natural black beginning to show at the roots. I wonder if I'll finally let it grow out this time.

By now, night obscures most of the room. The gloom softens the hard lines of my jaw but deepens the perpetual shadows under my eyes that have plagued me since childhood. *Those bags are designer, honey*, Zaza likes to joke.

On the far wall, an ocean of Polaroids fans out from corner to corner. In the darkness, they melt into one another, but I know them all by heart. There's my big sister, Maura, adopted pre-Vanishing, laughing in the tiny box of a kitchen of her tinier new apartment. She doesn't even have enough room to open the fridge door fully, but the place is all hers.

Zaza is everywhere. Painting in the kitchen, applying lipstick in the bathroom mirror. Standing with me outside FD Prep on the first and last days of school each year, matching in our prim, starchy little uniforms. From left to right, we grow up frozen in time. Whereas Zaza's grins are dazzling even on grainy film, mine have been reduced to reluctant smirks over the years.

As for my parents . . . I have all but two photos, handed down to me by my aunt, the rest burnt to ashes in the dead of nightfall. Swirling fumes of gray. Unbearable heat. Waves of it, choking the air. As I'd stared up at the inferno consuming our home, I thought the fire had taken everything from us. But that was before what came next.

Now these photos are all I have left to remember my mom and dad.

The first, taken by my aunt, is of their wedding day. Mom wears a red lace cheongsam adorned with a gold dragon winding around her waist. Though Dad wears a classic tux, his bow tie bears the same dragon motif as Mom's dress. As always, his glasses sit slightly askew.

In the second photo, my parents stand together on the steps of the repurposed Grand Central Station at 42nd Street and Park Avenue—now better known as the Central Headquarters of the Syndicate. Their first official day of duty: Mom as an enforcer, and Dad as the head curator of the Archives. As a professor of urban history at Columbia University best known around the world for his research in contemporary archaeology, the Syndicate requested that he lead the collection and preservation of the Artifacts. Back then, the Scholar Division—or the Archives, for that matter—didn't even exist yet. But with the government scrambling to figure out what the hell to do and Manhattan already on the brink of a catastrophic meltdown, the Syndicate had no choice but to step up. So they did—employing the city's finest expert to catalog and study the capabilities of all the Artifacts from day one. Dad carried that honor above all else. I'd never seen him beam so brightly as the day they bestowed upon him the title of head curator, not even in his wedding photos. History had been his first love, after all. Mom and I came after.

My gaze flicks to the bottom drawer of my desk, where I keep one other box of photos, gathering dust in the dark. My box of endings, you could say. Another reminder of what—who I've lost. I can't bring myself to look at the pictures inside, but neither can I bear to throw them away.

Maybe it's the leftover stress from my brush with the Deathling, but my eyes start welling up before I can stop them. I frown at myself.

Crying won't save anyone. Then again, neither will revenge, but at least it'll keep me busy. So I force my blurry gaze to the window and blink the tears away.

Then I watch the city that never sleeps fall very, very dark.

The electric lights are the first to extinguish. The traffic lights, the streetlights. The light on my desk. In our dorm. We tumble headfirst into the blackness. From the ground upward, floor by floor, every building winks out like a galaxy strangling to death.

In contrast, the sky overhead explodes with stars. Just across from the southern banks of Battery Park, I can picture the Statue of Liberty, her torch pointed to the heavens. Every nightfall, as though the dying breath of day bestows life to the dormant flames, the torch erupts in a blaze of fiery light. In place of embers or ash, billions of glowing particles ebb and flow over Manhattan. They drift down like they're falling from the stars themselves, until the entire city shimmers in dazzling defiance.

We call it stardust.

And because of it, Lady Liberty is not only the largest Artifact in the collection, but the most crucial.

I grab an empty jar on my bedside table and open the window right as Zaza returns with a handful of glass vials and a pipette. While she sets up,

I stick the jar outside and wait for the stardust to fill it up. It won't melt like snow, nor does it need to be released like fireflies. Come dawn, it will simply vanish.

I screw the lid on to keep the particles from floating away. Both the window and the jar illuminate my room with a soft, ethereal glimmer. Nowhere near as bright as your average lightbulb, but with all fire-making devices such as gas lighters ruthlessly forbidden—besides electric ones that don't work past sundown anyway—a jar or two is more than enough to see by. Even if fire hadn't been banned, everyone knows how fatal the risks are. As I learned the nightfall my parents were murdered, masters and mavericks aren't trained to combat that type of threat, and the firefighters who were selfless enough to try have long been devoured.

"Lie down," Zaza tells me. She begins the arduous process of collecting the pus. A wayward breeze whisks a tongue of stardust inside my room. It sets Zaza's bronze skin agleam in a luminescent sheen of amber, and mine in a honeyed glow.

I swear under my breath. The stardust stings my open wounds, similar to the sensation of rubbing alcohol. Slowly, it forms clots, which causes an unbearable itch that only intensifies as the wound rapidly scabs over.

Zaza seals the half-full vial with a black rubber stopper and holds it up to the window. "You going to be okay?" she asks in a too-casual tone.

I lift my button-down to my ribs and brush the smooth, unmarred skin beneath the remaining crusts of blood. "Good as new."

"I'm talking about the final exam."

"What about it?"

"We've only got one day left."

I gasp. "Really? I totally forgot."

"Are you sure you'll be ready?" she presses.

I peel off the scabs—gross, but a little satisfying. "Why wouldn't I be?"

Zaza raises an eyebrow. "Oh, I don't know. Maybe because you've spent every day after school hunting monsters instead of studying like everybody else?"

"That *is* studying." Sort of.

"Just because the scholar exam has no physical component doesn't mean the striker exam will be any less academically difficult," Zaza says lightly. "You've been working toward this for years, Rei. All I'm saying is don't chuck your future down a nightfang's throat. You can hunt as many Deathlings as you want *after* you join the Syndicate."

"You're starting to sound like my aunt."

Zaza smiles at that and gives the vial a small, experimental shake. "Do you know where I could find any nanopore sequencers lying around?"

Before I can reply, a midnight blur disturbs the shower of gold on the street below, kicking up swirls of stardust in its wake.

I leap to my feet and plunge my head outside of the window, squinting hard. It's dark enough that I almost wonder if Roland's decided to come by and torment me, but the mav is over six feet tall while this thing is so much . . . tinier.

"Oh my god," I whisper.

"What?" says Zaza.

The nightfang pup scrabbles to a halt, its ears perked, nothing more than a dirty smudge in the middle of Wall Street. Slowly, it looks upward.

Our gazes lock.

"What is it?" Zaza says again.

Heart racing, I drag her closer to the window and thrust my finger down below. But by the time she looks—

The pup is gone.

CHAPTER FOUR

Swirling fumes of gray. Unbearable heat. Waves of it, choking the air.

"Take her and go!"

Eyes stinging. Small hands, soft cheeks.

"You take her—"

"Wait. Be silent."

Something is here.

Everything stills.

Eyes like lumps of burning coal, blacker than black against fiery orange. Searching. Finding.

A wail erupts.

Found.

Hearts beating into overdrive.

"Take her, I said!"

The last thing said.

Footsteps thundering into the open.

Teeth like knives. Blood like blood.

Humans bleed so easy.

Buildings flying past. Monochrome glass, catacomb stone.

Everything stops.

They're here.

"Rei."

Fingers scrabbling. The clink of metal.

Brown eyes, gone black in night. "Wear this. Always. Never let it go. Never let them take it from you. Now run. RUN!"

Arms up, elbows locked, finger on the trigger.

BANG. BANG.

"Run, Rei!"

BANG.

"REI!"

BANG.

"REI! Wake up!"

I jolt awake in a cold sweat, my heart racing and the sheets crumpled in my clammy fists.

"You dead or something?" Zaza yells through the bedroom door. She gives it another kick. *Bang.* "We're going to be late!"

"Shit," I mutter, shooting upright. I take one second to touch the gold talisman around my neck and allow myself a shaky sigh of relief. It's a handmade rendering of a Chinese calligraphy character:

Shǎn: it can mean *lightning* or *flash*, but Mom's favorite definition was *to shine.*

My mood is the opposite of shining as I fling off the covers and stagger over to my closet. I yank on a skirt and lift the hem to strap my gun holster to my thigh.

Run, Rei.

Stuffing one arm into the sleeve of my blazer, I skid into the foyer, my staff sheath and duffel bag for combat education swinging wildly from my shoulder.

Zaza leans against the open doorway. She raises one perfectly plucked eyebrow. "Wow, did you tie your tie with your feet or something?"

"No, with these." I scowl, flashing her my middle fingers.

"Real mature, Rei. Real mature."

We hurry to the elevators. When the doors *ding* open, we find a boy with rich brown skin and short black curls styled in a high-top fade grinning at us. Just like me, he carries his gear in a duffel, though his staff is held fast to his back with a repurposed yoga mat strap. Though staffs have never been my Deathling-slaying weapon of choice, especially since I can't carry them near curfew without drawing hefty amounts of suspicion, they do eliminate the dilemma of running out of ammo in the middle of a life-or-death situation—which, following yesterday's events, does sound quite appealing.

"Good morning, Mr. President," I greet in my most serious tone.

"'Sup, Reynolds." Bomani holds out his fist. I bump it. He adjusts his cuff links and shoots a wink at Zaza. "Morning, Alvarez."

My best friend flips her hair over her shoulder, the picture of nonchalance. "Ciao."

He only grins wider and jerks his chin in my direction. "Did Reynolds tell you?"

"Tell me what?"

"That I'm going to kick her butt later."

She tilts her head. "You mean, you begged Coach Lee to assign you as sparring partners again so you could *try* to?"

"What can I say?" Bomani shrugs cheerfully. "Today might be our last chance to properly beat each other up. Without repercussion."

Zaza shakes her head. "Just another reason why I'm so grateful I never enrolled in combat ed."

"You had other reasons?"

"Being sweaty all the time. Everyone else being sweatier. And then you have to"—she shudders—"touch each other's sweatiness."

Bomani bursts out into such full-bodied, genuine laughter that the tips of Zaza's ears turn rosy. He wipes a tear from the corner of his eye. "If it makes you feel better, Alvarez, I'd wear a full stick of deodorant just for you."

She looks away, grumbling, "And I'd eat one if it would shut that loud mouth of yours."

"Aw," I say. "That's so romantic."

Right as Zaza attempts to bodycheck me into the wall, the doors open to the lobby, and a blond girl and a boy with bubblegum-pink hair strut out of one of the elevators to our right. The girl's skirt is rolled up five inches shorter than regulation. She brushes past me and Zaza with a haughty sniff. She does, however, send our president a saccharine smile. "Good morning, Bomani."

"Oh, for liberty's sake," Zaza groans under her breath. "It's too early for this."

Bomani nods. "Sharon."

She gives him an appraising look up and down while Justin simpers behind her. "Prom is coming up soon. I heard you haven't found a date yet."

Bomani doesn't falter. "Haven't quite gotten around to the asking part, I'll admit."

Sharon reaches forward to straighten his collar, causing Zaza's eyes to pop wide. *The audacity*, she mouths to me. Sharon dutifully ignores us and says, "Is that so? Well—"

"Sharon doesn't have a date yet," Justin pipes up helpfully. "No one wants to go with her. Like, literally no one. Not even me. So you should—"

A mortified Sharon yanks him away by the scruff and drags him off, hissing at him all the way out of the lobby. "What is your *problem*? Every time, Justin, I swear to god!"

Zaza releases a long sigh once the duo is out of earshot. "Oh, FD Prep. Truly home to some of the most extraordinary students in Manhattan."

I smile wryly. The admission rate at all ten elite preparatory schools established and operated by the Syndicate is capped at one hundred acceptances per school, per year, despite tens of thousands of applications. Breezy odds, compared to winning the Tournament, but still cutthroat. And everyone knows there are two ways to increase your chances: make rank or make bank. Sharon's daddy is the CEO of some major sports conglomerate. Justin's family invested in coffee stocks early on. There are dozens of kiddos just like them paying their way in with their parents' money, robbing spots from hard-working students who rightfully deserve them. But the schools' bills don't pay themselves, and with leading-edge facilities in premium real estate spaces, they certainly don't come cheap. Though it's a hard truth to swallow, it's impossible to ignore the benefit— external funding and generous "donations" mean scholarships that allow about half of the students to actually attend the school, like Zaza, whose entry test scores earned her a full ride.

Bomani spins around, walking backward with his arms spread wide, never missing a step. "Our last day. Can you believe it?" Though school doesn't end officially until next week, seniors get out early for the final exam. Expression wistful, he shoulders the exit door open. "I might even miss this place."

Before we can fully step out onto the sidewalk, we're ambushed by an explosion of shouts and flashing lights. I cover my face as a storm of media reporters descends upon us, their voices rising, overlapping, all clamoring for our attention. Once in a while, Wall Street fills with protesters condemning the travel ban or curfew rules or the Syndicate itself, but nothing like this. Never like this. And the authorities have always kept them in check. This time, there's no one here to protect us, not even Dean Abigail.

A reporter with a pixie cut shoves a mic into Zaza's face. "Do you believe the Tournament—and its costs—is truly a viable way to appoint the Syndicate's next generation of mavericks?"

"How many students fail the final exam every year?" another reporter shouts at Bomani. "With less than a day to go, do you feel adequately prepared?"

"Rei, come on! We have to get out of here," Zaza exclaims, tugging my hand as the crowd presses us inward, slowly but surely suffocating us. But there is nowhere to go, and she's made a big mistake.

"Rei? Did you say Rei?" someone yells, overhearing her. "Rei Reynolds? Current top ranker of FD Prep?"

And just like that, the rest of them home in on their new target. They swarm around me, assaulting me with their questions, no cease-fire in sight.

"What do you think are the consequences of forcing developing teenagers and young adults to compete against one another at such high stakes?"

"How do you feel about potentially competing against Tim Beckett, seven-time Prep League wrestling champion and current top ranker of your previous school, Upper West Side Prep?"

"Given the risks, do you even wish to compete in the Tournament?"

I am jabbed and jostled around like a scrap of bread tossed into a pack of feral geese. I try to stand my ground, disoriented by the mass of soulless camera lenses trained on me from every direction—the blinking red lights, the relentless white flashes.

"What does it feel like to be at the top?" someone hollers. When I fail to respond, they ask, "Do your friends ever get jealous of your rank?"

Zaza clings on to me, hiding behind my shoulder. A pudgy bald man has the nerve to nudge her aside to stick his mic directly into my face. "What makes you think that you've got what it takes to win?" he demands.

I wrench the mic right out of his hand and hold it over his head. "Want me to show you?"

BANG.

A shot shatters the din. The mob of reporters ducks to the ground to reveal a man in a midnight-blue leather trench coat looming over them all. He keeps his face lowered and his N.N. gun pointed to the sky. But one glance at his golden ponytail, the intimidating double shoulder holsters peeking out from underneath his coat, and the vicious, puckered scar engraving his face from cheek to chin like a sinister smile is all it takes for my heart to start pounding out of control.

At last, the man lifts his chin, gun still raised. His frigid blue eyes sweep over the reporters, leaving them wordless and trembling. The same eyes on the front covers of his autobiographies—the ones I've worshipped for so long that I feel like I already know him.

"Rei," Zaza whispers. "Don't you have posters of that dude all over your bedroom?"

I kick her in the shin.

Everyone stares between the man and his gun, too terrified to be the first to move or speak. Several flinch as he reaches into his pocket with his broad, calloused hand, only to pull out a colorfully wrapped candy. We all stare as he removes the foil and pops it into his mouth.

"What is meaning of this?" he says, every word even more heavily accented than I've heard from him on TV, while he sucks around the candy.

"These are public streets, Master Sasha," the bald jerk from earlier manages to reply.

"Hm. You seem to know rules around here, eh?" says Master Sasha in a mocking tone. "If you want, I make *you* Master of Financial District, so when Deathlings hunt these *public streets*, they will have many delicious, crunchy humans to enjoy . . . just like you." He opens his mouth to display the candy slowly dissolving on his tongue. With a morbid, mangled grin, he crushes it between his back molars.

The silence is deathly.

"Well?" he bellows, causing the reporters to scatter. "What are you blabberheads waiting for?"

But before we can hurry off as well, the man's gaze lands on me.

"You," he says in that gruff accent.

I clasp my hands behind my back to hide how hard they're shaking. I have to crane my neck up just to look him in the eye. "Master Sasha. It's such an honor to—"

"Yesterday afternoon. Rector Street Station."

My stomach lurches. *He knows.* He knows I broke in. I curse Roland. That bastard must have snitched on me. Master Sasha waits expectantly. Filled with dread, I nod once.

"And three days ago," he adds. "Last week, too."

Surprise flashes through me, followed by a rush of humiliation. No one caught me those times—or so I'd foolishly thought. Despite Master Sasha's order, some of the reporters still loiter nearby, attempting to eavesdrop. My face grows hot. Am I about to get exposed in front of all of them?

He considers me for an agonizingly long moment. Finally, his lips curl up at the edges in what might be a grimace—or a smile. "Not bad."

Then, without a word of elaboration, the Master of the Financial District spins on his heel and strolls away.

CHAPTER FIVE

I stare blankly out the window of the classroom, my fingers steepled beneath my chin. Far below—twenty-two floors below, to be exact—hundreds of boats cut through the churning gray waves of the Hudson River, leaving trails of white froth. Their steel hulls crisscross the water around the Statue of Liberty like sharks. Each rushes to dock and unload massive crates of imported goods into the hulking concrete complexes littering Battery Park. Thanks to global relief aid—worldwide pity, as we like to call it—we've been lucky enough to avoid any major food or medicine shortages. And while the government refuses to send in troops from the outside, they've got no such qualms about shipping in expensive tech and weaponry to help the Syndicate combat our pest problem. Nowadays, with the barbed wire and the enforcers patrolling the gates from dawn till dusk where truckers pick up all the deliveries for distribution, anyone could mistake the greenspace for a maximum-security prison.

"—answer for question thirty-three?" Ms. Livingstone asks, glancing down at the review sheet. When her inquiry is followed by awkward rustling and students shifting their gazes elsewhere, she sighs. "Rei?"

Without taking my gaze off Lady Liberty in all her oxidized, greenish-blue glory, I recite, "The purpose of the drug zircadiazicazine, better known as Triple-Z, is to artificially trigger the ventrolateral preoptic nucleus into rapidly releasing neurotransmitters that abruptly inhibit wake-promoting hormones such as norepinephrine, histamine, and serotonin." I catch Sharon rolling her eyes in my peripheral vision. "This allows for strikers in the field to remain unconscious for precise, remotely controlled amounts of time with virtually no risk of neural damage."

"Well said, Rei, thank you." Ms. Livingstone adjusts her bedazzled spectacles and pauses. "Sharon, perhaps if your eyeballs spent less time rolling and more time reading your textbook, you might've known the answer, too."

The class titters. A bright red flush swells across Sharon's cheeks. As soon as Ms. Livingstone turns her back, the girl shoots me a glare nasty enough to daunt a Deathling.

I can't even muster a glare back. I'm tired of school, anxious for the final exam and the Tournament, sick of the recurring nightmares. I also can't shake the fear that Master Sasha could show up any minute to arrest me.

Not bad, he'd said. What the hell did that mean? I can't decide whether to be deeply offended or to take it as the finest compliment I've ever received. To make matters worse, the sense of doom in my stomach only intensifies every time I think about my imminent visit to the Manor this afternoon.

Every class period rushes by, half the time they usually are to allow seniors to leave school early to prep for the exam and rest. Even so, it feels like an eternity before last period rolls around.

And god, am I itching for a fight.

I grab my staff and duffel from my locker and head down to the gymnasium. Only when I'm about to enter does it hit me that I've forgotten to stash my gun in my locker. I'm running late already, so I slip it into the sheath along with my staff. Even a license to carry won't mean shit if I get caught with a firearm on school premises—particularly since it's "borrowed."

A dozen of my fellow classmates already line the wall, stretching or doing warm-up exercises. I spot Bomani chatting with Coach Lee. As I pass, he grins at me and pummels his fist into his open palm. I shake my head and jog into the locker room with a wicked little grin of my own.

There's another girl already changing as I throw my gear onto one of the long wooden benches. She pulls the fabric of her exosuit up her dark, slender legs and slides her arms into the sleeves. One hand grasps around for her back zipper.

"Need some help, Anika?" I ask.

Anika turns, brightening. "Rei! I was so worried you weren't going to make it. Too bad we're not sparring partners, huh?"

"Blame Bomani," I say, zipping her up just like I've done since our first day in combat ed together. Neither of us actually need the help anymore, but we certainly did back then. Now it's simply tradition.

I rummage through my duffel for my own exosuit. A cross between a diver's wetsuit and sleek combat armor straight out of a cyberpunk movie, these replicas of a striker's most crucial weapon for survival look and feel almost identical to the real thing. From the outside, at least. What they lack are the premium bits and bobs: self-healing fabric, camouflage, jump propulsion, and most important of all, the complex internal system that harnesses a striker's kinetic energy to power their strength and speed tenfold. But it sure beats the standard, shapeless jersey and knee-length shorts any day.

As I slip off my skirt, Anika sneaks a glance at my thigh. As if I'd make the mistake of leaving my holster on in front of her again. She missed her opportunity to report me the first time, and I have a feeling that she's regretted not doing so ever since.

Reaching for my zipper, Anika says, "Remember when you thought it would be funny to put your head into one of the leg holes and you got stuck?"

"And you had to get Coach Lee to call the fire department to cut me out?"

She giggles. "How long did he make you serve detention? A month?"

"A full semester!"

Anika takes up her staff and claps me on the shoulder. "Sounds about right. Listen, we'd better get our butts into the gym before Coach blows his top, but I just wanted to thank you."

My brow furrows. "For what?"

Her soft brown eyes are all innocence. "For motivating me to work harder and *rise higher* and all that. You've always inspired me to be the best this school has to offer."

My smile is stiff. I hold out my hand. "Best of luck on your final exam, Ani."

In a way that could be interpreted as fierce, sisterly affection, Anika crushes my fingers in her iron grip. "Thank you, Rei. It means a lot. *Especially* coming from you."

"Maharaj! Reynolds!" a voice bellows outside the door. "Trying to get ready for a class or a beauty pageant in there?"

Anika scampers out. I grab my staff sheath—gun and all, I realize, too late—and rush after her.

As soon as I step out of the locker room, a familiar stench invades my nostrils. I halt in my tracks. Before us stands Coach Lee, wearing his double-extra-large FD quarter zip, the midnight-blue fleece straining against his bulging pectorals. And at his feet is a mass of gnarled black flesh heaving on the glossy floor.

A Deathling.

"So kind of you to join us," Coach barks. "Get in line."

I bite my tongue and hurry over to my place between Anika and Bomani. Like the others, they can't stop gaping at the creature bound in thick leather straps. Double pairs of ebony tusks jut out from its upper and lower mandibles. Four half-lidded eyes droop from sedation. Its mighty five-foot-long tail drags across the ground in sluggish sweeps. Powerful enough to smash through skulls like a human flyswatter. Unlike the Deathling pup I saw in the subway, this one is hairless and wrinkled, like a naked mole rat dipped in black tar.

"Congratulations on making it to your final combat education class," Coach Lee declares. "We have a special guest joining us today. Please give your warmest welcome to Agent Storm."

The main doors to the gymnasium are opened by two men in black suits. The *click-clack* of heels echoes in the silence. A slender woman in five-inch stilettos strolls through; her chic black sunglasses reflect streaks of fluorescent light from above. A slick platinum-blond bob frames the sharp lines of her face, rippling like mercury whenever she moves. Blood-rose lipstick, with immaculate nails to match. She wears white from head to toe, her blazer pristine and her pencil skirt fitted to every curve. A sleek bionic limb extending from below her left knee peeks out from beneath the skirt, all smooth silver and lustrous titanium.

My breath catches in my chest. Even in our exosuit replicas, we look like unkempt street rats next to her.

"Good morning, seniors," she addresses us in a voice as perfectly polished as her appearance. Although her sunglasses make it impossible to see her eyes, I can feel her gaze weighing upon us one by one.

"On behalf of the Syndicate, I will be observing your final combat education class today."

Around me, my classmates straighten, their stances widening. My own pulse quickens.

On behalf of the Syndicate.

The Syndicate sent a striker to scout our class. Better—an *agent*. Compared to the other three types of strikers—masters, mavericks, and enforcers—hardly anyone talks about agents because nobody knows how to *become* one. The process has never been made public, so we know less about agents than we do the anonymous Board of Directors.

First Master Sasha, and now this. I force myself to take a deep breath. Of course, the Deathling tied up mere feet away must be some kind of test. I steal a glance at my classmates, noting the feverish gleam in their eyes, the anticipation rolling off them in waves. Anika is practically bouncing. Like them, part of me knows that I would run face-first into a wall if this woman told me to. But then my stomach clenches with the memory of the throbbing pain from yesterday's wounds.

I need to keep my head on straight.

Agent Storm gestures toward the Deathling. "Can anyone tell me the three methods of incapacitating a Deathling in order of feasibility?"

Every hand shoots up. Agent Storm points. A boy named Pete Figley puffs out his chest while the rest of us stew in envy. "Combustion, i.e., shooting them with nitro-novae bullets, followed by electrocution, and lastly, thorough dismemberment."

Agent Storm nods. "Very good." She strides over to Pete, grabs his hand, and places something small and red in his palm.

And then she raises her bionic leg and kicks the Deathling in the ass.

An unholy shriek ruptures from its mouth hole. The straps restraining its body tremble. It bucks upward. All at once, they tear in half like cardboard.

So much for sparring.

I whip out my staff. As soon as my fingers wrap around the insulated handle, the weapon purrs to life. Electricity crackles through the gym as my classmates activate their own rods. We dive into action, forming three semicircle rows before the Deathling just like we've practiced all year. Frontline positions are first come, first served, and I end up in the middle of the last row with Bomani and two other students.

Though sluggish at first, the Deathling quickly shakes off the lingering effects from the sedation and charges directly at a wide-eyed Pete.

Closest to Pete are the Nguyen twins, Fiona and Khan. Fiona yanks Pete backward while Khan swipes his staff in a zigzag over the monster's ugly head. The motion triggers a surge of electricity to the end of the rod. With a confident smirk, Khan hurls his weapon forth with all his might. But at the last second, the Deathling leaps into the air. The staff skims its belly and clatters all the way to the opposite side of the gym.

Agent Storm tilts her head in assessment. Khan gulps.

Pete finally opens his fist to take a good look at the object in his palm. A mixture of confusion and disbelief dawns on his face. "What the—a lollipop?"

The monster swivels on him.

Deathlings love sweets.

Pete panics and stuffs the lollipop into a bewildered Fiona's hand. The Deathling snorts and lunges for her with its jaws stretched wide. Khan cries out as tusk meets flesh and bone, piercing through his sister's forearm. Fiona manages to jab her staff into its stomach, causing it to release her with an irritated grunt.

When the Deathling whips its tail through the air, only three of us duck in time. With the speed and force of an oncoming train, it flattens the rest of the students to the floor.

Anika, Bomani, and I zap the beast from behind, forcing it to charge toward us rather than all over our fallen classmates. Bomani manages to slice off a chunk of its tail. Anika takes a running leap onto its back, getting in a stab before it bucks her off. Foul brown blood splatters across the gym floor, but the Deathling refuses to die.

"Aggregate!" I yell. We band together, intersecting our staffs above our heads, and sweep them in an arc in perfect sync. Cords of lightning spiral into a single thunderbolt. There's no hesitation, no uncertainty in our movements, the choreography long drilled into our muscles from thousands of hours of practice.

As one, the three of us thrust our weapons upward. The thunderbolt torpedoes straight into the Deathling's face and engulfs it in a fireball. The blast sends us staggering backward. A cloud of charcoal smoke and the scent of charred flesh waft over us.

"Nice work," Bomani pants. Our rods give one last crackle before petering out, out of juice.

From afar, Agent Storm and the two men in suits dogging her continue to observe us. They don't speak, much less congratulate us. They simply wait.

Eventually, when the smoke has thinned to a gray veil, Bomani approaches the Deathling to get a closer look. Anika follows him while I take stock of the casualties. Some students are groaning, nursing fractured ribs and sprained wrists, and Coach Lee sends Khan to take an ashen-faced Fiona to the nurse's office, but we'll all live to see another day.

As I fetch my sheath from the floor to pack up my dead staff, I catch a spasm of movement through the clearing smoke.

Four black eyes snap open. Full of mania. Desperation.

"Coach, look out!" Anika screams as the Deathling lurches upright and makes a final lunge.

BANG.

The Deathling lurches sideways. Sways one stride closer to Coach. Then, with a revolting *squelch*, it collapses to the ground.

I stand with my gun raised, watching as my N.N. bullet combusts its chest into a sticky, oozing crater.

It takes me too long to realize that everyone is staring at me—or rather, the gun in my hand.

Including Agent Storm.

Shit.

If Agent Storm reports me to the headmaster, it won't matter that I saved Coach Lee's life. I won't get to write the final exam, I won't get to compete in the Tournament, and I'll certainly never become a maverick. Everything I've worked for, every vow I made to my parents will fall to dust through my fingers. My career will be over before it begins.

How could I be so *careless*?

Agent Storm removes her sunglasses, revealing wholly black eyes with no whites at all. A strange, overwhelming feeling of déjà vu washes over me. "Who are you?" she asks me.

"Rei," I reply, my heart hammering. I search her face, trying to place her in my memory. "Rei Reynolds."

"I see." She puts her sunglasses back on and addresses the entire class. "As part of today's evaluation, I expect full confidentiality on the preceding events from each of you. That will be all, seniors. Good luck on the final exam."

Her two dogs follow her out the doors, gone without ever having made a sound.

I watch her go, not knowing whether to feel sick with relief or just . . . sick.

Anika waits for the *click-clack* of Agent Storm's stilettos to fade away before speaking up. She hasn't looked at me since Storm left. "Coach, I think you've got something stuck to your back."

After a moment, Coach reaches behind him. He rips off the tape attached to a second red lollipop. He stares at it for a moment before dragging his gaze to the Deathling's steaming corpse.

In all my years at FD Prep, I don't think any of us have ever heard Coach speak at a normal volume. But when he finally finds his voice, we can hardly hear him at all.

"Class dismissed."

CHAPTER SIX

Through the window of the bio lab, I spot Zaza sitting at the table closest to the front of the classroom. While everyone else struggles to complete their work in time, she's already packed up and ready to go. As soon as the bell rings, she books it out of the room, grabs me by the elbow with a grin, and hurries us to the elevators so we can beat the rush. We ride the twenty-two floors down to the street and step into the sunlight. Seniors spill out onto the sidewalk around us, hooting at each other like animals freed from captivity.

There's a black limousine parked at the curb. The chauffeur hops out and opens the passenger door for me. The corners of his roguish brown eyes crinkle, a handsome grin lighting his weathered face. His hair is neatly styled back, raven-black dashed with a few strands of silver. "Miss Reynolds."

"Hello, Declan," I say. My smile for the man is genuine. Beneath his scrupulous uniform and punctilious manners is a heart of gold. He drove my aunt's family around even before the Vanishing. When I was six, I set his pants on fire. We've been thick as thieves ever since. He's bailed me out of some deep shit over the years, and in return, I never set fire to his pants (on purpose) ever again.

Declan takes my things. Before I can get into the car, Zaza blurts, "Wait!" She rummages in her bag and pulls out a Polaroid camera. "Almost forgot." She thrusts the camera at Declan and hauls me toward the front of the limo. "Come on, get on the hood."

"The hood?"

"Yes, the hood! Quickly!"

Giggling like fools, we abandon our bags on the sidewalk and clamber up onto the front of the car, smearing fingerprints all over the gleaming black hood. Declan winces when the car groans slightly beneath our collective weight but graciously keeps his mouth shut.

I reach out to flatten Zaza's flyaways, and she helps tuck my skirt down so I don't accidentally flash the camera.

"Smile, Rei," Zaza orders without even looking. "Our final last day of school ever deserves your dimples." I obey. She rolls onto her side and drapes herself over the car, cocking out her hip and propping her chin up with one hand. "All right, Declan, I'm ready for my close-up."

Click. A little white square of undeveloped film whirs out of the camera. Declan beams. "Wondrous little devices, these things are. I ought to get one for Antonio."

"Isn't your wedding anniversary coming up?"

"Two weeks from tomorrow," he replies. "Lovely of you to remember. It'll be our twentieth."

Zaza sighs. "That's so romantic. Rei should give you guys a shout-out during the Tournament broadcast."

Declan chuckles and snaps one more shot. "I appreciate the thought, Miss Alvarez, but I'm afraid that would be terribly embarrassing for all parties involved."

My grin falls away. I hop off the hood. "And that's only assuming I qualify for the Tournament in the first place."

Zaza frowns and slides off after me. "Of course you will, honey. You deserve it more than anyone." She speaks so matter-of-factly, without a shade of doubt. After squeezing me in a tight hug, she ushers me into the still-open car door. "See you bright and early tomorrow."

Declan pulls the car onto the street. I roll down the tinted black window to blow Zaza a kiss.

"Good luck at the Manor!" she calls, waving goodbye.

I slump against the leather seat. If luck alone could save me, I'd buy myself a horseshoe and hang it around my forehead.

The car swings onto Trinity Place, heading uptown. I prop the side of my cheek against the glass and watch the city ebb by. Grandiose Beaux-Arts buildings cozy themselves between sleek, modern office skyscrapers, while jumbles of opulent stone facades nestle among intimidating fortresses of glass and steel. The bone-white spindles of the Oculus at the World Trade Center cleave like a whale's tail through the sea of people milling around it, the trade tower itself stabbing through the sky like a titanium harpoon. Right beside it, vibrant graffiti covers the entirety of a squat brick museum. None of these buildings should really fit together, let alone complement each other, yet I struggle to picture the city without them. That's Manhattan for you—so many things have changed, but somehow we manage to find harmony in the chaos.

Declan turns the car right to merge onto the West Street expressway. "So," he says, raising his voice over the roar of wind from my still-open window. "How was—"

SCREECH!

He slams the brakes. I catapult forward. The seat belt jerks, cutting deep into my chest.

Across from us, a young man on a tarnished blue bicycle runs the red light.

HOOONK!

He scrapes by the limo's bumper and turns, his ash-brown hair tossing in the wind. Striking green eyes narrow into a death glare at the front of the car. My heart drops.

At first, I can only stare back in disbelief.

"Is that . . . ?" Declan begins.

It's him.

It's that son of a bitch.

Kieran Cross stares back at us for a second longer, now with no emotion flashing across his face whatsoever—let alone remorse. Then he pedals away, swift as a swallow as he weaves through the opposing traffic.

Declan auto-locks the door before I can burst out into the middle of the highway to hunt him down.

"Don't be reckless now, Miss Reynolds."

"Me? He was the one biking the wrong way at forty miles an hour! *Without* a helmet." A big white truck barges rudely into my line of view. I crane my neck farther out, but the bike is long gone.

Declan sighs and continues driving. "You two really were meant to be."

I stiffen and sink lower in my seat. Eyes closing, I try to think of anything else. Anyone else but *him*.

It's been over a year since the day he turned his back on me, but no matter how badly I want to incinerate every memory of him—of *us*—they refuse to fade.

"Miss Reynolds, please refrain from destroying your seat belt," says Declan, sending me some major side-eye in the rearview mirror. "The parts have to be flown in from overseas."

The seat belt I unwittingly tried to strangle slithers out of my grasp.

"Fate does seem to have a way of sticking its nose where and when it's least desired," Declan muses. "Maybe it's a sign that the two of you should re—"

With a touch of desperation, I interrupt. "Hey, have you heard of anyone who works for the Syndicate by the name of Storm? Agent Storm?"

Declan hesitates. "I don't believe so." He sounds slightly put out at the abrupt change of subject but intrigued nonetheless. "Why?"

"She crashed our combat ed class today. To scout us, apparently. Somehow, she got her hands on a Deathling and brought it for us to take down."

"I see." Declan pauses. "That doesn't sound terribly . . . legal."

I shrug and prop my chin on my hand. "Who knows? Seems like the rules are constantly changing these days. Deathlings are changing, too. They've always been hard to kill, but recently . . ." I trail off and arch one eyebrow, leveling Declan with my most critical look. "Something's amiss. Heard anything about it?"

When Declan's expression flickers, I know I've struck gold. "Perhaps."

I blast him with full-on puppy dog eyes. "Declan . . ."

He drops his gaze from mine in the mirror and sticks his nose up. "Whether or not I possess recent Deathling-related intel, you know more than well that I'm sworn to secrecy and can't divulge any of it."

"So that's a yes."

Declan eases the car into the exit lane for West 79th Street. We pass underneath a pole tacked with three signs, all pointing in the same direction: AMERICAN MUSEUM OF NATURAL HISTORY, METROPOLITAN MUSEUM OF ART, and lastly, UPPER WEST SIDE MANOR.

"If you really want answers," says Declan eventually, "there's only one person you can ask."

My stomach clenches. He's right, of course. "Yeah, but do you really think I'll get them?"

A beat. "Probably not."

Before long, we're driving downtown on Broadway. Above the clusters of yellow taxis swarming between lanes rises a lofty eighteen-story château on the corner of 74th Street. Balustraded balconies and elegant swirls of metalwork wrap around the weathered limestone exterior. Sunrays glint off the Parisian-style mansard roof, the enormous bay windows, the grand turrets in turquoise splendor that once housed distinguished artists and celebrities before the Syndicate converted the residence into their largest uptown member headquarters.

"Here we are," announces Declan as the limo glides to a halt at the entrance.

A pair of guards in full uniform await our arrival. One of them approaches the car and opens my door. "Welcome home, Miss Reynolds."

With my bags and staff slung over my shoulder, I step out underneath the forest-green awning and smooth down the pleats of my skirt. The second guard escorts me inside to the security check. Once my weapons and bags are cleared, I head to the elevator bank, where three people are already waiting for the next car. The first wears a scholar's lab coat with her name and BIOCHEMICAL TECHNICIAN embroidered below. The same specialty Zaza is gunning to land a job in. The biochemtech hits the button for the sixth floor, where most of the research laboratories are located. The remaining two scholars couldn't be dressed more differently—poppy-red armored vests with gleaming bronze visors concealing their faces. They each carry a metal briefcase labeled WEAPONS TESTING AND DEVELOPMENT.

"Top floor, please," one of them says to the biochemtech.

To me, she asks pleasantly, "Which floor?"

"Eleven, please," I reply.

Surprise flickers across her features, and then recognition. She takes a discreet step away, avoiding my gaze, and jabs the button like she's afraid it might bite her. Or maybe that I will.

A second before the doors slide shut, a leg shoots through the gap, too quick for the sensors to react. I wince as it gets squashed by the elevator's steel jaws. Then the doors reopen, revealing the leg's owner—a young man wearing a disgruntled expression and a school uniform nearly identical to mine but for the color and the crest: crimson instead of midnight blue, with the Upper West Side Prep logo embroidered on his heart. He glances up.

The moment his green eyes land on me, all the oxygen sucks out of my lungs like a vacuum.

Kieran.

My breath hitches. Of all people, of all places, why him? Why here? My eyes dart to the doors for escape, only for them to close with an air of finality. Leaving me trapped in a tiny metal box with three members of the Syndicate . . . and my ex-boyfriend.

"What the hell are you doing here?" he blurts out.

"What the hell are *you* doing here?" I retort.

"I got an internship at the Manor."

A snort of laughter escapes me. "As if the Syndicate would hire *you* to work here."

He arches an eyebrow. "Why, because I'm such an atrocious human being?"

I mostly meant it because he hasn't graduated yet, but his reason is pretty valid, too. Despite my best efforts, I can't help but notice how different he looks than the last time I saw him over a year ago. Trousers pressed, hair styled. His broad shoulders and chest fill out his blazer, and as much as it pains me to admit it, he's grown taller. Or maybe, more than anything, it's the attitude he gives off—head held high, posture laid-back but confident. Like he finally takes himself seriously now.

I turn my face away, fuming, my voice stuck in my throat.

He gives me a nudge. "Well? How have you been?"

My fist clenches around the handle of my duffel. So *now* he wants to know, after over a year of total radio silence? How can he be so casual, so nonchalant? As if he had no problem moving on, whereas I'm barely restraining the urge to sock him in the eye?

"None of your business," I respond coolly.

"All right, I see how this is gonna go," he mutters. "Guess I shouldn't be surprised. You always liked to make things difficult—"

I whirl on him, dropping all half-assed pretenses of cordiality. "Excuse me?"

The elevator stops. "Pardon me," the biochemtech interrupts, visibly sweating. "This is my floor."

There's an awkward moment as Kieran is forced to shuffle out of her way. Much to my delight, he accidentally bumps into the briefcase of one of the weapontechs.

"Watch it!" the weapontech snaps, cradling the briefcase.

"Sorry—"

"*Pardon me!*" the biochemtech exclaims again, panic edging her voice. Kieran flounders. Finally, he has the sense to step out of the elevator completely, allowing her to flee into the maze of bright white laboratories beyond.

I'm tempted to hit the button that will close the doors before he can make it back inside, but I can feel the eyes of the weapontechs on the back of my head. Once we start ascending again, I glance at the elevator panel. Besides my floor, the only button lit up is for weapons testing and development. Is that where he managed to snag his internship?

"You look tired," I remark, just to kill the unbearably tense silence.

He smiles straight ahead. "And you just look fresh as a daisy yourself, don't you?"

I grind my teeth. Touché.

"You never told me what you were here for," he says after a brief pause. "I take it you're still hell-bent on joining the Striker Division?"

At that, I shoot him a scathing glare. "What do you think?"

He merely nods. "Good. So am I."

I purse my lips. Our shared ambitions had been what drew us together in the first place, but I wish I could have known what disaster it would lead us to. Maybe it wouldn't have made a difference. Either way, it's pointless to think about it now. Even if we both rank top of our respective schools, only one person can win the Tournament and become the next maverick.

And it's going to be me.

Before he can interrogate me further, the elevator stops and opens to the eleventh floor. A long corridor stretches out toward a gargantuan pair of oak doors. Like earlier, Kieran steps out. But rather than waiting for me to pass, he continues down the corridor.

It takes me a solid three seconds to recover from my shock. I rush out after him, hating that I almost have to jog to keep up with his long strides.

"Where do you think you're going?" I demand.

"Work. Stop following me."

"I'm not. This is Master Minyi's floor."

"I'm well aware, thank you very much."

I'm too stunned to speak. Right then, the oak doors swing open. Light floods into the corridor as an empress in shining crimson robes steps out, her sleeves flowing like rivers of red silk. Her hem sweeps all the way down to the black-and-white checkered marble tiles like a peacock's tail. The sunshine basks her silhouette in a halo of shimmering gold.

"There you are," she says in a voice as bright as morning dew. She reaches for me and leans in to kiss me on both cheeks. A wedding band glints on her left hand. Despite its age, it's polished like new. She glances between me and Kieran, the briefest flicker of surprise crossing her expression. But to my confusion, she doesn't accuse him of trespassing. "Have you two already met?"

I elbow myself in front of him before he has the chance to respond. "I don't know what he's doing here. I can call security to escort him out."

"Ouch," he whispers.

Master Minyi's smile only widens. "No need. Allow me to formally introduce you both. Rei, this is Kieran Cross. As I'm sure you've probably guessed, he's a senior from UWS Prep. He's my new assistant."

I start laughing for approximately two seconds before I see the slight smirk on Kieran's face and I realize this isn't a joke. My voice goes flat as I try to hide my disbelief—and dismay. "You don't take assistants, Auntie."

"*Auntie?*" Kieran repeats, bewildered.

"Yes." Master Minyi rests a hand on my back as slow horror dawns across his features. "I'm Rei's aunt."

"And . . ." I chime in, resting my head primly on her shoulder, my smile dripping with sweet, sweet satisfaction. "My dear, beloved adoptive mother."

Kieran looks like he just found out that his puppy got hit by a bus. His accusing eyes find mine. I refuse to acknowledge him at all.

Silence ensues.

"So!" My aunt claps her hands together. "Who wants ramen?"

CHAPTER SEVEN

I've booked a table for four at Yūki," Master Minyi says, beckoning us into the tasteful foyer. A crystal chandelier throws multicolored rainbows onto the giant arrangement of orchids below. Natural sunlight streams in from every direction thanks to the floor-to-ceiling glass panels she replaced the old walls with when she moved in. Before I started high school and she got hired at her current job, Maura and I would wake up before dawn, bundle ourselves in a shared blanket, and sit in front of them. We'd watch the sky lighten tone by tone between the gaps in the skyscrapers as we waited for nightfall to end and the Master of the Upper West Side to come home. "Your sister will be there."

I whirl around. "Maura's back? Since when?"

My giddy delight makes Aunt Minyi smile. "She can't stay long, but she wanted for us to have a late lunch together, at least."

"She can never stay long," I mutter.

"Rei," she warns.

"Yeah, yeah. I know."

My aunt pats my back. "Cheer up. I've heard amazing things about the restaurant. They had a feature in the *Times* two weeks ago. Six-month-long waiting list, isn't that outrageous?"

"Yet you somehow managed to get a table?"

She winks. "Being the Master of the Upper West Side does come with its perks. Kieran, are you hungry? You're welcome to join us for lunch."

My entire body goes cold. The mere thought of sharing a meal with him makes my skin crawl. He's been hanging back this whole time, glowering at framed photographs of what Manhattan once looked like at night—yet it's impossible for me to ignore him. His presence has always been magnetic. Only now I'm repelled by it.

With very little subtlety, I make eye contact with him and make a cutting motion across my throat behind Aunt Minyi's back.

"Thanks for the offer," he tells her without dropping my gaze, "but I already ate. Maybe next time. Should I get started on the report on last night's stats while you're at lunch?"

My aunt beams. "Yes, that would be very helpful."

Kieran hesitates. "Could I have a quick word with your . . . daughter? Just about the final exam."

"Ask her, not me," my aunt says with a chuckle, already heading for the kitchen to make herself a cup of tea. Without turning, she adds, "Rei, I'll be waiting for you in my office."

Her tone makes me shiver. "Be right there." Before Kieran can protest, I grab him by the strap of his backpack and drag him into the nearest closed space—the hallway bathroom. I shove the door closed and lock it to be safe.

"When were you going to tell me the Master of the Upper West Side was your *mom*?" Kieran exclaims.

"Keep your voice down," I hiss. "And she's my adoptive mother, not my mom. My mom's dead. Also, I *was* going to tell you."

"When?"

I throw my hands in the air. "When the time was right! It's not my fault you ended things before that time came."

He leans against the porcelain sink and blows out a long breath. I fold my arms over my chest, realizing belatedly how cramped we are in here.

"Why did Master Minyi hire *you*?" I ask bitterly.

"Why not?"

Jealousy sears through me. I don't want to admit how many times I've offered—no, *begged* her to take me on as an assistant.

So instead of responding, I simply leave. I don't owe him an explanation. I don't owe him anything.

I make a last-ditch attempt to sneak by Master Minyi's office and escape into my bedroom at the end of the hallway, but I can't get two steps past the door before it swings open to reveal her unimpressed expression.

I'm screwed.

I trudge into her office, skirting around the colossal mahogany monstrosity she calls a desk. While another floor-to-ceiling window and a full wall bookshelf behind her desk take up two sides of the room, the third wall is dominated by a framed canvas print of pre-Vanishing Times Square at night. Out of all the works in Aunt Minyi's collection, this one has always been my favorite. Every inch is rendered in stunning detail. The tiny human specks packing every street, every corner. Every LED screen demands your attention, all bright colors and beautiful, enticing people. The dazzling splendor of the billboards and lights is a distant memory now, only captured by images like these. But for my aunt, it's more than a photo. It's a reminder of her life's greatest ambition.

Besides her desk, the only furniture decorating the rest of the office are two wingback armchairs and a large, out-of-place potted plant with waxy dark green leaves that I'm only sort of confident are real. I dump my duffel and staff on the floor and collapse into my usual chair with a *whump*.

With effortless grace, Aunt Minyi seats herself across from me. I keep my delinquent eyes glued to the plant as if that will help forestall the inevitable.

"If you're wondering why I hired Kieran," she begins, "he never spends his afternoons breaking the law." When I open my mouth to protest, she levels me with a look sharp enough to make me shrink. "Don't bother. Master Sasha flagged several hunting sprees in the Financial District during our weekly council meeting today. Imagine my embarrassment when he confronted me afterward to inform me that he'd tracked them to *you*. You explicitly promised me that you wouldn't go off-grid and put yourself in danger. Most importantly, you promised that you wouldn't get *caught*."

I stare stubbornly at the plant. The disappointment in her voice stings harsher than a slap in the face.

"On that note, I believe you have something for me."

With great reluctance, I unzip my duffel bag. I pull out my gun and place it into her waiting palm. "I'm sorry," I say, though it sounds unconvincing even to my ears.

"So this is your new strategy? Steal first, apologize later?"

"I slayed forty-one Deathlings this semester." The confession tears out of my chest. How many months have I held it back from her, waiting for the perfect moment to tell her, to stun her speechless? "Forty-one! It has to be some kind of record, considering I haven't even graduated from high school. Of course, it can't be officially recorded, but I don't care." All that matters is that those kills are mine, and that she knows it.

But when I look up at her face, I see nothing. My heart sinks.

"You know how dangerous it is," my aunt says, "to enter the subway tunnels. Even during the day."

My hands twist in my lap. "Of course I know it's dangerous. But so is your job. You risk your life every time you step out onto the streets at nightfall. And if I become a maverick, so will I."

"Danger is a force beyond our control," Aunt Minyi tells me. "When a tsunami comes, we accept that it will take as it pleases. But that doesn't give you an excuse to walk into the ocean." She reaches over to place her hand on mine. "You are my *daughter*. There is nothing more that I want from this world than the very best for you. You are privileged with opportunities, education, and life itself—you know better than to abuse them."

I bite my lip.

"No more hunting, Rei. No more underground escapades, not unless you become a striker. Or there *will* be consequences. Are we clear?"

I give her a grudging nod.

The melodic chime of the antique clock on the fireplace mantel breaks the silence. My aunt glances up, and just like that, her demeanor transforms. By the time she stands up, she's exchanged her stern expression for her loveliest smile as effortlessly as switching hats. "Look at the time! I'll call Declan to see if he's eaten yet."

Ten minutes later, the three of us head east on 74th past rows of cozy, quintessential Upper West Side townhouses. Rust red, worn white brick, classic brownstone, no two facades alike, shaded by tall, lanky trees swaying in the noon breeze. Cars park bumper to bumper on both sides of the narrow street. A woman wearing sunglasses half the size of her face walks a yappy little poodle. A young couple struggles to maneuver a secondhand couch through a building's door. On the surface, it seems like almost nothing has changed since the Vanishing. But when you take a closer look, you'll start to notice the differences, inching across the city like fractured glass. The barred windows all the way up to the top floors. The old coffee beans left on sills and stairs crunching beneath your shoes. The deep gouges in the asphalt beside a recently replaced manhole cover. A splatter of dried blood on the pavement leading from a sewer grate. We thought about sealing them off like the subways, but if a pipe broke down, we'd find ourselves in deep shit. Quite literally.

We find Yūki easily enough, thanks to the obscene line of people outside the understated entrance. And by understated, I mean you almost have to look twice to confirm its existence. Its only marker is a traditional Japanese noren that hangs in front of the door, two flaps of navy fabric hand-painted with koi fish and calligraphy in broad white strokes.

Despite the line wrapping all the way down the sidewalk, the host instantly spots Aunt Minyi in her crimson master's coat and hurries over to us. Of course my aunt starts conversing fluently with him in Japanese, just one of the many languages she's picked up over the years for work.

"What do you think they're talking about?" I murmur to Declan.

"Wild guess, but maybe ramen," says a voice from behind us.

I spin around to face a tall girl with smooth brown skin and a smile as radiant as the sunrays glinting off her gold hoop earrings. Her floral maxi dress flows in the breeze, paired with a stylish leather jacket and white sneakers.

A massive grin breaks out across my face. Maura throws her arms open. I run into them, laughing. She gives me a spine-cracking hug. "Hey, sis. It's been a hot second."

I do my best to sound disgruntled. "Try five months!"

"Over here!" Aunt Minyi calls from the entrance. She motions for us to follow and slips past the noren. Declan waits patiently for us while we skirt past envious onlookers, lifting one flap so we can duck beneath.

Before I pass, he taps me on the shoulder. "How'd it go with Master Minyi?" he murmurs. "Did you get your answers?"

I merely shake my head. After Aunt Minyi's lecture, I didn't get a chance to ask her about much of anything.

As soon as we step inside, the warmth of the restaurant enfolds us like a welcoming embrace. Paper lanterns hang from the walls, casting a soft golden wash over the tawny plank-wood walls and ceilings. The air is full of the aromatic curl of steam from teacups and bowls, as well as the hushed but lively chatter of patrons, the slurp of noodles, and satisfied sighs.

Our waitress seats us in a corner booth near the bar. After Maura exchanges hugs with her mother and Declan, we slide into the booth across from each other.

Aunt Minyi places her coat on the bench beside Maura. "I'll be in the restroom. Feel free to order in the meantime."

Declan decides to go as well, leaving me and my sister to ourselves. As soon as they're out of earshot, Maura grabs my hands, her eyes alight. It's almost like she never left at all. "Okay, spill."

I have to smile at her enthusiasm. "The final exam is tomorrow at seven a.m. sharp."

"On a *Saturday*? Is that even legal?"

"Apparently."

Maura shakes her head, her grin devilish. "Just another reason why you should've dropped out like I did."

"If it wouldn't mean the death of my career prospects," I reply. "Though you seem to be doing fine."

She waves me off and veers away from the topic like she always does when I mention her job. The job that steals her away for months at a time, yet I know absolutely nothing about except that it's some prestigious, Syndicate-related position. By now I should be used to her vague responses, her dismissive smiles, her evasion tactics. I know her work is classified, but that doesn't make it any easier. "What about in the romance department? Any updates?"

"I saw Kieran today."

She slams her palms against the table. "Where? In jail?"

"Actually, I saw him twice. Declan almost hit him with the car near West Street, and then he showed up at the Manor. Auntie Min hired him as her new assistant."

Her eyes pop wide. "Wait, what the hell?"

"Yeah, it was a really close call. He was riding his bike in the wrong lane—"

"No, no. I meant the assistant thing."

"She wouldn't explain it." I pause. "Maybe she'll be more willing if *you* ask."

Despite the fact that she's mostly absent these days, Maura will always be Aunt Minyi's first daughter. Unlike me, Maura was adopted as a baby by my aunt and her husband, Uncle Elliot, long before the Vanishing. Due to the demanding nature of her parents' normal, pre-Vanishing jobs—Uncle Elliot as a neurosurgeon at Mount Sinai and Aunt Minyi as a special ops agent—she ended up spending a lot of time with my family. We might have just been cousins back then, but she's always felt like my sister.

Then came the Vanishing. That fateful morning, Maura left home for track practice. Thirty-five minutes later the first explosions shook the city. I picked up her call as my parents were cooking and getting ready for work. I remember the sound of her crying, and then looking out the window of our living room and seeing the foreboding swaths of white smothering the skyline, spire by spire. I remember screaming her name into the phone, over and over again, waiting for an answer that would never come.

I didn't understand when my parents sat me down a few days later and explained that Maura was one of the half million people seemingly lost to the fog. At the time, no one really understood it. How it had happened, or why. If we were being punished, if the end of the world was nigh. Even as a child, I knew these things only happened in stories. But maybe my generation knew so little of the world of "before" that we didn't have any other choice but to adapt to our new, harsh reality. And for me, to adapt to a world without my jiě jie—my big sister.

That is, until two entire years later, when she became the first person to ever *come back*.

"So what did Mom say? About your relationship with Kieran, I mean."

I blink to attention and focus on the living, breathing miracle sitting across from me. "Nothing."

Maura smiles. "See? I told you she wouldn't care."

"No, I meant she said nothing because I never told her about him at all."

My sister groans. "Rei, you can't keep this secret from her forever."

"You know how she gets about either of us dating!"

"She can be overprotective at times," Maura allows. Her voice goes soft. "We're her only family left, mèi mei."

I press my lips together to kill the temptation to ask the question that has burned in me for years, ever since Maura returned from the Vanishing to the doorstep of Upper West Side Manor, unconscious and covered in blood that was not her own.

What happened to Uncle Elliot?

Uncle Elliot, who, in his grief, buried himself in work and research after Maura Vanished. Who spent every waking hour in the labs at the Manor, dissecting Deathlings by the light of stardust while his wife battled them on the streets. Who broke curfew without explanation or reason the exact nightfall before Maura was found, only never to return himself.

"Overprotective doesn't describe it," I say instead, swallowing the urge as I always have. "Distrustful, maybe. She never even allowed us to bring any friends over, let alone someone we were dating."

"You can't blame her. There are too many people out there that might use us to get to her, which would put all three of us in harm's way."

I shake my head. "Who would be stupid enough to try and target a master?"

She sips her tea. "You'd be surprised."

Deep down, I know she's right. After all, it's the very reason why I never told Kieran that the Master of the Upper West Side was my aunt. Though I do wish Maura could have seen the look on his face when he found out.

"Something else is bothering you," Maura murmurs, her eyes filled with concern. I've always loved that, despite our other differences, they're the same color as mine. Black as coals, until the light hits them just right. "What was Declan saying to you outside the restaurant about answers?"

I lift my teacup and blow at the steam, savoring the heat seeping through the glazed clay. "Have you ever seen a Deathling pup? In real life?"

"You know talking about Deathlings violates my work contract."

"Does it?" I say innocently. At her stern look, I add hastily, "It's not what you think it is."

"Isn't it? You're asking because you want to hunt them down, don't you? Cull the children to snuff out the rest, that sort of thing. Pretty ruthless, even for you."

"No," I exclaim in shock, loud enough to cause several people to glance over. I lower my voice to a hush. "I mean, I would be lying if I said that hadn't occurred to me at some point or another, but that doesn't mean I actually did it."

Maura stares at me. "You saw a Deathling pup?"

"Yeah, down in the old station at Rector Street. I—I couldn't bring myself to kill it." I tighten my grip on my teacup until it sears my skin. The image of its teeth flash in my mind. "I should have. It probably wasn't big enough yet to kill anyone, but it will be soon."

"So why didn't you?"

I glance up. "Huh?"

My sister watches me carefully. "You hate Deathlings. Why did you choose to spare its life?"

"I—" I falter. An awkward huff of laughter escapes me. "I don't know. A true striker wouldn't have hesitated. I guess I was too . . . weak."

"Weak?" Maura echoes. She reaches across the table and grips both my hands in hers. "Humanity is not a weakness. Don't view it as yours. It's a mark of strength. Always remember that, mèi mei."

"Oh yeah? Have you forgotten what happened to Tofu? If it wasn't for my so-called strength, my dog wouldn't have—"

"Yes, but imagine." Her grip tightens. "Imagine if you could have proved all of us wrong."

I'm about to snap back at her when I realize that this might not just be about Deathlings anymore.

Something happened to Maura during the two years she went missing. Something she won't talk about to anyone but her mom.

With Uncle Elliot and my own parents gone, sometimes I feel like an outsider in my own family. We're like a patchwork quilt—our broken fragments stitched and bound together to form a whole. Each of us has our own boundaries that we must respect, like how I don't ask about Uncle Elliot, or how Aunt Minyi is okay if I never call her "Mom" even if that's what it says on paper.

That's just the way it's always been.

Maura glances over her shoulder and leans in, her voice hushed and urgent. "She's coming back. You know I have limits on what I can communicate to you, but if there's anything else I can do . . ."

An idea strikes me. "If I had the password to the database, you'd never have to get your hands dirty."

"Don't you always guess her password?"

"To her computer. I'm talking about the master key."

Maura purses her lips and releases my hands as Aunt Minyi slides back into her seat. Time's up. "I'll see what I can do."

"About what?" says Aunt Minyi.

"Nothing," we chorus.

"Are you girls keeping secrets from me?"

Maura points her chopsticks accusingly at her mother. "Forget us. You hired an assistant?"

"Yes, I hired Kieran Cross. Arrest me." At our unimpressed glares, she sighs. "What's the big commotion about?"

"Oh, nothing," says Maura. "Except that you've flat-out refused to take on an assistant for years, even when you were drowning in work."

Aunt Minyi picks up her menu and hides her face behind it. "Look, let's just say that Kieran is in a difficult situation. I'm just lending him a hand to right some wrongs. He's a temporary assistant, nothing more. And he makes great coffee."

"Rei makes great coffee."

My aunt sighs again. "Could someone please pour me some tea?"

I fill her cup, resisting the impulse to pour the tea into her lap instead.

"By the way, Maura," Aunt Minyi goes on. "Rei's hoping to compete in the Tournament next week. I doubt she's asked you yet since she knows how swamped you are at work yourself, but I'm sure she'd love it if you could swing by and show your support."

"It's fine," I rush to say. "I don't even know if I'll qualify yet. And you're really busy, so I don't want to be an inconvenience—"

Maura grabs my hands again. "Are you kidding me? Of course I'll be there."

"Really?"

Her smile warms me from the inside out.

"Promise."

CHAPTER EIGHT

On Saturday morning, Zaza and I arrive at Grand Central Terminal, the main headquarters of the Syndicate, to sign nondisclosure agreements about the contents of the exam and to undergo identity verification. Every year, a handful of geniuses hire stand-ins to take their exam for them, but they're better off not showing up at all.

A few hundred students linger about the terminal as scholars and strikers clock in or out of work. Their footsteps echo off the great walls as they hurry down the grand marble staircases, mingling with the passive female voice that recites a constant stream of announcements on the intercom. Being the transportation hub of Manhattan, it's a wonder that it wasn't simply shut down. Now the largest Syndicate facility in all of Manhattan and the state-of-the-art headquarters for all operations only a decade later, this place is truly a testament to the sheer will and influence of the organization's founders—the richest, most powerful, and most forward-thinking New Yorkers this city had to offer. If not for the groundwork they laid (and their money, of course), the Syndicate wouldn't exist.

A few enforcers offer us good luck on their way to the kiosk in the middle of the terminal. We watch as they enter. There's a brilliant flash of golden light in the windows and the chime of a bell, and then they vanish. Whisked to their off-grid destinations, to the laboratories and offices and control rooms below.

"Look," says Zaza. Atop the kiosk, like an opalescent jewel, is the iconic, four-faced Grand Central Timekeeper clock—perhaps the most famous and beloved Artifact besides Lady Liberty herself. And priceless—bringing true meaning to the phrase *time is the only luxury money can't afford*, for the Timekeeper's magical ability is to power not only itself through nightfall, but all the other clocks in Manhattan, too. "Isn't it extraordinary?"

I manage a nod back, fixated on the black swirl of a mav coat in the crowd. I rub my sweaty palms against my uniform and try not to get overwhelmed by the fact that I'm finally *here*, in this immense hall, minutes away from the moment I've spent my entire life preparing for.

The first half of the exam, the core evaluation, is the same for everyone, covering your standard Syndicate-designed curriculum, everything from physics to war strategy, American history to anatomy—human *and* otherwise. Then we split up for specialized testing depending on our study track: striker or scholar.

No rule says you must pass the final exam. Whether or not you receive your diploma depends on your performance during the school year. But any student who wishes to be chosen to join the Syndicate, whether as a striker like me or a scholar like Zaza, must aim for a top score. And if I want my shot at competing in the Tournament to become the next maverick, I need *the* top score in the FD Prep pool.

To calm myself, I touch my left pinkie finger to my thumb. Then my left ring finger. Then both middle fingers to both thumbs. I repeat the pattern in a loop.

This morning I slipped the two photos of my parents into my wallet so I could carry them with me. Just minutes ago, we walked up the very steps my mother and father once stood upon on their first official day in the Syndicate. I gaze out into the station and can't help but imagine them somewhere in the sea of people, their presence soaked in the tiles beneath my own feet and the walls towering around us in every direction.

I will not let them down today.

As we wait for our announcement, we stargaze at the vast cerulean-blue ceiling sprawling high above our heads, marveling open-mouthed at its majesty. A celestial mural of the zodiac constellations dances across it in gold. On the far wall hang two flags: the American flag, and next to it, the Syndicate's—eleven gold stars instead of fifty, the biggest one surrounded by a ring of ten smaller ones to represent the neighborhoods of today's Manhattan, united against a backdrop of the darkest black.

The Timekeeper strikes half past six. The woman's voice makes the announcement over the intercom.

"All Prep League students, please report to the kiosk for transport."

And just like that, the final exam begins.

CHAPTER NINE

For eleven years in a row, along with the rest of my classmates, I sat in the cool darkness of the school gymnasium and watched as the upperclassmen attended the graduation ceremony on live TV. For days, I'd be humming the sweeping orchestral fanfare, majestic enough to bring a tear to any maverick's eye. One thousand uniform-clad students would be packed into the lavish Rose Hall above Columbus Circle, sectioned off by school into a ten-petaled blossom. Crimson, emerald, pearl, plum, honey, charcoal, steel. Midnight blue, of course, for our beloved FD Prep. Midtown Prep is famous for their blisteringly beige uniforms that do nothing for their wearer's complexions but are still nowhere as offensive as the orange eyesores from Tribeca, which according to legend once prompted a police officer to use a Tribeca student in uniform to block off a pothole from traffic until a safety pylon could be found.

Today—now—walking into Rose Hall with Anika and Zaza is utterly surreal. My steps are featherlight, almost tentative, as we let ourselves be carried by the flow of the crowd. The graduating seniors of all ten Prep

League schools stream into the hall, students from every neighborhood of Manhattan. I crane my neck to stare at the spirals of rosewood rafters soaring high above our heads. The tiny gold orbs of light embedded in the floors and walls and ceiling, millions of them, a cascade of twinkling constellations close enough to run our fingers along as we find our seats. Bomani mills about the aisles, chatting with our classmates. He sends us a wave.

Dozens of operators flit about, manning sleek cameras or nimble drones that zip up and down the aisles at dizzying speeds. Last-minute directions rise over the babble of the students as the crew readies for the broadcast. Almost all the cameras point at the center, circular stage, empty but for a podium. A pennant of shimmering black silk spills down the front of the podium, dotted with the Syndicate's eleven stars.

Zaza jerks her chin at the school directly opposite us—Soho Prep. "Pick your champion. Mine's the girl with the undercut and braids in the first row."

It's the game we've played while watching the graduation broadcast over the years. A guessing game. A crapshoot of who we thought would rank first as the cameras panned across the legions of graduating seniors.

"The blond one in the third row, far left," I whisper back. She holds herself like she's already won the Tournament itself, her charcoal-black blazer and matching trousers hugging her lithe body like a glove. Shoulders thrown back, chin tilted upward, blood-red lips pressed together in disdain. Sapphire-blue eyes glittering with cunning. "She's gorgeous."

Anika snorts. "She looks like a cold-hearted bitch."

Zaza elbows me. "Three sections to our right. *Someone's* staring at you."

My gaze slides past the steel-gray wash of Lower East Side Prep and the honey-yellow of Harlem to Upper West Side's sprawling legion in crimson. Of all the schools, they're the rowdiest, propping their legs up onto the seats in front of them, arguing loudly, laughing and jeering at one another like chimpanzees. Everyone except for the boy sitting in the center of the first row, long legs splayed out in front of him, his brow furrowed and his arms folded sullenly over his chest.

"What does he want?" Zaza murmurs.

"Watch this," I say. I wait for his eyes to meet mine. When they do, I blow him a kiss. His cheeks flush the angry red of a newborn. *Take that, shithead.*

"Aw, he's blushing," says Zaza. "Are you finally going to get back together again?"

I scowl. "Of course not."

"I just don't get it," she sighs. "Things were going so well between you two, and then . . . you just what? Fell out of love?"

"Something like that," I mutter.

"Did you see him at the final exam?" she asks. I shake my head. I can tell she's dying to know how the exam went for me, but we both know we're legally forbidden from speaking of it.

My fists flex. "I still can't believe that Auntie Min hired him as her new assistant."

"But your aunt doesn't take assistants," Anika pipes in. And she would know, too—she's tried to get her foot in that door at least a half dozen times.

Before any of us can say another word, the lights dim to near darkness. The chatter falls to a hush. The cameras on standby blink at us like menacing red eyes in the sudden twilight. My blood thrums, my stomach clenches with a strange feeling I can't quite place.

A voice echoes through the hall. *"Going live in 3 . . . 2 . . . 1."*

Spotlights dazzle across the seats. The fanfare theme I've been waiting to hear in person for over a decade blossoms around us. We burst into applause.

"From Rose Hall in New York City, it's the eleventh annual Preparatory League Graduation Ceremony! Ladies and gentlemen, pleeease welcome your host . . . Nick Valentine!"

Every spotlight swivels onto the podium, where a tall man in a glittering black tuxedo has materialized before our eyes. Broad shouldered, dark-skinned, and achingly handsome, the darling of the Syndicate throws his arms outward to us in greeting.

"Welcome!" he booms over the thunderous cheers, his deep voice sending us into further furor. He takes in every single one of us with those warm brown eyes, that electrifying charm. Zaza swoons. We all do. "Welcome to your graduation, Prep League seniors!"

"Phantom! Phantom!" the crowd begins to chant.

Nick Valentine is known by many names, but best by the Phantom due to his chosen Artifact: an ivory half mask that renders its wearer both invisible and invincible. With it, he's untouchable. Although most mavs borrow Artifacts from the Archives' collection on an as-needed basis, the Mask refuses to indulge anyone but Nick as its master. Together, they've recorded over two thousand Deathling kills—the second-highest kill count *ever* after Master Sasha. Which makes Nick Valentine the Syndicate's most lethal maverick. So the Archives was only too happy to grant him— and the Artifact—a more permanent partnership.

Our master of ceremonies holds up his hands, ducking his head with a bashful grin. He waits for us to settle down. "Thank you, thank you. It's my honor, as always, to be your host on this momentous occasion.

"Today marks the culmination of your dedication and diligence. Years and years of studying, training, and grueling work have led you to this moment. Deathlings are a virus in our society, and you—all of you who have devoted yourselves to the Syndicate's vital mission—are the cure. The Syndicate was built to eradicate the abominations plaguing our streets. From the scholars who perform crucial research and oversee the Archives to the strikers defending our lives, all our brave workers and warriors are willing to sacrifice anything to restore the city for all future generations to come." Nick Valentine punches his fist into the air. "A city liberated from monsters and massacre!"

I've never seen the Phantom in the flesh, and I can't help but marvel at the man. No screen could ever do his stage presence justice. We are the air to his flame as he fills the hall and draws us into his light, all-consuming and inescapable.

"So go forth and set us free! Today, you are seniors no more, but graduates! You rise above us all! And tomorrow, you shall rise higher still!"

"Rise above!" I chant alongside the crowd, the Phantom's fire igniting inside my chest, my heart burning with the desire to exterminate all Deathlings. "Rise—"

My voice catches in my throat as my gaze snags on Kieran. Amid hundreds of fanatical students, he is a statue. Silent. Still. He observes the Phantom. And the look in his eyes is so, so cold.

"Now, the moment you've all been waiting for," Nick continues. "The release of the striker rankings!"

The spotlights flare brighter, sweeping outward toward the audience. A 360-degree hidden screen lowers from the ceiling, playing footage from the drones to capture our live reactions to the results. I dismiss Kieran from my thoughts instantly. Some students wave enthusiastically when the cameras land on them, while others offer nothing more than a prim smile.

"First up, Harlem Prep!" The tension thickens, making it hard to breathe. The cameras pan over white-knuckled fists, drawn faces of people whose hearts are about to be broken. For some of us, working toward this moment is all we've known.

A drone flies to the podium and deposits an envelope in the Phantom's waiting hands. He tears it open.

"In third . . . Juan Olivier!"

The spotlights center on a boy in the second row. He makes a show of wiping his brow and looking relieved. Ranking third is perfectly commendable. Maybe he's even glad that he won't have to compete.

"In second . . . Molly Black! And your top ranker . . . Mia Knight!"

The Harlem students cluster around Mia, hugging and congratulating her, some of whom probably aren't even her friends—just desperate for some screentime with the champion of their school.

"And next, Upper West Side Prep!"

I meet Kieran's eyes as Nick Valentine reads off the first name. My hearing fuzzes. I don't hear it clearly, I just know it's not his. And then—"In second, Kieran Cross!"

I expect to see his face crack with disappointment, that strong set of his shoulders break. But as his classmates cheer for him, he just looks . . . resigned. I can't decide whether to pity him or take pleasure in his loss. It's only when Nick Valentine announces the top ranker, a boy—no, a *giant*—nearly seven feet tall and bulging with muscle, Tim Beckett, that true rage flashes across Kieran's face. Tim lets out a roar of triumph loud enough to drown out the rest of the cheers altogether.

Try as I might to memorize all the rankers, the names soon begin to blur together. Only the top rankers stick in my mind. UES Prep's is a boy with a tattoo of a basilisk spreading its wings behind his ear. There's a girl from Chelsea Prep, her nose more crooked than her devious smirk.

The spotlights convene over Soho Prep. "And your top ranker . . ." Valentine pauses for dramatic effect. "Noëlle Cartier!"

Zaza nudges me as the cameras land on the blond girl I wagered on earlier. As we applaud, Noëlle flips her hair over her shoulder with a sniff. She doesn't even look pleased with her ranking. I note that none of her classmates move to congratulate her.

Something trembles in my lap—my hands. They're shaking. I almost ache for the comforting weight of my gun to steady them. Instead, I force my fingers into the patterns—left pinkie to thumb, left ring finger to thumb, both middle fingers to both thumbs. A silent mantra to remind myself of what they promise. Nick continues to list off the top rankers, but I've stopped listening. Killing Deathlings is a cinch compared to this unbearable suspense. Why am I so nervous? I've been top ranker for years and years. Untouchable, just like the Phantom himself.

Because you didn't study enough during the final weeks before the exam, says a voice in my head. *Because you were distracted. Because—*

"And last but certainly not least, Financial District Prep!" Nick announces. Our legion goes wild, as if we could outshine all the schools that came before us just by screaming at the top of our lungs.

Zaza notices me fidgeting and grips my arm. "Breathe, Rei. Do you want to hyperventilate on live television or something?"

"Uungh." I swallow hard, trying to dispel the foreign fluttering in my stomach. My heart pounds against my chest, demanding escape.

"In third . . ."

Rei Reynolds, I hear him saying in my head.

Third is perfectly commendable, I tell myself. *It's good enough.*

But how can it be?

"Please," I find myself whispering through clenched teeth, my lips barely moving. "Please, not third."

"Fiona Nguyen!"

My shoulders sag in relief. My applause is genuine for my classmate.

But I don't even have time to brace myself before Valentine continues.

"Ranking second from FD Prep is . . . Bomani Malick!"

"Yes!" Zaza shouts. My distress momentarily forgotten, we jump to our feet in a standing ovation. Everyone goes wild for Bomani. He blinks in disbelief for a second before a shit-eating grin rises to his face. People slap him on the back, tousle his hair. Once he shakes himself out of his daze, he leaps into the aisle. To everyone's delight, he runs along it, high-fiving outstretched hands like some celebrity athlete scoring the winning goal. Although he didn't rank first, I have no doubt that the Syndicate will pay very close attention to him.

Secretly, I'm even more ecstatic because he had the best chance of outranking me. Zaza shoots me a knowing look.

"You know what this means," she whispers.

"And finally, the top ranker of Financial District Prep . . ." Nick can't keep the grin off his face as he lifts up the note card to read out the last name.

I can't move a muscle. I watch the screen, resisting the urge to projectile vomit onto the drone that zooms toward my row. I watch as the camera slowly tracks from right to left, passing over Zaza . . .

And onto me.

The tension drains out of my body. I exhale with a tiny smile. Zaza grabs my hand and squeezes as if to say, *See? All is right in the world.*

And then the camera glides over me and lands on Anika. My stomach drops. *No,* I think to myself. *No, no, no, stop, come back, this can't be happening—*

Nick's grin widens. *"Anika Maharaj!"*

CHAPTER TEN

When I was nine years old, Aunt Minyi got me a very special gift for summer solstice. As the longest day of the year, we're allowed to eat, drink, and frolic in the streets for an entire evening—so it's basically better than Christmas, even though we only get one day off school since we're supposed to make the most of the extra daylight during the summer months.

I remember she sat me down and made me cover my eyes before placing something in my lap. Something soft and squirmy.

I opened my eyes to a puppy.

He was golden and fluffy, so I named him Tofu. He peed all over the apartment and chewed my shoes to tatters. He wanted belly rubs from every stranger we passed on every walk, and he liked to flop down in the middle of intersections so that I'd have to carry him across the street like a baby.

He was perfect.

But then, one nightfall, I made a mistake.

That night, I learned what it meant to lose all hope.

That feeling floods back to me now, leaving my body ice-cold while my legion celebrates Anika's triumph.

"Oh my god!" she cries beside me, hugging herself. "Oh my god. I can't believe it. Oh my god!"

As I die on the inside, I'm forced to smile and congratulate her because I know the cameras are watching. I applaud, one mechanical clap at a time.

It's over. I lost.

A high-pitched whine fills my ears. I feel the tightness of Zaza's hand gripping my wrist. She's the only one holding me back from doing something very, very rash, and she knows it.

"Wait a moment," Nick exclaims as a drone delivers him yet another envelope. "What's this?"

Anika wavers in her celebration. The students settle down, exchanging confused glances. This is off-key, a dance step gone wrong. The order of business hasn't changed in twelve years, and even Nick looks a little flummoxed. He breaks the seal and slides the note card out.

"A message from the Board of Directors," he reads aloud. The hall fills with whispers. The one and only thing everyone knows about the Directors is that they run the Syndicate, and therefore the city. Anonymous and all-powerful, they don't answer to the masters—the masters answer to *them*. "Due to extraordinary and unprecedented circumstances," Valentine goes on, "and after close consultation with the masters, the Directors have decreed that the roster of competitors for this year's Tournament shall be . . . *doubled*."

His hand shoots into the air to silence the rising wave of commotion.

"Each of the masters has been requested to propose one candidate at their own discretion and submit their nominee as soon as possible. Candidates will be announced no later than noon tomorrow. All decisions," Valentine concludes, looking up from the note card, "are final."

He shakes his head in amazement. "Well, ladies and gentlemen, it seems like we've got ourselves ten wild cards."

"Rei," Zaza whispers, shaking me. "You know what this means? You can still—"

I don't give her a chance to finish. I'm already leaping out of my seat and running for the doors.

✳

"Hello, you've reached the personal cell of Minyi Reynolds, Master of the Upper West Side. Please leave a messa—"

"Dammit," I hiss, jabbing the end call button on my phone. *Seven outgoing calls to Minyi Cell,* my call history reads. Another seven under *Minyi Office.* Whether she's ignoring me, occupied, or asleep, she's not picking up.

I weigh my options and curse again. There's no other choice. I'll have to go to the Manor. Part of me knows she'll choose me as her candidate regardless, but after today's events, I need to make sure.

Of course, when I burst out onto the street to hail a cab, they're all taken. I wish I'd brought my skateboard with me—twenty minutes rattling down roads riddled with craters from Deathling skirmishes beats a forty-five-minute trek any day. Bus then—but no, with the current rush-hour traffic, I'm better off on foot. I'm sprinting down the second block when a black limo glides up to the curb beside me. The window rolls down.

"Get in!" shouts Declan.

I nearly dissolve into a puddle of tears right then and there. Instead, I throw myself into the back seat. "Have I ever told you how much I love you, Declan?"

He revs the engine and shoots into traffic to a cacophony of blaring car horns. "As I believe the kids like to say: I've got yo' back."

"The kids don't say that. How'd you get here so fast?"

"I was watching the broadcast on my phone a few blocks away. Saw you dashing out of the hall like a woman possessed and figured you might need a lift. What were you thinking, trying to run all the way to the Manor?

"No thinking involved," I say grimly. "Just desperation."

Nine minutes later, we pull up to the entrance of Upper West Side Manor. Soon I'm riding the elevator up to Master Minyi's floor. I stride across the black-and-white-checkered tiles and raise my knuckles to the door at the end of the corridor.

The door opens before I can knock.

Aunt Minyi gazes down at me. "Hello, Rei." She's wearing her nightgown, but obviously, she's wide awake.

And she does *not* look happy.

CHAPTER ELEVEN

To be fair, I *did* call her fourteen times in a row.

"What can I do for you?" says my aunt.

I open my mouth to reply. Then hesitate. I prepared a speech on the way here, but suddenly none of it sounds right anymore.

A painful silence stretches out.

My voice is hoarse when I finally confess to her, "You've always been my hero."

Her eyebrows lift.

I let the words spill out. "I've always looked up to you. Even before the Vanishing. Everything I've done, everything I want to be." My voice grows pitifully small. "I want to do what you do. I want to save this city and wipe out Deathlings once and for all."

Master Minyi folds her arms over her chest. After considering me for a long moment, she lets out a sigh and steps out of the entryway. "Come inside."

I trail a few steps behind her as she leads me into her office. She motions for me to take a seat in one of the chairs by the window.

"My dear, there is one thing every maverick must learn before they might one day become a master. It is that this city cannot be saved. Nor does it need or want to be."

"What do you mean? It's not . . . conscious."

"Isn't it?" When I don't respond, she extends her hand toward the window, to the fever rush of the streets below, the honking cars and pedestrians hustling up the sidewalks with their heads bent down, always chasing their next destination. "Don't you feel it?"

"Totally," I say. "The streets and the sidewalks, like arteries and veins, the rhythm of life, the footsteps like beating hearts, the songs of the pigeons—"

"I'm serious. The Vanishing proved that some things cannot be explained. Stardust. The Artifacts."

"Well, they're . . . magic," I answer half-heartedly.

"Do you remember when the Artifacts came into power?"

I nod. I was only three years old, but I'll never forget how they illuminated the sky on the first nightfall like searchlights projected against the clouds, guiding a city still reeling from the inexplicable disaster to their locations. One hundred and fifty-one Artifacts in total—well, technically one hundred and fifty-two since the records claim one went missing.

"Of course, we couldn't retrieve them until the eighth day after the fog had lifted," she continues. "Which is when—"

"Stardust began to fall, and the first Deathling appeared," I finish, tapping my foot impatiently. "So most people believe that they're all linked, especially since stardust couldn't heal injuries from before the Vanishing." The image of the bionic limb belonging to Agent Storm flashes through my mind—a scar from long ago.

My aunt nods. "Some believe in a divine power that bestowed the Artifacts upon us to arm ourselves against the monsters . . . or the city did.

Either way, each of the Artifacts serves one ultimate purpose."

"To kill Deathlings."

"No, Rei. To save the city."

"Same difference."

She only smiles at my mounting frustration. "You grow defensive because I'm pressuring you to seek out what you'd rather ignore. The law of thermodynamics rules that energy—including magic—must give rise from one source to another. We can't just pull it from thin air. You've heard a hundred times that the Artifacts are fickle things. That they have their own personalities. Their own wills. Choosing their masters as the Mask chose the Phantom, for example. They have good days and bad days, just like us."

"You mean the masters?" I ask, confused.

"No, the Artifacts. The Phantom noticed that the Mask's strength varied from day to day. So our analysts began collecting data on its energy levels. We matched the results up against countless variables, and we discovered that the data showed an almost perfect inverse correlation with the city's energy usage. In other words, the more energy consumed by the city during the day, the weaker the Artifacts were at nightfall, and vice versa."

"I've never heard that before."

"That's because the Syndicate hasn't disclosed it to the public."

"Then shouldn't we be cutting citywide energy consumption to give masters and mavs their best fighting chance at nightfall?"

"My point is, you can't—and shouldn't—deny the connection between the Artifacts' powers and the city itself. So who's to say that Deathlings are any different?"

The fervid gleam in her eyes unnerves me. But she's not a conspiracy theorist, she's one of the Syndicate's most powerful weapons of all time. Who am I to doubt her?

"Different or not," I say firmly, "why tell me all this now? You know that's not why I'm here."

"No, I'm simply—"

A leaden feeling settles in my gut. She's never been one to stray off topic. I shove myself out of the chair, fists balled. "You're stalling," I realize. "Fourteen missed calls. You *were* avoiding me. Why won't you propose me as your candidate?"

She rises too, somehow maintaining superiority even though I stand a half head taller. "Four reasons."

"Four?"

"First and foremost, logic asserts that the masters elect candidates capable of contending with the top ranker. Meaning second or third rankers, of which you are neither."

"I was the undefeated top ranker for years!"

Master Minyi tilts her head. "Then why aren't you now?"

I grind my teeth. "Because I—because . . ." I curse and bite my lip. All those excuses swirling around in my head, hiding the truth. I was arrogant. I saw the finish line and assumed it was mine because I couldn't see anyone else behind me.

"Regardless, I'm sure you'll learn from your mistakes," my aunt goes on. "Which brings me to reason number two. When your mother and father died—"

"Were murdered," I correct.

"Yes, *murdered*. From before the day you were even born, I made a vow to my sister to guard you with my life if she could not. To never *intentionally* put you in harm's way."

"You gave me a gun!"

"I gave you training and helped you register for a *permit*. My job comes with its dangers, and I never wanted to leave you defenseless. I may not have the right to control which paths you choose in life, and I'll always support your goals. However, I would be breaking my promise to your mother if I nominated you for the Tournament."

"Tournament or not, I've been training my whole life to join the Syndicate, and I *will* earn my place among you." Despair corrodes a hole through my stomach. "If you claim you support my goals, why stop me when it matters most?"

"Reason number three: it would be a gross display of nepotism."

I roll my eyes. "Oh, *come on*—"

"I'm your aunt, Rei. Only your classmates know you were the top ranker at FD Prep. Even if they all got together to shout it from the rooftops, it'd be worthless now that the official results have been televised. To outsiders, I'd be picking favorites."

"Who cares about favorites?" I demand, desperation clawing my throat. I hate how I must appear to her now, my shoulders trembling, my voice cracking with rising tears. "You raised me. You know what I'm capable of. I can win the Tournament. *You know I can.*"

Aunt Minyi reaches out and envelops me in the warmth of her arms. I cry into her shoulder like a goddamn child. "I know, my dear. I know."

It's the sincerity in her voice that makes my heart—and the last of my hope—plummet. "Then why?" *Four reasons—what could possibly be the last?*

She rubs my back and kisses my temple. "I'm so sorry, Rei. I thought you were going to rank first, I truly did. But this isn't the end of the road. The Tournament is just the fastest way to become a maverick. You can still apply to become an enforcer next cycle and work your way up the ladder like your mother—"

"*Why?*"

"This morning, before your graduation ceremony started, the masters received a message from the Board of Directors. I submitted my proposal right after the Phantom announced the rankings for Upper West Side Prep."

Upper West Side Prep.

"You didn't," I say, suddenly aware of exactly what she's going to say next yet wishing I could deny it all the same. *Let it be anyone else.* Because *of course* she would choose him, why wouldn't she, who else but—

"Kieran," she says. "I chose Kieran."

CHAPTER TWELVE

I want to rage. I want to kick the door down, to smash everything within reach to ruin. Instead, I take a slow, deep breath, untangle myself from her embrace, and step away.

"Thank you for your time," I force out, my voice astonishingly steady. Bowing my head once, I turn on my heel and make for the door.

If this were a book and I were the hero, Master Minyi would call out to me at this exact moment—*Rei, wait! I've changed my mind. Let me see what I can do.*

But she doesn't. She watches me go without a word, or maybe she doesn't watch me at all. I'm too busy escaping into the black-and-white-checkered hallway to turn around.

The exhaustion strikes me out of nowhere. I lean against the wall in the middle of the hallway and sag onto the floor. All my efforts, all those years, all that damned hope and perseverance amounting to nothing but defeat.

I close my eyes and try to reassure myself. There *are* other ways to become a mav. I could apply for an internship. Work my way up. Befriend the right people. Rise above—

RIIIIIIIIING! RIIIIIIIIIIIIIIIIIING!

"Mother*trucker*!" I jam my hand into my pocket and angrily withdraw my phone.

Unknown Caller.

Probably a scammer. I raise the phone to my ear, my voice sarcastic. "Swole patrol, how can I help you?"

"Hello, Miss Reynolds," rumbles a voice deep enough to penetrate my soul. "This is Headmaster Darwin."

My phone slips from my grasp. It clatters to the floor. I scramble to put it back to my ear. "Headmaster Darwin!" I squeak. "Hi! What's—how can I help you?"

"Apologies for the sudden notice, but your presence is needed at school immediately. We can arrange a car to pick you up from wherever you are, just let us know your location."

Shit. Did he see me run away during the ceremony? Is he going to revoke my diploma? My grip on the phone tightens. "Sir, with all due respect, this really isn't the best time—"

"Miss Reynolds, I currently have a very distinguished guest sitting in my office wishing to speak with you. Trust me, you do not want to keep him waiting. Should I send the car?"

"N-no, sir, I—"

"Very well. Make haste, Miss Reynolds. See you soon." With that, he hangs up.

For a long moment, I simply stare at my phone. Then I wipe the snot from my nose and hit speed dial. The call connects on the first ring.

"Hey, Declan. Could you give me a ride?"

✳

The final bell rings right as I step out of the elevator onto the twentieth floor of FD Prep. I thought I'd already said goodbye to this place, yet here I am. Underclassmen pour into the hallways, but everyone gives me a wide berth. Whispers catch like wildfire in my wake.

I quicken my pace.

Inside the administrative offices, the plush carpet muffles my footsteps as I approach the receptionist.

"Excuse me, I'm here to see the headmaster—"

Headmaster Darwin barges out of his office. He ducks his head to avoid colliding with the top of the doorframe. "Ah, Miss Reynolds! There you are." His hand dwarfs mine as I shake it, but I make it a point to match the strength of his grip. "A pleasure as always. Come in, come in."

His beefy torso blocks my view of the office as I follow him through the door. Once inside, I marvel at the vintage maps of Manhattan framed on his walls and the grand floor-to-ceiling shelves brimming with thick leather volumes. The sharp scent of cedar and old books clings to the room as much as it does him. He takes a seat behind the colossal cherry-wood desk in the center of the room.

"Sweet?" asks a familiar, thickly accented voice. A figure lounges on the windowsill overlooking Battery Park. His golden hair slopes down his neck in a sleek tail, a wicked scar in the shape of a crescent curving from his cheek down to his stubbled chin. His midnight-blue trench coat billows about his crossed legs, carried by some invisible draft. Bright, pale blue eyes like lucid diamonds observe me, somehow unhaunted by the endless horrors he's witnessed during his seven-year stint as Master of the Financial District.

"Master Sasha," I stammer out. I resist the ridiculous urge to curtsy.

Having watched and memorized a hundred hours of his combat footage, I struggle to affiliate the godlike striker I know with the person I see sitting mere feet away.

He produces a little bag of candy from his pocket and offers it to me. I take one, wishing I could preserve it forever, but knowing it'll probably melt before the end of the day. Sucking on the sweet, milky toffee, I'm pleasantly surprised by a burst of tangy fruit jam in the center. I've never tasted anything like it. I don't recognize the packaging, either.

"I watched you on broadcast," says Master Sasha, unwrapping two more candies and tossing them into his mouth one after the other. "Your face like soap opera. Where did you scurry off to afterward?"

I blink. For a split second I think about lying, but he'd probably sniff out my bullshit before it even came out of my mouth. "To Master Minyi."

"I thought so." Master Sasha gets to his feet and begins ambling around the office. His coat ripples open to give us a glimpse of the iconic leather shoulder holsters where his twin N.N. guns nestle. He looks so out of place in this tidy little office, this warrior of blood and violence and cruel cunning. "Do you know why I never arrested you for sneaking around underground like little rat?"

"Master Minyi let me use her key code," I begin, trying to decide how I feel about being called a small rodent by one of my lifelong heroes. He shoots me an unimpressed look. "Er . . . unknowingly."

"No. I'm talking about cake traps you set for the Deathlings. Very creative, I must admit. I only saw aftermath, while I patrolled tunnels, but better than most mavs with years of experience." Master Sasha strokes his chin and grins at me so wide it comes off as frightening. "I thought to myself, this little rat impresses me. So I let you roam the sewers to see what might happen. You had no access to Artifacts, yet your kill count could put rookie mavs to shame. That takes more than talent. It takes finesse. And a certain fire."

Yesterday, I would have been beside myself to hear those words from a master. But now they just ring hollow. I stare at my feet. "Thank you, sir."

"Hmph. You are just as infuriatingly humble as your father was." His grin settles into a rueful little smile. "Even if it is all just an act, I would have hoped that Minyi had beaten it out of you by now."

My head jerks up. "You knew my dad?"

"Of course I did. He was the most knowledgeable curator the Archives would ever have. In the early days, no one knew how to use Artifacts. Ru Chen's work was groundbreaking, even if it was short-lived. No need for top rank at snooty private school."

"I believe what Master Sasha might be trying to say," Headmaster Darwin interjects, "is that your exam scores may not have been what you hoped for, but you *were* the top ranker for six years in a row."

"Even if you weren't," says Master Sasha, "working hard is one thing. Working smart, another. But both?" He leans down and wags his finger in my face. "That's the way to make it to the top. And I believe that you have what it takes to stay there, too."

Something stirs deep inside me like cinders catching ablaze.

"Rei Reynolds," the Master of the Financial District declares, "I have chosen you as my champion for the Tournament."

I grab the edge of the headmaster's desk to steady myself. "You want me to be your candidate?" I say with a shaky laugh.

"No." Those diamond eyes glitter. "I said champion."

Dazed, I take a moment to consider what this will mean—representing Master Sasha in the Tournament, and if all goes according to his ambitions, possibly further. *Maverick Rei of the Financial District.* I wonder what Aunt Minyi would say. Speaking of . . . "How do you know that Master Minyi didn't already nominate me?"

With a scoff, Master Sasha starts unwrapping another candy from his pocket and tosses it into his mouth. "She's favored that Cross boy for long time. Besides that, we get notification of each master's pick." He pauses, noticing that I've gone eerily still. "Something wrong?"

Aunt Minyi's words bounce in my head. *Kieran is in a difficult situation. I'm just lending him a hand to right some wrongs. He's a temporary assistant, nothing more.*

All lies.

I shake my head and force myself to focus on what lies before me now: an opportunity. A second—no, a *third* chance.

Master Sasha extends his hand, waiting for me to accept his offer.

But I hesitate.

"You want to know why I picked you, and not second or third rankers," he says.

I nod.

He leans close and lowers his voice to a whisper. "Roland."

My jaw drops. *"Roland?"*

"The little prick told me what you said to him a few days ago." His face grows dark. "You were right. A master must never lose sight of what they rise for and who they rise against. Some already have. Will you, I wonder?"

I rise to my feet and stick out my hand. Master Sasha's grip is unyielding. As we shake, I can't help but release a soft huff of laughter.

His scar dances with amusement. "What is so funny?"

"I was just thinking about how Roland will react when he finds out that you picked me *because of him*. He's going to be so pissed when—"

"He won't."

My smile wavers at the sudden grief in the master's face. "Why not?"

Pain flashes through those stark blue eyes. Maybe diamonds can break after all. "Roland. He's dead."

CHAPTER THIRTEEN

By noon sharp, twenty hopeful candidates will wait in front of the doors of the Archives to begin the first phase of the Tournament. I am the seventh to arrive at the stately mansion of red brick and white stone columns, a midnight-blue armband marked with FD Prep's crest that Master Sasha gave me after our meeting tied around my left bicep.

Shimmering webs of red light encase the mansion in a giant impenetrable cube of death, with enough juice to fry Deathlings—and humans—to ash. The only way through is a rectangular entryway surveilled by security officers toting humongous assault rifles in the courtyard beyond. Though the electricity dies at nightfall, the Artifacts do not, and the Syndicate's best Innovators have figured out a way to harvest a small supply of their energy to safeguard our most valuable assets once the sun goes down.

After I get my face and fingerprints scanned by an officer, I ascend a short flight of stone steps into the courtyard. Of the six competitors that have already arrived, I recognize three. Only one is a top ranker: Yuna Park of Flatiron Prep. According to my research, she was a tae kwon do prodigy. Not to mention that this year she led the team that won the grand prize at the annual STEM competition sponsored by the Syndicate.

One of the competitors I don't recognize approaches me with an easy smile. "Hi, I'm Everly. They/them. I'm the nominee from Midtown Prep."

I shake their hand. "Rei Reynolds, she/her. Nice to meet you."

Everly points out the other competitors. "That dude over there is Langston, from Soho, and Clover's from Upper East Prep—she/her." A young, bronze-skinned man with an emerald band around his bicep and short, black sponge twists raises a hand. Beside him is a short, pale brunette with freckles and a cute smile. She flashes a peace sign before returning to her conversation with a stunning girl with legs for miles. Her deep brown, almost black skin is speckled with lighter patches. "That's Mia, from Harlem Prep. If she looks familiar, it's 'cause you've probably seen her on the billboards at Times Square. She models."

Everly nods at the remaining nominees, who stand in stony silence at opposite corners of the courtyard. "Those two prigs won't deign to interact with me, so I have no clue what their names are. Guess we'll just have to find out on the battlefield." They grin.

"Rei!" a voice exclaims from behind us. We both turn to see Anika bounding up the stairs, an ear-to-ear grin lighting her face. "So happy to see you here! Thank god for your aunt, huh?"

I force a smile. "Actually, Master Sasha nominated me."

"Oh!" Her eyebrows shoot into her bangs. "I see. That's . . . great. Did you meet him through your aunt?"

I let out a dramatic sigh and gaze off into the distance. "Nah. Apparently, he's been scouting me for quite a while. You know how it is."

Anika gives me a curious look that I can't quite discern. "Totally." She spins on Everly, her voice bright. "Hi!"

Everly watches our entire interaction with growing amusement. "I take it you two know each other?"

I bump my armband playfully against Anika's. "Yep. Same school. Anika, this is Everly from Midtown. They go by they/them."

"She/her. Nice to meet you," Anika replies with a handshake. She glances toward the stairs, where several other competitors are arriving. One wears a leather biker jacket covered in a gratuitous number of metal spikes, whereas another, strangely enough, wanders around in a mouse kigurumi—a cute, cozy onesie. In my black button-down and trousers, I feel oddly underdressed.

At one minute before noon, all the competitors but one have arrived. While everyone else gathers by the doors, I lag behind, scanning the streets for Master Minyi's nominee.

Did Kieran drop out?

Do I want him to?

Across the street, a breeze ripples through the trees of Central Park. I check the time on my phone. No sign of him.

Then, with seventeen seconds left on the clock, a speck appears on the horizon of Fifth Avenue and East 102nd Street. A boy on a battered blue bicycle careens toward us at breakneck speed.

Ten seconds left. *He's not going to make it*, I realize.

He screeches to a halt in front of the mansion. The bicycle crashes onto the sidewalk as he sprints and dives for the electrified entryway. Flecks of rubber incinerate off the soles of his shoes as it seals itself behind him a moment later.

Everyone stares as Kieran runs a hand through his wind-tousled hair and saunters over to me.

"Hey," he says.

"Hel-*lo* there," replies the girl in the spiked jacket before I can say anything. She looks him up and down with a smirk lewd enough to make my face grow hot.

Bastian Guerra, the top ranker from Tribeca Prep, evidently does not feel the same way. He adjusts his gold cufflinks and wrinkles his nose at Kieran's bike, which gives him a remarkable resemblance to a pug. "What a piece of junk."

As if on cue, the sun drifts out from behind the clouds to shine down on Kieran's rickety little bike, showcasing its multitude of dents and scratches and chipped paint in a dazzling burst of light as if to say, *Try me.* Kieran merely grins.

The doors of the mansion swing open, and a dreadfully pasty man in white with a dusting of gold hair steps wearily out into the sunlight like an unenthusiastic angel. He checks his watch while simultaneously cradling a bowl-sized mug of coffee in his hands.

"I'm Mr. Humphreys, one of the assistant curators here," he drawls. "Seeing that it's officially noon, you may now proceed inside the Archives." Under his breath, he mutters, "Or don't, see if I care."

With that warm welcome, we file silently into the mansion, only to be greeted by more officers. Rather than normal rifles, these ones carry sleek, state-of-the-art taser rifles humming with lethal electricity.

"Nice guns," someone calls out. It's the human porcupine in the leather jacket. She shoots the rest of us that devilish smirk. Along with her crooked nose, she's hard to forget—Taz Diaz, the top ranker from Chelsea Prep. She curls her arm up and flexes. "But not as nice as these."

Tim, the brute who outranked Kieran, explodes with laughter. Each guffaw echoes like a cannon blast against the sandstone walls. "You call those nice?" He flexes both arms. They're almost twice as wide as his head.

Kieran, who has somehow fallen into step next to me, rolls his eyes so hard that his irises disappear completely.

Taz tries to look unimpressed. "You know what they say about brains versus brawn."

I expect a crude retort from Tim, but all he does is give her a chilling smile that speaks volumes. He *did* outsmart everyone else at Upper West Side Prep, including Kieran—who's been stealing sideways glances at me for the past minute like I won't notice.

"Happy to see me?" I mutter as Mr. Humphreys leads us through long, winding corridors filled with workshops and research labs where the scholars toil, puzzling out the secrets of the Artifacts.

"Always. How'd you get the Master of the Financial District to pick you?" Kieran asks.

"I didn't *get* Master Sasha to pick me. He *wanted* me."

"I don't blame the guy, but . . ." He wiggles his eyebrows. "He's a tad old for you, don't you think?"

I wish he'd been late. I hiss back, "At least he'd be mature enough to face his relationship problems rather than run from them like a childish coward."

"All right, we're here, everyone shut up!" Mr. Humphreys hollers. We draw to a halt before an intimidating set of steel blast doors, the kind designed to resist ballistic strikes. And Deathlings, of course.

Not giving Kieran a chance to respond, I squeeze myself through to the front of the group and ditch him at last.

"Welcome to the carousel," Mr. Humphreys proclaims. "Beyond these doors lies our collection of Artifacts. Currently, we have made fifty accessible to you lot for the Tournament. When these doors open, you will each have ten minutes to choose *one* Artifact to aid you during the competition. You will receive it *only* at the start of each task and must return it promptly at the end. Once you have made your selection, you shall report it to the desk clerks."

Everly raises their hand. "How will the order be decided?"

Mr. Humphreys's smile is wan. "Oh, it's first come, first served."

I try to edge closer to the doors, but another girl blocks my way. I curse in pain as she stomps on my toes in her high-heeled boots. She raises a haughty eyebrow at me and purses her blood-red lips. Noëlle Cartier, the top ranker from the ceremony whom none of her classmates liked. Now I can see why. Rather than giving her a kick in the shins, I send her a disturbing little smile à la Tim. She recoils slightly, giving me just enough room to slip past her.

As Mr. Humphreys inputs a series of codes and biometric scans to unlock the doors, excitement rears through me. For years I've contemplated which Artifact I might choose. The Lexow Gavel, perhaps, which when struck against the ground slows an oncoming enemy for three seconds. Or perhaps the Jellyfish from the Museum of Natural History, which glows whenever your enemies are near. Or even Bernstein's Baton, which lures Deathlings into the open when you conduct anything by Gershwin.

Beep.

The doors heave open, spilling the carousel's scarlet glory into the hallway.

We surge forward like a pack of hungry wolves, but Mr. Humphreys throws one hand up. We freeze. His eyes flash demonically in the red lighting.

"One last thing," he growls, unsheathing a hidden taser baton from his voluminous sleeves and switching it on with an ominous *click*. The black rod hisses and spits electricity at the ceiling. *"No running inside the carousel."*

As we pour inside, most of us can't help but take a moment to simply admire the space. Since there are no publicly disclosed photos or videos of the carousel's layout for security purposes, this is our first look at the legendary home of the Artifacts. Glaring red lamps line the ceiling, bathing our faces in hellfire. Half gallery, half curio emporium, the room contains three concentric rings where the Artifacts hover above the ground, revolving in alternating directions like horses on a carousel, contained inside a sphere of golden light without a lock or latch in sight.

I had no idea that it would be so dark. But it makes sense. Cone and rod cells in human eyes take time—hours, even—to sensitize fully to darkness, and the last thing any mav wants is to have to pick an Artifact and then go out in the middle of nightfall with impaired vision. Hence the lower-wavelength red light illuminating the carousel instead.

I make a beeline for the outer ring. There's no way to tell which of the Artifacts I'll find, nor where they're located. Those records are confidential. Like every good student, however, I have painstakingly memorized the name, appearance, and ability of every single Artifact. I recognize them all on sight: the glazed terracotta Fang from the exterior facade of the Flatiron Building; the shiny NYC Taxi and Limousine Commi-ssion Medallion; the green-and-white 6½ Avenue Street Sign from the intersection at 52nd Street. I weigh the pros and cons of each in my head. The Flatiron Fang grants one extremely amplified sense in exchange for the temporary dampening of another. And whereas the Medallion can increase your reflex speed to help you dodge any attack, the 6½ Avenue Sign allows you to teleport one-quarter of a mile in any direction of your choosing.

If only I knew what the three tasks would involve.

"Tasks change every year," Master Sasha had explained to me as we waited in line at the local ice cream shop he insisted on taking me to after we sealed the deal in Headmaster Darwin's office. "So no way for you to prepare. Just like in the real world. You like chocolate chip cookie dough?"

"Uh, absolutely," I said, distracted by all the stares I could feel boring into us. Master Sasha artfully ignored the attention in favor of the bountiful ice cream flavors displayed behind the glass. "Couldn't you give me some sort of hint?"

"A hint?" he said while ordering two extra-large scoops on waffle cones.

"Yes."

"You need hint to win?"

I blinked. "No, but—"

"Good." He handed me my ice cream. "Now eat."

And that was the end of that.

Langston skirts past me, a little ball of light hidden in his cupped palms. He's not the only one heading for the desks. How did the others choose so quickly? Unless they came across Artifacts so powerful that they didn't have to think twice . . .

Shouts rise into the air. A fistfight breaks out between Taz and Clover by the middle ring as they grapple for the same Artifact. Mr. Humphreys descends upon them with his taser baton. Two zaps, and both competitors fall to the ground, limbs twitching in a macabre dance. The Artifact in question is confiscated.

How much time do we have left? I chew my lip. I'm about to swerve into the innermost ring when something flashes in the corner of my vision. I glance over my shoulder.

An Artifact. And . . . it's following me.

Double-checking to make sure no one else is watching, I hurry closer and realize it's one that I'd already dismissed. A subway token, no bigger than a dime, with a cutout Y in the center. Unused for decades, even prior to the Vanishing, since New Yorkers switched over to MetroCards and contactless payments, and unused now, too. Out of all the Artifacts, this is the only one whose abilities are still unknown—or nonexistent.

The tiny brass coin hovers closer, bumping repeatedly into my chest.

"You're choosing me," I whisper. Slowly, reverently, I reach for it. As soon as my fingers brush the surface of the sphere, the Token within blazes pure gold. Its aged patina withers away, leaving the surface shining like brand new. A strange warmth blossoms across my skin.

But just because it seems to have chosen me doesn't mean *I* should choose *it*. I need to pick an exceptional Artifact. Picking this one should be inconceivable. From my memory, it's only been borrowed from the collection *once* in nearly fourteen years. If no scholar could figure out what it does, what chance do I have?

"Two minutes left," intones Mr. Humphreys from somewhere in the gloom.

Only four competitors remain inside the carousel, zigzagging through the rings, still searching. I hear someone fall into step behind me. I steal a glance over my shoulder. It's the girl in the mouse onesie. She glares at me, her eyes glinting satanically in the lamplight. I suddenly notice the scaly pink tail dragging behind her. Not a mouse. A *rat*.

I pick up my pace.

Only to skid to a halt in front of an unclaimed treasure etched in gold. Randel's Map.

My heart twists as I think of Roland. Could he have been the last to use it? I reach for it, but it floats out of my grasp, the corner of the parchment wagging down at the Token cupped in my palm. Unless I return it, I can't take Randel's Map. But before I can choose between them, the rat girl swoops in front of me and snatches the map right from under my nose.

"Hey!" I exclaim, but it's far too late. I swear, regret stinging my stomach.

"Ten seconds left," announces Mr. Humphreys.

The checkout desk is on the other side of the room. I have no choice. I sprint for the desk. A useless Artifact is better than no Artifact at all.

I'm mere feet away from safety when the furious crackle of electricity fills the air. Mr. Humphreys appears out of nowhere with a malicious grin, his taser baton aimed directly at my face.

No running inside the carousel.

Too late do I remember his warning. Terror jolts through me. As he swings, I try to duck, but he's too close, too fast. I clutch the Token to my chest, shielding it, my eyes squeezed shut as I brace for the pain—

With a rocking *BOOM* and the shatter of glass, the world explodes in a flash of blinding gold.

Then everything goes black.

CHAPTER FOURTEEN

I awaken to the sweet scent of jasmine and Mom hovering over me with a steaming mug of honey-lemon tea.

"Here," she tells me. "Drink this." Her face is turned to the window. Her necklace—*my* necklace—winks gold in the fading daylight.

I take a sip. It soothes my throat and fills my veins with molten warmth. I sigh and set the empty mug on the bedside table, snuggling deeper into the blankets, my eyes already drooping shut.

I hear her slippers padding across the carpet. Her step is so light, as if the ground is the back of a beast and she's afraid to wake it. Something wet trickles onto my face as she presses a kiss to my forehead and whispers, "*They're coming.*"

My eyes fly open. Her face looms inches away from mine, glistening with gore, four scarlet claw marks gouging each cheek. Half her jaw is nothing but a gaping crater, ringed by the outline of teeth raking across her lips and neck. Blood spills off her chin into my eyes, blinding me as I try to cry out, to escape, to forget that night, as a monster devoured her whole and I could do nothing but *scream*—

Her hands wrap around my throat. They cut into my skin, cold and stinging, like metal chains. *"Never let them take it from you,"* she hisses as I thrash beneath her, slowly blacking out. *"Never!"*

I yank myself out of the nightmare with a gasp. As my mind races, my body is still soft with sleep, totally oblivious to the nightmare so fresh and violent and vivid in my mind. For a minute I lie in the darkness, unmoving except to touch the talisman at my neck, to trace the ridges and grooves of the character. *Shǎn.*

It takes me too long to realize that the pillow underneath my head feels totally unfamiliar. I shoot upright and grope around in the dark. The pajamas I'm wearing don't belong to me, either.

I search my memory. Running for the checkout desk, that vulture in white descending upon me. The Taser baton. The explosion of gold. As for the rest, I have no recollection.

Carefully, I slide out of the bed to investigate. My bare feet brush the cold linoleum floor, then there's a soft *whirr* to my left. A rectangular panel in the wall glides open, flooding the sparse, compact room with purple light. There's nowhere to hide, and it's too late to pretend I'm still asleep. I grab the nearest object to use as a weapon and leap into a fighting stance.

My aunt strides inside, a mug in hand. The strips of light flickering along the ceiling bathe her face in an eerie, bruised indigo. She stops short.

"Have mercy, O Fearsome One," she finally says, eyeing the pillow I'm fiercely brandishing over my head. She holds out the mug. "Tea?"

My nose wrinkles at the faint scent of lemon and honey. I shake my head vigorously. Not while Mom's mutilated face still haunts my mind. Also, it feels like too much of an unsaid apology, which I'm in no mood to accept.

Aunt Minyi sits herself on the edge of the bed. Beside her, I now notice, is a neatly folded garment in black. My FD Prep armband rests atop it. "Do you know where you are?"

"The Sanctuary?"

"That's right. Ordinarily, only strikers and essential personnel have access to these facilities, but as usual we've extended our hospitality to you and the other nineteen competitors for the duration of the Tournament. Until elimination, at least."

"Will the rules for elimination change now that the roster's been doubled?"

"You'll find out with everyone else at breakfast, along with instructions for the first task."

"So what are you doing here?" I ask.

"I just got off duty. I heard about what happened at the carousel. I wanted to talk to you about it in private first."

"I know, I know. I should have picked something better. I should have gone for Randel's Map or something—"

"I was talking about when Mr. Humphreys tried to intercept you near the desks. And then . . ." She splays her fingers outward. "*Boom*. Mr. Humphreys sustained first-degree burns and a minor concussion—he's fine now, of course—but you made it out utterly unscathed."

I'd have better luck cracking an optical illusion than her expression. Her pleasant smile conflicts with the grave crease of her brow. I read a dozen different signals from her features, none of which I can discern to be real or a facade.

"I just assumed that someone else stepped in because they thought he was going too far."

"No one stepped in, Rei."

"Wait, are you implying that *I* caused the explosion?" I shake my head. "I wasn't trying to hurt Mr. Humphreys, I swear."

"That's not what I meant," my aunt reassures me. "Being in the carousel surrounded by Artifacts, it's impossible to say exactly who or what triggered the explosion."

"Could it have been the Token?" I dare to ask.

She touches my shoulder. "Try not to get your hopes up, Rei. There's a reason why hundreds of scholars haven't had any luck whatsoever with that particular Artifact."

The lights on the ceiling begin to flash, accompanied by a bell-like chime.

My aunt rises. "That's your wake-up call. You're meeting the masters at breakfast in fifteen minutes, so get changed. Oh, and enjoy the toast," she adds with a coy smile.

I follow her to the door, befuddled.

She rounds on me just before leaving, her expression shifting into a new mask within a single blink. "One last thing, Rei. Do not tell anyone about what we discussed here. Not Kieran. And especially not Master Sasha."

I barely hear the second part, feeling only the stab of her lies again at the mention of Kieran. I stare at the floor, stomach twisting. "Aunt Minyi, wait—"

But she's already gone.

✳

At breakfast, there is no breakfast. Not for us, at least.

Three masters lounge around one-half of a round table laden with a lavish feast, observing the twenty high-strung teenagers crammed elbow to elbow across from them like a chain of dynamite set to erupt at the slightest spark.

I sweat quietly in my newly issued Tournament uniform, identical to everyone else's apart from my name, emblazoned vertically along the left sleeve above my FD Prep armband. The uniform resembles an exosuit, but the center of my chest and back have been equipped with two circular discs aglow with green light.

I'm caught between Anika and Bastian, the pug-faced top ranker who sneered at Kieran's bike. His buggy eyes are glued to the tower of frosted cinnamon rolls. He drools a little.

"Ah, the smell of bloodlust," muses the Master of Tribeca, a stocky woman with a flame-red Mohawk. She crosses her bulky arms and leans back in her chair, balancing the front legs precariously in midair. Her N.N. gun hangs from her hip, modified into a fat, triple-barrel blaster thick as a fist.

"Smells like bacon to me, Master Eliza," quips a man with kind eyes and curly hair graying at the temples. While Master Hassan of Midtown may be the oldest of the masters in age, his genteel manner belies his true lethality.

"No, I smell it, too," says Master Sasha. It's jarring to see him, mostly because he all but ignores my presence. Despite being the master to have chosen me, he cautioned me not to expect anything beyond the nomination itself during the Tournament. It's only fair to the top rankers who earned themselves a seat at this table with their scores.

We all watch hungrily as Master Sasha cleaves through a poached egg in one deft stroke. He deliberately lets the ruptured yolk dribble onto his toast as slowly as possible. Bastian moans aloud. Master Sasha chuckles.

The main door glides open. In walks Nick Valentine, dressed in a burgundy velvet suit. He flashes us a grin so roguishly charming that even Tim blushes. "Morning, competitors. I need two volunteers. Anyone?"

Everyone's hands shoot into the air.

He picks Noëlle and Everly. "Stand against that wall, will you?" he asks Noëlle. As she complies, he fishes into his blazer and hands Everly a gun. "Now shoot her."

Everly fumbles with the weapon for a second. But before the shock has fully settled over some of us, they raise their arm and fire point-blank into Noëlle's chest.

Several of the competitors flinch, but stony-faced Noëlle doesn't even blink. Nor, unfortunately, does she fall. Instead, her disc flashes, changing from green to red.

Valentine gives Everly a jovial pat on the back. "Splendid aim. For this task, each of you will be assigned one of two roles: Raider," he declares, taking the gun from Everly and holding it up dramatically for all to see, "or Evader." With a flourish, he reveals three brightly colored flags hanging from his waist belt like fall's hottest new fashion trend. "You also have two objectives: to collect as many flags as possible, and to avoid getting shot at all costs. At the end of the hour, each flag in your possession will be worth one point."

"So only Raiders get guns?" someone interrupts. Her sleeve reads DAWN CHO. It takes me a moment to recognize the girl who snatched Randel's Map from me yesterday. She's not wearing her mouse onesie today, but she's done her hair up in two cute space buns, which does nothing to detract from her petite stature. It's clear she's the smallest of all the competitors, but judging from her vicious glower, she couldn't care less. My sister always told me that it's the fun-sized ones you have to beware of—their bodies can't contain the extent of their rage.

"Correct," says Valentine. "And I know what you're thinking—why would anyone want to end up as an Evader? To even out the advantage, Evaders will receive *three* flags right at the start of the task while Raiders only get one. Each will be marked with their initials. If they manage to successfully evade the Raiders and keep possession of their own flags until the end of the task, the value of those flags will be worth triple the points."

A trio of servers file in, bearing trays of crystal tumblers filled with a finger of some amber liquid. They begin handing them out to all the candidates. A separate server brings glasses for the masters and Valentine. I can't help but notice that Tim gets double the amount that the rest of us do. He gloats.

"What an asswipe," Anika mutters under her breath. She nudges me beneath the table with her knee. "You can bet I'll be giving him a good slugging at the first opportunity I get."

"Get in line," I mutter back.

"There are three ways to get eliminated," Valentine goes on. "Obviously, getting shot. The boundaries of the playing field will be clearly defined. Cross them, and you're out as well. Finally, any candidate that does not finish the task with a top ten score will also be eliminated."

Disbelief falls over the room. Under normal circumstances, only three candidates would get eliminated during the first task. I was expecting that the number would be doubled to six, like how the roster was doubled from ten to twenty, but it looks like they're hoping to cut us down—fast. Everyone at the table scrutinizes one another in a new light.

Valentine smiles at the sudden shift. "Oh, and one last thing. If a fellow competitor scores a hit on you and the disc on your exosuit turns red, you will surrender all flags—and points—in your possession to them."

"Today, neither the strong nor the clever will rise," Master Hassan proclaims. "Only a combination of both will allow you to prevail."

"The Tournament is your stage," says Master Eliza. "Year after year, the Tournament outperforms every single international broadcast. There's more than just a trophy or title at stake. Whoever wins," she says, looking at each of us in turn, "could determine this city's survival."

Valentine raises his glass. We follow suit, albeit uneasily. "Around the world, everyone is watching. *Hoping.* For someone to bring Manhattan and all its people to liberation, so that one day we may once again open our doors to the world."

"Also, it is marvelous entertainment," Master Sasha adds. "For us."

"Indeed, we will be watching you," Master Hassan amends with a wry smile, "as will every member of the Syndicate—including the Directors. Every single one of you sitting in this room has the potential to become a maverick at the snap of their fingers . . . but only if you can prove yourselves worthy."

A thrill runs through my veins.

"The time has come!" says Valentine. "Show us that you have what it takes to become one of us. To rise, and above all, to defend the people of New York City. For where Deathlings dwell . . . here be champions!"

"Here be champions!" all of us chorus before downing our toasts.

I choke immediately. Coughs fill the room as the other competitors struggle to keep the unbearably bitter drink down—even prim and proper Noëlle can't help but gag. The masters regard us, completely unaffected. Perhaps it's an acquired taste—taste that's pure *shit*.

"So, do we get to decide who's a Raider by fighting each other or . . . or what?" says Tim. His voice slurs. He makes a face at his empty glass. I don't blame him—my own head is swimming from that awful concoction.

Master Eliza snorts and takes a bite of one of the humongous cinnamon rolls that poor Bastian was salivating over. When the hell do we get to eat? Aunt Minyi said we'd get toast, didn't she? "You wish, kid. You either *wake up* as a Raider or you don't."

Beside me, Anika slumps into the table face-first with a loud *thunk*. Bastian follows a second later, his tongue lolling out of his mouth.

Toast.

The toast.

"You drugged us!" Everly accuses, struggling to keep conscious.

"Triple-Z," says Master Eliza. "Works like a charm every time."

Tim slumps sideways onto Kieran, his glass slipping out of his limp hand and shattering on the floor. I force my eyelids to stay open as the other candidates drop cold.

Master Sasha chuckles at my efforts. Before anyone can stop him, he walks over, places two fingers over my eyelids, and slides them gently shut. "Good luck, little rat," he whispers.

I remember nothing else.

CHAPTER FIFTEEN

I jolt awake to the hard press of stone digging into my back. Lush trees sway above me, their red and gold leaves vivid against the overcast sky. Past them stretches a dome of shimmering red light, identical to the energy shield at the Archives. Beyond it, the rugged Midtown skyline.

It's impossible not to recognize this place.

I'm in the middle of Central Park.

The disc on my chest pulses. The sky flashes. Projected in bold block numbers onto the ceiling of the dome, the clock begins its countdown:

60:00

59:59

59:58

I see no other competitors, but based on the size of the dome, they can't be far. I scan my surroundings. To my left, a playground usually crawling with squealing children lies lifeless, the iron chains of the swings creaking ominously in the wind. The outcropping of rock I'm standing upon can only be Rat Rock—a colossal mass of reddish-gray Manhattan schist allegedly named after the rats that once swarmed its nooks and crannies.

A small cloth sack on the ground near my feet catches my eye. Grabbing it, I loosen the top to find my chosen Artifact—the Token.

"Might as well have showed up with a potato," I mutter.

I pat my hips. My hands brush not the hard, comforting solidity of a weapon, but three soft squares of fabric pinned to my hips.

Humiliation creeps up my neck. So I'm to be hunted.

The way Valentine explained the rules made the game sound fair to both Raiders and Evaders, but it still boils down to the same thing. Humans versus Deathlings. Predator versus prey. Without a gun, I have no choice but to run and hide.

I clench my jaw. Fat chance of that.

A high-pitched *buzz* pervades the air. I spot a flash of black soaring over the trees. The drone dips down to hover nearby, all four of its camera lenses focused on my face like shiny insect eyes. Like every other New Yorker, not to mention people from all over the world, I've watched the Tournament broadcasts for years. It feels strange—almost alienating—to imagine my face televised on millions of screens, my every movement watched, analyzed, and criticized. Could the Directors be watching me at this very moment?

One thing's for sure: I could use an ally. Unfortunately, Anika's my best bet. But right as I step out into the open, a menacing guffaw cuts through the air. I duck back behind Rat Rock, my heart hammering, just as four figures appear on the path leading to the playground.

The one in front towers over the rest. It's Tim—and he's got a gun.

Of course he's a Raider, I think sourly.

Then I see the object in his other hand, and my heart plummets even further. It almost looks like the jagged beak of some gargantuan, prehistoric bird, but in fact it's a pair of colossal crab pincers: the Chela. It was once part of the Peace Fountain, symbolizing the struggle of life, of good against evil. Tim obviously didn't get that memo. Despite the unwieldy weight and size of the Artifact, he swings it around like a chainsaw without breaking a sweat. With its power, he's more than just a threat. He's unstoppable.

The competitor yapping loudly at his heels must be Bastian. One glimpse of the lustrous blond ponytail belonging to the third figure is enough to recognize Noëlle.

When I see they're both carrying guns, a foul suspicion strikes me.

At that moment, a fourth figure appears through the foliage. Anika joins her new allies, her sweet smile tipped with malice. She, too, holds a weapon.

The four of them share one thing in common: they're all top rankers.

As I lean out to get a better look, the grit beneath my boots crunches. Anika turns in the direction of the rock. I fling myself behind it and hold my breath.

After a minute of silence, I glance around the corner to check—

And find myself face-to-face with Anika.

Keeping her gun leveled at my chest, she puts a finger to her lips. I search for an opening, but she's put enough distance between us that I can't take her down without getting hit.

"What happened to giving Tim a good slugging?" I hiss back at her.

She tosses her hair over her shoulder. "You'd have done the same if you were a Raider."

"How do you know that I'm not?"

"You'd be pointing a gun at me by now. Now hand over your flags."

"Like hell I will."

She shrugs. Her confidence is sickening. "Do it, and I'll let you go. Otherwise I'll eliminate you from the Tournament right here, right now, and you'll have to give up your flags to me anyway."

I grind my teeth. "Why bother giving me the option?"

"What can you even do? You're an Evader." Her lips curl into a smirk. "Also, it's your fault I could never rank first at FD Prep. So consider it a thank-you for screwing up your final exam and letting me take your spot."

It takes every ounce of willpower in my body not to punch her in the face. But she has me at a devastating disadvantage.

"Anika!" Bastian's voice yells from afar. "Tim said you'd better move your ass, or we're leaving you behind."

I tense, preparing to flee the second she exposes me, but she shouts back, "One sec!" She gestures at me with her gun. "Hurry up."

I have no choice. Hating her with every cell in my body, I toss my flags down at my feet.

With a glare, she bends down in front of me to pick them up, keeping her gun carefully trained on my disc all the while. She scrunches up the flags as tight as she can and stuffs them into her boots. Right before she runs off to rejoin Bastian, she sends me a sugary smile. "For what it's worth, I'm sure you would've made a great Raider."

I bite my tongue hard and wait for her to disappear. Only once her footsteps have completely faded away do I allow the air to collapse out of my chest.

I'm furious.

Furious that Anika was chosen to be a Raider and I wasn't. Furious at myself for getting caught so quickly and being forced to surrender my flags.

Screw this. I'm done squatting in the dirt. I'm not waiting around for some worthless Raider to gun me down.

I stick to the trees while I scout the area, but everyone seems to have steered clear of Tim and his posse. If only I had taken Randel's Map at the carousel—with it, I could have asked it to track the locations of all the competitors.

The pressure of time winding down ticks like a bomb in my chest. Out of desperation, I take the Token out of my pocket. I do my best to recall the confidence I felt at the carousel when the Token chose me, when I thought myself capable of unlocking its secrets. Taking a deep breath, I try to summon the golden light.

Nothing.

I murmur magic words. I wave it around in ridiculous, whimsical patterns. I even try begging.

A peculiar rumbling rises from the distance. Hope surges through my chest until I realize it's not coming from the Token. I crouch behind the trunk of an elm tree, its shaking branches raining leaves down upon the path.

A creature large as a grizzly bear and white as snow bursts out of the trees up ahead. My eyes widen. Not a bear, but a massive lion. An actual, *live* lion. Before I can panic and think some maniac broke into Central Park Zoo and freed the big cats, I catch sight of a girl riding upon its back. It's Yuna Park, top ranker of Flatiron Prep. In one hand, she totes a gun. In the other, three colorful, rumpled flags. As she blurs past, her short black hair streaming in the wind, I realize the lion isn't flesh and blood at all, but solid marble. It's an Artifact, brought to life.

I hurl the Token into the dirt.

Yuna and her lion are gone in a blink, but they leave behind a cloud of dust that shrouds the main path. The perfect cover, I realize. As I'm about to head for the path, another competitor sharing my opinion crosses over onto my side. The boy with cruel gray eyes that I recognize as the top ranker of Lower East Side Prep. If he's anything like the other top rankers so far . . .

Then he's got what I want.

I press myself behind the elm tree, keeping just out of his line of sight. When he darts onto the grass, oblivious, I pounce. He lets out a cry as I wrestle him to the ground and shove his face into the mud, muffling his screams. I clamber onto his back and pin him down with all my weight. He jams his elbow into my side, knocking me off. Silver flashes in the corner of my vision. He rolls over, aims the gun directly between my eyes, and pulls the trigger.

Nothing happens. In his moment of confusion, I rip the weapon out of his grasp and point it at the center of his chest—at his disc. I grin as he realizes his mistake.

He gasps. "Wait! You can't shoot me, I'm a Raider."

"Says who?"

"The masters, you idiot! They chose me to have a gun."

"This gun, you mean?" With fake surprise, I glance at the weapon in my hand right before I fire it at his disc. The disc that's on *every* competitor's chest, regardless of their role in the game. It flares from green to red.

A drone descends from a nearby tree, propellers buzzing. "Lars Hendriks, LES Prep, top ranker. Eliminated by Rei Reynolds, FD Prep, nominee. Please exit the arena."

Lars purples with rage. "You low-ranking trash. I'll make you pay."

Stunned by his words, I barely manage to stumble out of the way as he lunges for me. His disc blazes white. He screams and falls to his knees, his entire body convulsing and crackling with electricity.

I back away, my eyes wide. I don't want to stick around long enough to find out whether he'll get escorted out of the arena on his feet or on a stretcher.

Low-ranking trash.

I shake the words from my head as I forge deeper into the park.

I can't let them distract me right now, no matter how hard it is to push away the shame that they're partly true.

My grip tightens on my newly acquired weapon.

After all, trash or not, I've got a tournament to win.

CHAPTER SIXTEEN

Thirty minutes before the end of the first task, a *CRASH* like the clap of thunder splits the air, and the dome of shimmering red light marking the boundaries of the arena begins to shrink. The walls press inward, herding together sheep and wolf alike. Soon, even those in hiding will be forced to clash.

The transformation reduces the arena to three main locations: Rat Rock and the playground; the swath of trees and footpaths surrounding them; and the softball diamonds to the north, a wide open plain of grass fields and sand that encompass nearly half of the remaining territory.

The trees whisper in the breeze as I skirt around the edge of the fields, determined to scope out the area before it's too late. While Tim's posse roots out the Evaders, I need to find the best place to spy on them.

My plan to run into some lone stragglers and catch them off guard fails miserably. The outskirts of the arena are utterly deserted.

It isn't until I arrive at an old merry-go-round at the northeast perimeter of the boundary that I realize I'm being followed.

An eerie, grayish gloom casts the merry-go-round horses in darkness. Their painted manes and saddles are chipped and faded, remnants from another time. I hop onto the platform, my fingers brushing the cold steel bars impaling each steed midair. The shiny veneer does nothing to hide their grotesque expressions, their mouths open in silent, soundless laughter—or screams.

On the other side of the merry-go-round, I slip into an ornate chariot pulled by a black stallion.

Something whooshes through the air behind me.

"Hey, sunshine," says a familiar voice.

I whip around to find a mud-streaked Kieran leaning against the horse to my right. Without thinking, I shoot him directly in the chest.

His disc stays green.

My jaw drops. There's no way. Just to make sure, I shoot him a second time. And a third.

"Done yet?"

His cheeky smirk tells me I'm missing something. And the only satisfaction greater than catching me off guard will be letting him see my frustration grow.

"How did you find me?" I demand instead.

He simply pulls out a sheaf of aged parchment from behind his back and waves it over his head.

"That's—that's Randel's Map," I stammer. "That was Dawn's Artifact!"

"Yeah, I know. I stole it." He makes a face. "It was the least I could do. She stole my flags first."

I still can't believe my eyes. "You've got the map now! Just track her down and steal them back."

"I *would*," he says, his nostrils flaring, "but unfortunately she bought her own protection by giving two of them up to Tim."

Of course she did, the weasel. Even as an Evader, she found herself a way to survive.

I take a deep breath. "Well then? What do you want from me?"

"Hey, no need for such hostility. I'm just looking for an ally."

I scoff. "I'd rather lick the mud off Tim's boots."

His gaze hardens. "No, you'd rather win this task. And no offense, but you don't look like you're doing a very good job of it."

"Like you could do any better."

"Face it, sunshine—"

"You do *not* get to call me that anymore," I snarl.

He winces. "Look, at this rate, both of us barely stand a chance of passing this task. But I have the map, and you have a weapon. Together, we can get our flags back—and maybe even eliminate Tim and the other Raiders while we're at it."

My heart jumps at the possibility. Even so, I can't trust him so easily. He's still hiding something. "Why don't I just force you to give me the map right now?"

He spreads his arms open in invitation, exposing his disc once more. "You can try, but I'm afraid the map and I come as a package deal."

My eyes narrow.

"If I wanted you eliminated, I could've chosen any other competitor to help me out. But we're almost out of time. And regardless of your lack of trust in me, you're the only person *I* trust." At my stony silence, he throws his hands in the air. "Come on, Reynolds. What's your alternative? Spend the rest of the task hoping to randomly pick off competitors? Even if you get lucky enough to cross paths with someone, there's no guarantee they'll have any flags."

"You should know better than to underestimate me."

He regards me for a long moment. "I thought you were the one who believed in working things out, but obviously I was wrong. I'll stop wasting both of our time and find someone else to be my ally."

I'm too stung to come up with a witty retort. As he turns away, I bite my lip. Strategically, I'd be a fool to miss this chance—or maybe not. No matter what he says, there's no trust between us. Not anymore.

Yet at the last second, something propels me forward. "Wait." I reach out to grab his wrist—

Only for my fingers to pass straight through his arm.

My mouth drops open.

"Don't underestimate me either, sweetheart." Kieran tilts his head. "I've got a few tricks of my own up my sleeve."

The turn of phrase lights a spark of understanding. I drop to the ground and thrust my hand through his boot. Like before, it passes right through him. This time, however, my fingertips brush against something thin and smooth. As I lift the object off the ground, Kieran vanishes into thin air.

I hold an otherwise plain-looking playing card up to the light. Flipping it over, however, reveals the Ace of Hearts, scrawled with the carelessly elegant signature of the most famous magician of Manhattan: Harry Houdini.

Kieran's Artifact flies out of my grasp and whizzes into the sky, too quick for me to trace. No wonder nothing happened when I shot him—he was never standing before me to begin with.

"Fine," I declare to the empty trees. "I'll work with you. But I won't hesitate to pull the trigger if you even *think* about betraying me."

A figure slides off the roof of the merry-go-round above me.

Kieran lands on the ground in a crouch with Randel's Map clutched in one hand and the Ace of Hearts in the other. His green eyes meet mine in the morning light, dancing with mischief.

"Oh," he says with a smirk, "I wouldn't dream of it."

✳

"Twenty minutes left," Kieran mutters from below me, his neck craned up at the countdown clock projected into the sky. "You sure about this?"

"I'm happy to eliminate you, if you'd prefer," I answer without taking my eyes off Randel's Map. By folding it down to the square where Central Park is situated and opening it back up again, the map enlarges to fill the entire parchment, giving me a perfect close-up of our location—not to mention the locations of the remaining thirteen competitors. Nearly half have already been eliminated. Unfortunately, that tally doesn't include any other Raiders besides the one I eliminated myself.

The leaves rustle softly as Kieran grabs the branch I'm perched on and hoists himself up beside me.

"I never gave you permission to sit on my branch," I say.

"My bad," he replies without moving.

I roll my eyes and return my attention to the dots representing each competitor moving through our corner of the park. My neck tingles as Kieran leans over my shoulder to study their positions.

The surviving Evaders are scattered across the park. A few allies travel in pairs at most. As expected, Tim's posse dominates the rest of the competition. Then I spot Dawn loitering around the boundaries, avoiding Tim's pack. After losing her Artifact to Kieran, I don't blame her for making herself scarce.

"Eighteen minutes," Kieran warns me.

I point at Tim's dot. "Look. They finished surveilling the west side. They're on their way."

Kieran traces a path across the softball diamonds. His arm brushes mine gently. "So you'll cut them off over here?"

I shift away from him ever so slightly. Even the way that he touches the map makes my stomach flip, his fingers gliding along the paper like bare skin, dredging up memories best left forgotten. "Right. Meanwhile, you'll—"

"Find somewhere to hide."

"I was going to say get into position. *Where* is another question entirely."

He winks. "Don't worry. Wherever I end up, I won't take my eyes off you."

"Or Tim," I remind him.

He grimaces at that. "Or Tim."

Back on the ground, we split ways. I head south, choosing speed over stealth. The tree cover here is painfully sparse, leaving me almost completely exposed. But as long as my timing is right, it won't matter.

A familiar hum invades my ears. I glance to my left to find the boundaries of the dome creeping closer to me with each passing second. I shift course to give it a wide berth.

Rat Rock rises in the distance. I search the ground and grab the first stone I can find in the right size. Then I hurry behind a tree around eighty feet away.

Now, we wait.

I hear the Raiders before I see them. Tim's heavy footfalls against the rock, Bastian's wheedling voice. Leading the pack as usual, Tim surveys the area from atop the highest crest. A whopping seven flags hang from his sides. Bastian trails at his right hand, ever the loyal lapdog. Behind them, Noëlle wears her own trio of war trophies captured from fallen Evaders. Anika brings up the rear, my flags nowhere to be seen.

Movement darts across the field ahead. Tim's head snaps up like a wolf catching a scent. He rolls off commands to the rest of the pack, then clambers down the rock and takes off into the distance with Noëlle.

Before Anika or Bastian can take another step in their direction, I fling the grapefruit-sized stone I picked up earlier with all my might. It sails high over their heads and bounces down the other side of Rat Rock with a series of explosive clatters.

The two of them whip their weapons into the air. Turning in circles, they scan the area for the source of the noise. I slink a little closer. Anika descends the other side of the rock to investigate. A reluctant Bastian follows her a moment later.

After they've disappeared, I dart out from the tree and scale up the face of the rock closest to me. Once I reach the summit, I crouch behind the tallest peak and peer over it.

"I thought you would've learned your lesson by now," calls a voice from below.

I dive back just as Anika opens fire at me. How the hell does she keep predicting exactly where I am?

Then I glimpse something glowing in the palm of her hand. A luminescent, tentacled creature ensconced inside a crystal sphere, blazing bright as a torch.

The Jellyfish.

The closer Anika gets to me, the brighter her Artifact glows, like a compass guiding her straight to my location. No wonder she discovered my presence earlier, too.

Together, she and Bastian surround Rat Rock on both sides, blocking any hope of my escape. I scramble from outcropping to outcropping, trying to prevent them from getting a clear shot of my discs. But I can't just wait up here for them to shoot me down.

I leap toward a narrow column of rock when my foot skids out from underneath me. This early in the morning, some patches of the worn stone surface are still slick with dew. Sharp bursts of pain ricochet through my body as I tumble gracelessly down Rat Rock. At the bottom, I stagger to my feet, bruised and more than a little bloody. But now the adrenaline pumps through my veins, numbing the pain, setting my veins abuzz. I lunge at a bewildered Anika. I kick the inside of her knee, causing her to buckle. I lock my grip on her arm and shoulder.

Her eyes widen. She's always known she can't beat me one-on-one in combat education, but I remind her of it anyway.

Twisting sideways, I hook one leg around hers, using her own momentum to throw her forward and slam her into the hard-packed earth. Her gun ricochets out of her grasp and flies into the air. I catch it by the grip.

"Bastian!" screams Anika as I pin her down with my boot. "Help me!"

Bastian scrambles around the bend. But as soon as he lays eyes on Anika squirming like a trapped insect beneath me, her own gun aimed at her disc by my hands, he spins on his heel and flees for the fields.

Anika spits a curse at his retreating figure, then returns her gaze to me, simmering with spite. "It's always you. *Why is it always you?*"

I shake my head. "Don't blame anyone but yourself, Ani. It's your fault that you could never catch up to me."

Fear no longer fills her eyes—only pure, unadulterated loathing. "I should have finished you when I had the chance."

I shrug. "For what it's worth, I'm sure you would've made a great maverick."

Even if I had any mercy to spare, she has too much dignity to beg for it. So I pull the trigger instead.

CHAPTER SEVENTEEN

Trouble arrives in the form of a swishy blond ponytail and a magic gavel.

I'm sprinting around the field to rendezvous with Kieran when the earth quivers beneath my feet and the world grinds to a standstill, slamming my body to a halt. No—not the world. Only me. My limbs. My lungs. The race of my heart nearly stops dead, no more than a dull, sluggish *thud . . . thud . . . thud* in my ears.

My mind struggles to compute this new reality—my arms and legs pumping in mid-run, the trees blurring past, yet I've moved less than an inch.

Thud, goes my petrified heart.

Struggling against the inescapable force trapping my muscles in slow motion, I raise my head to see none other than Noëlle Cartier.

She strolls over to me like she has all the time in the world. And thanks to the Gavel, she does—at least, for a few seconds.

She lifts her gun to my chest.

For the first time during the Tournament, I'm truly helpless. My brain sends desperate fight-or-flight commands to the rest of my body, but there's simply no response. Her smug smile tells me she knows it.

Thud.

A gust of wind blows through the trees at Noëlle's back. My eyes linger on the leaves flurrying down around her. Through the haze of panic clouding my mind, an idea emerges. My body may refuse to obey my will, but that doesn't exempt it from obeying the laws of nature.

So when my foot strikes the ground, instead of trying to keep running, I force myself to trip.

Gravity takes care of the rest.

There's no way to control the fall, so I faceplant into the ground. Noëlle shoots. I get a mouthful of dirt, but my disc stays green. She falters in disbelief, which buys me a precious second.

But that's all I need for the effects of her Artifact to finally lift.

A shudder passes through me from head to toe. As my body lurches back into real time, the momentum from all the restrained energy bubbles up and sends me barreling forward. I take a flying leap and tackle her to the ground. We roll through the dirt. She bares her teeth at me. I grab her ponytail and yank it back hard enough to make her neck crack. She throws her punches with terrifying precision and grace. But with her slight, willowy frame, she's built like a bird, not a boxer. Between that and the adrenaline cavorting through my veins, I barely feel her hits—but I make sure she feels mine.

The sky flashes. We both waver and glance up as the clock begins counting down the final ten minutes of the task. The boundaries that have been inching toward us all hour suddenly surge forward with a vengeance.

White static explodes across my vision as Noëlle plows her fist into my face. I howl. Something warm and wet floods down, filling my mouth with the sharp, metallic tang of blood. I spit it into her eye. She shrieks in revulsion and reels back. Crimson fury paints her expression. She lifts the Gavel above her head to deliver the final strike.

But then the dome begins to warp. Like a cell undergoing the last stage of mitosis, it begins to split straight down the middle, right above us.

"The boundaries," I gasp, pointing.

She realizes her dilemma. If she finishes me off now, neither of us will make it out of the way in time. The split will devour us both.

She meets my gaze. I'm not worth getting herself eliminated over. She shoves me away just as the new boundary sweeps between us, sealing the two halves of the arena in separate bubbles—as well as separating us from each other.

She pins me with her frigid blue death stare. *Next time*, her eyes say. *Next time you won't get so lucky.*

I merely grin at her and hold up three flags. *Her* flags, which I ripped from her belt when she shoved me back.

Her hands fly to her waist, searching for what's no longer there. The hairs on my arm rise at the absolute *murder* written across her face. For a moment I worry that she'll cross the boundary anyway just to wring my neck. But after she takes a deep breath, she turns and sprints off in the other direction to find a new victim.

Before I can so much as sigh in relief, a bellow of rage echoes across the newly divided arena, sending flocks of birds scattering into the skies.

The countdown clock passes the five-minute mark. *Shit.* I'm late.

The adrenaline high has already started to wear off, leaving my body aching, but I force myself to break into a run toward the grove of trees just west of the softball fields.

Then the grove comes into view—or what remains. I skid to a stop in the middle of the field, unable to tear my eyes away from the destruction. Even from afar, it looks as if a hurricane touched down in the middle of the park. Branches and limbs litter the ground like fallen soldiers.

My resolution wavers. I touch the flags at my sides. Six of them—twelve points in total, since the three I dug out from Anika's boot were originally mine. More than enough to make it to the next round. Maybe even enough to win the first task. I could squat behind a rock for the rest of the task and walk out of the arena as the champion. Why should I risk it all?

I never made any promises to Kieran. In fact, it's in my best interests *not* to help him.

Abandoning him now would just be payback for what he did to you, a little voice in my head whispers.

But if he hadn't shared Randel's Map with me or stuck out his own neck to distract Tim and Noëlle and lead them away from the rest of the pack, I would have never gotten my flags back.

We made a deal, and I won't be the one to break it.

I arrive at the grove just in time to see Tim decimate a bush with the Chela. White spittle froths from his mouth as he lets out a rabid scream. His biceps strain through his exosuit as he swings the crab pincers left and right without the slightest regard to his surroundings. With a single careless swipe of his Artifact, an entire tree limb severs and crashes to the ground.

"Come out, come out, wherever you are!" he roars.

I hunch behind a tree at the edge of the grove, breathing hard. I struggle to suppress my fear at the monstrosity that Tim has become armed with the obscene power of his Artifact. Few people could even lift the damn thing, let alone wield it. Tim's attacks *are* sloppy. Poorly aimed. Unpredictable. But the volatility of a loose cannon doesn't make it any less deadly.

My attention snaps back to reality as Tim lets out a triumphant howl. My heart seizes as he bulldozes through a cluster of young pines to reveal Kieran crouched in the foliage.

A scream rips from my throat. *"Kieran!"*

Tim whips his head at me. His eyes are glazed with the fervor of battle. He lifts his Artifact. Not to strike, but to use it as a shield, blocking his disc from the hail of gunfire I release upon him.

Then, in one swing, he turns back to Kieran with the Chela to cleave his head right off his shoulders.

CHAPTER EIGHTEEN

My scream wavers as the Artifact passes through Kieran like a blade cutting through mist. The illusion of Kieran grins up at Tim, unharmed, and flips him off. Then in a blink, he's gone.

Now I understand why Tim's gone batshit ballistic.

Kieran throws up clone after clone, never waiting long enough for Tim to catch up to them before recalling the Ace of Hearts back into his hand. He plays the big brute like a magician does an audience, using his surroundings as equal parts distraction and diversion. It's an endless game of three-card monte, and his opponent is losing. For now.

Tim gnashes his teeth and lashes out with the Chela. The crack of wood echoes like gunshots as a birch tree topples down. In his frenzy to find the real Kieran, he seems determined to raze the whole grove to the ground.

"You made it," a voice pants directly beside my ear. I jump. Sweat glistens on Kieran's brow. "I was getting worried. Watch out." His arm encircles my waist just in time to whisk me out of the way of a falling tree branch. Holding up two fingers, he calls back the Ace of Hearts and catches it between them. In the background, Tim screeches in frustration.

"What now?" I gasp.

"Pray that I don't run out of trees to hide behind." He casts out another clone and dashes off.

Meanwhile, Tim hacks through the trunk of a towering maple. Except, he doesn't stop. He keeps chopping, seemingly in rage. The tree lets out an ominous groan, but Kieran doesn't notice. He's so caught up in outsmarting Tim at his own game that he misses the one Tim has been playing all along.

I watch in frozen horror as the maple wobbles—then tips forward.

Plummeting straight down onto Kieran.

From one heartbeat to the next, I'm flying through the air, the shadow of the maple descending upon me like a guillotine. Then I collide into the hard planes of Kieran's chest, and we tumble head-over-ass into a tangle of roots. The wind gets knocked hard out of my lungs.

The maple falls. The earth convulses from the shock of the impact. My face is pressed into Kieran's neck. His arms tighten around me. Only when the echoes fade do I dare look at him. He stares at the ruined tree and the place beneath it where he stood seconds prior. I feel him tremble against me.

A new shadow engulfs us. When Tim sees me draw my gun at him, his lips twist into a morbid grin.

"Go ahead," he rasps, his voice like the scrape of bone on bone. His massive bulk blocks out the sky above us. "This is all just a stupid, fake game. In two minutes, we'll all walk away. But I promise that if you pull that trigger, I'll snap your spine in half for real. And no one will be able to stop me."

In my millisecond of hesitation, Tim laughs and swings the Chela. Every thought evaporates from my brain except for one:

He's actually going to kill us.

Without thinking, I shield Kieran with my own body, as if I'm anything more than flesh and blood.

Eyes squeezed shut, bracing for the pain.

The world erupts in a shower of gold fire. Even from beneath my closed lids, the light is searing. There's a scream of agony.

When the light has faded, I pry my eyelids open to discover Tim lying inert on the ground. Black smoke rises from his exosuit. Both his discs have shattered.

A hand appears in the corner of my vision. Dazed, I grab it and allow Kieran to pull me to my feet. We gawk at the aftermath.

"See?" he says after a moment. "I told you I had more than a few tricks up my sleeve."

"You did?"

He grins. "Yeah. You were my best one."

A hysterical huff of laughter escapes me. The sky pulses—only ten seconds left on the clock.

Kieran picks his way over to his nemesis and checks for breathing. "Still alive, unfortunately." Then he grins and bends down to start untying the flags fastened next to the gun tucked in Tim's belt.

Something rustles in the foliage behind me. Kieran glances up.

In the first task's final seconds, he snatches up Tim's gun—instead of the flags—and shoots right at me.

CHAPTER NINETEEN

I stagger backward. My hand flies to my disc.

But it doesn't turn red.

A startled cry pierces the air behind me. I whirl around to find Bastian standing a few feet away . . . with his gun still aimed at my back. Flabbergasted, Bastian stares down at his disc, which flashes an angry scarlet.

It wasn't me who Kieran shot.

The countdown clock hits zero with a clangorous *BUZZZZ*. The dome over our heads disperses into evanescence.

The first task is over.

"Wait!" I exclaim, frantically looking back at Kieran. Besides the gun, he's empty-handed. "You didn't—"

"I know," he interrupts, tossing Tim's weapon away in disgust.

"You just gave up the opportunity to win the first task!" I yell.

"I know."

"But *why?*"

"Don't ask why," he replies, almost pleadingly. "You know why."

I curse and turn my face away so he can't read my expression. I know all too well how badly he wants to win the Tournament. How badly he wants to become a maverick. And he sacrificed all of that for what?

A drone floats out of the sky. Besides cameras, this one has a screen, too. And on it, Nick Valentine's grinning face.

I shove myself in front of Kieran. The words start tumbling forth before I even know what I'm trying to say. "Mr. Valentine, Kieran Cross was in the position to acquire enough points to win this task when he chose to sacrifice them all to save an ally, so—"

Valentine raises an eyebrow. "So?"

"So . . ." I stall, scrambling for an idea. "So I demand that the council allow me to split my points with him."

The Phantom's grin disappears. "Miss Reynolds, I'm afraid you can't simply dole out points as you please. The only way to give your ally any points would be to give up *all* of them."

I falter. Kieran goes still as stone. Then he grabs my elbow, expression pained. "Rei . . ."

Valentine lets out a giggle.

"What's so funny?" I snap at him.

"You two should see the looks on your faces," he says. "I'm just teasing! In fact, I'd like to congratulate *both* of you on passing the first task."

"What?" Kieran and I blurt at the same time.

"One of the rules I shared prior to the task is that you must surrender all flags in your possession to whoever eliminates you. Mister Cross eliminated Mister Guerra," he explains, "who happened to possess a grand total of one flag."

We both turn to Bastian, who looks like he swallowed a rotten lemon.

"Bastian," Kieran begins, "I never thought I'd say this, but I could kiss you right now."

He glowers back. "Just take my damn flag."

We emerge from the southwest corner of Central Park and ascend the granite steps of Columbus Circle to frenzied chaos. Enforcers struggle to hold the barricades keeping the press and fans at bay. We're exhausted and filthy, but we smile and wave, playing it up for the sake of the cameras.

A squeal pierces the air, and Zaza elbows her way out of a throng of people, an access badge hanging around her neck next to her strand of coffee beans. She strangles me in a hug.

"You were *sooo* good. And god, that suit makes your butt look amazing."

"Thanks," I wheeze.

"Here," she says, handing me something crinkly. "A random girl told me this was for you."

I open my palm to find an unmistakable little toffee candy. The familiar, almost addictive sweetness brings a smile to my face. I search the crowd, but of course, Master Sasha wouldn't let himself be seen here.

In his place, a candy might not seem like much, but for some reason it means more to me than I can explain.

"Where's Maura?" I ask, standing on tiptoe to try to catch a glimpse of my sister.

"Haven't seen her," says Zaza. "Did she say she'd come?"

I brace myself for the disappointment, just like all the other times—the missed birthdays, the countless last-minute cancellations. Yet all I feel is a dull sense of resignation. "Forget it. Kieran, you remember Zaza, right?"

Kieran steps forward, a boyish grin on his face. "I presume you're still hoping to land that apprenticeship with the head of the Syndicate's biochemtech program?"

"Hoping?" She smirks. "Oh, honey, I already did. And I presume you're still single?"

"*Zaza!*" I exclaim.

"I am, actually, yeah," Kieran cuts in without quite meeting my gaze. "Trying to stay focused on school and all that."

I scoff.

But Zaza only beams. "How perfect. You're coming to senior prom, right? The Syndicate is hosting it at the Penthouse this year, so you know it's going to be lit."

I blink. I'd totally forgotten.

Kieran shrugs. "Sadly, I didn't get a ticket."

"Well, lucky for you," my best friend replies, oozing with glee as she reaches into her pocket, "I've got an extra one right here. It would be *such* a shame to let it go to waste, don't you think?"

"Hang on," I say. "Is that the extra ticket you asked me to buy you last week? You told me you needed it for someone important!"

"Yeah, your *date*." She gives the air a haughty sniff. "Lord knows you weren't going to find one for yourself."

"What about *your* date?"

"I've got one, thanks very much."

"Who? Since when?" I growl, attempting to snatch the ticket from her. She jumps out of the way. I'm about to dive-wrestle her to the ground when Kieran steps up behind us and plucks it from her fingers.

"Actually, I'd love to go," he says to me. "If . . . you're cool with that."

Suddenly, I notice how quiet it's gotten. My neck burns from the intensity of the curious stares from nearby onlookers, not to mention the media. None of them know my history with Kieran. If the Directors are watching right now, they wouldn't care even if they knew. Mavericks need to be able to cooperate with anyone, no matter what. All they'll see is me acting up, right on the heels of our shared first task victory.

I hear the murmur of Nick Valentine's voice in my ear. *You have the potential to become a maverick at the snap of their fingers . . . but only if you can prove yourself worthy.*

So I grit my teeth into my nicest smile for the cameras. "Why wouldn't I be?"

"Splendid," Zaza coos. "We'll meet you there in two hours. Text Rei for the address. You *do* still have her number, right?"

"Of course I do."

My head snaps to him, but he merely looks the other way. I was certain he'd deleted it. After all, why keep it?

"See you then," Zaza sings, slipping an arm around my waist and steering me toward the street where Declan awaits in the limo.

Only once Kieran's safely out of earshot do I hiss, "What were you thinking back there?"

"That you should totally wear your new red dress tonight. The silk one with the slit and the sequins and the sexy little straps on the back—"

"*Zaza!*" I glance over my shoulder to find Kieran still staring after us. Heat rises to my cheeks. "In case you've forgotten, he's my competition. And my *ex.*"

"Look, normally I would never advise someone to get back together with their ex. But you should have seen the two of you during the Tournament." She flutters her eyelashes. "There was so much unresolved *tension*—"

"Yeah, it's called a rivalry," I interject quickly. "One of us has to make it out on top."

Zaza wiggles her eyebrows at me. "Oh, I'm sure you'd love to be on top again. *Of him.*"

I stop walking. "Zaza?"

"Yes?"

"I'm giving you three seconds to run."

Music blasts from the living room of our dorm as we rush to get ourselves glammed up. Most of our belongings are already packed up and stacked in cardboard boxes scrawled with thick black marker. In a week we'll be ready to move out, forced to say goodbye. My photos and posters and memories have been stripped off the wall, leaving a blank, white expanse that makes me wonder how it all ended so quickly.

Right now, however, I'm turning my room upside down.

"Zaza!" I bellow. "Have you seen my tweezers?"

"*No!*" she yells back from the bathroom.

"Ugh." I dig through the desk drawers. I toss aside notebooks, old birthday cards, useless textbooks I had to buy but never ended up reading.

I pause at the bottom drawer. An unassuming box gray with dust peeks out from within. Gingerly, I lift the lid.

With a sharp inhale, I clap it closed, warmth rushing to my face. I fix my gaze at the ceiling. My heart turns somersaults in my chest. After a moment, I regain my composure and remove the lid once more to reveal the stack of old photos.

In the first shot, Kieran lounges on the windowsill of his dorm room, lost in a book. Shirtless. The sunlight catches on his eyelashes, the sharp line of his jaw. The contours of his neck, his bare chest.

In the next, we stand in front of his mirror, his arms wrapped around my waist, *shirtless again*. Laughter spills across both our features, probably at some ridiculous inside joke. I wish I could remember it.

Then come the snapshots from our Sunday study sessions at the library. My stomach tightens. I sift through them: his profile, captured between the spaces in the shelves; his hands, splayed across pages covered in his meticulous handwriting; his cheek, pressed into a stack of textbooks as he dozes peacefully, his lips parted in a perfect O.

I catch myself suppressing a smile and immediately feel a familiar wave of guilt. I shouldn't have kept these. The day Kieran walked out of both the library and my life a year ago, I should have burned them to ashes.

I flip to the next photo. A little golden puppy with a half-eaten sock in his mouth blurs toward the camera. A lump forms in my throat. There are at least a dozen more pictures, but I shove them all back into the box and out of my mind.

✷

Half an hour later, I'm bundled up in my leather jacket with a little black clutch tucked under my arm. I hurry after Zaza down Wall Street to the car, trying to avoid getting the heels of my stilettos wedged between the cobblestones. My phone buzzes.

Unknown Caller
Are you here yet, it's past 3

I frown.

Who is this?

ur mom

I stare.

SHIT WAIT IM SO SORRY I take that back.

Please tell me you're not gonna ghost me

I chew my lip and fire a text back.

still debating tbh

Well, debate faster please. If people keep trying to

interact with me at this rate I may actually perish.

I snort. As we pile into the car, Zaza peeks over my shoulder. "Who are you texting?"

"Nobody."

She smirks. "Tell Kieran I say hi."

Declan pulls the car into drive and raises his eyes to the rearview mirror. "What are you talking to that ruffian for?"

Zaza's smirk widens. "Haven't you heard, Declan? He's Rei's prom date."

"He's not my date!"

"Seat belts please, ladies."

Zaza pats my knee consolingly. "Relax. No one said you have to make out with him or anything. You guys won the first task! Just live a little. You can go back to being mortal enemies tomorrow."

I groan loudly and let my forehead fall against the tinted window with a defeated *thunk*.

Too soon, we're cruising along Sixth Avenue, past the shops and cafés flurrying with pedestrians hoping to beat the dinner rush before everyone gets off work and curfew starts. My favorite bakery is already boxing up whatever sweet confections remain and selling them at a heavy discount. Whatever gets left over must be eaten or incinerated before curfew.

Declan swings the car onto 49th Street, giving us a brief glimpse of Radio City Music Hall on the next block. When I close my eyes, I can picture it before the Vanishing, the neon red-and-blue lights bleeding into the night. It's just not the same during the day.

We pull up beside a chic marvel of glass and crystal spiraling into the sky, with a long red carpet leading to the entrance. The windows on the uppermost floors are blacked out—a day club in masquerade.

When Declan opens the passenger door, I don't move. Zaza peers at me. "You good?"

I grip the leather seat. "I don't know. Can we go home?"

She rolls her eyes. "Rei, you hunt monsters for fun. You're chickening out over *this*?"

I blow out a breath. She's got a point.

Declan levels me with a hard look. "Tell that boy of yours that if he tries anything funny, I will beat the living shitsticks out of him."

I clap one hand over my mouth, my anxieties momentarily forgotten. "Did you just say *shitsticks*?"

He lifts his chin high. "Yes, well. Drastic times call for drastic measures and all that. Don't tell your aunt. Now, run along. And for the love of Lady Liberty . . . have some fun. For once."

"Okay, Dad," I quip, which makes him beam. With a fond shake of my head, I follow Zaza into the lobby, where a mob of people surround a guy in a white suit. At first I worry that it's Kieran, but then the guy turns around and spots us. A huge grin overtakes his face. "Reynolds! Alvarez!"

I wave to Bomani. As our class president navigates his way through the crowd, Zaza seizes my arm. "How do I look?"

"Hot," I reply off-handedly, busy searching for Kieran.

"*Rei*," she says urgently. "Seriously."

"Why are you—?" It clicks. "Oh my god, is he your date?" She shoots me a look. "Oh my god, he *is*! Why didn't you tell me?"

"I didn't want to make a big deal out of it! Dios, why am I sweating so much?"

Looking her up and down, I can't help but smile in spite of my own nerves. She's done a smoky rose eyeshadow and bold black eyeliner, highlighted by a fine line of dazzling gold that brings out the flecks in her hazel eyes. Her hair falls in soft, loose ringlets that frame her round, dimpled face. Her dark, wine-colored dress, the same shade as her lipstick, is all gloss and satin with a flirty, low cowl neckline. The fabric clings to her in all the right places, showing off her gorgeous curves.

I reach for her hands and squeeze them tight. "You look like a damn *queen*."

After a second of hesitation, her expression transforms. "Yeah. Yeah, you bet I do." She strides over to him.

He takes her hand and presses a kiss to her knuckles, his eyes shining in reverence. "Good *god*."

Zaza lets out a delicious laugh. "No, honey, it's just me."

As an enamored grin overwhelms Bomani's face, I spot a figure hunched in a gloomy corner beside the elevators, staring at the blank screen of his phone like he's forgotten how to use it.

I approach Kieran tentatively, wishing I had even half of Zaza's confidence. But when he looks up, straight at me, and his face illuminates with pure awe, I wonder what I ever had to worry about.

He shakes his head when I reach him, almost as if he can't believe himself. "You look . . . devastating."

His sincerity makes my cheeks flame. I'm grateful for the dim lighting. "Don't I always?"

"Most of all when you're covered in mud and sweat and the blood of our enemies." He pushes himself off the wall. As the light falls on him, my thoughts turn to mush—*how is this the first time I've seen him in a suit and why is his shirt so tight over his pecs and why am I so turned on and please lord have mercy on my soul?*

"I like your hair," I manage to blurt out instead.

Which I do—styled in a neat, debonair side part. He runs a hand through it, which is absurdly hot for absolutely no good reason. "Thanks. Er . . . this is for you." He produces a small carton from behind his back and hands it to me.

For a second, I can only stare at it. "Banana pudding," I finally say. "You got me banana pudding."

"From that bakery down the street that you like. I was going to get you a corsage, but I figured you might like this better," he rambles. "Actually, I don't know what I was thinking. Of course you wouldn't want pudding at *prom*—"

He tries to grab it back, but I snatch it out of his reach and hold it protectively to my chest. "No. It's mine now."

He bites down on his bottom lip like he does whenever he's trying to hold back a smile. Once I manage to fit the pudding carton into the pocket of my leather jacket, he offers me his arm. "So. Can I buy you a drink?"

I tuck my hand into the crook of his elbow. Unthinkingly, our steps line up like muscle memory. It's so natural, so *easy* to slip back into the familiarity of him. The contours of his body, the sureness of his touch reawakens a deep, aching longing for the intimacy we once shared.

Not that I'd ever admit it.

I can hear the dull thud of music from upstairs as soon as we step into the elevator. We ride up to the Penthouse in silence. I'm hyperfocused on the steady pressure of Kieran's arm, the faint scent of his cologne, the warmth radiating from his body to mine—

Ding.

The doors slide open. A thousand colored strobe lights assault us from the rafters. They reflect off the walls, crafted from shattered mirror shards, so that the entire space dazzles even in the dark. We navigate one of the crisscrossing walkways suspended over the dance floor, peering over the railways to glimpse the sea of bodies and sweat and seduction writhing below.

"*Welcome to the hottest party in New York City!*" the DJ yells into the mic. Howls of delight go up from the crowd as one song glissades into the next. Students from all ten Prep League schools chant the lyrics at the top of their lungs like a moonstruck cult in prayer. I spot Bomani twirling Zaza across the floor like a pro.

Kieran turns to me and hollers something.

"*What?*" I shout back.

He tries again. I shrug hopelessly. He takes me by the shoulders and leans in close. The throb of my heartbeat reverberates through me, almost louder than the bass of the club music.

"*Do you want to go somewhere quieter?*" he bellows directly into my ear.

"The bar upstairs?" I shout.

"*What?*"

I snort in exasperation and grab his hand. I lead him up the walkway to the stairs. We skirt around couples dancing to the music, couples grinding against one another to the music, and couples full-on eating each other's faces to the music. Kieran shoots me a horrified look. We make a break for the club's top floor, taking the steps two at a time.

By the time we get to the top, we're both giggling and slightly out of breath. Thankfully, the music here is fainter, subdued enough that we don't have to scream at each other anymore. I realize I'm still holding his hand. I drop it and clear my throat as he regards me in amusement.

A whirlwind of emotions churns in my chest. Now that we've stepped away from the exhilaration of the party, the high that carried me here wears off.

I look him dead in the eye.

"I haven't forgiven you."

His smile fades. He swallows. "I know."

"Well, good." I spin on my heel and head off toward the bar.

"What can I get for ya?" the bartender asks over the loud rattle of ice as he prepares cocktails for two girls in a silver shaker.

I scan the drinks menu, my fingers tapping against the counter. "One Honey Trap, please."

"And for you, sir?"

"Uhhh . . ." Kieran scrutinizes the menu as if it's written in hieroglyphics. After much deliberation, he glances up helplessly. "Vodka? Or something?"

The bartender doesn't even blink. "Sure. One Honey Trap, one vodka or something coming right up. IDs?"

We show him our Prep League identification cards, then linger to the side of the bar to wait for our drinks in uncomfortable silence.

"Have you ever . . ." I begin at the exact same moment he goes, "Do you . . ."

We both trail off. "You first," I say.

"I'm sorry," says Kieran without meeting my eyes. "About the way things ended."

I fold my arms over my chest. "Are you actually?"

"I never wanted it to end. Us, I mean."

"It was your choice."

His jaw tightens. "It wasn't, really."

I scoff. "Whatever helps you fall asleep at night."

He looks up suddenly. My breath catches at the pain engraved in his expression. "You have no idea what it was like."

"What?"

The regret shining in Kieran's eyes hits me like a punch to the gut. "To lie awake, unable to sleep," he says, voice rough, "wondering if you were missing me as badly as I missed you."

I can hardly believe my ears. I grip the counter, feeling light-headed. "You kept my number. But you never called. Never texted."

"Of course not. You wanted to get as far away from me as you could. As much as it tortured me, what right did I have to disrespect that?"

I can't do anything but stare at him. How do I even respond to that? I'd almost pity him—if not for how *colossally* infuriated I am by his senseless, self-righteous logic.

Kieran rubs his face. "Look, I think I should just go. You obviously didn't want me to come in the first place. I don't want to ruin your prom."

"No," I rush to say. "I mean, I didn't want you to come earlier, but it was because I was worried that . . . that . . ."

He searches my face. "Yes?"

I open my mouth. *That I would realize how much I still want you.*

I close my eyes. "Kieran, I—"

Thud.

We both startle at the impact of glass against wood. The moment shatters. I can't decide whether to be relieved or not as the bartender slides a shimmery gold cocktail and a dark blue mystery concoction in a tall glass over the counter. He winks. "Enjoy, you two."

Kieran elbows himself in front of me and hands the bartender a twenty before I can reach for my wallet. "This one's on me," he says. At my expression, he adds, "Don't be difficult."

I huff and hold up my Honey Trap. "Fine. But next one's on me. To victory."

He clinks his glass against mine. "To *our* victory."

The corner of my mouth twitches upward. I take a sip of my drink, rolling the flavors on my tongue. Floral bourbon, sweet with honey and a kick of lemon. The burn on the way down fills my chest with warmth. Not for the first time, I'm thankful for the reduced drinking age. With all the responsibilities we were expected to bear starting so young, it only made sense to give us this small privilege, too.

I look up to see Kieran with the bottom of his glass pointed to the ceiling. His throat bobs as he gulps down his drink to the last drop.

"What the hell, Cross?" I exclaim. "Slow down!"

He slams the empty glass on the counter and blows out a fierce exhale. He points at my shoes, his eyes blazing with new resolve. "Can you dance in those?"

"Of course, but—"

"Dance with me. Just a little."

"Why?"

He holds out his hand. His pupils are blown wide, but it can't be from the alcohol, not yet. They rove across my face, lingering on my lips. "Because I'd hate myself forever if I didn't ask."

I abandon my drink and follow him back downstairs. He laces his fingers with mine tightly, as if he's afraid we'll lose each other in the crowd. Just as we reach the bottom, something blurs in my peripheral vision.

BAM!

Someone barrels into me at a full sprint, nearly knocking me onto my ass. Kieran catches me by the elbow just in time.

"Oh my gosh," the girl exclaims, her short bleach-blond hair disheveled and her cheeks pink from inebriation. She tugs on the hem of her body-con dress and wipes at the mascara streaking her cheeks. She looks up at me with big brown eyes. "I am *soooo* sorry! My boyfriend just b-broke up with me in the m-middle of the dance floor, and I was so embarrassed and I just—"

"It's fine," I interrupt, holding her up as she sways forward. "Are you okay? Are you hurt?"

She sobs. "Obviously I'm hurt! He broke my heart!" She sniffles and hangs her head, still leaning into me. The sweet scent of vanilla envelops me. I glance at Kieran, but he's staring at the girl with the most bizarre, unreadable expression. Right when it seems like he's about to say something, she loudly wails, "I just . . . I just loved him so much, and I thought he loved me too, and I can't *believe* he broke up with me at the *prom*! Prom of all places! Like, you'd think that he'd at least have the *decency* to choose a different place—"

It's at that moment when someone brushes past me and I feel the tiniest tug at my wrist—barely noticeable. By the time I glance down to my purse, I discover the flap hanging open.

I shove the girl back. She stumbles away. In her hands, my phone. My wallet. Too late, I realize that despite her intoxicated behavior, she doesn't smell of alcohol in the slightest.

She's also wearing sneakers.

Without hesitation, she turns on her heel and bolts into the crowd—but not before sticking out her tongue and throwing the middle finger at me.

I cuss loudly. I'm wearing four-inch stilettos.

But that doesn't stop me from chasing her onto the dance floor.

CHAPTER TWENTY

As soon as I dive into the horde of sweaty, flailing bodies, I know I've made a terrible mistake. The floor is jam-packed with teenagers possessed by raging hormones and the stamina of the undead. I shove my way through them with increasing violence, barely garnering more than a bewildered look here and there from faces bathed in glitter and euphoria. The music throbs through me, mocking me, drowning out my thoughts, trying to lure me off course.

I think about giving up and just reporting the theft to the police when I realize—

Shit. The photos of my parents.

They're still in my wallet.

With a burst of fury, I fight through the living, writhing maze of bodies pressing into me from every direction. The thief is much smaller than me. She dodges elbows and weaves beneath arms with ease. She throws a smirk over her shoulder, only to flinch when she finds my snarling mug mere feet away like a homing missile set to strike.

She doubles her efforts, lunging for the ever-shifting gaps between bodies. She manages to break free of the crowd and sprints for the stairwell exit. I curse. I might be able to run in heels on flat ground or even up stairs, but going *down* stairs is an entirely different story.

I burst into the stairwell, weighing my options. While the elevator could get me to the ground floor faster than running down twenty flights of stairs, I'll have no idea if the thief decides to exit on some other floor.

"Rei!" someone shouts from behind me in a hoarse voice. "Wait!"

I turn to find Kieran staggering after me. He opens his mouth, but then the beat drops, and his words are lost in an explosion of bass. He tries to yell over the music, but it's useless. Eventually, he points to himself and then the elevators. I nod, beyond grateful for his understanding, and clatter down the first flight of stairs.

The thief's footsteps echo up to me. I estimate she's about five flights below—there's no way I can catch up to her like this. My eyes dart to the smooth stainless-steel handrail: a flat, sloped bar one inch thick.

No time for hesitation. I yank off my heels and boost my butt onto the railing, nearly flipping over and smacking face-first into the concrete thanks to the silken material of my dress. It takes me a few precious seconds to figure out how to distribute my weight and exactly where to splay my limbs out for balance, but soon enough, I'm flying down the rails at truly breakneck speed.

I'm exactly one flight above the thief when she makes it to the ground floor and barges into the lobby, where Kieran will be waiting for her. Anticipation courses through my veins as the end of the hunt draws near.

But when I reach the lobby, I'm met with a livid, red-faced Kieran, shoving the thief not to the ground, but out the door.

Onto the street.

To freedom.

The stairwell door clangs shut at my back. Kieran whips around, stiffening at the sight of me.

A roar fills my ears, drowning out every other thought, more deafening than the music in the club.

Without a word, I strap my heels back on.

Kieran holds his hands up as I storm past him. "Rei, wait, I can explain—" he begins desperately.

My only response before I run out onto the street is to whirl around and punch him in the face.

✷

When Kieran and I first broke up, Sundays became my least favorite day of the week.

On that day, we'd meet up at the library right after breakfast to catch up on homework or cram for tests, grateful for the simple comfort of one another's presence. Every Sunday, without fail—until the day I found myself sitting alone in the library for five hours before he finally texted an apology that he wouldn't be able to make it. Something about a doctor's appointment he'd forgotten about.

No worries, I texted back. *Mistakes happen.* I was disappointed, of course, especially since school had gotten so busy that we couldn't find time to see each other during the week anymore, but I could understand.

Then next Sunday came around. This time, it was a plumber who needed to fix a bad leak caused by the storm a few days prior. The Sunday after that, it was a last-minute promise to babysit a friend's kid. For the next two weeks, he professed that he'd caught a terrible cold. When I offered to come by and take care of him, he refused, insisting that he was extremely contagious and didn't want me to catch anything.

I wanted to be understanding. To be sympathetic. Even when I thought his behavior seemed bizarre, I believed his back-to-back misfortunes.

Only after he canceled on me for the sixth Sunday in a row, claiming that he was *still* sick, did I give in to my suspicions. That Friday, I snuck out of last period and took a taxi to Upper West Side Prep.

The entire cab ride, I berated myself for acting so paranoid. I told myself to turn around, but next thing I knew I was sitting at an outdoor table in a café across from UWS Prep with a perfect view of the school's main exit.

I ordered myself a hot chocolate to go and settled down to wait.

As the minutes dragged by, I tried to convince myself to leave again. But the doubt had already crept in, like mold and mildew seeping through hidden cracks, weakening my resolve, rotting my trust in him.

Maybe he didn't want to spend time with me anymore. Maybe he'd lost interest in our relationship. In me. Or maybe . . .

Maybe there was another girl.

Maybe all those flimsy excuses had just been a ruse all along. Maybe he'd stopped showing up to the library because he was busy spending time with her. Laughing with her. Holding her. Or even—

I shook myself and drained the rest of my drink. *Get yourself together.*

A flurry of commotion rose from across the street. I glanced up just in time to see the wave of students in crimson uniforms flooding out the doors. I scanned the crowds, looking for his face, his hair, but he was nowhere to be seen.

Relief flooded me. And shame. I couldn't believe I'd stooped low enough to stalk my own boyfriend. And then—

I spotted him. Strolling out onto the street amidst a chattering group of students.

Without thinking, I picked up my cell phone and speed-dialed his number.

From my seat at the café, I watched him fish through his pockets for his phone. Blink at the screen. Hesitate. Then slowly lift the phone to his ear.

"Hello?"

"Hey. It's me," I said.

"Of course it's you. How's my little Rei of sunshine?" he teased.

"Are you still sick?" I asked. My heart pounded. Even from here, he looked tired, but obviously not bedridden. When the line went silent, I added hastily, "I just need to know if you'll be there this Sunday. At the library."

I watched the guilt play out across his face at my question. "I don't know, I'm still pretty sick."

The empty paper cup crumpled in my grip. "Where are you right now? Why do I hear traffic?"

"Stop worrying. I went to pick up some medicine, that's all."

Hearing one thing come out of his mouth and seeing a different reality entirely . . . I felt detached from myself, from the phone gripped to my ear and the voice I spoke with. "Can I come over? I'll bring you soup."

"No, you shouldn't be around me right now," he replied hurriedly, as one of his friends slung an arm around his shoulder and another offered him a piece of gum. A girl with blond hair and a killer smile said something to him that I couldn't hear. He waved her off. "But I promise I'll be there next Sunday, okay?"

"Okay," I whispered, and hung up before the tears could start to fall.

✳

The thief almost manages to lose me. *Almost.*

I catch a glimpse of her rounding the corner of 49th and Broadway. She crosses the street and races down the bike lane. Though she's flagging, she's still pretty damn fast. I sprint after her, my breathing even and my lungs thankful for fresh air after the stifling heat of the club.

Coach Lee made us run ten miles up and down West Street before school every day for six months in a row, and I'm glad it's finally paying off.

The thief looks like she's heading for Times Square, but the whole area is crawling with officers. She veers left at 47th instead, right before the pedestrian-only zones where people used to watch the ball drop at midnight on New Year's Eve. A turning taxi slams on the brakes and blares its horn at me, just barely grazing my behind as I rush across the intersection at the tail end of a yellow light.

When I've got the thief an arm's length away, I leap forward and tackle her into the concrete. She cries out in pain as her bare knees scrape the sidewalk, but I feel no sympathy.

Drenched in sweat, she gasps for air beneath me. Her whole body trembles in fear and exhaustion. I yank her to her feet and drag her into the unlit foyer of an abandoned building, the doors shattered by Deathlings or vandals.

I slam her into the wall and pin her elbow behind her back. "Where's my stuff?"

"You can't hurt me," she says confidently. "You're competing in the—" She cuts off in a whimper when I give her arm a hard twist. "I don't even have your shit!"

"Oh," I hiss into her ear. "You know who I am?" She nods frenetically, cowering away, trying to squirm out of my grasp even now. "Then you should know exactly what I'm capable of."

In my head, it's like she's not there anymore. All I can see is Kieran, offering his arm to me with a smile. Following me through the crush of bodies, calling out my name. Pointing to the elevator and waiting in the lobby, like we were still allies in real life. Making me think I could trust him, only for him to make a fool out of me again and *again*—

"*Ow!* Pl-please, stop! You're hurting me! I don't have your things anymore, I swear!"

I startle back to the moment, realizing my grip has tightened hard enough to bruise. I let go of her. She slides to the ground in a sobbing heap. The rage drains out of me. What the hell am I doing?

People only ever rise for two reasons: to serve those who look up to them, or to look down on those they serve.

I take a few steps back, broken glass and stale coffee beans crunching underfoot, and crouch down awkwardly. "What's your name?"

Before she can answer, a voice drawls out behind me.

"Her name is Cassie."

I whirl around as Kieran stalks through the door, one step at a time. He keeps his posture slack, but his eyes are harder than iron. A red, knuckle-shaped welt has already formed on his left cheek.

I rise to my feet, fists clenching, about to gift him a matching one on the other cheek when he adds, "Short for Cassandra. Cassandra Cross."

I falter.

He stops at my side and glares down at the thief. "AKA my baby sister."

CHAPTER TWENTY-ONE

Your sister," I echo weakly. He'd mentioned having a sibling in passing, but despite having dated for two years, we'd never visited each other's houses or families. Aunt Minyi hadn't allowed me to bring guests to the Manor, and Kieran always flat-out avoided the subject of home.

Even so, I can't believe that this is the first time I'm seeing his sister. The resemblance is difficult to spot at a glance, what with her blond hair and brown eyes, but when I look closely, I can detect it in their high bone structure, the curve of their cupid's bows, their heart-shaped faces.

"I'm sorry," Kieran says to me. "I grabbed her in the lobby and realized she'd already passed off your things. I was going to explain it to you myself so you wouldn't beat the shit out of her, but—well." Wryly, he touches his bruise.

Whoops.

Kieran leans down and grabs Cassie by the arm. "Where's your partner in crime? Call her, now."

"With what phone?" Cassie retorts.

Kieran's nostrils flare. After a moment, he digs through his pocket and slaps his phone into her waiting palm. "Hurry up."

She purposely enters the number as slowly as she can. The phone rings out.

"Put it on speaker," Kieran says.

A moment later, someone picks up. "This is Big Italy Pizza, how can I take your order—"

Kieran swears and grabs the phone from his sister. "You little—"

"Wait, wait!" she squeals. "Bea, it's me."

A pause. "Are you with someone?"

"She is," Kieran cuts in, his voice deeper than usual and menacing enough to send a shiver down my back.

A much longer pause. Then— "Ah, shit."

"Yeah. Get your conniving ass back over to Times Square."

"I already used my free transfer for the bus ride home. I guess I could use some of the money in your girlfriend's wallet—"

Kieran pinches the bridge of his nose. "Don't even think about it. We'll be waiting by the tennis courts near your apartment in forty minutes. If anything is missing . . ."

He doesn't need to finish his sentence.

"Just don't tell my mom about this" is all Bea says before the line goes dead.

Plumes of foul black smoke sputter out of the bus's exhaust pipes as we rattle uptown. Kieran, Cassie, and I stand near the back of the bus, having given up our seats for a pregnant woman and her two squabbling toddlers. The bus pulls around the south bend of Central

Park, the pedestal at Columbus Circle where we just were earlier today rising past the grimy windows. There used to be a marble statue of the famous explorer on top of it until a Deathling somehow crashed into it and took his head clean off. Now his scraggy bit of neck is occupied by pigeons.

While most of Manhattan's vehicles have switched to clean, electric power, the Transportation Authority has yet to fully replace their outdated fleet of buses. Even before the Vanishing, it was a slow, costly process, and without the revenue from the subway system and the out-of-city commuter trains, they lost almost everything they had.

"Are you a better maverick than my brother?"

I blink down at Cassie. She stands in the middle of the aisle, swaying erratically as the bus bumps and jostles us along. "You should hold on to something," I tell her.

She links her arm with mine in response. "Well, are you?"

"Stop bothering her," Kieran berates from my left. She sticks her tongue out at him. To me, he says, "She likes to pretend she doesn't understand anything because she doesn't go to a Prep League school."

"Neither of us are mavericks yet," I tell Cassie. "I'm trying to become one of them by winning the Tournament, and so is your brother."

Cassie smiles sweetly and rests her head on my shoulder. "I hope you beat him."

Kieran spends the remainder of the fifty-minute bus ride glowering at her.

The bus wheezes along Riverside Park, a long sliver of green that stretches up the west side of Manhattan. Joggers and couples pushing baby strollers soak in the afternoon sunshine for as long as they dare. Some even picnic on the shoreline of the Hudson River, gazing across the expanse of choppy gray waves to the not-so-far-off New Jersey coast.

Close enough to swim—after the city went into lockdown, some people snuck out after curfew and did just that. They became the first to find out that Deathlings could swim, too—at least, well enough to hunt. Once New Jersey and the other boroughs caught wind of that little fun fact, the government quietly installed several "coastal defense mechanisms." No Deathlings ever seem to have made it across the river, but some guys in a homemade canoe tried to. Only the shredded remains of their boat ever made it back to shore.

"The next stop is Riverside Drive," announces a pleasant voice over the speaker system.

We disembark. Traffic rushes past on the West Side Highway a mere few feet away from the path as we trek through the park in total silence. Intimidating black clouds creep along the horizon. Cassie wraps her skinny arms around herself to ward off the chill.

Kieran lets out a long-suffering sigh. He takes off his blazer and thrusts it at her. "Here."

She makes a face. "Thanks, but no thanks. What if someone saw me wearing that thing?"

"Aren't oversized blazers supposed to be a fashion statement?"

"The size isn't the problem."

I slip my leather jacket around her shoulders. "There. Now you'll be warm *and* stylish."

"Now *you're* going to freeze," Kieran grumbles at me. Before I can protest, he drapes his blazer over my shoulders, enveloping me in the warmth of his lingering body heat and the scent of cologne and . . . him.

With curfew fast approaching, it's no surprise that the brick-red tennis courts are almost totally deserted when we arrive. We wade through the rampant sea of grass and shrubs toward a chain-link fence overrun with crawling weeds. Against it leans a short girl in a baggy gray hoodie and ripped black jeans, examining her chipped nail polish. She pops her gum and cocks out a hip.

"Sick jacket, Cas."

"It's hers," Cassie replies, flicking the zipper a little self-consciously.

Bea lets out a derisive snort. "Course it is. Even more reason to *not* hand over her stuff." At Kieran's withering glare, she reluctantly digs a hand into her hoodie pocket and pulls out my wallet and phone.

"Did you guys steal anything from anyone else?" I ask her.

"If only."

I grab my things and make sure my parents' photos are still here, anger swirling in my stomach. "I could've had you reported. Arrested, even."

"So?"

"*So?* So you'd have a permanent violation on your record. That kind of irresponsibility could ruin your future *forever*. You think you're young, that it doesn't matter—"

"Shut up," Bea snarls. Fists clenched, she storms right up to my face, spittle flying. "Just *shut up*. You don't know anything, you rich, entitled bitch. You don't know the first thing about struggle or hardship."

"Bea," Cassie warns.

"No, Cassie. You know how much cash she was carrying in her wallet? You think she knows what it's like?" Bea turns on me. "To have to watch your parents work themselves to death and your four younger siblings *still* starve, because it's either food or rent? And you have no choice but to pay rent because if you don't have a door to lock, you get killed by monsters! And because of the monsters we're not allowed to move away, so we're all stuck living in this cesspool of a city until the day we die. So yeah, I don't give a shit about my future. *Because I don't have one.*"

Kieran steps toward her, one arm out. "Bea, you—"

"You're no better," she hisses. His shoulders go rigid. "You think you're above all of us now that you've made it out, but you're still the same piece of shit as you've always been."

Cassie grabs her. "Don't talk about my brother like that."

Bea shoves her off, but Cassie seizes a fistful of her hair and yanks her to the ground. They scream at each other, biting and kicking one another in the dirt. Kieran swoops down to intervene. Bea nails him square in the crotch. He goes down. I manage to drag Cassie away and hold Bea at arm's length as both struggle against me.

"Stop it," I shout. Neither listen. So I let them keep struggling for a few moments until the fight leaches out of their bodies. Their chests heave. Sweat drips down their reddened cheeks. When I release Bea, she stumbles forward and falls in a heap at my feet. Cassie sags down next to her, panting hard.

Kieran limps over. "Done?" he asks them.

They don't respond, staring emptily at the ground.

Finally, Cassie speaks up, her voice hoarse. "Bea has a point, you know. About the rent crisis. And the lack of choice."

When everyone first found out the borders were closing, landlords all over the city took the opportunity to hike up rent from already sky-high prices. Which left two options: pay up or face eviction. With Death-lings prowling the city after sundown, being homeless for longer than an afternoon is as good as a death sentence. Which is why the shelters are perpetually at capacity, but never over—the Deathlings see to it.

"You would think that one-third of Manhattan's population disappear-ing to god knows where would've freed up some real estate," Bea grunts.

"There were people that came from elsewhere," I say. Workers com-muting in, university students. Tourists and foreign visitors, like Roland. "They got trapped here, too."

In the distance, the curfew bells begin their haunting toll.

"Bea, I—" I begin before realizing I have no idea what to say. Sorry? For what? Our collective failings as a society? The existence of Deathlings? Her family's struggles? All the apologies in the world won't take any of those problems away.

In the years since the Vanishing, the Syndicate built up an empire to protect the streets of this city. But for over a decade, those streets have been full of cracks, growing wider every day. And thousands of people are slipping through.

At last, I take a deep breath and meet Bea's glare. "If there was something I—I mean, the Syndicate—could do for you, what would it take to make you believe in your own future?"

The barest flicker of surprise passes over her features. Then her expression hardens. "For starters? Help us pay rent. Or cancel it. My parents each work three jobs. We filed for financial relief, but the application has been pending for months. We're already living in the cheapest one-bedroom we could find."

A one-bedroom for seven people.

Whatever I could say to that is nothing I should say. Bea was right—it's not my place to judge her. It will never be.

"Here." I remove the bills from my wallet and hand them to her. I know it's not a long-term solution, but it's the only thing I can think of to do in the moment. "Take this for now. I'll talk to my aunt and see what else we can do to help you and your family."

Bea hesitates but a second before she grabs the money and stuffs it into her bra.

Cold drizzle peppers our faces. We glance up at the blackening skies.

Bea pulls her hood tighter over her head and shifts her feet in the grass. "I'd better go," she says. Just before she rounds the bend beyond the tennis courts, she turns back and calls, "By the way, I hope you're not expecting me to say thank you! Because I'm not going to."

An inadvertent smile rises to my face as she disappears. I think of Roland's sneering face, waiting for my declaration of gratitude. Even if he was a dick, at least he taught me something.

Kieran regards me for a moment and shakes his head. "You didn't have to do that."

I look down at my wallet, empty but for the photo of my parents' first day. They gaze back at me. There's only so much money from the funds they left me, mostly from their death benefit. But I think they would have been happy to know that, even in death, they were helping another family—another daughter, just like me.

"Everything has changed because of the Deathlings," I whisper. If the Deathlings are a plague, then this city is dying. The fury of a million lost futures—my parents', Bea's, and those of every citizen murdered because of *them*—blazes in my chest. But then I think of how helpless I felt when Bea was the one in need. I shut my eyes, wondering what the hell I'm doing.

Because what is one girl against a city full of monsters?

We hear the pounding of the rainstorm before we feel it. It sweeps across the Hudson, battering the trees, dousing the tennis courts and the stone paths and finally us. Cassie squeals and holds my jacket over her head, running for the cover of the trees, but Kieran and I stand frozen in the rain.

His eyes are cold, but I can tell the ire in them is not for me. While my anger is the volcanic, explosive kind, his is a quiet rage that seethes like a flow of lava, slowly but surely consuming all that stands in his way.

He tilts his face down to look at me, raindrops cascading off the bridge of his nose. I watch them trace the soft outline of his cupid's bow, drip down the pale column of his throat. When he speaks, his voice is rough as concrete scraped raw. "Sometimes, this world makes me sick. The Syndicate makes me sick. *Rise*, they say. As if rising will save the people we've left behind."

The rain intensifies, beating down against the earth until I can barely hear him, drowning out even the toll of the curfew bells. Somewhere in the distance, I hear something like a scream.

"I'd rather fall," he goes on. "All the way to hell, if I have to. And I'll be damned if I don't take every single one of those monsters down with me." The rain plasters his hair to his forehead, making the wet strands glisten darkly. With his face twisted in a snarl and his soaked clothes clinging to his rugged frame, I can almost imagine him as a different kind of monster, crawling out of the Hudson, thirsting for Deathling blood.

In a trance, I reach up to touch his cheek. "I believe you."

A shriek shatters the air. We whip around to find a wide-eyed Cassie stumbling toward us through the curtain of rain, her sneakers squelching and slipping dangerously in the grass.

Kieran draws away from me. "What?" he demands.

Cassie raises one trembling hand and points toward the trees: the branches pitching in the wind, the impenetrable downpour pummeling the leaves. *"Deathling."*

CHAPTER TWENTY-TWO

The first thing Kieran does is shove his little sister behind him. Then he yanks me toward him by the lapels of his blazer. Before I can protest, he shoves his hand inside and pulls out a switchblade from the inner pocket.

"You brought that to *prom*?" I exclaim.

He ignores me. "What did it look like, Cassie?"

"It—it had so many *arms*," she sobs.

"What are the chances?" I breathe. While it's close to curfew, the likelihood of a Deathling aboveground before nightfall should be nonexistent.

Kieran curses. "Rei. Take Cassie and run. Find somewhere safe, call Minyi."

Run, Rei, my mother's voice echoes in my head. Right before a Deathling—

"No," I snap, banishing the thought. "I'm not leaving you on your own." I scan the trees. The wind blows away from us, masking the monster's stench, so there's no way to tell exactly how close it really is.

"Rei, please—"

"We'd have to make it out of the park to find cover, and it might be too late for that. Our chances of survival will be much higher against a Deathling if we stick together. Any chance you've also got a spare staff or N.N. gun hidden in your pockets?"

Kieran scowls. "How big do you think they are?"

"Big enough to fit—" Realization dawns upon me. "Pudding," I whisper.

"Pudding?" Kieran repeats in confusion. Then his eyes widen, and the color drains from his face. *"Pudding."*

Cassie stares at us like we've lost our minds. "What?"

Kieran snatches her by the sleeve of my jacket to dig out the carton when the stench hits. That pungent, stomach-turning concoction of rot and decay and misery. Cassie freezes. Kieran brandishes his knife. Against a fully fledged Deathling, he may as well be wielding a thumbtack.

Kieran passes me the pudding. Between our combined arsenal, our best hope will be to buy Cassie enough time to get a head start.

We wait, unmoving, ready to bolt.

The rain covers the sound of the girl's footsteps until she emerges from the trees, her gray hoodie totally soaked through. As she jogs toward us, she keeps one hand in her pocket. With the other, she shields her eyes from the storm.

The tension drains out of Cassie's body. She lets out a loud sigh of relief. "Bea! Oh my god, you scared the crap out of us!" She's about to step toward her best friend when Kieran jerks her backward sharply. "Wha—"

Bea breaks into a dead sprint and leaps five feet directly into the air, her teeth bared in a grotesque smile.

A smile glistening red with blood.

Her hand comes out of her pocket midair, as bloodstained as her teeth. There's no doubt now who the scream I thought I heard earlier belonged to. Kieran vaults into the air to meet Bea halfway, his knife aimed straight for her neck.

A choked cry escapes Cassie. She lunges forward, but I wrench her back. Kieran and Bea—or rather, the monster wearing her skin—tumble to the ground, grappling in the mud.

Cassie's skin is dangerously slippery as she thrashes against my restraint. She kicks me in the shins. "No!"

I give her a hard shake. "Look, Cassie! That is *not* Bea!"

Of course, everything about the Deathling *seems* like Bea the human: her appearance, her height, and her clothing. But the way the monster moves—the way it *attacks*—is nothing but a pure killing machine. Kieran snarls and dodges its strikes, driving the little switchblade into its body again and again, but it barely slows.

"But it's not nightfall yet," Cassie whimpers, unable to tear her horrified gaze away from the Deathling masquerading as her friend. She's right. The curfew bells continue to ring in the distance, almost tauntingly.

My nails dig into Cassie's shoulders. "Listen to me, Cassie. You have to get out of here. *Carefully.* Do not run. Do not bring attention to yourself." I thrust my phone and wallet at her. "Once you make it out of the park, find shelter and dial emergency services. Understand?" She only gapes at me. I give her another shake. "*Cassandra.* Your brother's life is on the line."

"Y-yours too," she stammers.

"Don't remind me." I give her a hard shove toward the nearest exit out of the park. "No matter what happens, don't look back. We're counting on you."

Finally, something in the girl hardens. Without another word, she darts away.

Kieran lets out a howl of pain. I whirl around to find Bea's jaws locked around his arm. I grab the biggest rock I can find off the ground and jump the Deathling from its blind spot, driving the sharp edge between its eyes with all my strength. Something cracks. The monster releases Kieran and staggers back. Blood pours down its forehead, obscuring its vision. I wrench the switchblade from Kieran's grasp and slash a clean line down the middle of Bea's throat. My gut roils. No, not Bea.

Not a human. A Deathling, I remind myself as I leap onto its back. I plunge the knife deeper, drowning in the scent of rot. When I try to make the last cut to cleave off its head, the blade snaps in my hand.

The Deathling flings me off. I roll in the muck next to Kieran. "We need a new plan," I gasp, hauling myself to my feet.

He pants, stanching his bleeding arm with his other hand. "Didn't know we had one in the first place."

My eyes search the ground again as the Deathling wraps one hand around its neck to keep its head in place as its wounds heal. It lumbers toward us. With each step, it sheds Bea's skin and shifts into its true form. It contorts backward to walk on all fours, its head rotating to lock on to our locations. Its skin begins to char and crack, like driftwood held over a flame, until all that remains is a blackened husk. Arms sprout from every direction—one out of its neck, two from its ribs, a cluster swiveling out of its head like Medusa's serpents. Elongating, doubling in number, until it walks on all eights, then sixteens. Each arm ends in a sickle-shaped talon.

"Hey!" I shout at the Deathling. I wave the carton of banana pudding and pry the lid off. "You want this?"

The heavenly scent of bananas and sweet cream and sugar cuts through the stink. The Deathling wavers. A long web of drool dribbles down its muzzle.

"At my signal, run for the other side of the tennis courts," I murmur to Kieran from the corner of my mouth. "The fence won't give us much time, but it's better than nothing."

He inhales sharply. "Rei."

"Smells good, doesn't it?" I call out to the Deathling, feigning a wide, easygoing grin. "It's all yours, if you want. What do you say?"

"Rei," Kieran says again, his tone low and urgent.

Keeping my grin in place, I hiss at him through gritted teeth, "Can't you see I'm a little busy here?"

"There's another one!"

With the barest of movements, I turn my head. My heart shoots to my toes as I catch sight of the second monster. Covered in red spots that blink like eyes, it creeps toward us from the opposite direction, cutting us off. It must have smelled the pudding, too. Or our flesh.

I curse the bells still clanging away in the distance like nobody's business. The chances of us surviving a Deathling encounter by fighting it two-against-one is higher than running from it. But *two* of them . . .

Kieran shuffles closer to me as the Deathlings draw nearer, until we're pressed back-to-back. "Well? What now?"

"We die."

"Splendid," Kieran mutters sarcastically. "Just *splendid*. Go to prom with Rei Reynolds, Zaza said. It'll be fun, she said."

"It was until your sister came along!"

I hold the carton of pudding above my head. My heart pounds harder with every step closer the Deathlings take toward us. I calculate the distance, take aim, then throw.

It lands perfectly between the two monsters. They pounce for it at the same time, crashing heads, spitting and snarling and clawing at each other.

"Go!" Without hesitation, Kieran and I both barrel into a run. I estimate that the pudding will buy us at least twenty seconds.

I'm way off.

Less than fifteen seconds later, the Deathlings give chase, the stampede of the taloned one's many limbs louder than thunder. They're gaining *fast*. Like, fourteen-additional-limbs fast. While Kieran struggles not to slip in the mud in his dress shoes, the Deathling's talons only give it better purchase on the slick terrain. I'm almost grateful for the heels of my stilettos.

"We're not going to make it," Kieran gasps.

In that second, the world goes quiet. I can feel death dancing upon my shoulders, our final, violent moments flashing before my eyes. Panic threatens to swallow me whole, to override all logic with fear-driven instinct, but I don't let it. I grab ahold of it, taking advantage of my sharpened senses, the primal terror screaming at my legs and heart to work harder, faster.

This is what we've trained for.

The Deathlings' hot, rancid breath gusts the back of my neck. I still have the broken piece of blade in my hand.

Before Kieran can stop me, I spin and duck to the ground, holding the edge just right to slice off one of the first Deathling's many limbs. With the talons facing upward, I rake its own severed leg across its belly as it speeds over me. Hot blood splatters onto my face.

But it's not enough.

The other Deathling swoops down on me. I stab upward. There's a horrible screech and the sickening *crunch* of bone . . . but it's not because of me.

"Rei!" Kieran hollers from up ahead. "The hell are you doing? Get up!"

I wipe the blood from my eyes, disbelieving, as I watch both Deathlings get ripped apart by a small black ball of fur and teeth. Not just any ball of fur and teeth, though. A nightfang pup.

My nightfang pup.

CHAPTER TWENTY-THREE

Teeth flashing, jaws snapping, the nightfang pup clambers over the first Deathling and tears off limb after limb, too nimble for its flailing talons to slash. The shrieking monster falls to the ground, squirming and useless without its appendages.

My pup has grown significantly since we last saw one another. But even with its coat soaked to the bone and though it's grown as large as a full-sized chow chow—with twenty times more teeth—there's no world where I wouldn't recognize it.

The pup rips out the eyeballs of the second Deathling, then its throat with one well-aimed *chomp*. The mangled beast sways for a heartbeat before toppling into the mud with a repulsive *squelch*.

In a daze, I crouch down to the pup in absolute wonderment. It prances over to me like a proud show pony, unable to fully close its mouth for the sheer number of fangs protruding forth. With its short stubby legs and disproportionately large head, I simply can't help but think it really does look kind of adorable. Especially after saving our skins.

"Hi there," I murmur as it playfully butts its head against my knee.

"Thank you for the rescue. I'm sorry I didn't save any pudding for you, but I promise to bring you a truckload next time."

Kieran skids over to me as the pup continues nuzzling my leg. "W-what the hell *is* that thing?"

"It's not a thing." The pup's round black eyes shine at me. Inspiration sparks. "His name is Boba."

"Boba," Kieran repeats slowly. "Like . . . bubble tea."

I smile as Boba makes a high-pitched chirping noise that I read as approval. "Yeah, his eyes look like tapioca pearls. See?"

"All I'm seeing is teeth. How can it have so many teeth? Like, it's just four legs and teeth."

"Boba's just a pup right now," I explain. "You'll grow bigger eventually, isn't that right?" I ask the pup in an adoring voice, scratching at the soft tuft of fur above his eyes. His entire body vibrates with pleasure. I think.

Kieran massages his temples. "But what *is* he?"

"Well, I don't actually know if Boba's a he, but—"

"You know what I'm talking about!"

"What does it look like?" I tickle Boba's tummy. "He's a nightfang pup, of course."

"But—but *how?*"

I make a face. "We just got attacked by two Deathlings in broad daylight, and *this* is what you're having trouble believing?"

"Actually no," Kieran says, gravely serious. "I can't believe we're going to miss seeing who gets crowned prom queen."

We stare at each other in silence for a long moment. Then we break into a fit of hysterical giggling.

All of a sudden, Boba skitters away from me, growling at the parkway. A moment later, we hear the screech of tires against asphalt and the slam of van doors, followed by shouting and the heavy thud of boots. The pup bolts away, disappearing into the tall grasses without a trace.

A squad of eight Syndicate enforcers emerge from the trees in full tactical gear, their eyes hidden behind bronze visors and their weapons humming with electricity. Weapons they're currently pointing at *us*.

"Hands in the air!" one of them shouts. The squad fans out into formation, barricading us and the two incapacitated Deathlings lying on the ground from all sides.

Kieran and I are quick to comply. Once they've confirmed we're not Deathlings in disguise, they give the all-clear to the rest of the squad.

"Are you in need of immediate medical attention?" the chief enforcer asks.

I'm about to point out Kieran's arm, but he shakes his head. "Where's my sister? I assume she was the one who called you."

"She's been escorted to a secure location," they reply. "You may reconvene once you have both completed questioning."

Questioning? That's not standard procedure.

"What for?" Kieran demands, his tone so blatantly hostile that I do a double take. "We were nearly killed by two Deathlings, *before* curfew! If anything, we should be questioning *you*. You assure us that we're safe as long as we follow the rules, and yet—"

A loudening roar cuts him short. A motorcycle revs toward us, the thick wheels kicking up waves of mud. Atop it leans a woman in a red trench coat, her face hidden by a gold visor. She halts beside us and kills the engine. "Stand down!" she orders, leaping off the bike. The enforcers obediently drop their weapons to their sides, though they don't power them down.

My knees nearly give out. "Aunt Minyi!"

She gives my shoulder a squeeze and positions herself between us and the enforcers. "Thank you, Chief," she says as four more motorcyclists ride into view. They, too, wear the same coats, silver visors concealing their eyes instead of gold. Mavericks. "We'll take it from here. Kaplinsky, Yang, it's your show."

The two mavs standing on the far left withdraw their N.N. guns and stroll toward the Deathlings. Using harnesses, they begin securing the corpses for transport back to the labs.

My aunt reaches into her coat and pulls out some takeout napkins. "Are you hurt?"

I use them to wipe my face. "Kieran's arm got bitten, but I'm fine. Aunt Minyi, how could there—"

"Not here, Rei," she murmurs, guiding us toward the motorcycles. The remaining two mavs pull out helmets from underneath the passenger seats of their motorcycles and hand them to me and Kieran. We strap them on. One of them takes out a small first aid kit and wraps his arm.

When my aunt and the mavs are turned the other way, I grab Kieran by the wrist. "Not a word about Boba," I whisper. *"Please."*

Brow furrowed, he holds my gaze for a tense moment. Long enough for my heartbeat to quicken with dread. My grip tightens. At last, he nods almost imperceptibly. We separate and mount our bikes behind each of the two mavs.

"You good?" my maverick asks as I wrap my arms around her waist.

"Define *good*."

"Alive," she answers simply.

I glance at Kieran, only to find that he's already watching me. I wonder if he has any idea how much of his face is covered in mud. He must, because he puts one hand on his cheek, bats his eyelashes, and sends me the prettiest of smiles.

I let out a shaky laugh. "Then yeah. I'm good."

✳

We make it back to the Manor with less than thirty minutes before curfew to spare. As soon as we step out onto the eleventh floor, Aunt Minyi shepherds us directly into her office. She moves the two armchairs by the window in front of her desk, gestures for us to sit, then returns to the door.

The lock slides into place with a foreboding *click*.

Taking her seat behind the desk, the Master of the Upper West Side steeples her fingers beneath her chin and stares at us.

We stare back.

At last, she says, "I'm sure you both have questions. But before that, I want you to know how glad I am that you're safe."

"We barely made it," says Kieran.

Aunt Minyi's hands flutter in a placating gesture. "I know. And I can only imagine how terrifying it must have been for both of you. And yet you managed to dispatch those Deathlings on your own. How—"

"Let's just call it luck," I interrupt. If she finds out about Boba, she'll be forced to report him to the Directors. There's no telling what they'll want to do to him. What they might force *me* to do to get their hands on him.

"We need to notify citizens that Deathlings aren't waiting until nightfall to attack," says Kieran. "Especially those living near the Riverside Park area."

"I'm afraid we must do the exact opposite of that."

I blink, certain I've misheard. "The opposite?"

Master Minyi leans forward, bracing her hands on the table. "Listen closely, both of you. What happened today must stay between us."

"But *why*?" I demand.

"If the media catches wind of this, panic would break out like a plague. The very credibility and integrity of this entire organization would be thrown into question. To put it frankly, the two of you are currently the Syndicate's biggest security threat. Understood?"

I glance at Kieran to share my disbelief, but all he does is stare into his lap. I want to grab him by the shoulders and shake some sense into him. How can he just sit there and obey?

When he finally speaks, all he says is, "What about my sister?"

"I've already spoken to her. She's asleep in the guest bedroom right now, which she's welcome to occupy for as long as she needs. You can see her before you return to the Sanctuary."

My fists clench in my lap. "Those Deathlings were on killing sprees. Before nightfall. How is that even possible?"

"Adaptation," Aunt Minyi replies simply.

"But they've always been dormant during the day—"

"So far, yes." She rubs her temple. "Do you know how many billions of dollars we've spent on research and weapons development? We've got exosuits, electrocuting rods, and biochemical bullets. Yet we've barely made a dent in their numbers. Every time we get a little better at killing them, they find a way to evolve. It was only a matter of time."

"Attacking before nightfall isn't evolution," I argue. "It's against their very nature."

"Rei, I understand your frustration. Trust me when I say we're doing everything we can to safeguard the city. The Directors have already been working with scholars and strikers alike around the clock to revamp protocols to combat the recent attacks."

I struggle to keep my tone in check. "Did you . . . did you just say *already*? As in, these daytime attacks have happened before?"

Aunt Minyi's mouth presses into a thin line.

"When?" I demand, shoving myself out of my chair onto my feet. "And why the hell hasn't the public been warned yet? They have the right to know, to protect themselves!"

"I'm not in the position to divulge any more details—"

My voice shakes. "An innocent girl was *killed* today! A girl with a family and a life and a future! Her blood isn't just on the hands of the Deathlings—it's on the hands of the Directors. And yours!"

Aunt Minyi slams her fists into the table hard enough for me to flinch. *"There's enough blood on my hands to paint this damned city red!"* she yells.

I sit down.

In all the years she's raised me, I've never seen my aunt like this. So . . . *uncontrolled.*

Judging by Kieran's wide eyes, neither has he.

My aunt is a fortress. Never allowing any emotion to escape through her walls, separating each version of herself. Caring mother of two daughters by day, ruthless killer by night. Guardian of hundreds of thousands of lives. Bringer of peace through bloodshed. She fulfills so many roles, wears so many masks. She does it all with unshakable poise, no matter the circumstance. No matter the pressure.

But at the end of the day, she's human. Just like the rest of us. And at some point or another, we always break.

"Five," my aunt grits out, breathing hard.

Kieran and I exchange a glance. Timidly, he ventures, "Five?"

When she speaks, it is to the table, as if she can't bear to face our judgment. "Lina Beaumont. Bryant Liu. Alana Gonzalez. Isiah Lincoln. Roland Winchester."

A cold lump of foreboding settles in my gut.

Kieran frowns. "Aren't they all mavericks?"

"Yes." My aunt sinks back into her chair. She steeples her fingers beneath her chin again, but this time it looks more like a prayer. "And as of exactly four days ago, they're all dead."

CHAPTER TWENTY-FOUR

I've never had trouble falling asleep.

But tonight, I lose track of the hours I spend tossing and turning, until I finally throw off the covers with a frustrated grunt and slip into the Sanctuary's empty hallways. Ornate crystal bulbs affixed to the walls swirl with stardust, refracting bursts of light along the floor. I've never seen anything like it, not even at the Manor.

I have no idea what time it is, except that it's very early. Or very late, depending on whom you ask. Despite my exhaustion, there's an itch in my veins. A need to get on my feet and *do* something. Anything.

So I head to the gym.

I let myself in quietly. The room is cool and dark, feebly illuminated by the row of square windows set high above the ground on one far wall. There's just enough moonlight for me to distinguish the vague outlines of the equipment. After a quick stretch, I feel my way over to a rack of dumbbells and get to work.

I lose myself in my usual routine, completing my sets with razor focus. It's all I can do, really, to prevent my mind from spiraling. I try to concentrate on that familiar ache, try to get Aunt Minyi's words out of my head. *There's enough blood on my hands to paint this damned city red.*

I should have known something was wrong when Master Sasha told me Roland died. His death—and the deaths of the others—should have headlined every news source in the city, but instead they were silenced like nothing ever happened.

With the semifinals of the Tournament tomorrow, I can't stop thinking about Kieran, either. The burden of the secret we've now been forced to share.

I wish I could ignore the truth, but I can't deny the way my body reacts to him, to his closeness. The chemistry is still there. It always has been, since the moment I confronted him in the library because he was about to check out the book I needed for a physics paper on exosuit aerial dynamics—and he refused to give it up to me unless I gave him my number.

And then he had the gall to use the transferring of the book as a decoy for our first date.

I shake my head, biting down on an involuntary smile.

Even though we went to two completely different schools, we always shared the same devotion to our goals. And to each other.

At least, that's what I'd thought.

I switch over to the bench press, adding more weight. I lie down on the bench and grip the barbell. The darkness makes it too hard to block out the memories.

To Kieran's credit, he did show up to the library the following Sunday as he'd promised. He found me sitting in the relative privacy of the stacks, staring blankly at my notes.

"Hey," he said, sitting down beside me. "Are you okay? What did you want to talk about? I can't stay too long."

I tried to keep my voice even. "Why not?"

He didn't answer. This time, he hadn't even bothered to prepare another pitiful excuse.

That was when I snapped.

"I thought you cared about your future," I hissed. "But you'll never qualify for the Tournament slacking off like this. At this rate, you might not even get scores high enough to land an entry-level position in the Syndicate."

Despite his initial shock, he recovered quickly. "You think I can't even scrape together three brain cells to pass my classes?"

"*Pass* your classes? Oh, so now just *passing* is good enough for you? What happened to climbing to the top of our schools' rankings?" I throw my notebook at his chest. "Together?"

"Not everybody can be as good as you all the time, Rei!" he burst out. Someone shushed him violently from the other side of the shelves. He ducked his head and reached for my hand. "Sorry. It's just—"

I wrenched it from his grasp. "Seriously?" A storm of outrage swept away my disbelief. "Not everybody can be as good—are you kidding me right now? So all this time . . . how ironic. How goddamn ironic."

His jaw tightened. "What is?"

That all this time, you made me doubt myself. You made me believe that I *wasn't good enough for* you.

"That after everything we've been through, I thought I'd finally found an equal in you. But it turns out that you were just *jealous.*"

"What? No! That's not—"

"Not what?" I spat.

A dark shadow passed over his features. He straightened his shoulders and tilted his chin to look down at me. "You know what? Maybe you're right. Maybe my ego is so fragile that I do feel threatened by your success."

"Or maybe you're just an asshole," I muttered.

He huffed out a strangled little laugh. "Probably."

"Was any of it true?"

"What do you mean?"

"Those excuses you made. The doctor's appointment, the plumber, the babysitting. Being sick."

A beat of silence. "No."

"Then what have you been doing this whole time? Why did you lie to me?"

"I can't tell you."

My stomach filled with sinking dread as my mind flashed with hazy images of the faceless blond girl who had been plaguing me for over a week. I didn't want to know. Yet, at the same time, I *needed* to.

"Tell me, Kieran," I said. "Tell me why you've been lying, or I swear we're through."

At that, he stilled. His face turned ashen. "What?"

"You heard me. Unless you give me the truth, it's over between us."

For an eternity, he didn't utter a sound. His green eyes drank me in slowly, gleaming with a terrible sadness that I didn't understand until he finally spoke. "I'm sorry, Rei. I really am."

It wasn't the words themselves that chilled my blood to ice. We'd had fights before, of course. But he didn't sound merely apologetic. He sounded . . .

Final.

I hated how small my voice became. "Am I not good enough to deserve your honesty?"

"You're *too* good for me, Rei. We both know that you're better off on your own."

That fateful Sunday afternoon, before he turned his back on me, he tried to give me one last smile. It came out as more of a pained grimace, like he never knew how badly a smile could hurt—while I never knew how easily he could rip through my chest and walk away with my bleeding heart still in his hands.

✳

Panting hard, I thrust the barbell upward one more time. Sweat runs into my eyes. My arms shake from the strain. Only now do I notice the feeble rays of sun trickling through the window. How long has it been? How many reps have I done?

Turns out it's one rep too many.

My entire body trembles as I try to raise the bar higher, but my muscles refuse to obey. My back arches off the bench. I try to tip the bar off to one side.

The gym door opens.

I swear through my gritted teeth. The weight crushes me downward. Just as my arms give out, a pair of hands grab the bar, braced on either side of mine, and lifts. I breathe out a sigh of relief as the burden disappears and the bar settles onto the rack with a gentle *clank*.

"Thanks," I gasp, sitting up. "I really—oh. It's you."

Kieran raises an eyebrow. "Please, you don't have to sound *that* excited."

I lift the hem of my T-shirt to wipe my brow. "How's your bite doing?"

"Hm?" I catch him checking out my abs. He blinks back to attention and clears his throat. "Oh. It's fine."

He rolls up his sleeve to show me the healed wound, exposing the veins carving down his impressively sculpted forearms. It's obvious he's been working out recently—and hard.

I bite my lip, wondering what the rest of him looks like now, too.

"Reynolds?" He smirks. "Am I interrupting something?"

"Yeah, my examination of your injury." I grab his wrist and twist it over, where the skin around the Deathling bite has regenerated, courtesy of a little stardust. Dammit, this side of his arm looks even hotter. "Looks good," I say carelessly.

He grins. "Yeah, I bet it does."

I scowl and drop his wrist. "What are you doing here, anyway?"

"Couldn't sleep."

"Join the party." I gesture at the barbell and lie back onto the bench for one more set.

Wordlessly, he positions himself at the head of the bench to spot me. I keep count this time. After a slight hesitation, he asks, "Do you think we're doing the right thing?"

"You're going to have to be a little more specific," I grunt out.

"I trust Master Minyi. But to sit back and do nothing when a civilian was killed feels . . . wrong. And Bea wasn't the only person to die. What about all those mavs? They would have been armed with weapons and Artifacts, not to mention years of training and experience." He shakes his head. "From what it sounded like, they were all killed on the same day. Maybe even at the same time. What kind of monster could have wiped them out like that? It must have been huge. Or impossibly strong."

"Or smart."

"Deathlings aren't exactly known for their critical thinking skills, Reynolds."

I exhale hard and finish my last rep, easing the barbell back onto the rack. "That doesn't mean it's impossible. Have you ever seen any records of a Deathling pup?"

"No, but now that you mention it, you still owe me an explanation about that. I take it that you never bothered to inform the Syndicate of your little discovery?"

I sit upright. "No, I didn't. But given that my *little discovery* saved our necks yesterday, I don't regret it, either."

"I'm glad."

"What?"

"I'm *glad*. I know how much you worship the Syndicate and everything they do. It's nice to know that you can still think for yourself."

My eyes narrow. "What is it with you and your vendetta against the Syndicate?"

His expression shutters. In all my years of knowing him, he's never acted like this. "That's beside the point. There must be something they can do, right? We could propose an earlier curfew to Master Minyi, but with the days so short, New Yorkers are already restless enough as it is. I heard that one of the protests last weekend in Washington Square Park escalated to multiple injuries. Forcing more rules might trigger full-blown riots. The last thing the city needs to deal with right now is people getting killed by *people*."

I mull over his suggestion. "If we're trusting what my aunt said, shouldn't we just let the Syndicate handle it?"

"The Syndicate isn't all-powerful, as much as they'd like to pretend otherwise. They might've done a lot of good for this city, but we'd be fools to trust that they can save everybody—or would even want to."

His words hang ominously in the air.

"Where is this coming from?" I ask quietly.

He averts his gaze. "It has to do with Cassie, mainly. With my family. It's not something I'm ready to talk about yet with anyone," he admits. "Except for Master Minyi."

A strange suspicion settles over me. Kieran had always danced around any talk of his family, but I'd never questioned him why. Now I think of what my aunt told me about why she decided to hire Kieran. *Let's just say that Kieran is in a difficult situation. I'm just lending him a hand to right some wrongs.*

I swallow the urge to pry. "So you trust her, but not the Syndicate itself?"

He raises an eyebrow. "You don't trust the Syndicate enough to turn in that Deathling pup."

A memory flashes through my mind. *Snowy banks. Gold fur. Blossoms of red on white.* I shut my eyes. "My instincts have been wrong before."

"So have mine. But for what it's worth, I don't think yours were this time."

I sigh and sit down on the floor to stretch my limbs. Kieran lowers himself onto the ground across from me, long legs splayed outward. The silence spools out amid the smell of sweat and steel and rubber, but it's a lot less agonizing now than what I expected.

Not that you could tell by the look on Kieran's face.

When I can no longer stand the suspense, I say, "What's wrong?"

"There's something I've been wanting to tell you since last year."

I tense.

"You said I was jealous of you. I was, but not of your success. You always ranked first while I could barely scrape the top five, even when you devoted so much time to helping me study. I felt like a burden." He closes his eyes. "You were there for me. I couldn't do the same for you. I didn't tell you about the internship with Master Minyi because I wanted to prove to myself that we could be equals. And then I went and got outranked by Tim of all people anyway."

For a second, he looks so discouraged, so powerless, that I can't help but despise the system that quantifies us—our intelligence, our determination, our worth—with a single number.

"Is that why you stopped showing up to the library?" I frown. "You felt insecure?"

"Yes. Sort of." He flexes his hands into fists, opening and closing them. "Not exactly."

"Then was it that other girl? The one you were seeing."

His head snaps up. "What other girl?"

"Come on, you can admit it. We're not together anymore. I don't care."

He turns his body fully to me and says in the most serious tone I've ever heard from him, "There was no other girl. There's never been another girl besides you."

"Then what in the name of liberty were you lying to me for, week after week?"

A long pause. "I—I didn't want the truth to make you think any less of me," he says at last, averting his eyes.

"But you thought lying wouldn't?"

"It was a personal family matter. To be honest, I didn't think you would understand. I still don't. But that doesn't mean I'm any less sorry."

Before I can push him any further, the door opens and Everly pokes their head in. "Yo, you guys working out?"

"Yes," I say at the same time Kieran goes, "No."

Everly shoots us a perplexed smile. "Okay, then! Do you mind if I use the treadmill?"

I glance at Kieran. He stubbornly continues avoiding my gaze. So, conversation officially over. Fine. It's just as well—he made his choices, and the reasons behind them are none of my business now.

Everly's appearance is just another reminder that this competition is far from over. Only one of us can win—which means that my success depends on Kieran's failure.

And I'm perfectly fine with that.

CHAPTER TWENTY-FIVE

At dinner Kieran and I enter separately and sit at different tables, so no one gets the impression that our alliance from the first task has stuck. Tonight's extravagant menu includes herb-and-honey-roasted salmon imported from Alaska and braised short ribs from Nebraska. I load up my plate and sit with Everly and Mia instead, while Kieran joins Yuna, Taz, and Langston a few tables down. Tim tries to sit with Noëlle, but she pins him with her frigid gaze as she slices her salmon until he gets the hint and leaves. Dawn sits by herself, nibbling at a plate stacked with cookies from the dessert bar.

I check the clock on the wall. By now the curfew bells should have started ringing, but we can't hear them through the Sanctuary's walls. It's the first time I haven't heard them since the day they started ringing. But they've become so integrated into my brain that I swear I keep hearing them, faintly, only to fixate on the sound and realize my ears are hallucinating them entirely.

A buzz in my pocket distracts me. While Everly and Mia carry the conversation, I sneak a peek at my phone.

jie jie

hey mom told me what happened at the park.

you ok??

Maura. My grip tightens around my phone. No mention of missing the first task from my big sister. Part of me doesn't even want to bother to respond, but I choose to be salty.

I didn't see you at the Tournament.

work is killing me . . . sorry. :(

i have the recording on my laptop.

i'll watch it as soon as i can.

I press my lips together to curb my irritation. It's always the same thing with her. Why did I expect anything different this time? There's another buzz.

i know this doesn't make up for me not being

there in person, but i hope it helps.

do NOT tell Mom!!!

ENCRYPTED FILE RECEIVED

The doors to the cafeteria burst open. My head jerks up as Nick Valentine comes strolling in, ensorcelling us with his familiar ear-to-ear grin. Instead of a tux, the Phantom wears an exosuit beneath his long black trench coat. "I'm on duty tonight!" he announces to the competitors. "So finish that last bite and follow me."

I bite my lip and pocket my phone. Decrypting the message will have to wait until later.

After we put away our empty plates, the Phantom leads us out of the cafeteria through the clean, austere halls of the Sanctuary, then down several flights of stairs. We halt before a black door with a gold, cursive *S* carved into the center. It opens of its own accord to reveal the pitch-black void beyond.

The Phantom makes eye contact with the competitor standing closest to him: me. He gestures at the darkness with a flourish and a wink. "After you, Miss Reynolds."

With my heart fluttering, I step into the unknown.

The darkness pours into my eyes. I keep my arms raised in front of me as I walk deeper into the space, my fingers outstretched. There's nothing but the sound of my own shallow breathing and the hollow echo of footsteps as the other competitors file in. The door falls shut, sealing us in true and total blackness.

"Welcome," resonates the Phantom's voice, enfolding us from every direction, "to the second task."

I gasp softly as the floor flickers to life. Lines of silver light race and weave between our feet, crisscrossing higher and higher to form intricate structures. A familiar skyline rises into existence. Soon, a small-scale 3D replica of Manhattan's parks, buildings, and skyscrapers sprawls out all around us in holograph form.

"As you know"—Valentine's voice floats toward us—"the streets are fraught with danger and Deathlings come nightfall. For mavericks and masters, this is no exception."

We each marvel at the mind-blowing details of the cityscape as it bathes our faces in a silver glow. We're a pack of hulking giants with a perfect view of the gridded streets, all the way from the northern tip of the island down to the docks at Battery Park. The spire of the Empire State Building tickles my waist. My feet are currently submerged in Koreatown.

"Once the sun sets, we can no longer access the transportation we take for granted during the day: cars, motorcycles, and even horses, which grow paralyzed in fear at the scent of Deathlings," Valentine continues. "We must travel by foot. But that doesn't mean we can't take to the skies."

A list of names flickers over the hologram.

TEAMS FOR THE SECOND TASK:

DAWN CHO & TAZ DIAZ

EVERLY EVANOFF & YUNA PARK

KIERAN CROSS & TIM BECKETT

LANGSTON BROWN & MIA KNIGHT

NOËLLE CARTIER & REI REYNOLDS

Noëlle's icy glower burns me from across the room. Her crimson lips pinch like I'm a wad of chewing gum she just discovered besmirching the bottom of her shoe.

I guess she hasn't forgiven me for looting her flags *quite* yet.

"For the next two hours, study the map with your teammate. I can't reveal the specific instructions prior to the commencement of the task, but I strongly advise you to take advantage of this particular view of the city. Try to think like mavs, if you will. And remember: successful candidates must be capable of dealing with any situation that gets thrown their way."

He waves a hand, and the list of names is replaced by a timer, set to two hours. "Good luck, all of you. If you have any questions, I'm afraid you'll have to find the answers for yourselves, as I've got monsters to kill."

Then he pulls out the ivory half mask from the inner pocket of his mav coat and dons it. As soon as he fits the legendary Artifact to his face, he just . . . *vanishes*.

We startle as his deep voice booms around us, nowhere and everywhere all at once.

"Your time begins now."

I muster up all my will and make my way over to the tall blond surveying the West Village. I take a deep breath and paste a grin onto my face. "Looks like we'll be working together."

She turns her sharp gaze down at me in a way that screams *unworthy peasant* but says nothing.

"What, don't you know how to talk?" I ask, already irritated.

"I have no desire to associate with you."

A snort escapes me. "And you think I do, Your Highness?"

A thinly veiled flicker of outrage flashes across her features. "Don't call me that."

"Then stop acting like a pretentious little bitch."

The room around us goes abruptly silent. Maybe I said that a little too loudly.

Noëlle has gone still as stone. In a voice so low I barely catch it, she says, "Take it back."

I set my jaw. "No."

Her nostrils flare. She starts forward, fists clenched. *"Take it back."*

"Okay, fine," I snarl. "I take it back. But that doesn't make it any less true."

Her hand flies at my face. I grab her wrist and knee her in the stomach. She hooks her ankle around my other leg and sends us both toppling to the ground. She wrestles me into a chokehold. I bite down on her arm hard enough to make her screech.

"Fight! Fight!" Tim chants joyously.

Everly and Langston grab Noëlle by the arms. I try to get in one last punch as they drag her away from me, but Kieran seizes me from behind and holds me back. "Save it for the final task," he murmurs into my ear, but I think he's just jealous that he didn't think of beating up his own teammate first.

Everly does not look impressed. "Can you guys chill, or do we need to call the Phantom?"

We both grumble something unintelligible in response. After releasing Noëlle, they return to Yuna's side to continue planning for the second task. The other teams also quickly lose interest, redirecting their focus on more important matters. Well, not all of them—Taz and Dawn stand in opposite corners of the map, blatantly ignoring each other's existence.

Noëlle crosses her arms over her chest and stares emptily at the hologram.

Successful candidates must be capable of dealing with any situation that gets thrown their way. The Phantom's words weigh in my mind. In the field, mavericks don't get to choose who they work with.

I have to find a way to cooperate with her. My future depends on it— and in fact, so does hers.

I swallow hard and make my way over to her again. Her shoulders tense, but all I say is, "You're right. I shouldn't have called you what I did. For that, I'm sorry. I don't blame you for not wanting to work with me, especially considering what happened during the first task. But that's why the masters put us together on the same team. They want to see if we can figure out a way to put aside our differences in order to work toward a common goal."

Her brow furrows. "Which is?"

"Winning, of course."

The sharp glint returns to her eyes. She turns to me and drawls, "And why would someone like you have any chance of winning?"

"Why wouldn't I?"

"Isn't it obvious? You're a nominee."

The way she says the word curdles in my stomach like spoiled milk. "Look," I growl. "You might have gotten all the perfect scores in the world on your final exam. But I was *chosen* by the Master of the Financial District. If he believes in my abilities, so can you. Do we have an agreement?"

She lets out a long-suffering sigh. "Do I have a choice?"

It's certainly no heartfelt declaration of allegiance, but at least we're not trying to claw each other's eyes out anymore.

And for the first time, I truly believe that maybe—*just maybe*—we can make this work after all.

CHAPTER TWENTY-SIX

Two hours later, I realize that I am an idiot, and we will *never* make this work.

CHAPTER TWENTY-SEVEN

The second task of the Tournament begins where the first ended. A massive crowd has gathered on the sidewalks surrounding Columbus Circle, waving posters of our faces and names with one hand and filming us on their phones with the other as we pull up in a huge black van. An army of drones buzz through the sky, capturing aerial shots of our arrival, ready to follow the competitors to wherever the Tournament takes them.

I wait my turn, flexing my fingers anxiously beneath the cool black fabric of my exosuit. My heart hasn't stopped pounding all morning.

I touch my thumb to my left pinkie finger, then my left ring finger, and then both middle fingers. But this time, it's not just some comforting ritual. My exosuit whirrs against my skin, coursing with electricity, with life. These are the real deal, not the mock-ups I fought in during combat education class. Each in-body command engages a different function: touch the thumb to the pinkie for camouflage, ring finger for shielding, and double middle fingers to engage the boosters that allow you to jump two hundred times your own height. *Pinkie.* The fabric covering my legs blends into the leather seat. *Ring finger.* It expands, inner layers filling with gel, while the surface ripples and hardens into a rigid, scale-like shell. Nothing happens for the last command—yet.

Due to the exorbitant manufacturing cost, only mavs and masters wear real exosuits, so none of us were expecting this opportunity. It isn't until I catch Kieran's grim gaze that I realize where—or *who*—the spare suits must have come from. A shudder runs through me. I examine the fabric for any trace of rips or tears or teeth marks, but of course I find nothing. The self-healing nature of the material ensures that it will outlast the wearer. Who wore this suit last? And how did they die?

Langston is first out of the van. Seconds later, Tim squeezes out of the van to an avalanche of cheers. He is something out of a nightmare in his new exosuit, his biceps bulging even larger than usual beneath the thick sinew running up and down the sleeves of his suit that houses all the internal tech like muscle fibers..The fibers along his calves ripple with enough strength to crush Deathling skulls underfoot like candy apples. When he stomps his feet and lets out a roar, the concrete actually trembles. It isn't hard to imagine why he's one of the favorites to win.

After Dawn and Everly step out the door, it's my turn.

I lift my head out of the van to a thunderous greeting. My boots settle upon the sidewalk. I take my first step. My exosuit calibrates to my movements beautifully, rendering every effort effortless. I feel weightless. Airy. Like I never realized the physical burden of my own body until my exosuit set me free.

The dark eyes of the cameras bore into me. I can't find it in myself to smile for them this morning. How many people are watching the broadcast? Including the Directors? Right here, right now, I could speak the words I'm sworn not to speak, and every single person in this city would know them.

My lips part.

But then Yuna emerges from the van, stealing the attention. The cameras swing away, and the moment passes. I take my place in the line of competitors beside Everly. Exhaling shakily, I withdraw Mom's necklace from my collar and clench the talisman in my fist. I can't forget I have more than one promise to keep.

"I can't believe these people have nothing better to do than stand here for hours on end just to see *us*," Everly mutters to me out of the corner of their mouth, watching Mia strut down the length of the plaza like she's on the catwalk, her long legs eating up the distance. I *almost* sympathize with Taz, who has no choice but to plod out in Mia's wake like the surly little goblin that she is. She scowls at the crowd's lukewarm response to her arrival.

"At least it's only September," I murmur to Everly. "Before the Vanishing, my aunt told me that around one million people would freeze their asses off in Times Square on New Year's Eve every year just to watch a ball drop."

"Sounds pretty miserable. Unless you're a Deathling. Then it sounds like an all-you-can-eat feast. Bon appétit!"

I grimace weakly. "And a happy New Year."

Once Noëlle and Kieran have taken their places, completing the lineup, we wait for the inevitable.

At last, Nick Valentine emerges from the van. It's a miracle that the windows stay intact from the explosion of screams. At least seven people faint. Some guy unzips his jacket and begs the Phantom to autograph his pecs.

Eventually the Phantom makes it over to us, a metal briefcase tucked under his arm. "Welcome to the second task, semifinalists," he announces in that rich, honey-sweet voice that he reserves specially for when the cameras are rolling. He opens the briefcase to reveal five cream-white envelopes with black seals bearing the Syndicate's insignia. "The rules of the second task are very simple. In teams of two, you will solve three riddles. Each of these envelopes contains a first riddle—and each riddle is unique. The solution to each riddle will lead you to three locations around the city, where you will find answer keys that will help you determine the location of your final, shared destination. You *must* travel by foot. Any form of transport is forbidden, such as—but *not limited* to—cars, buses, and bikes. Only the first three teams to cross the finish line will advance to the final round of the Tournament."

So it's a race. Noëlle casts a judgmental look at me, probably assessing whether she could complete the task faster if she shoved me into oncoming traffic and finished it on her own. Well, tough shit. If she tries to take me down, I'll grab her nasty, swishy blond ponytail and take her down with me.

I step forward to select an envelope, but Noëlle yanks one out of the case first. She breaks the seal and turns away to read it. I enviously watch as Langston and Mia already start discussing their game plan, heads bent together over their envelope. They might not have come out on top during the first task, nor are they the strongest of the competitors, but their ability to work as a team gives them a serious chance of winning this thing.

To my disbelief, Noëlle folds the riddle back into the envelope. As she heads off toward the west corner of Central Park, I grab her wrist.

"Where do you think you're going?" I grit out through a forced grin, all too aware of the cameras trained upon us.

Noëlle exhales loudly, as if *I'm* the one testing her patience. "Look, I simply don't have the time to deal with you. Just follow my lead and stay out of my way. The task will be over before you know it."

"Follow your lead," I echo. "And stay out of your way."

"Exactly!"

"Don't you realize that this task is supposed to test our ability to cooperate with each other in spite of our differences, just like mavs?"

"I'll have no trouble cooperating with *real* mavericks. You'll never make it that far. Master Sasha might have chosen you, but I ranked first. I actually deserve to be here."

Her words turn my blood to ice. For a second, I have no idea what to say—because she's technically right. But just as she spins on her heel again, I yank her back and hiss into her ear. "You're right. You worked hard. You proved that you're the best. Everyone is expecting you to win. But I have no reputation to uphold. I'm the wild card, which means I can do whatever I want. And right now, there is nothing in this world I'd love more than to rip you to pieces."

The second I release her, she reels away, rubbing her bruised wrist. "Maniac."

I blow her a kiss and tear the envelope from her grasp. I begin to read:

House of Glass, floating high.
Neptune, Saturn, Jupiter's eye.
The cosmos' secrets one by one
Orbiting a second sun.
Unravel these vast mysteries,
And there you'll find the first of keys.

Orbiting a second sun? My mind whirls. "The planetarium at the Museum of Natural History," I murmur. "They have relative-to-scale models of the planets hanging from the ceiling, revolving around the Omnisphere theater where the shows are played. The sun is represented by the planetarium itself."

"Wow," Noëlle says flatly. "How very clever. Whatever would I do without you?"

With that, she jogs off in the same direction she was heading in earlier—uptown, via Central Park West. The fastest route to the museum. A flush creeps up my neck, but any lingering embarrassment evaporates when my first running stride launches me five feet into the air.

I flail through the air as my boots propel me up and down like pogo sticks. I struggle to adjust my gait. Less height, more distance. The exosuit stores the kinetic energy created by my every movement and converts it into power, but it's up to me to learn how to harness it.

Somehow, Noëlle already has the hang of it. I copy her until I catch up. We bound across the intersection, tailed by drones. Onlookers cheer from the sidewalk. Soon, I settle into my stride. I am the picture of elegance, smiling for the cameras, my every leap as graceful and nimble as a gazelle's, until I miscalculate the angle of a left turn and nearly crash headfirst into a hot dog cart. After that, I keep my ego in check and focus on the task.

We leave Columbus Circle behind, the wind dancing along the streamlined curves of our exosuits and carrying away the faint odor of horse manure. We race taxis up the avenue, never needing to stop for the lights at the crosswalks. When the sidewalk grows too crowded, we veer into the bike lane, the clamorous honks and whooshes of cars passing a little too close for comfort.

We hit the bustling intersection where the museum, all rustic, reddish stone in the sunlight, sprawls out before us like a fairy-tale castle, until it transitions into an imposing white marble fortress. A stretch of grass separates the entrance from the street. We catch our first glimpse of the glass cube known as the Center for Earth and Space. It gleams in the sunlight, the neat rectangular panes reflecting whimsical swirls of drifting clouds. A huge white sphere lies within—the planetarium.

Bang!

In the distance, a plume of bright yellow smoke shoots into the sky. Could one of the teams have already found their next riddle?

Beyond the revolving glass doors, the atrium stands eerily empty. I approach first. Noëlle trails a few steps behind me, her gaze flitting uneasily around the area.

"Where is everybody?" she asks.

I push the revolving door, but it doesn't budge. I frown. We try all three sets of revolving doors and the two double doors on either end. All of them locked.

"They must have locked them on purpose," I say. "Either that, or we misinterpreted the riddle entirely."

"Unlikely. *Neptune, Saturn, Jupiter's eye.*" She points at the models of Jupiter and Saturn with its rings, and the rest of the planets suspended from the ceiling. "I can't see anyone inside this section of the building. It's probably been blocked off."

"*Unravel these vast mysteries,*" I recite, starting to pace in front of the doors. "What mysteries, exactly? We're trying to become mavericks, not astrophysicists."

Noëlle rolls her eyes. "I'm going to try a different entrance."

A familiar hum reaches my ears. For the most part, the drones seem to be trying to stay out of sight, pursuing us clandestinely, but I glance up now to find several flying over us. One in particular hovers much higher than the rest, higher than even the tallest of tree branches.

"What was it that Valentine told us last night?" I ask suddenly.

"Think like mavericks?"

"Not that. 'We must travel by foot. But that doesn't mean we can't take to the skies.' We must have spent two hours studying Manhattan from above for a reason."

Noëlle drags her eyes up the smooth surface of the glass structure and pales slightly. "You think there's an entrance up there? That's easily a hundred feet high, without footholds or a harness."

"But we won't have to climb at all if we jump. You've seen that unreal compilation video of Master Hassan launching himself onto a building—"

"Over two hundred times his own height? Don't be patronizing, of course I have."

"So this should be easy."

"What?"

I crack my knuckles and get into position, knees bent, one foot behind the other—

"Wait!" Noëlle cries out in a strangled voice. "I don't . . . I can't do it."

I stare at her in utter disbelief. "Come again?"

She raises her hands and brings her thumbs toward her middle fingers without quite touching. Her expression is carefully smooth, cold with indifference, but the tremor in her voice gives her away. "It's one thing to watch a video of it, and another thing entirely to—"

"Actually execute it?" I finish. She nods. "For once, I agree with you. But for better or for worse, this is the kind of challenge you signed up for."

"I didn't sign up for anything. I just aced the final exam."

"Good for you! Do you want to wipe your tears on your perfect transcript while someone who might've gotten straight Cs snatches away the greatest opportunity of your life just because you weren't willing to make this jump?"

"You got *Cs*?"

"No! And why does it matter anyway? Look, we're a team. I couldn't leave you behind even if I wanted to, which, trust me, I do. But I won't, because that's not what a mav would do, and that's what matters to *me*."

"Fine!" she exclaims. She takes a deep breath, widens her stance, and bends her knees. "*Fine*. But I'm warning you. If this doesn't work and I break my neck, my uncle will make you pay."

The corner of my mouth twitches upward as I mirror her position. "Tell him he can take it up with my aunt." I press the pads of my middle fingers and my thumbs together, forming the shape of a teardrop. My breath hitches as my suit whirrs and compresses downward like a spring coiled tight. I raise my eyes to my target—a stone balcony running along the perimeter of the glass cube. It's an easier target, only about thirty feet off the ground. When the pressure threatens to buckle my legs, I nod at Noëlle. "On go?"

She nods back.

"Okay. Three. Two. One. *Go!*"

My teeth snap down hard on my tongue as I'm fired into the air like a human rocket. The ground below rushes away, too fast, too far. I overshoot *way* past the balcony, so high that I might actually make it to the top of the glass cube.

Almost there—

I strain my arms, reaching for the edge. But I'm still a foot short when my trajectory reaches its peak . . .

And I fall.

Panic seizes my chest. My stomach plummets to my toes. I'm six years old again, on my first roller coaster as it tips over the summit and crashes down, wind roaring, steel shrieking. Except now there is nothing but the free fall— no seat belt, no safety, too paralyzed with fear to even think of screaming.

It is only the sight of Noëlle staring up at me from the ground, open-mouthed, that brings me to my senses. Because she's staring up at me. From. The. *Ground*.

This ho didn't jump, I realize.

The rage is enough to unfreeze me. With a snarl, I smash my ring finger to my thumb and feel my suit whirr again, deploying shield mode. I've never fallen from nearly a hundred feet, but I've also never been wearing a state-of-the-art, multimillion-dollar piece of tech while doing so, either.

The balcony rushes up to meet me, and Noëlle is screaming, and gravity is laughing at me, nudging me even faster.

My feet strike the balcony. I try to roll, but my suit locks around me, controlling every movement. The shock of the impact shudders up my ankles, my legs, my torso. It skitters along my arms to the very tips of my fingers, the nape of my neck, my body vibrating like a metal gong pummeled by a dozen different hammers. I wobble as it fades, my knees reduced to jelly, and collapse onto my back.

A buzz fills the air above me. Three drones glide out of the sky, broadcasting my brush with death to millions of screens across the city. One of them lets out a little whine, like it's disappointed I didn't splatter into the human equivalent of a Jackson Pollock painting.

Noëlle sails over the railing and hits the balcony in a crouch. "Are you all right?"

I stagger to my feet. "No thanks to you."

"I know," she says. I detect what might possibly be an undercurrent of apology in her voice. "There were a few variables I wasn't sure of. Watching you jump first helped me figure them out."

A dozen searing replies scorch my tongue, but before I can fire any of them off, another bang echoes through the city. A red flare rockets above the buildings a few miles uptown, marking both the location and progress of another team. We're falling behind.

My mistake during the first attempt was to interfere with my exosuit's computations by forcing it to my will. This time, I let my suit do the work for me, just like how it took control when I crashed onto the balcony, calculating the best method for my survival.

I keep my eyes perfectly level as I press my fingers together. Slowly, I raise my gaze until it hits the top of the glass cube. My suit whirrs into action, calibrating my target based on the angle at which I crane my neck, the hardness of the ground beneath my feet, the weight of my body. My knees bend of their own accord, and I feel that compression again as energy courses along my skin like a live wire.

Without a word to my so-called teammate, I release my fingers and shoot into the sky. No longer am I a loose cannonball careening through the air, but a bird of prey, arms tucked close to my body, then extending above my head, stretching—

My fingers latch on to the edge of the cube, solid as steel. I hoist myself up onto the roof. In its center rests a silver briefcase. *Bingo.* I jog over to it and grab the handle just as Noëlle swings up onto the roof. I don't spare her so much as a glance as I flip the clasps open and swipe the envelope waiting within.

"Reynolds," she says.

"Save it." I rip the envelope open. "The sooner we cross the finish line, the sooner we can be rid of each other." Before she can protest, I read the riddle aloud.

Among red velvet, in dazzling light,
Stars are born and soon take flight.
A triumph of Black art and expression
Rise, despite decades' oppression.
The Duke, the Queen, countless greats,
All blessed by the god where your next key awaits.

"*A triumph of Black art and expression*," Noëlle murmurs. "Another museum, maybe? But what god? Where stars are born . . . red velvet, dazzling light . . ."

"Not a museum. A concert hall or theater. The Duke . . . they're nicknames." I close my eyes and imagine myself back in my dorm room with Zaza, the bright notes of a trumpet and the warm, soulful croon of a woman drifting from her record player. "The Duke has to be Duke Ellington. And the Queen—Ella Fitzgerald. The Queen of Jazz."

"Wouldn't she have performed at dozens of places in the city?"

"Yeah, but there's one that's famous for kickstarting her career. The Apollo Theater."

Her eyes gleam. "The Greek god of music and poetry."

Bang!

We both jump as a plume of orange smoke surges over our heads, marking our progress. But before we can rejoice, a blue flare erupts several blocks east.

I flip the riddle over. Three letters are printed in bold on the back. "A, R, M. What's that supposed to mean?"

"Valentine called it an answer key. Maybe we can't solve it until we retrieve the other keys."

As we get ready to make the jump back to the ground, I decide to speak up. "Cartier, you know competitors have died in past Tournaments, right?"

She takes a subtle step away from me. "And you're mentioning that right now because . . . ?"

"I need to know whether I can trust you when you give me your word about something. Forget about winning—if either of us breaks that trust, we could both end up dead."

By the disturbed look on her face, I'm certain I've gotten through to her until the only thing she replies with is, "I'll take that into consideration."

Then she immediately leaps off the side of the building.

I suppose it's the best I can ask for.

CHAPTER TWENTY-EIGHT

Every few months, there comes a storm where you hear the thunder roll into the city before the rain falls. The New Yorkers hurrying to and fro will look up and frown, the wind whipping at their skirts and ties. Empty plastic bottles will rattle among stray newspapers whirling across the emptying street like tumbleweeds. The tension crackles through the air, as tangible as lightning, as everyone silently waits for all hell to break loose.

It's exactly how I feel as we cross into Harlem. Noëlle was never talkative, but the silence separating us now tastes like the expectation of violence.

We sprint past vibrant street art flourishing from brick and concrete like a secret message and a declaration all at once. We pass a crowded sports bar playing the live coverage of the Tournament, catching Langston's triumphant grin flashing across the screen as he and Mia locate their third and final riddle.

I swear under my breath with a mixture of dismay and amazement. They've got two answer keys with one to go. We haven't even *arrived* at our second location, much less begun searching for the next key.

Noëlle surges forward in a burst of speed. Not one to be outshone, I push myself faster, too. Seconds later, I hear a warning beep from my suit. I'm depleting the suit's energy resources faster than I can regenerate them.

"Cartier! Slow down!" I shout after my teammate as she bolts through a gap between moving cars at the intersection.

"Slow down?" she shouts back. "And lose? Be my guest."

"If your suit burns out and I have to carry you to the finish line, you can bet your ass we'll lose! Cartier! Are you even listening to me, dammit?"

The beeping turns into a shrill wail, intensifying until my eardrums can't take it anymore. I slow my pace by a tiny fraction—but even then, the distance between us grows stride by stride.

By the time she turns right on 125th, I'm an entire street behind her.

HONK! Screeeeeech!

I round the corner, my heart in my throat. There, lit by the marquee and vertical letters spelling APOLLO in red neon lights, I find my teammate sprawled facedown on the pavement.

I vault over the hood of a car and dash over to her. I skid across the asphalt and crouch by her side, preparing for the worst. Before I can so much as lay a finger on her, however, she lets out a loud groan and rolls over on her own.

"Son of a biscuit," I gasp. "Your *face*."

Haltingly, she raises a hand toward the blood dripping down her cheek, then thinks better of it. "Don't say it," she croaks.

"Say what? 'Your face'? Which, by the way, looks gruesome as fu—"

"No," she moans. "Don't tell me *I told you so*. Only I get to say that to other people."

I have to deliberately keep my eyeballs from rolling out of my skull. "Well, you'd better get your ass off that high horse, Your

Royal Majesty, because *I emphatically told you so.*"

"Hey!" someone calls, standing halfway out the open door of their car. "Does she need an ambulance or something?"

I glance over my shoulder to discover the crowd of concerned onlookers gathered around us, then back down at Noëlle, who shakes her head. It seems that her suit absorbed most of the damage. "No thanks, we'll be all right."

"I have some Band-Aids and hand sanitizer in my purse," says another person, while someone else offers me an unopened bottle of water out of their backpack to give to my teammate.

"Thanks," Noëlle mutters in a tight voice, one hand held over her face. At first, I think she's trying to conceal the wreckage, but I realize a second later that she's hiding the steady stream of tears leaking down her cheeks.

"Okay, okay," I say, waving my arms and stepping in front of her to block as many of the oglers as possible. "Thanks for your help, everyone. She's going to be fine."

As the crowd disperses, I put my arm around Noëlle's waist and help her onto her feet. She smells sweet, like magnolia blossoms and honey. "You need to get your suit charged back up. Jog around, do jumping jacks, whatever." I eye the roof of the theater—thankfully, it's much lower than the planetarium's. "I'll check the roof for the second key."

She brushes me off. "You do that. I'll try the front door."

Amidst the chaos, I hadn't even noticed the glamorous chandeliers lighting the lobby from inside, nor interpreted them as an invitation—especially after the locked doors at the museum. But when she grabs one of the long metal handles and pulls, the door swings wide open. Without looking back, she treks down the faded red carpeting, the suit's dead weight visibly dragging down on her every step.

I shake off a faint sense of unease and chart my course for the roof, leaping onto the edge of the marquee. I wince as it creaks in protest beneath my feet. Might be best if I avoid testing the structural integrity of a century-old roof lest I accidentally endow the theater with a brand-new skylight.

Instead, I lock my fingers onto the narrow window rail of what appears to be an office above the entrance. Dust and old paint flake off at my touch, drifting to the street in swirls of ashen white. I boost myself onto a window ledge, then swing onto the rickety metal bar jutting out horizontally from the stonework that holds up the giant APOLLO sign and haul myself up. It groans beneath me. Muttering an unending stream of apologies under my breath, I shinny up the sign as quickly as I can, reaching over my head for the last stone ledge. From there, I dangle precariously above the street before finally hoisting myself onto the roof.

My gaze sweeps across the maze of vents and ducts, searching for a briefcase. I almost think Noëlle might have been right when I spot a glint of silver to the left. Bingo.

But before I can bask in the afterglow of my own self-satisfaction, a bloodcurdling scream pierces the air from inside the theater.

Noëlle.

By the time I burst inside the old theater, Noëlle's screams have gone quiet. The silence prickles at the nape of my neck, like the silence of a dark basement that's supposed to be empty.

I know I'm not alone.

The door to the lobby slams shut behind me. Gripping the heavy metal briefcase in front of me—half shield, half weapon—I squint into the pitch-black darkness.

"Noëlle?" I hiss.

A sob. "Rei? Is that you?"

Is she hurt? Or is this just part of the game? Do I charge into the dark to save my teammate or retreat and wait for backup? I chew my lip, know-ing the cost of each second of indecision. "Where are you?"

"Over here, on the stage." The acoustics only amplify the pain in her voice. "Help me, please—"

"How badly are you hurt?"

"My leg," she cries. "I can't—I can't move it."

I curse under my breath. "Just stay calm, keep talking to me. What happened?" With one hand, I feel along the ridges of the velvet seats and use them as a guide as I begin creeping toward the stage. The aisle slopes downward, like a ramp, covered in carpet that silences my steps—as well as the steps of anyone or anything else that might be lurking nearby.

"I don't know," she moans.

"The hell do you mean, you don't know?"

"I—I just came in here to look for the briefcase, and then the lights went out."

My toe bumps into something solid with a hollow *thud*. I bend down, my fingers skimming a set of steps that must lead to the stage. I ascend them one at a time until I reach level ground. I clutch the briefcase tighter, trying to steady the wild stampede of my heart. "And then?"

"*And then,*" her voice says directly into my ear, "*it was too late.*"

Multiple hands grab me from every direction. A single shout escapes me before a meaty palm clamps over my mouth. I bite down on the hand and ram the briefcase behind me as hard as I can. A man grunts. There's a bodily thump as he stumbles back and trips off the edge of the stage. Someone grabs my elbow. I swing the briefcase up and hear the satisfying *thwack* of metal hitting bone.

But the assailants don't stop coming. Noëlle set me up, and now I'm sightless and obviously outnumbered. I lose track of the flurry of hands as I get tackled and pinned to the ground. The briefcase gets ripped out of my grasp. A gag is stuffed roughly into my mouth as I'm dragged offstage.

I'm trying to piece together why she betrayed me when a blood-curdling scream pierces the air, and it all makes sense.

Because the scream doesn't belong to Noëlle.

It belongs to *me*.

But *I'm* not actually screaming. I'm just hearing a simulation of my voice played on a speaker that must have been placed somewhere on the stage in order to trick my teammate. Just like I was tricked by the simulation of her voice. It's exactly what a Deathling could do in real life—steal someone's voice and use it to kill you.

It was a test all along, and I just failed it.

The theater blazes alight. I wince and blink up at my startled attackers—six of them, wearing infrared goggles and Syndicate-branded uniforms. Caught by surprise, they make the mistake of loosening their grip on me. Now that I can see exactly what I'm up against, and exactly where I need to hit to make it hurt most, I don't hesitate.

Only, before I can throw the first punch, they all put their hands behind their heads and file into the wings as if following a scene direction in a script. The only thing they leave behind is the briefcase.

"Reynolds! Over here!" a voice calls. I squint past the dazzling spotlights to the back of the theater, where Noëlle stands before a large, complicated-looking control console. She messes with some buttons until she figures out how to turn on the house lights, then jogs over to me. "Well, that happened. Good job, I guess."

I groan. "Falling for the trap and getting myself captured, you mean?"

She shrugs. "I ended up going backstage first, where I found cameras showing two guards surveilling the controls, but they were forced to abandon their posts when you started taking down the others like an angry badger on steroids."

I don't know what to say to that.

"Did you find the next riddle?" she asks.

"In here," I say, turning the briefcase toward her. She opens it and removes the envelope. As she breaks the seal, I expect her to read it herself first, but instead she holds it out for both of us to see. I'm oddly moved.

> *Bridging worlds, where land meets sea,*
> *Earthen souls stand in soliloquy.*
> *Silent sentries lost in mist—*
> *Granite, quartz, Manhattan schist.*
> *An act of balance, strength, and skill,*
> *To win this challenge, you must fulfill.*

Before I've even finished reading the riddle, Noëlle says, "I know where we need to go."

I glance up. "Where?"

"There's a little spot on the banks of the Hudson River, right by the George Washington Bridge." It fits the clue—the bridge that once connected Manhattan with New Jersey, a world separate from ours. "It's about three miles uptown."

"Then we'd better get going."

"Wait, don't forget about the second key."

I flip the riddle over and read, "O, R, Y. Plus the first key, it spells . . ."

"*Armory*," Noëlle murmurs.

I wrack my brain. "There's an old armory on the Upper East Side that the National Guard occupied until the government abdicated all local jurisdiction to the Syndicate. That must be where the finish line is."

Noëlle shakes her head. "We can't know for sure until we get the third key."

"But the Armory is in the opposite direction of where the third riddle is telling us to go. If we went straight there, we could save valuable time. We could beat the other teams."

"Only if you're right."

"What else could *Armory* mean?"

"Depends on what the third key tells us."

"But—"

"What would your aunt do, Reynolds?" she questions. "Would she take the shortcut? If you truly believe that she would, then . . . I'll trust your judgment."

I stop short. She's trusting me with the choice. The choice that could lead to both of us winning this task. Or being eliminated entirely.

"Master Minyi is efficient," I begin slowly. "But she's also meticulous. She's never cut a corner in her life."

"So . . . ?"

My chest fills with newfound resolve. I nod at my teammate. "You're right. She wouldn't take the shortcut. She would find the final key."

Noëlle smiles the tiniest of smiles—but a smile nonetheless. "Then follow me."

CHAPTER TWENTY-NINE

The waves of the Hudson River dance with sunlight. It's almost enough to distract from its polluted, brown tint. Noëlle leads me north along the bike path next to the Hudson, a belt of asphalt and trees sandwiched between the river and the roar of cars on the parkway. The George Washington Bridge rises over the treetops, spanning across the width of the river, transformed into a delivery port to process goods entering the city.

Noëlle catches me staring at the bridge. "Do you ever wish you could leave?"

Have you ever thought about leaving this place? Roland asked me, too. "No," I tell her honestly. "I've never even thought about it."

"Really?"

"My family—what's left of it—are all here. And my friends." I frown. "Do you?"

Her eyes settle on the horizon. "Always." She lowers her head and quickens her pace, forcing me to hurry after her.

The path opens up to a peculiar sight at the water's edge. From afar, it looks like a crowd of slender figures have gathered by the shore, curving along the length of the river like spectators at a concert.

Except every single one of them stands completely, utterly still.

At first, I wonder what they're waiting for. And then I realize what they actually are: stones. Stones of all sizes—small, fat, smooth, and jagged. Stacked one on top of the other, in threes or fours and sometimes fives, perfectly poised, perfectly balanced.

"Here we are," Noëlle murmurs. "The Sisyphus Stones."

For years I've heard the name spoken—always in hushed, reverent tones. In fact, the Stones existed decades before the Vanishing, risen by the hand of an artist called Ulysses. Every time the sculptures toppled, by wind or sea or the hands of assailants, through his persistence and hard work, they would rise anew.

Ever since the Vanishing, they've taken on a new kind of magic. No one tends to the sculptures anymore, but through high tides and hurricanes and vandals, they stand eternal.

"*Silent sentries lost in mist*," I recite from the riddle, gazing at the rocks. "My aunt thinks the sculptures have minds of their own, like Artifacts. Choosing who to appear before and when."

"That's just part of the myth. They're always here when I come."

Gooseflesh prickles across my skin. Of all the times I've walked this path, I've never seen them once.

Noëlle reaches forward to touch the nearest sculpture.

A deep boom resounds across the waterfront. We reel back in alarm as the river begins to churn and the earth rumbles beneath our feet. The sculptures sway but don't fall.

My eyes widen as a flashing object cleaves through the roiling waves and ascends past the surface. A submarine? The mast of a boat? No—a street sign, attached to a mangled steel pole and glistening with river water. ONE WAY, it reads.

The sign is soon joined by a lamppost, a chain of Chinese red lanterns, the railing of what looks like a fire escape torn off the side of an apartment building. The bizarre amalgamation of objects continues rising higher and higher out of the Hudson. At the bottom of the structure, closest to the shore, seven rows of narrow brass columns emerge from the water at increasing heights and intervals. The eighth row supports a platform, upon which a huge, rusted metal wall scattered with holes is mounted.

"Good god," Noëlle whispers with a mixture of horror and awe. "What *is* that?"

When the rumbling finally stops, the ONE WAY sign dangles seventy feet in the sky. The whole thing just looks like a mess of rust and scraps, like some trash leviathan salvaged from the depths of metropolitan misery. I'm debating between calling it a shipwreck or an art installation when the realization hits me.

"*An act of balance, strength, and skill.* It's an obstacle course. We probably have to get to the top to retrieve the final key."

Noëlle can't tear her eyes away from the top of the course, her complexion sheet white. "Sounds simple enough."

"Maybe a little too simple." I study the obstacles carefully. The first part should be fairly straightforward—leaping from column to column. But I have no idea how to get up that rusty metal wall. The holes are too small to fit my hands and feet into. I glance around us, searching for some tool or object to help, but there's nothing except rocks.

I approach the shore, where the first column awaits like a stepping-stone. Gingerly, I place one foot atop it to test its strength. The waves around it recede, exposing the riverbed in a semicircle as they lap the bases of the next two columns, which stand equally distant from the first column, like the other two points of a triangle. I choose the column on the right and jump.

It crumples beneath my weight. My heart plummets to my toes as I fall and splash into the frigid water with a gasp.

"Reynolds!" Noëlle shouts.

"I'm fine," I splutter. Thankfully, the column was only a few feet off the ground, but the remaining columns only extend to greater, more lethal heights. I heave my dripping self back onto the first column. The river sloshes again, receding toward the next two columns. "I don't understand. They look identical. How do I choose?"

"Wait." Noëlle points. "Look, down here. At the bottom of the column you're standing on."

As soon as I step off to check it out, whatever force holding the river back releases, and the base gets submerged before I can catch so much as a glimpse. "Switch with me."

Noëlle steps onto the column. The river sloshes. I bend down to find something inscribed at the base—a big, bold arrow, pointing to the left. To the column I didn't choose.

She leaps onto the left column. The waters recede a little farther, revealing another arrow pointing at the next correct column.

"One of us will have to stay on the ground to give the other instructions on how to complete the course," I realize.

She avoids looking at the rest of the obstacles, her jaw clenched.

If I perform the course, I'll have no choice but to give her the full extent of my trust. One mistake in directing me, and I could end up at the bottom of the Hudson. But if she takes on the course and freezes halfway . . . we're equally screwed.

Which leaves me with only one option.

"Noëlle." I wait until she turns to me to extend my hand. "I'm counting on you this time, so don't let me down. Got it?"

For the briefest second, I swear she's not going to take it. But then she grabs it, jumps down, and says, "Don't fall. I won't catch you."

I huff and set my attention on the course. *Just get to the top.* How hard can it be?

I give myself a running start and bound across the first three rows of columns. The water parts to expose the next arrow.

"Second from the left," Noëlle hollers from the shore. "Far right!"

I leap from column to column, trying not to glance at the swirling waters down below. Instead, I focus on the sound of my teammate's voice and the path ahead. But soon the columns grow out of my reach, too tall for me to jump onto. The wind buffets me from every which way, trying to tear me down. I shiver and wrap my arms around my dripping self. The column quivers from the impact of the waves assaulting it from below. There's barely enough room for my feet, let alone any errors.

"Stop overthinking!"

I whip my head around to look down at Noëlle. "What?"

"Use your body, not your brain. I'll do the thinking for the both of us. Just concentrate on your target and hit it."

Easy for her to say. I press my middle fingers to my thumbs to engage my exosuit. What little surface area I had to land on suddenly seems all the more minuscule. But I listen to her. Bend my knees. Take a deep breath—

And *jump.*

The wind lashes at my face as I hurtle toward the final column. I land off-center, half of one foot slipping off the edge. My heart shoots straight from of my chest. I wobble, my arms flung out for balance. The river froths hungrily below.

Somehow, I manage to hold steady. I've arrived at the final row of columns—seven, straight across. Beyond, the platform leading to the next obstacle, the metal wall. "What's next?"

"Dead center!" Noëlle hollers back.

I launch myself toward it. But as soon as my feet leave the ground, I know I've overshot. I fly well past the column, my legs floundering through empty air. The toe of my left boot clips the edge of the column. I muster every ounce of strength and kick out as hard as I can to propel myself up the last ten feet.

With one hand, I latch on to the edge of the platform. Teeth gritted, I reach with my other hand and hoist myself up. Panting, I look down to discover the river has receded enough to expose the metal briefcase anchored into the riverbed. Noëlle scurries across the rocks covered in slimy lichen and muck to grab it. When she touches the handle, the wall behind me flares. I turn to discover the holes carved into its surface glowing with light. No, not glowing—pulsing, flickering on and off at random.

"*It's stuck!*" Noëlle yells from below, yanking at the briefcase. It doesn't budge.

My thoughts race. "What's inside? Maybe you're not supposed to move it."

She casts an uneasy glance at the murky brown wall of waves suspended inches away from her face. At any second, whatever force is holding it back could give way and drown her. Eventually she gets the case open. Instead of another riddle, she withdraws two long, narrow cylinders . . . like climbing pegs. I look at the rickety, corrosion-ravaged holes in the wall with sudden dread.

A yellow flare rockets past the buildings in the distance. My stomach tightens. Could another team have found the final key?

"Throw the pegs to me!" I order Noëlle.

Hastily, she hurls them into the sky. A gust of wind sends them astray. I lurch forward to catch them, teetering dangerously over the edge of the platform. Below, the river swells forward like a balloon about to burst.

Noëlle scrambles away. The glowing holes in the wall behind me go dark. I recover my footing, and the water stills. Only when she steps toward the briefcase does the wall flicker back on again.

It's all connected, I realize. She can't move from that spot or else I'll fail the obstacle. And if I fail, she'll get swallowed up by the Hudson. *An act of balance, strength, and skill, to win this challenge you must fulfill.* So the true challenge isn't about the obstacle course at all—it's about trust. I'm counting on her, but she's counting on me, too. Neither of us will pass the task without the other.

I grip the pegs like daggers and stab them into the first pair of glowing holes. I have to be swift—the light jumps from one hole to another by the second, constantly changing, like a game of Whac-A-Mole.

A blast of wind knocks me sideways as I'm straining for the next peg hole. I slam against the wall, dangling by a single precarious peg. It scrapes against the metal, slowly slipping out of the hole. With a groan, I twist my body around and manage to thrust the other peg into the wall just before I lose my grip.

At last, I drag myself over the top of the wall.

A loud rumbling rises from below. The invisible dam breaks free. Noëlle flees for the shore as the water crashes down upon the riverbed, surging after her heels.

She scrambles safely onto the bank. I let out a whoop. Even she can't help the begrudging grin on her face. We've reached the final obstacle.

From here, the end of the course is close enough to see, lying across the other side of the wild jungle of metal scraps and abandoned relics. I grab the first, a lamppost hanging horizontally, and swing myself in a graceful arc onto the handlebars of a bicycle frame missing both wheels. Arms out, I skirt across the wire cable hung with red lanterns onto the hood of an ancient taxi, the bold letters and checker print emblazoned across the faded yellow paint warped from time. The metal caves beneath my feet as I launch myself toward the fire escape, but I manage to seize the bottom of the railing and clamber over the bars onto the landing.

The ONE WAY sign glints at me, pointing eastward. The only thing that stands between me and it is fifty feet of absolutely *nothing*. An emptiness wide enough to stretch across four lanes of traffic, promising a very, very long fall.

I make the mistake of looking down. My head spins with vertigo. My breath comes too fast, too hard. I don't even have the space to take a running start—I have to rely fully on the abilities of my exosuit.

From afar, I pick up the sound of my name. *Reynolds. Reynolds.* Everything is muted, as if my ears are clogged with water. Then—

"—on your feet, you useless nominee!"

My fingers curl into fists around the iron railing. I haul myself upright to find Noëlle screaming insults at me from the edge of the water. "Useless? How can you call *me* useless when you're just standing there doing *nothing*?"

"It's not like I have a choice! The final obstacle is right in front of your face, you coward!"

"Me? *I'm* the coward?"

"You're worse than a coward! You're a gutless, pants-wetting, pigeon-hearted weakling!"

"Just wait till I get my hands on you, you little—"

"And do what? You can't do *anything* until you finish the stupid course!"

"Fine then, I'll finish the stupid course!"

"Fine!"

"*Fine*," I hiss, smashing my middle fingers to my thumbs. My exosuit powers up. Only when the usual whirr turns into a high-pitched whine do I let myself fly like a bullet into the air. The wind shrieks past as I shoot toward the final obstacle and collide into it with a *clang*. My foot gets lodged in the gnarled metal pole holding it up, but it doesn't matter. I made it to the end. I beat the challenge.

A flare hidden on the shore blasts into the sky, announcing our victory to the entire city. I turn triumphantly to Noëlle—but instead of annoyance, her face bears a matching grin even more smug than my own.

Creeeeeeak.

The smile vanishes from my face. I freeze. The pole I'm clutching on to begins to tip forward. "No," I whisper to it pleadingly. "No, no, no—"

With an earsplitting *crack*, the pole rips in half, and I plummet straight into the Hudson.

CHAPTER THIRTY

The cold stabs into me like a thousand needles. A cold so cold I forget how to breathe, so cold that it *burns*.

I choke on the water's foul taste. Like sewage. Like Deathlings.

It's a losing battle from the start. My foot is still shackled to the sinking pole. I struggle to free myself as it drags my head beneath the frigid waves.

The letters on the ONE WAY sign blur in my peripheral vision. For a second, I could swear that they spell out a different word entirely.

TRACK.

Track what? I wonder to myself dully. I look up, my lungs throbbing, hoping to glimpse the light of the surface one last time, but the water is too dirty.

As my consciousness fades, I hear a splash. Something latches on to my foot. Wrenches it. *Hard.* The pain is sharp enough for my eyes to fly open. I see a halo of gold hair floating below me. The weight around my ankle jerks free. Arms slide around my chest from behind. I feel the movement of water against my skin, the powerful kicks propelling us upward.

The next thing I know, I'm on my back, staring up at the eye-wateringly blue sky as rocks dig into my spine. I turn my head to the side and vomit out several lungfuls of filthy brownish-green water.

"Damn you," a voice spits beside me. "Damn you all the way to hell and back." Noëlle wrings out her soaking-wet hair. She retches at the stink and shudders violently.

I cough. "You dove into the Hudson for me?"

"Didn't I tell you I wouldn't let you down? I was trying to piss you off enough to compel you to make the last jump, but you just had to go overboard as usual, didn't you?" When I fail to respond, she glances at me and recoils. "Are you crying? Stop. Stop that immediately. We still have to find the key. Unless you happened upon it while drowning in the Hudson?"

"The one-way sign," I mumble, wiping my eyes. "There was something on the back of it, something about searching . . . *track?* The word was track."

Noëlle frowns. "Track what?" Then her eyes widen. "*Armory.* Armory Track, the track-and-field stadium on Fort Washington Ave. It's right there, on the other side of that parkway," she exclaims, pointing behind us.

The scent of burnt rubber and sweat fills my memories. "My sister used to run track-and-field competitions there. I used to go to her meets to cheer her on."

"But how are we going to get there? There aren't any pedestrian pathways we can use, and it'll take us ages to go all the way around the traffic."

"So we don't go around it," I say, recalling the map we studied yesterday. I push myself onto my feet. "We cut straight across."

Noëlle stares, first at me, then the cars on the road screaming past us at fifty miles an hour. "No, thank you."

"Come on, just *follow my lead.*" I grin at her glare. "Last one to the finish line is a useless nominee."

I take off toward the parkway, her footsteps thundering after me. We race each other to the traffic barricade and launch into the air at the same time, soaring across as one.

Less than three blocks separate us from our final destination. This time, I don't even have to stop and think as I propel myself into the sky. I hit the first roof running. When I reach the second roof, neck and neck with my teammate, I spot the triangular-shaped roof of the Armory. At one end, a giant checkered banner ripples in the breeze, with a gleaming ribbon stretching from one side of the roof to the other to mark the finish line.

My jaw goes slack. "The ribbon. No one's crossed it yet."

Against all odds, we're the first team here. The realization fuels us with a fresh burst of speed. We slip and slide our way up the Armory's roof tiles, trying to adjust to running across the sloped surface.

Less than a hundred feet away from the finish line, two figures leap onto the north side of the roof. It quakes as Tim the Brute crashes down and staggers up the slope, followed by Kieran. Tim's bulk doesn't do him any favors as he's forced to scrabble up the tiles on all fours. Kieran skirts around him easily, his light steps pattering behind us like rain.

But we're ahead of them, and they know it. Tim swears loudly. As soon as he finds his footing, he barrels after us like a runaway steamroller, the sheer length of his strides allowing him to gain on us in a heartbeat.

Twenty feet from the finish line, he calls out to Kieran. I glance over just in time to see him lunge forward. At first, I think he's going to make a dive for the finish line. *There's no way he'll make it*, I think. But it turns out that he's not aiming for the finish line at all.

Instead, he plows into Kieran. With a mighty shove, he sends his teammate flying straight into mine.

Kieran cries in warning, causing Noëlle to turn around. She veers out of his path at the last second. Unable to catch himself, Kieran comes down on one foot at a grisly angle. His knee twists out underneath him with a horrific *CRACK*. He hits the tiles and tumbles headfirst down the slope of the roof.

I forget about everything else—the task, winning the Tournament. All I can think is that he doesn't deserve to die—not here, not like this.

"Reynolds!" Noëlle shrieks as Tim flashes us a monstrous grin and barges past her, bursting across the finish line with a roar of triumph. "What the hell do you think you're doing?"

But I'm already sprinting down the roof after Kieran. I dive onto my stomach right as he topples over the edge. His fear-stricken eyes find mine. My hand locks around his elbow. My arm socket screams in protest as we jerk forward. I dig the toes of my boots into the roof ledge to anchor myself.

"Climb up," I snarl.

For a nauseating second, we simply dangle over the precipice, the sidewalk looming far below. The ledge begins to buckle beneath the strain of our collective weight. Kieran feels it.

"Rei," he gasps. "Let me go."

"Like hell."

He relents and grabs my forearm, using me as a ladder to climb his way back onto the ledge. But right before he makes it all the way up, the ledge lets out a horrible keening noise.

And then it snaps.

A sharp yank at my ankles cuts off my scream halfway. A brief scuffle ensues somewhere above before Kieran's weight vanishes off me. Hands drag me back up to safety. The grip on my ankles releases.

Noëlle dumps me on the roof and manhandles me back onto my feet. I've never seen her look so furious.

Yet she still jerks her chin at Kieran, whose face is contorted in agony as he tries to limp away from the edge of the roof. Without a word, she helps me prop him between us.

Together, we half carry, half drag him across the finish line.

＊

The paramedics transport Kieran down to the street and strap him into the ambulance. As the sirens fade around the corner, Mia and Langston burst onto the east side of the roof, only to witness Everly and Yuna cross the finish line just seconds ahead of them.

"We went to the East Side," Mia gasps, hands braced on her knees. "To the wrong Armory." They took the shortcut and missed the final key, costing them their place in the final round of the Tournament.

If Noëlle had listened to me, it would have been us.

We wait for Dawn and Taz to show up, but they never even make it. Of all the obstacles we faced in the second task, it seems that teamwork was the one they simply couldn't overcome.

Later that afternoon, Nick Valentine asks the finalists to return to the Sanctuary. We arrive to find it emptier than ever. As we gather in the cafeteria, Everly and Yuna are the only competitors who share a table. Kieran's undergoing surgery for a tear in his knee, not that he'd want to sit with Tim anyway, and Noëlle makes a deliberate effort to sit as far away as possible from me. She hasn't spoken a word since we crossed the finish line. I can't blame her. Thanks to me, we let Tim steal the victory that should have been ours.

The Phantom enters without any of his usual pizzazz.

In fact, he looks *pissed*.

"I'm sure all of you are exhausted," he begins, "and you deserve as much well-earned rest as you can get before the final round, so I'll keep this short." He nods at me and Noëlle. "First off, on behalf of the masters, I would like to commend Miss Reynolds and Miss Cartier for their act of heroism. You may very well have saved a life today."

Across the room, Noëlle folds her arms over her chest and glowers at the floor. Commendation or not, we still lost. To *Tim*.

The Phantom's voice turns frighteningly stern. "As you know, one of your fellow candidates is currently receiving treatment for a severe injury."

Tim has the audacity to snigger.

"Every striker prides themselves on upholding a strict code of honor," Valentine says, louder. "Those who break it *will* face the consequences." The Phantom strolls to Tim's table and slams his palms against it, his usual warmth and charm replaced by nothing but cold, hard contempt. He leans down over Tim, a wicked smile curling his lips. "As a result of the treacherous behavior displayed by a certain Mr. Beckett, the masters have voted unanimously that only five of the six remaining competitors will be moving on to the final round."

The cocky grin on Tim's face freezes.

And then, for what may be the first time ever, Noëlle begins to laugh.

CHAPTER THIRTY-ONE

That afternoon is the last we see of Tim. He has no choice but to leave, but he doesn't realize it until a squadron of eight enforcers show up to remove him from the premises. He's kind enough to leave us a parting gift: smashed plates and glasses in the cafeteria, broken furniture littering the hallway, and dented walls that by the next day still are in the process of being repaired. As I head back from the showers with my damp hair wrapped in a towel, I pass a crew refitting the door to Tim's room onto its hinges, and another scrubbing four rust-colored words written on the wall in what may actually have been his own blood.

YOUR END WILL COME

I head back to my own room with a shudder.

Preoccupied with thoughts of the fried chicken on tonight's dinner menu, I let myself in and nearly trip over the bloodstained corpse slumped against the foot of my bed.

I scream.

The corpse jolts up, eyes darting wildly and mouth spitting curses in a thick accent. It takes me a hot minute to recognize the rugged, bearded face, the slash of a crescent-shaped scar from cheek to chin.

"Master Sasha?" I splutter.

"Hello, little rat," he coughs out.

A thousand questions blitz through my head. Will I get eliminated for speaking to him? And how the hell did he get into my room? But then the Master of the Financial District staggers to his feet, and I get my first good look at the big man.

The sickening realization that the blood on his face doesn't belong to a Deathling comes first. His blond ponytail is disheveled, streaked with dirt and more blood from the gash at his temple. The outside of his exosuit is unmarred, but his heavy limp and the crooked, awkward way he holds his left arm tell a very different story. In the end, a single question rises to my lips—a question that no one would dream of asking a master.

"Who did this to you?" I whisper, my hand pressed to my mouth.

Master Sasha juts his jaw out. "*What*, Miss Reynolds. What did this to me. Go on, guess."

"Deathlings," I say, because that is the only possible answer.

"More."

"What do you mean, *more*?" Could it be the things that killed Roland and the other mavericks?

He shakes his head impatiently. "You won't understand, not yet. Tell me, have you heard of legend of missing Artifact?"

"I've heard rumors—"

"Imagine an Artifact so powerful it could level entire city to rubble like atomic bomb. If it came into your possession, what would you do?"

My brain stutters. I'm terrified of giving the wrong answer. "Return it to the Archives?"

"Where it would be available for anyone with access to exploit? What if it fell into wrong hands? Would you be so irresponsible as to let that happen?"

I bite my lip and reconsider. "Maybe I'd hide it."

He nods in satisfaction. "Now tell me, you have been to Master Minyi's office?"

"Yes, sir."

"Is there a box?"

"Pardon me?"

"*Box*," he thunders, slicing his hands in the air in the shape of a square. "For putting things. For locking and hiding things."

"Like . . . a safe?"

"Yes! Yes, a safe."

"I-I'm not sure. I don't think I've seen one." I pause. "Why do you want to know?"

Master Sasha suddenly advances on me, his hulking frame and bulging muscles blocking everything else from view. Terror shoots through me as he grabs me by the shoulders, his calloused hands strong enough to crush my bones in an instant. Something feral glows in his eyes.

"You must find it. And then you must steal whatever is inside."

I gape at him. "You want me to steal something from my aunt?"

"You have to."

A very compelling argument. I notice an empty plastic packet on the floor behind him—the toffees. If he's been carrying sweets around at nightfall, no wonder Deathlings have been targeting him like mad. It is an invitation for death. "How many of those have you eaten?"

"No more," he says softly. "Finished."

Part of me wonders if I'm hallucinating this entire encounter. "You want me to find you some more or something?"

"You cannot. They come from my home."

I pick up the packet and read the foreign text printed on the front. "Just give me your address, I can—"

He grabs the packet from me and crumples it in his fist. "Thousands of miles, just for little candy. The costs of transportation could feed families for weeks, do you understand? But it is my vice. A small piece of home, a small price to pay when cost of fighting for this city is so great. Yet now it is unjustified. I am unjustified."

"With all due respect, Master Sasha . . ." I look him up and down, realizing that he must be delirious from his injuries. There are still a few hours until nightfall, which means that he'll have to resort to mundane means of medical treatment. "I think we need to find you a doctor."

"No time," he grunts, even though the simple act of shifting his weight from one foot to the other makes him wince. "All my sources lead to her. I will take you to Upper West Side Manor, right now."

Conflict rages inside of me. Of course part of me wants to obey him. To show the master who chose me that I'll follow his word as faithfully as a sailor follows the stars. "C-could we discuss this again tomorrow, please?" I say. "After the final task. I need to focus—"

"Too late by then. They are coming."

My mouth dries. "Who's coming?"

"The Forsaken," he growls. "They are coming for us all."

But before I can demand any further explanation, I'm cut short by the ringing of a cell phone. Master Sasha pulls out his phone from the inner pocket of his leather trench coat and glances at the caller ID. He curses. "I must go."

Then he stuns me by getting down on one knee, groaning in pain all the while. He clasps both hands over his chest. It's utterly surreal, seeing someone I've held higher than the gods kneeling down to me— especially for all the wrong reasons.

"Miss Reynolds," he begins. "For the sake of the Syndicate, for every human being living in this accursed city . . . to save us, you must uncover truth. I beg of you. My driver waits outside, ready to take you to the Manor. You are only person I entrust with this secret."

It feels like the riddles from the second task all over again. "You believe that there is an Artifact out there capable of total annihilation. And you believe my aunt is hiding it in her office."

He nods once.

I exhale heavily. "Master Sasha, even if that were true, which I *highly* doubt, how am I supposed to find the safe and break into it without getting caught?"

"I have been searching for this Artifact for very, very long time, Miss Reynolds. With its power, we could eradicate Deathlings for good."

My heart quickens. *Eradicate Deathlings for good?* "What in the world could have that kind of power?"

"How am I supposed to know?"

That gives me a pause. "Er . . . well, you're . . . you."

He scoffs loudly. "I am no divine prophet, Miss Reynolds. I know I have not told you much, but it is all I know. I do not have the answers. It is why I come here to ask *you* to find them. You are clever, little rat," he adds, tapping my forehead lightly. "Very clever. I am certain you will find your way. I fear that fate of Manhattan may depend on it."

I waver. The fate of Manhattan?

He hauls himself to his feet and taps at his phone, finally cutting off its incessant ringing. Before he raises the phone to his ear, he bows his head to me. "Good luck tomorrow, Miss Reynolds. I do not know what for, but I think you will need it."

With that, he sweeps out of the room in a swirl of midnight blue.

✳

After I clean up the bloodstains on the floor, I lay sprawled on my bed, staring emptily at the ceiling. Outside, I can hear people heading to the dining hall for dinner, but I've lost my appetite.

With a great sigh, I grab my phone and check the time. I have less than an hour before nightfall. If I'm going to the Manor, I have to leave now. Unfortunately, I can't bring myself to get out of bed, much less breach a heavily guarded facility and commit a severe felony without getting arrested—or worse, caught by Aunt Minyi—by sundown.

So instead I open up my messages and tap out a quick text to the only person who knows more about my aunt than I do.

yo

I sigh again, wondering if I'll even get a response, when my phone buzzes one back at record speed.

jie jie
Sup sis

nothing much. just chilling after a surprise visit from
a master who looked like he died but ended up
getting rejected from the afterlife and then
resurrected himself straight out of a gutter

huh?!?

never mind . . . also totally unrelated but do you
know if auntie min keeps a secret box in her offi

My fingers hesitate over the keyboard. I chew the inside of my cheek, and then hold down the delete button to tweak the message.

never mind . . . also totally unrelated but the
holidays are coming up soon and i was thinking
about what to get for auntie min.

we could bake her some cookies

what about a lockbox? or a safe?
to put jewelry inside or whatever.
we could decorate it together.
but do you know if she already has one?
like in her office

I count every nail-biting second that ticks by before my phone finally buzzes. I scramble to check it.

zaza♡
hey idk if you'll see this but i took your hairbrush! don't ask why

why

need some of your dna. might try to clone you.

I stare at her bizarre response for a few moments, but when Maura's message comes in I decide to worry about it later and type back lol ok sounds cool as quickly as possible and switch chats.

jie jie
she does actually

My stomach drops. So Master Sasha was right?

really??? what does she keep inside of it?

Not totally sure but probably not jewelry lol

"No, Maura," I whisper to my phone screen. I'm definitely not *lol*-ing. After I gather my thoughts, I type out another message to her.

hey if someone super important asked you to
do something dangerous, would you do it?

Yeah probably why

what if it meant stabbing someone really close
to you in the back? figuratively, not literally

Depends. Are they family?

Yes.

Then no. Never. Our family always comes first, mei mei. Always.

Especially after everything we've been through together.

Guilt washes over me. Of course, my sister is right. What was I thinking—breaking into my aunt's office, stealing from her—just because Master Sasha asked me to? Despite how much time I've spent admiring him from afar, not to mention my gratitude for his nomination, he's still practically a stranger to me. Albeit a venerable, powerful stranger whom I've respected for years, but a stranger nonetheless. How could I ever have even let the notion of betraying my own family for him cross my mind?

After sending Maura a quick thank-you, I slip out of my room. The lights in the east wing of the Sanctuary flicker on, identical doors to sleeping quarters and communal bathrooms stretching all the way down the corridor. As the sounds of chatter and the delicious aroma of food waft through the air from the dining hall, I almost laugh at myself. Poor Master Sasha must be sleep-deprived. Or plain paranoid. But as I walk farther and farther away from the entrance to the Sanctuary where his car idles at the curb, waiting for a passenger that will never arrive, I can't help but remember his warning—

The Forsaken. They are coming for us all.

With a shiver, I banish the words from my mind and head off to find myself some dinner.

CHAPTER THIRTY-TWO

On the morning of the final task, five keys await us at the table at formal breakfast. Actual keys, forged from iron and inscribed with our names.

"Morning, Rei," Everly greets me, nursing a glass of water like it's hard liquor, the tight smile on their face not quite reaching their eyes. Our breakfast feast lies on the table completely untouched. While almost all the finalists have arrived, the chairs on the masters' half of the table still sit empty.

"Good morning," I reply, taking the middle seat. Now that twenty spots have been culled to five, we've each got plenty of personal space. "Morning, Yuna."

She nods curtly in response as she folds a napkin into a swan and places it onto Everly's empty plate. A congregation of them surround her—it seems she's building an army.

Noëlle, sitting on Yuna's other side, drops a sugar cube into a cup of coffee. I watch her drop a second into the dark liquid, then another. And another.

"Stop staring, Reynolds," she snaps without even looking up.

"Sorry, I've just never seen anyone take coffee with their cup of sugar."

To my surprise, she softly admits, "It's how my mother drank it. Not sure why I picked up the habit."

"That's sweet."

"Of course it's sweet, I've got four sugars in it."

"No, I meant about how you still take your coffee like your mom."

She stirs her coffee for a moment. The melodious tinkling of the spoon clinking against the inside of the mug fills the silence. "I don't have much else to remember her by. She fell victim to the Vanishing, as did my father." She pauses and frowns down at her cup. "I don't know why I'm telling you these things."

"It's probably the sugar." At her glower, I sigh. "My parents are dead, too. Killed off duty by Deathlings."

Her eyes narrow judgmentally. "Did they break curfew?"

Swirling fumes of gray. Unbearable heat. Waves of it, choking the air.

My chest tightens. "No. There was a fire." I glance at Everly and Yuna, who go back to pretending that they're not eavesdropping. "No one knows how it broke out in the middle of nightfall while everyone was asleep, but it did. We had to wait outside for help to arrive. But . . . the nightfangs came first. My mom and dad sacrificed their lives to save mine."

There's an immediate look of *oh shit* on Noëlle's face. "I'm sorry."

"You're sorry that they saved me?"

Her expression only grows more horrified. "No! No, that they died!"

"Why do you keep reminding me of it?" I moan.

"Sorry. I'm sorry!" she exclaims, waving her hands in such distress that she nearly knocks over her coffee.

I snicker and lean back into my chair. "I'm just messing with you. But thanks for the condolences." I turn to Everly and Yuna. "What about your families?"

"My sister and mom Vanished, too," says Everly.

"My dad and both of my older brothers Vanished on their way to work. My younger brother, Jae . . ." Yuna fiddles with the wings of a swan, not answering for a moment. "He went missing two years ago."

I blink. "Missing?"

"For now. I'm going to find him. And when I do—" Out of nowhere, she crushes the swan in her hands back into a crumpled napkin and looks up. "I'm going to kill him."

"She's joking," Everly exclaims finally. "Right, Yuna?"

Yuna nods. It convinces no one.

Everly lets out a flustered laugh. "It kinda feels like we're at a slumber party playing a really depressing version of Never Have I Ever." They hold up one hand. "Put one finger down if at least one member of your family disappeared during the Vanishing. Put another down if they were brutally murdered by night demons."

"Come again?" an incredulous voice interrupts from behind us. We find Kieran at the door, staring at us like we've grown extra heads.

Everly shrugs. "Well?"

Kieran blinks at them for a moment. And then he sticks up his hand and folds two fingers down. Without any further explanation, he flops into his seat and helps himself to a cup of coffee. "Is no one hungry?"

"We're waiting for the masters to arrive," I tell him, refraining from asking about his family—or the mysterious family "situation" he can't bear to share with me.

"And to think that *I* was the one worrying I was late," he mutters.

As if on cue, Yuna's stomach gurgles. She blushes and casts a longing look at a silver chafing dish filled with bacon. "Sorry."

We all share a collective glance. In unspoken agreement, we start loading up our plates and dig in. I go straight for a platter of powdered donuts filled with strawberry jam.

"You don't think this is part of the task, do you?" I ask Kieran mid-chew.

"You have powdered sugar all over your chin," he replies, mixing a spoonful of cinnamon and peanut butter into his oatmeal.

I ignore him and steal a bite from his bowl. "It's already nine. The other tasks started way earlier."

"But it's not like they ever told us what time the—" He scowls abruptly and brandishes one of Yuna's napkin swans in my face. "Seriously, you look like a coked-up Santa Claus."

Without breaking eye contact, I stick my tongue out and slowly suck a stray dollop of jam off my fingertips, leaving my lips sticky and sweet with the taste of strawberries.

"You missed a spot," he says, voice low.

I cock my eyebrow. "Did I?"

Reaching forward, he drags his thumb across the corner of my mouth and licks the sugar off. "Wipe your damn face, or that jam won't be the only thing I'll make you lick off your lips."

Something tight coils deep in my gut. I grab the napkin from his hand, my cheeks burning. I should have let him fall off that roof.

When the clock strikes nine thirty, Everly pushes their chair back and stands up. "Okay, either something's gone terribly wrong, or we're missing the obvious. I think we should look for the masters. Or Valentine, or anybody else that might know where to find them. Yuna and I can take the north corridor."

"I'll cover the west wing," says Kieran.

"Great. Cartier, you check the east wing."

"I don't take orders from you."

Everly smiles pleasantly. "Could you *please* check the east wing?"

Noëlle sniffs delicately. "I suppose."

"Fab. Rei, do you think you could try to get in touch with Master Minyi? You have her number, right? I know we were told not to use any electronic devices during the first two tasks, but they never said anything about the final task."

"Already ahead of you," I respond as I press send on the text I was typing.

They nod. "Keep us updated. Let's report to the dining hall in fifteen minutes in case any of us find anything."

As the others break off and file out of the room, I find myself lingering behind as words from earlier echo through my mind.

Either something's gone terribly wrong or we're missing the obvious.

Slowly, I slink around the table, crossing over to the masters' side. I run my fingers along the gilded ornamentation on the backs of the chairs, decorated like thrones compared to our simple wooden seats. I pull out Master Sasha's chair and settle into the plush velvet.

They are coming for us all.

The hairs on the nape of my neck stand on end as I remember his warning from yesterday. Could it have been more than paranoia after all?

My foot bumps against something underneath the table. I lift the tablecloth and bend over, peering into the gloom.

My mind stutters to a halt.

"Oh my god," I whisper, eyes wide.

"Reynolds?"

My head whips up, accidentally banging the edge of the table on the way up. "Ow. What?"

"You coming or not?" asks Kieran, leaning against one of the chairs. Then he catches sight of my expression. "What's the matter?"

In response, I beckon him over and lift the tablecloth higher for him to see. It takes a moment for the shock to register on his face. "Oh hell."

"Find the others," I say grimly. "Tell them to get them in here. *Now*."

CHAPTER THIRTY-THREE

By the time the five of us have gathered once more, the time is nine forty. I've pushed the furniture against the far wall, out of our way. We stand in a circle where the table was, surrounding my discovery.

Everly lets out a low whistle. "That is a *big* hole."

"It *is* a big hole," I agree. It's the length of my arm span, dug right through the floor.

"Big enough for a master to fit through," says Kieran. "Or two."

"You think the masters burrowed a hole through the floor of the Sanctuary and crawled into it?" Noëlle asks flatly. "Like gophers?"

I crouch down to examine the hole more closely, looking for blood or some other evidence of a scuffle. Nothing. I sit back on my heels and stare down into the darkness in resignation.

Then I glimpse a glint of something below. I pull out my phone and turn on the flashlight, pointing it at an object half-buried in the rubble.

Kieran squints over my shoulder. "Is that a coffee mug?"

My eyes sweep the table, checking the masters' untouched place settings—no. *Nearly* untouched. Among all the food, none of us noticed, but sure enough . . . "Their coffee mugs are missing."

"Maybe the masters came to breakfast super early, though they were already gone by the time Yuna and I showed up. Maybe the servers just cleaned their dishes away."

Yuna leans down into the hole. Fishing the mug out, she brings the rim to her nose to give it a sniff. Immediately, she recoils with a gag. "Zircadiazicazine."

Triple-Z. The drug that the masters used on *us* to knock us out before the first task.

Everly laughs nervously. "Why would the masters have taken Triple-Z?"

"They might not have had a choice," Kieran murmurs.

"So you think someone drugged them? And then what, kidnapped the Masters of Manhattan?"

"It sounds far-fetched, but . . ."

They are coming for us all.

I shake Master Sasha's voice away. "Let's not panic just yet. This could be part of the final task." I scan the room, searching for hidden cameras even now.

Everly pinches the bridge of their nose and sighs. "Well, task or not, we should still investigate."

"You want us to jump down that hole?" Noëlle demands, as if they just asked her to lick the wheels on a taxi and guess where it drove from. "We don't know anything about it—where it leads, who made it, who might be waiting at the other end. If the masters *did* get kidnapped, I certainly don't want to get anywhere near who- or whatever managed to accomplish that."

We sink into an uncomfortable silence. She's right. If the masters are the closest thing we have to gods, who on earth would be strong enough to strike them down? The longer I think about it, the more unlikely it seems. Perhaps this is just part of the task after all.

Yet all the same, I can't get Sasha's warning out of my head.

"The keys," Everly says abruptly, pointing over to the table. "Did anyone figure out what they were for? Or what they unlock?"

"Actually, I think I did."

We all turn to Yuna.

She shrinks beneath our scrutiny, but eventually elaborates. "I've explored the entire Sanctuary over the last few days. And I think I found a secret door."

After we grab our keys, Yuna brings us to a library. The ceiling is low, but the walls are vast, the vibrant space complete with overstuffed armchairs, coffee tables, and an open electric fireplace flickering with silent flames. Floor-to-ceiling shelves surround us on all sides, bursting at the seams with books. Hundreds and hundreds of them—old dusty tomes crammed next to recent releases, biographies of the more notorious members of the Syndicate. I pick up a magazine resting on a nearby coffee table with a black-and-white close-up of Master Sasha's face deep in thought. In grayscale, his eyes are even more piercing—nearly white. On the back cover, his most famous quote is printed across the top: KILL WITHOUT REMORSE. LIVE WITHOUT REGRET.

We watch as Yuna walks over to the fireplace, the surface of her exosuit dancing softly from the blaze like glowing coals. She raises her hands, palms forward, as if to warm herself.

Then, without warning, she plunges her hands straight into the flames.

"Wait!" I exclaim, lunging forward.

But she merely withdraws her hands—no scorched skin or blisters in sight—and arches an eyebrow.

Tentatively, I reach forward and swirl my fingers in the fire. No heat whatsoever. And . . . "There's something behind the flames," I realize, feeling around until I find a switch. *Click.* The fire extinguishes to reveal a star carved into the stone wall beyond. Each point of the star bears a keyhole—one for each of us.

As soon as we slot our keys into place, a rumble shakes the floor. We back away just in time for the fire to roar back to life, this time with real, scorching heat. The books quake as the shelves holding them split into fragments, lowering to the floor until they disappear completely. In their place, row after row of display cases rise into the light.

They are full of guns.

Not just guns, but electrified staffs and protective gear, exosuit mods, gear for any kind of weather, weapons of all shapes and sizes.

Yuna turns to us, grinning wider than a child let loose in a candy shop.

"I call the grenade launcher."

CHAPTER THIRTY-FOUR

The tunnel, to put it delicately, smells like shit.

Behind me, Kieran gags loudly as we creep through the gloom. We must be near the sewers. Rubble crunches beneath our boots. Our flashlights sweep the rough edges of the makeshift passage, struggling to penetrate the stifling darkness. I stoop lower as the top of my head scrapes against the ceiling. Noëlle touts an impressive submachine gun, muttering an endless string of complaints under her breath. Everly and Yuna bring up the rear with extra firepower in case things go south.

The beam from my flashlight catches on the tangle of footprints marking the ground. My brow creases. Human boot prints mix with the claw gouges typical of nightfangs, almost blending together at times.

"Something doesn't line up," I murmur.

"This whole situation doesn't line up, Reynolds," says Noëlle.

I shake my head. "How could the masters have walked around after being drugged?"

"Who else could the footprints belong to? And in any case, Deathlings don't perform elaborate kidnappings, they eat people. That's the *only* thing they do."

Kieran and I exchange a glance. I silently will him not to mention Boba.

"Humans must have been involved," he says eventually. "But the prints could be from another time."

"Imagine if someone found out how to control Deathlings," Everly muses. "They could take over Manhattan, and only the masters would be able to stop th—*oh*. Oh god, what if—"

I wave my flashlight frantically. "Let's not jump to any conclusions yet! This could all just be part of the final test, remember? For all we know, there could be cameras planted anywhere."

"Either way," says Kieran, his flashlight shining on the gaping maw at the end of the tunnel. "I think we're here."

When we reach the other opening, I duck low and step over a pile of demolished concrete. My boot splashes into a shallow stream of muck . . . among other things. I hold my breath and look above to where a metal ladder bolted into the wall of the tunnel leads up to a circular hatch. Just enough light seeps through the cracks that I can stuff my flashlight into my pack.

As I hoist myself onto the first rung, I pause.

"What's the holdup?" Kieran says.

The *honk* of a car horn and the *clank clank* of wheels rolling over the hatch echoes down the tunnel.

I clamber up the ladder and press my ear against the cold, grimy grating. Suspicions confirmed, I brace my arms against the hatch. In one swift movement, I shove it off and burst upward into—

The middle of the street.

I blink furiously, disoriented, struggling to adjust to the daylight assaulting my eyes. Engines rev as the traffic lights switch to green. *HONK!* I duck my head back underground with a yelp right as a bus roars over the opening of the manhole, its filthy underbelly passing inches from my nose.

"What's going on up there?" yells Kieran.

When the light turns red, I retrieve the manhole cover and seal us back into the darkness. As I descend the ladder, my boot skids. I lose my footing. I scrabble for purchase, but the rungs are too slippery. I tumble down, limbs flailing, heart in my throat.

My back collides into something hard. Arms wrap around my torso. Kieran staggers back from the impact, holding me tight to his chest. "Got you," he gasps.

Between the fall and the way his body is wrapped around mine, my heart won't slow.

"Have you guys ever thought about dating or something?" says Everly while Noëlle and Yuna snicker behind them.

I disentangle myself from him as soon as he lowers my feet safely to the ground. I point up at the ladder, keeping my voice composed. "The tunnel doesn't lead to some secret villain's lair after all. It's just midtown Manhattan."

"That makes no sense," says Noëlle.

"Hey, I've got service!" exclaims Everly. They start typing furiously. After a few seconds of scrolling, their face goes slack in shock. They hold up the screen. "Take a look at this."

We gather around it. It's a news article, published several minutes ago.

"*Tournament Finals Delayed,*" I read aloud, hardly believing the words even as they're coming out of my mouth. "*Mobs gather outside Syndicate Headquarters, demanding answers.*"

"Delayed?" Noëlle says. "What the hell is that supposed to mean? Why didn't anyone tell us?"

Everly slumps against the tunnel wall. "It means that whatever happened this morning *wasn't* part of the Tournament after all. Only the masters know what the final task is supposed to be, so if they weren't there, no one would have known any better. But the kidnapping was all *real*. The masters are gone."

The realization ripples through all of us like an earthquake. How will Manhattan protect itself without them?

"So what now?" asks Noëlle.

"We go back to the Sanctuary," Kieran replies. "We check security footage, if there is any. How many hours do we have until nightfall?"

Everly checks their phone. "About seven hours."

Kieran nudges me. "Have you heard back from Master Minyi yet?"

I shake my head, lost for words.

He squeezes my shoulder gently. "For all we know, not all the masters were kidnapped. If she was on duty last night, she could just be asleep right now."

That burning hope is the only thing that keeps me moving. Once we all make it safely out of the tunnel, I say to the others, "You guys go ahead. I'm going to try to get through to her again."

As they depart, Noëlle turns to me, her eyes filled with sincerity and not a hint of contempt—an immediate cause for alarm. "I know what it feels like. To lose someone important. I really hope your aunt is okay."

I swallow the tightness in my throat. "She is. She has to be."

Noëlle nods once. "Even if she isn't, we're going to find her. We'll get her back—together."

For the first time, I wonder what kind of person she might have been if the Vanishing never happened. If her parents were still alive. I think back to the moment when Nick Valentine announced her name at our graduation ceremony and none of her classmates clapped for her. I wonder if the reason she's so cold is because the only way she knew how to cope was to harden her heart to keep it from breaking.

Then again, her surprising sympathy could all just be a cunning act. If the masters were kidnapped, there has to have been someone on the inside. We're not teammates anymore, and I can't be certain of her intentions, or where her true loyalties lie.

I have to remember that although the final task may have been derailed, this competition is far from over.

CHAPTER THIRTY-FIVE

Riiiiiiing. Riiiiiiiiiiiiiing.
    Riiiiiiing. Riiiiiiiiiiiiiing.

"*Hello, you've reached the personal cell of Minyi Reynolds, Master of the Upper West Side. Please leave a message and—*"

The ghostly, flickering white light of the security screens illuminates the faces of the others as they watch me hang up for the eleventh time. My hope has withered and died in my chest, but I stab my finger on the call button once more.

Riiiiiiing. Riiiiiiiiiiiiiing—

Kieran stops flicking through footage of the deserted Sanctuary. "Reynolds."

I ignore him. *Riiiiiiing. Riiiiiiiiiiiiiing—*

He places a firm hand on my shoulder. "*Rei.* I don't think she's going to—"

I throw the phone at his chest. "Shut up! I know, okay? Just *shut up.*" Shoulders heaving, I stare at the security display until my traitorous vision begins to blur.

"Maybe her phone's just out of battery," he says.

I falter at the slight quaver in his voice. I forgot how much he must care about her, too.

"*Tournament Fiasco*," Noëlle reads aloud from her phone. "*Finals Go Bust. Syndicate Scandal: Deathlings Fake After All?*" She snorts. "They're having a field day."

"The conspiracy theorists?" asks Everly.

"Nope. Mainstream media."

"Christ."

Bang!

We all jump at the distant echo of a door slammed open, followed by the thunder of boots down the hall. We turn back to the security screens just in time to catch the figure hurtling inhumanly fast toward us. Nick Valentine bursts into the room, Mask in hand, his mav coat clinging onto his frame in tatters. He takes three seconds to catch his breath.

Then he gives us the phoniest grin any of us have ever laid eyes on. "Hello, competitors."

We stare at him in silence.

And then Everly slams their fist against the table hard enough to knock a security guard's mug of tea onto the floor. It shatters, splattering onto the Phantom's polished boots. "Where the *hell* have you been?"

A soft exhale rushes through the maverick's parted mouth. I think it's supposed to be a laugh, but it's a broken thing. "You don't want to know."

Yuna walks over to him and takes his hands in hers. He seems touched by the gesture until she looks him square in the eye and bluntly asks, "Are the masters dead?"

He flinches. This man, the darling of the Syndicate, killer of over two thousand Deathlings, flinches. The hand clutching his legendary mask twitches toward his face, as if to put it on and disappear.

"No need to hide from us, Mr. Valentine," Everly growls. "We can't hurt you."

The Phantom grits his teeth and stuffs his mask into his pocket. He pointedly does not answer Yuna's question as he tells us, "Okay, kids, I have some really fantastic news for you, so listen up. The masters wish to congratulate you on your formidable accomplishments. Over the last week, you have displayed unparalleled skill, bravery, and acumen. Against fifteen other competitors, you five came out on top. You have proven yourself to be the future that this city deserves. As a result, we are honoring your achievements by officially promoting all of you to mavericks. Right now."

We can do nothing but gape at him.

He spreads his arms and offers us a weak smile. "*Surprise!* Welcome to the Syndicate."

CHAPTER THIRTY-SIX

Is this a joke?" Kieran asks.

The Phantom clasps his hands behind his back. "Nope!"

"Mavericks? Just like that?" says Yuna.

"Yes, Miss Park. Congratulations! Now, if you'll all just follow me right this way—"

"No," Everly mumbles under their breath. "What about the rest of the Tournament? There's something you're not telling us." They look up suddenly, eyes blazing. "Don't act like this is normal. Tell us why it's happening."

"I just did. Your achievements—"

"Cut the bullshit," Everly snarls, stunning even the Phantom silent. "Of course we're skilled and brave and smart. Hell, every competitor in the Tournament's history has been skilled and brave and smart. We're all technically qualified to become mavericks. But why *now*, and not after the final round of the Tournament when the true champion is declared?"

"Well . . ." the Phantom begins slowly. He points to the clock ticking on the wall. "There's about two hours until nightfall."

Horror dawns across Everly's face. "You can't be serious. We haven't received any real training yet."

"Well, you're about to. Besides, you won't be expected to perform the same tasks as seasoned mavericks. You'll spend most of nightfall as safe and as high aboveground as you can get."

"Hell no." Everly laughs harshly. "*Hell* no. Aboveground or not, we're supposed to shadow masters for two *years*, not two hours. On top of that, whatever killed the masters is still out there. You're not asking us to help. You're asking us to die."

"The masters aren't dead, they're just missing in action."

"Oh, that changes everything! My bad!" Everly yells. "I'm sorry, but this isn't what I signed up for. I wanted to become a maverick to help make this city a safer place for New Yorkers to live. Without training, without the masters . . . I'm not going to throw my life away to be Deathling fodder. I'm out."

With that, they sweep past Valentine and storm out the door.

Yuna starts after them. "Everly, wait—"

Valentine steps in front of her. "No, let them go. Trust me, I understand if any of you want to go home. This is the reality of being a maverick. The only way you can survive this job is to want it so badly that you're willing to die for it."

Kieran, Yuna, and I don't budge. Noëlle bites her lip, but ultimately remains.

"Thank you," says the Phantom with an undeniable touch of relief. "The four of you have my eternal respect and gratitude. Though your induction into the Syndicate seemed less than official, I have granted you unlimited access to all its resources, including the full collection of the Artifacts. Now . . ." He pauses to look at each of us in turn. "Your job tonight is not to hunt down Deathlings. Nor to provoke them, and especially not to try to kill them, unless it means the difference between the life or death of you or another human being. No matter what happens tonight, it is crucial that the four of you remember what you are fighting for. *Who* you are fighting for. You may wish to seek vengeance, but always remember that the greatest motivation is not to kill what you hate," he says, pinning us each with a knowing look, "but to protect what you love. To protect the future of the city that you have grown up in. To protect the millions of people surviving on the simple hope that tomorrow will be better, that one day they might live in a world without fear, without nightfall, and without Deathlings." He raises his fist skyward. "And only *we* have the power to make it happen."

A beat of silence.

"Cool," I mutter under my breath. "So . . . no pressure."

The Phantom sighs. "In the Tournament, the worst that could happen to you was elimination. Tonight, once the sun sets, there will be no room for pettiness or arguing. You're all one team now, whether you like it or not. Do you understand?"

"Will we have backup, at least?" asks Noëlle, twisting the end of her ponytail.

"The idea is that you *are* the backup. Meanwhile, I'll be working with other mavericks to hold the Deathlings at bay while simultaneously continuing our round-the-clock efforts to locate the masters."

"But even with the masters gone, shouldn't there be enough mavs to safeguard the city?" she pushes. "Why do you need us?"

Nick keeps his expression in check, but the grief in his voice is painfully fresh. "A week ago, there were. Not anymore."

Noëlle pales considerably, but Yuna frowns. "What happened?"

"There was a massacre."

"Be more specific."

"Excuse me?"

Yuna shakes her head impatiently. Her fiery black gaze would make a lesser man quake at the knees. "Most of those mavericks had over a thousand kills. The average Deathling couldn't dream of laying a claw on them. So *what*, exactly, caused their deaths?"

"They were ambushed."

"But Deathlings usually hunt alone, or in groups of two or three at most."

"It's still under investigation," he replies with a defensive edge to his tone.

Yuna surges toward him, a delirious shine to her eyes. Valentine sidesteps swiftly and grabs her by the arm, twisting it behind her. In one smooth motion, he pulls out his gun and jams it into her neck, his cool demeanor gone up in flames.

"Unless you're looking for a bullet in the skull, explain yourself immediately," he murmurs dangerously.

Rather than apologizing, she turns her head and rises to her tiptoes to whisper something into the Phantom's ear.

He recoils and snaps, "You have no idea what you're talking about. That's *impossible*."

"What's impossible?" asks Kieran.

"Nothing," Yuna replies quickly. "Just call it . . . hope."

An odd feeling passes over me. Something about the look on her face makes me recall her declaration at breakfast about her brothers. The two that went missing first, and then the youngest.

Jae.

Valentine dismisses her with a wave. "A fool's hope. And between now and nightfall, Miss Park, I suggest you forget about it completely. In the meantime, I think it's time for all of you to get dressed."

✳

The Token glints in the dying sunlight as I roll it back and forth across my knuckles. Of course, now that we have access to all the Artifacts, we don't actually have enough time to visit the Archives. Luckily for everyone else, their Artifacts were already at the Sanctuary. However useless the Token may be, tonight it's officially mine.

Cold bleeds through the back of my exosuit as I slouch against the marble facade of the Syndicate's Midtown Headquarters. The visor of my helmet covers my face, tinting the world with a silver sheen. Overhead, austere flags bearing the starred insignia snap in the brisk evening wind. I crane my neck farther, trying to see the top of the mighty spire of the Empire State Building across the intersection, but I'm thwarted by the fog spilling over the city like cigarette smoke.

My nose wrinkles as the dissonant harmonies of the curfew bells chime in the distance. Even my helmet can't deter the pungent smell of coffee beans clotting the evening air. The enforcers have finished making their rounds, scattering the beans on the doorsteps, leaving the streets desolate.

Manhattan: a ghost town.

The glass entrance opens behind me. Kieran saunters down the steps, two knives hanging from his waist and his staff slung across his back. He carries his helmet tucked under his arm. "Haven't seen fog this thick since the Vanishing," he says even though we both know there's no comparison. I'll never forget that impenetrable fog, so thick you couldn't see your hand in front of your face. Those who walked into that fog never found their way back out.

Except for my sister.

Kieran stops an arm's length away from me and leans against the wall. As if the height difference between us wasn't annoying enough, the way he gazes down at me with that lazy smirk makes my blood pressure spike. He gestures at the bandolier of ammunition hanging diagonally across my chest. "For a second I almost thought you were wearing one of those prom queen sashes."

"I wonder who won the crown."

"In my mind, there was only ever one clear winner," he replies. His eyes find mine, solemn and serious. My stomach flutters—until he finishes. *"Me."*

His laughter rings bright and joyous against the desolate city blocks. Cheeks hot, I shove him in the chest. He catches me by the wrists and tugs me with him. I lose my balance and stumble right into his arms.

Everything happens so quickly. Our bodies pressed together, our faces inches apart. His nearness, his touch, his warmth spark across my skin like live embers. My heart lurches, like I'm standing at the precipice of a skyscraper high above, looking all the way down. I've never been scared of heights, but this feeling . . .

Kieran's laughter fades. His eyes flick down to my mouth for the briefest second, then back up. Hesitant. Questioning. Slowly, he caresses his fingers up my arms and cups them around my jaw, his pupils dilated like dark moons in eclipse.

I tell myself to push him away, to resist.

But I don't.

Because I know what I want. What I've wanted, what I've never stopped *wanting* even since the last day I saw him as he walked out of that library. His other hand hovers over my waist. I can see all my desire, all the months of pent-up longing reflected at me in his eyes.

There are so many words between us that have been left unsaid, but maybe there are other ways to say them.

Like the city around us, he remains perfectly still, perfectly silent. Waiting for my answer.

My eyes slip shut as the sheer gravity of him tugs me closer, toward his lips—

BRRRREEEEEEEEEEEEEEEEEEEEEEEEEEEEEEEE!

The shrill wail of the siren cleaves through the air. The final warning before nightfall. I leap away from Kieran as if electrocuted. I rub my arms and curse myself. *What was I thinking?*

"Sorry," he mutters. "I didn't mean to—"

"It's fine," I cut in sharply.

"It's not." He scrubs his face with his hands. "I can't stop thinking about you, Rei."

"Kieran," I warn, even as my own heart twists. "Now is not the time."

"Will it ever be?" he says quietly.

I hesitate. "I—I don't know."

He nods, unable to meet my gaze. After a moment of tense silence, he asks, "Did you try to call Master Minyi again?"

The tension in my shoulders unwinds a little as he drops the subject. "I think I broke her voice mailbox."

"Jerk. No wonder I couldn't get any messages through."

A half-hearted smile touches my lips, but it vanishes just as quickly. "There's so much I wish I could say to her right now. Recently, things have been difficult between us, to say the least. I was really upset when she chose you as her candidate, but more at myself than at you or her. I just felt like I'd disappointed her. Like I'd failed her somehow."

"True failure is only when you've given up before you begin," Kieran replies. "Even if Master Sasha hadn't chosen you as his candidate, I know you wouldn't have just accepted defeat. You would have found another way. You would defy the stars themselves if they told you no."

"That doesn't change the fact that I didn't rank." It seems trivial now, but there's pain in dedicating years of your life to something only for you to fall short right before the finish line.

"I get that. You know I do. Both of us were taught that grades mean everything. Maybe that's just because the world we live in decided to turn everything into a competition. But in reality, any Deathling trying to bite off your face won't care less whether or not you got a perfect score on that Inhuman Anatomy midterm senior year."

I wonder how I would've taken that statement a year ago. Or even after the rankings were announced at the graduation ceremony. My end goal has always been to become a maverick, so I needed the grades. But I regret ever letting a percentage slapped on a piece of paper determine my self-worth.

"I mean, look at the finalists," Kieran goes on. "Only two out of the five are top rankers. You think that makes the rest of us any less capable than them? Be proud of who you've proven yourself to be, Rei. I know I am." Then, softly, he adds, "And so is your aunt."

I swallow the lump in my throat as the last of the sunlight fades and the city succumbs to the darkness. The curfew siren breaks off, suffocated into silence.

The glass doors behind us fly open with a *bang*. The Phantom emerges, followed by two helmeted figures. His white half mask rests upon a mysterious bundle of black.

Thanks to the opaque visors concealing their faces, it takes me a hot second to realize that the two figures are Yuna and Noëlle. The only way to tell them apart is by their height.

"These," Valentine declares, holding out the bundle, "are for you."

One by one, he presents us with the trench coats worn by every maverick and master.

I slide my arms into the sleeves reverently, feeling both the weight of the fabric and its responsibility settle onto my shoulders. Already, the thick, sturdy exterior layer paired with the buttery-soft lining of the coat helps to fend off the windchill.

As the first swirls of stardust begin to fall, I glimpse my reflection in the glass doors of the headquarters. My breath catches. A thrill runs through my veins at the maverick I find staring back at me.

I am a terror to behold.

And I look fashionable as all hell.

"You'll begin your patrol along the predetermined route in pairs, and then split up if things are going smoothly so you can cover more ground," the Phantom reminds us. "Remember to keep track of your ammo and proceed immediately to the nearest safehouse if you're running low. And whatever you do, don't lose these. They're your only chance of survival if something goes wrong." He hands us each a packet of emergency flares, which we tuck into a small compartment sewn into the thigh area of our exosuits. "Best of luck, mavs. See you at dawn."

The Phantom dons his mask. It gleams white as starlight for a split second, and then he's gone without a trace.

The show has begun.

As Yuna and Noëlle head east, Kieran pulls me back. "I have a favor to ask you. If anything happens to me tonight, I need you to give a letter to Cassie. I moved it here for safekeeping." He points at the inner chest pocket of his new coat. "Someone needs to keep an eye on her if I'm not around anymo—"

"No."

"What?"

I jab my index finger square into his chest. "Keep an eye on her yourself, Cross. You're not going anywhere, so don't even think about it."

After a moment, he smiles. "Whatever you say, Rei."

CHAPTER THIRTY-SEVEN

Walking the city in the dark is something out of a dream—or, depending on how it ends, a nightmare.

A strange sort of excitement flutters in my chest. How many years have I spent fantasizing this very moment? Finally, I'm free. Free of the rules and the bureaucracy that forced me to strike from the shadows like some unwilling vigilante. No more squatting in abandoned subway stations, no more scavenging for bullets behind Aunt Minyi's back. But tonight . . .

Nothing stands in the way of my wrath.

A tremor shudders through the ground beneath my boots. We barely have time to hurl ourselves out of the way as a jumble of limbs galumphs around the corner, frothing at the maw. Even the overwhelming stink of coffee pervading the air of my first official nightfall cannot mask the foul arrival of the Deathling.

So starved for flesh, the Deathling charging directly into the sight of my gun either doesn't notice or doesn't care about the weapon in my hand. A weapon that suddenly seems measly compared to five hundred pounds of muscle and bone—at least, until my bullet halts it in its tracks and explodes a gory crater through its belly. A downpouring of gnarled toes and glistening entrails slaps onto the sidewalk with the most repulsive of *plop*s.

"Should've brought an umbrella!" Kieran's voice crackles through my helmet.

"Six o'clock," I bellow, firing at another Deathling careening down the street, its jaws stretched wide enough to engulf a human head in one chomp. Yuna beats me there, leaping into the air with her staff aimed at its throat like a javelin. The beast implodes and dies.

"Watch it, Park," I growl. "You almost got yourself caught in the crossfire."

"As if I'm going to stand aside and let you get all the kills, Reynolds." I can't see her expression through the cold silver reflection of her helmet, but her tone says enough. She cocks her head at me. "And besides, I'd hate to see you run out of bullets."

I raise my gun toward her and fire. She flinches. Right behind her, a Deathling melts into a flesh puddle with a scream of misery. A perfect shot.

"Don't count on it," I tell her with a frigid smile.

"Cut it out, both of you," Kieran orders. "We need to get to higher ground."

"Let's split up. Cartier, you're with me." I start jogging off until I realize no one's following me. I turn. "Cartier?"

Noëlle starts when I call her name. "Yes. Coming." She lurches into motion like a broken windup figurine.

Before I can ask her why she's acting so strangely, a chorus of ghostly singsong cries rises with the wind. Not just three or four voices, but many. Too many.

Grimly, we begin patrolling the routes Valentine assigned to each of our pairs. We snake around each block, covering two sides per pair. Noëlle and I forge onward all the way to First Avenue, close enough to the East River that we can almost hear the lapping water against the squalid stone banks.

As I leap from one roof to the next, a hum floats into my ears. I whirl around, searching for a Deathling waiting to pounce from a nearby fire escape, only to realize that the sound is playing through my helmet.

"Noëlle, is that you?"

The humming stops. "I can't bear the quiet."

"Fine. Just keep it down."

She quickens her stride, a new melody flowing from her lips, the syllables from another language soft and round. Although her singing could distract us from approaching Deathlings, none of us seem to have the resolve to stop her. Secretly, I'm grateful—the silence felt too much like someone had nailed the lid of a coffin over our heads.

I squint down the narrow street as we blur past Madison Ave. "There's something up ahead. It looks like . . . a sign."

Yuna's incredulous voice channels into my helmet. "In the middle of Koreatown?"

"It's got legs," says Noëlle. We skid to a halt about three hundred feet away, at the mouth of the intersection.

"How many?" Kieran asks.

"Just the two. It's a curfew breaker. Or a Deathling in disguise."

Kieran and Yuna round the corner into view. "Only one way to find out," he says.

The lone figure stands in the middle of the street between a lifeless Korean barbecue restaurant and a karaoke bar, wielding a poster high above his head. NOT MY GOVERNMENT, it reads.

"That's no Deathling," I mutter.

"Worse," Noëlle mutters, her tone dripping with a scathing amount of disdain. "It's one of *them*."

Indeed, the protester wears a T-shirt with the words SCAMDICATE painted in red over the Syndicate's insignia. Stardust coats his bald head like the world's shiniest toupee.

"Citizens are prohibited from leaving their residences after sundown," I yell at him. "You must seek shelter immediately or face the consequences!"

"Or what?" he yells back. "You'll lock me up? Do it!"

Kieran steps forward. "Sir, we're going to need you to—"

He freaks. "Don't you touch me! Don't you dare!" he screams, spittle flying. "You're crooks, all of you! Cutting off the power at sundown, imprisoning us in our own homes! For what? *For what?*"

"Sir, are you not aware of the flesh-devouring monsters crawling the streets?"

"Yeah, yeah. Searching for fresh meat just like me. Blah blah blah!" He gives us the finger. "Well, I've been out here fifteen minutes already, and I haven't seen a damn thing!"

"By the time you actually see something, it'll be too late," I tell him as calmly as I can. "If you're in need of shelter, you should proceed to the nearest emergency housing center. Now."

"I don't need any damn shelter. The only threat to my life and liberty is your so-called government. I've listened to your rules for over a decade. I'm sick of it! I used to be able to do whatever I wanted to do in this city at night. Go to the club. Walk in the park. Shit in the subway—you Syndicate assholes banned all that!"

None of us point out that shitting in the subway was definitely banned way before the Syndicate even existed, but I grit my teeth and attempt to show some sympathy. "We understand your frustration, sir. But you have to believe that our only desire is to do what's best for the city and keep you safe."

He snorts. "Don't you get it? There's nothing I need to be kept safe *from*. Do you know anyone who's *actually* been killed by a Deathling?"

"Yeah," I answer flatly. "My parents."

"Okay, but did you *actually* see them get killed?"

"Yeah."

"Like, *in person*?"

"Yep."

He shakes his head, undeterred. "You're blind. All of you. It's what I've been saying for years. Deathlings—it's all just a damn hoax." He turns his face to the sky and screams, "*Come and get me, you assholes!*"

Without another word, Kieran strides up to the man and grabs him by the throat. The man chokes on his own battle cry, his rheumy eyes popping out like a rubber chicken's.

"The truth is, your life is worthless to us," he utters. There is no pity in his voice. There is no emotion at all. "The only reason I haven't speared you through your squealing piglet mouth yet is that I refuse to let your astonishingly thick skull dull my blade. Your death would be less significant than a birthday candle getting snuffed out by a blizzard. Not a single person would notice."

This is the Kieran I remember from the graduation ceremony, his eyes burning with nothing but cold, dark malice. A thrilled shiver runs through me.

The man gargles something, his face steadily purpling.

Kieran leans closer, his tone mocking. "What was that? You think the other anti-Syndicate protesters will notice?" He jerks his chin at the empty street. "Then why aren't they with you now? Why are *you* the only one here?"

For the first time, the man fails to find a response.

"I bet your leaders told you that everyone would rally together, didn't they?" Kieran murmurs. "That's what they tell all the newcomers naive enough to fall for their ploy. And yet they've abandoned you to the very monsters they claim they don't even believe in, because deep down, they *know* they're wrong. Deathlings are real, and your mutilated corpse will serve as the proof. Tonight, you will be sacrificed for a cause that no one—absolutely *no one*—believes in."

With that, Kieran releases the man. He drops to his knees, coughing and spluttering, clutching at his bruised neck. Noëlle starts toward him, but Kieran stops her.

"If he wants to die this way, then don't bother. We have more important matters to—"

"I believe in it."

Kieran stills.

"I believe. I have to," the man rasps, dragging himself onto his feet. "My wife . . . she was all I had. She couldn't have been killed by some make-believe monster straight out of a horror flick. Something else had to have killed her. Something real, like the Syndicate. You wouldn't understand."

As he speaks, I hear the grating of metal against asphalt. My eyes narrow. The manhole cover by his feet shifts ever so slightly.

"Sir," I exclaim. "Sir, step away from that manhole."

He's not listening. "Where did these Deathlings even come from? Ever since that pandemic all those years ago, people started moving away from the city. Companies took their business elsewhere. The city was dying, and the government knew it! Then the Vanishing happened, and they closed the borders to prevent anyone from leaving—"

I draw my guns. "Step away!"

"You can't convince me you don't think it's the least bit suspicious!"

he yells just as the cover lifts. "It's all just a damn—"

BANG! The cover rockets upward, shattering the protester's kneecaps with a gruesome *crunch*. He goes down with a scream as a creature with writhing tentacles for a face surges out of the ground and latches on to his flailing legs by the ankles. It drags him toward the hole.

"*Heeeeeeelp!*" the man screeches.

I fire. The monster jerks back as the bullets punch through its jaundiced skin. Rancid brown blood gushes onto the asphalt. A scream like a kettle about to blow pierces the air. It thrashes as the bullets explode inside its body.

Yuna and Kieran sprint over to the protester and grab him by the armpits while the Deathling bleeds out.

"My legs!" he wails. "I'm dying!"

"Shut up," says Yuna.

"I say we leave him out here," Kieran says darkly. "Survival of the fittest, right?"

The man pales. "Please. Please, no. I'll never break curfew again. The way it *grabbed* me." He shudders violently and dry heaves. "I don't have anywhere to go. But I don't want to get eaten, either. Please—"

Yuna sighs. "I'll take him to the nearest emergency housing center."

"You can't go alone," Kieran says. "I'll escort you."

"How am I supposed to walk?" the protester cries.

With a sigh, Kieran plucks him off the ground and hauls him over his shoulder like a sack of potatoes, ignoring every shriek of profanity. "Cover me, Park."

"Just try to keep up." Yuna takes off in the opposite direction, leaving him no choice but to race after her. As the thud of their boots fades, so does the connection through our helmets. In the hush of static, my eyes linger on Kieran's back.

I don't want him to leave.

But I tell myself that they'll both make it to dawn. They both will.

We regard the shriveled-up husk of the Deathling corpse at my feet.

"Did you hear the way it screamed?" Noëlle whispers.

I give it a kick and watch emotionlessly as it crumbles to dust. If only they could all disappear so easily. "Psychoanalyzing monsters won't help you kill them any better."

Rather than merely rolling her eyes, she asks, "Is that all you can think about? Killing them?"

I give her a weird look. "Isn't that what all of us became mavericks for?"

"Right." Like a switch being flicked, she's all business again. "Until the others return, we've got a lot of extra ground to cover. Let's move."

I don't say anything, but I can't shake off my growing suspicions.

We jog past a tall church of austere white stone surrounded by a wrought iron fence. Upon it, strips of vivid red silk have been draped between the pickets in memoriam of the victims of this week's Deathling killings.

I look away, heavy with the knowledge that the count is five off.

How soon before the city realizes its masters are gone, too?

CHAPTER THIRTY-EIGHT

A unt Minyi always told me that there were only two things that separated a master from a maverick: experience and patience. The former, she believed, I would acquire through time and hard work. She had no hope for the latter.

So as we continue our patrol, it's not surprising that the fourth time Noëlle flinches at the howl of the wind, I lose my shit.

I yank my helmet off my head and round on her, blocking her path. The frigid nightfall air is a blessing, relieving my flushed skin, cooling the sweat dripping from my brow. But more than that, taking off my helmet prevents anyone from eavesdropping on our conversation. I gesture vehemently at her to do the same.

"Why did you stay when Valentine told us that we were free to walk away?" I demand.

"Same reason as you. I want to be a maverick."

"And yet you cower at the first sign of a Deathling."

At that, she scowls. "You're trigger-happy enough for the both of us.

Why are you complaining? I thought you'd be eager to stack up more kills than Yuna."

"Stop turning this on me. What are you hiding?"

She clenches her jaw. Ever since the graduation ceremony, I've never seen her looking anything less than immaculate, even when her exosuit died and she wiped out in front of all those people at the Apollo, but between the hairs sticking to her sweaty forehead and the anger splotching her cheeks, she looks to be on the verge of a Vesuvius-level meltdown. "Nothing is wrong, okay? This is what I wanted! This"—she flings her arms at the empty streets, her eyes wild—"is the future I have been working toward ever since the Vanishing. Everything is going perfectly to plan."

"What plan?" I ask quietly, my grip tightening on my guns.

Noëlle falters. "What?"

"You said *everything is going perfectly to plan.*"

"My plan to become a maverick, obviously. Look, I don't want to talk about this anymore. Let's just survive the night."

"You can't just—"

"*Please*, Rei."

At the exhaustion and vulnerability bleeding through her voice, my objections die in my throat. I close my mouth.

Fine. I'll find another way past her defenses.

I shove my helmet back on and push her aside. The fog pooling around the buildings above like greasy clouds sinks lower and lower with each step as we trek through Midtown. As if monsters crawling out of the sewers and the ever-looming threat of slaughter weren't sinister enough. We're forced to slow as we strain to make out shapes through the fog.

"*Hmmmmm.*" I keep my gun trained on the shadows. "*Hmm-hmmmm . . .*"

"What the hell are you doing?"

"Humming," I say.

"You sound like a broken radiator."

"I'm doing my best."

"I know." An awkward pause. "Thanks." Is that a smile I heard in her voice? "But do shut up, you're quite awful."

"What song were you singing earlier?"

"A lullaby. My grandparents used to sing it to me. Regrettably, my grandmother sounded a lot like you, but my grandfather had a wonderful voice."

"They don't live in Manhattan?"

Noëlle hesitates. "No. Fortunately for them, the rest of my family is safe on the other side of the world. I'm the only one left in this forbidden city."

"Not the only one," I remind her. "And who knows what the future of Manhattan will be. If we destroy Deathlings for good, we can open the borders back up. People will be safe to enjoy the city at night. Maybe one day you'll be able to see your family again, too."

"Or shit in the subway," she adds wryly.

"Hey, if that's your dream, I'm not gonna stop you."

Noëlle halts abruptly. "Reynolds, I don't care about killing Deathlings like you. And I don't care about saving this city, either, like Everly. Or protecting people, like the Phantom."

Bewildered, I ask, "Then why are you here?"

"My uncle," she says after a moment. "He lives in New Jersey now, right across the river. He's a businessman who dabbles in politics when it suits his mood. He found a job for my mother here and convinced her to uproot our lives and move to this country. When my parents Vanished, he all but denied my existence."

"So . . ." It takes me a moment to form my thoughts. "You've been living all alone. For fifteen years."

"There was a family next door that helped me out for a while. But they tried to leave the city when I was ten, and I haven't heard from them since." She gazes toward an open patch in the fog where the stars twinkle from above, like she's searching for an answer they can't give her. "When my uncle found out I was the top ranker at my school, he decided to get back in touch. He promised me that if I became a master or a maverick— in other words, someone in a position of great power with connections to every major political figure in the city—he'd help me figure out a way to get out. To go home and reunite with the rest of my family."

I almost tell her that no matter how many strings her uncle thinks he can pull, unless he can rebuild obliterated bridges or tunnels with a snap of his fingers or sprout wings and fly, he'll never weave a miracle like that. But the glistening sorrow in her eyes tells me that she already knows.

"Sorry," she manages, wiping her tears. "Forget I said an—"

Before I can regret every decision leading up to this moment, I fling my arms around her and hug her as tightly as I can. For a few tense beats, she stands stiff as a pole. Then she releases a quiet exhale and relaxes into my embrace.

"I really hated you at first," I murmur, staring into the fog. "And I hate that you still look really pretty even when you're crying. More than that, I hate that you had to fight so many battles on your own. But you've got a team to back you up now . . . and a friend."

Before she can reply, a haunting cry pierces the night. Following it, a loud *bang* and a high-pitched whistle.

We break apart as the fiery red tail of an emergency flare soars over our heads, shearing through the fog.

My body goes cold with dread.

Something's gone wrong.

Plunged back into reality, we stuff our helmets back on. That's when the second *bang* blasts through the night. No more than a few blocks away from the first, another flare shoots into the sky, corkscrewing upward in a shower of scarlet sparks. We both freeze, shell-shocked by the sight.

"There are two," Noëlle whispers.

"We follow protocol," I say firmly, swallowing my own nerves. "That means—"

She nods and straightens her shoulders. "I'll take the flare from the east side."

"But—"

"I'll be fine. I've got a team to back me up now, remember?"

The last thing I want to do is let her go alone, but I can already feel every precious second wasting away, so we exchange a final nod before sprinting off in opposite directions.

I let my instincts take over, focusing on the familiar rhythm of my arms and legs pumping steadily in time with my breaths. As I fly down the street, a pair of Deathlings lurking behind a mountain of trash bags piled on the curb leap out after me. I can't see how close they are, but I can hear their savage grunts as they attempt to chase me down, the promise of violence in the scrape of talons against stone.

I run faster.

Eventually, the only noise that reaches my ears is the sound of my own panting. Less than a block away, the smoky tail of the flare has already begun to dissipate. With my back pressed into the worn stone wall of a bank, I hold my gun close to my chest and prowl to the corner, peering through the huge glass windows to discover a completely deserted street. Am I too late?

Something's off.

The street isn't just deserted. It's completely devoid of *anything*. No blood, no bodies, not even the empty shell of the flare.

Just as I'm about to step out into the open, the hush inside my helmet wavers. Hard breathing fills my ears—not my own. My head whips back around the corner. Through the glass, another mav sprints toward me from the opposite end of the street to investigate the flare. I can't tell who it is, but they don't hesitate like me, instead rushing from door to door to inspect every storefront for signs of life. It is because of their diligence that they don't see the shadow on the roof across the street, nor the glint of the round object sailing toward the concrete.

"*GRENADE!*" I scream at the top of my lungs.

With perfect aim, the grenade bounces once, twice, and rolls to a stop next to the maverick. The last I see is their head turning in surprise before the grenade detonates in a fiery explosion.

I throw myself onto the ground and cover my head. My ears ring from the blast and the shatter of glass. Staggering to my feet, I take aim at the roof with shaking hands, but it's too late. The shadow is long gone.

Black smoke churns in the street. I have no choice but to fight down my rising panic and force my legs to move, to run straight toward the carnage and whoever lies within.

CHAPTER THIRTY-NINE

I find the body under an awning a quarter block away from where the grenade detonated. A spiderweb of cracked polycarbonate spreads across the visor of their helmet. The helmet itself is peppered with dents and scratches from the shrapnel. They must have jumped high enough to avoid the kill zone, but not out of range of the explosion. Even with the exosuit's protection, the fabric is torn in multiple places. Bloody lacerations bespatter the flesh underneath.

"Come on, come on," I hiss, my fingers fumbling to undo the clasp on their helmet. I catch sight of myself in the fractured reflection of the visor. *This could have been you*, it seems to say. All of a sudden, everything becomes too much. My breath comes too short, too fast, fogging up the inside of my own helmet. Trapped in the dark, I'm overwhelmed by a wave of claustrophobia. I barely manage to rip the thing off. It's all I can do to throw it aside, to gasp in the cold air, to force down the bile rising in my throat.

I scramble onto my hands and knees. Ground myself. Dig my fingers firmly into the asphalt until they hurt. Until the world stops spinning.

I think about how Aunt Minyi would act if she were here.

Be calm, she would say to me. *Better to take things one step at a time than to lose your footing and fall.*

I glance over at the mav's chest. A small shred of relief eases the knot in my stomach—there's movement, however slight. And so long as they're still breathing, the stardust will help take care of the rest. But it won't be long before the scent from the growing pool of blood attracts every Deathling within the vicinity for a feeding frenzy.

At last, I manage to wrench the mav's helmet off. Short, jet-black hair tumbles across porcelain-white cheekbones and a delicate nose. With her eyes closed and her skin even paler than usual, Yuna looks worse than death. Blood dribbles down the side of her cheek from a gash that missed her right eye by no more than a half inch.

Biting down hard on my tongue, I start pulling out the broken polycarbonate from her face shard by shard. Then as much shrapnel as I can from the rest of her body. Under normal circumstances, I would never remove the projectiles keeping her wounds plugged up. During nightfall, however, leaving them in might cause the stardust to heal the skin *over* them, meaning in order to remove them she'd be forced to cut them out all over again.

I'm halfway through cleaning up a nasty gash in her stomach when she comes to with a gasp. Her glazed eyes land on me as I dig my fingers through her flesh like a graverobber hunting for organs. She screams in horror and promptly knees me in the face.

I fall flat on my ass, swearing violently. My hand flies to my bruised cheek. It comes away bright red and sticky. I stare at it in shock before realizing the blood actually belongs to her.

Meanwhile, Yuna desperately tries to scramble away from me, but she seizes up in agony, cursing and groaning, still delirious from the explosion.

"Yeah, I wouldn't move yet if I were you. The shrapnel basically turned you into a human dartboard. Falling from that height, I'm pretty sure you fractured a few bones, too."

Yuna pauses, her bloodshot eyes blinking in and out of focus until they settle on my face. *"You?"* She regards me with such incredible displeasure that her expression could rival every look of disdain I've ever received from Noëlle combined.

"No, it's the bastard that threw the grenade at you." I wipe her blood off on my leg, hoping that the Syndicate has some top-tier dry cleaning services. "Of course it was me. Now hold still, there's shrapnel stuck in your shoulder."

She glowers. "Thank you."

"You don't sound particularly thankful."

"I don't—" She gasps in pain as I finally manage to expunge the last stubborn shard embedded in her body. Her blood is already coagulating, the raw flesh and exposed tissue shimmering with gold. "I don't like being indebted to anyone."

I sit back on my haunches. "Well then, consider the debt already paid. If you hadn't barged in on the scene first, it might've been *my* organs festooning the block."

She feels the area around her eye, wincing slightly, but the majority of the skin around the gash has already knitted itself back together. "Where's the hitman? You shot him dead, I presume."

I swallow the bitter taste in my throat. "They fled as soon as the grenade went off."

"Did you see their face, at least?"

"Do I look like I've got X-ray vision?"

"To be fair, you did spot the grenade." Yuna massages her temple and mumbles, "It better have been one of those anti-Syndicate radicals. The last thing we need is more traitors roaming our midst."

I glance down the street. "Where's Kieran?"

"When the first flare went up, we hadn't arrived at the emergency shelter yet. So we split up. He was supposed to deliver that protester to safety and then meet me at the second flare after I'd cleared the first one." She pushes herself into a sitting position with a grimace. "We'd better hurry up and catch him before he gets there. Chances are that both flares were traps, so we need to—"

My heart surges into my throat. "Noëlle." I leap to my feet. "We split up, too. She went to the other flare alone."

"I'll have to catch up to you. I need more time to heal up."

"And leave you to fend for yourself?"

"Trust me, Reynolds, I've survived much worse. I'm more than capable of keeping myself alive in dire circumstances."

I shake my head in frustration. "You've never had to go head-to-head with a five-hundred-pound nightfang intent on tearing out your innards, much less a city full of them."

"How would you know?" she replies with a tint of amusement. What she finds funny, I have no clue.

"You'll understand one nightfall," I warn, "but not tonight. I'll carry you."

"The increase in required output energy will compromise the longevity of your exosuit's functionality. It'll burn out. You're better off leaving me behind."

"Too bad."

"Why are you so keen on sticking out your neck for me?"

"If our positions were switched, I'd count on you to do the same for me. That's it. Hurry up, we're wasting time."

She narrows her eyes at me, realizing that I won't take no for an answer. "Fine. So how exactly do you want to do this?"

✳

If any of the insomniacs of Midtown Manhattan found themselves staring out the window on this particular nightfall, they might have expected to see a maverick swooping through the fog. Perhaps even two.

Not, however, two bloodied teenage girls, one hitching a piggyback ride on top of the other as though it were the world championships of the newest track-and-field event.

"Come on, Reynolds!" Yuna yells as the rim of her helmet bounces against mine while we fly down the streets. Even without the visor, we figured that a dinged-up helmet beats a bashed-in skull.

My exosuit beeps in warning. I only tighten my grip on Yuna's thighs and push myself faster. The pavement beneath my boots glistens like an endless sheet of glass. I make every stride count, devouring the distance I'd normally need four or five minutes to cover while walking in mere seconds. But I can already feel the cost of my speed creeping up on me—besides the incessant beeping of my helmet, the fabric of my suit is heating up from overexertion, especially at the joints from all the friction. Steam rises off my shoulders into the chilly air. Soon it will turn into smoke—and knowing my luck, Yuna will have a human flamethrower at her disposal to use against the Deathlings by the time we reach 30th Street.

"Did you see that?" Yuna exclaims. "There, one block south. I saw someone on the roof!"

Unfortunately, I have no way of simultaneously looking up and sprinting down the sidewalk forty miles an hour without accidentally hurtling into a fire hydrant.

"Put me down at the next intersection," Yuna instructs me.

"That'll be four hundred dollars," I pant. "Plus tip."

"Ugh. Taxi fares these days."

"Inflation. What can you do?"

We stop only long enough for Yuna to slide off me before kicking it right back into top gear. Besides the bloodstains, it's hard to tell that Yuna almost got blown up. The self-healing fabric of the exosuit conceals any lingering traces of injury, and if she's still hurting somewhere, she hides it frighteningly well.

"We're close," she mutters. "Next street over, I think."

The fog hovering over the city at sundown now cloaks every block in a veil of ghostly white. Through the haze, towering lampposts and spindly young trees with skeletal branches jump out at us in stark relief. I suppress a shiver. Any nearby Deathlings might not see us coming, but we're equally as visionless.

"Should we—" I begin.

Yuna grabs my elbow and yanks me backward, dragging me into the shadows of an elegant marble archway. She puts a finger to her lips.

In the silence, the rustle of the trees in the park down the street is louder than the chatter of bones. The wind picks up, carrying with it the reek of rotten eggs.

But it's not a Deathling I see.

It's a broken heap in the middle of the street, too small to be a monster and too large to be anything other than human. From here, it's impossible to tell who it is, but it's clear enough from the glimmer of the exosuit that it's a maverick.

And the longer they lie unmoving beneath the thin but growing blanket of stardust without rising, the more I realize that they must be—

"We have to go and help them," I choke out. "We have to check if they're actually—"

"You can't," Yuna hisses. "When have you ever heard of a Deathling killing their victim and leaving the body behind? It had to have been a human. It's a goddamn trap, and you know it. There's no choice but to wait until dawn to retrieve the body."

I clench my hand to my chest, right over my heart, trying and failing to quell the storm tearing me apart from the inside out. "I have to know," I whisper. "I have to know who it is."

Yuna regards me for a long moment. "You're a reckless bitch, you know that?"

"I know."

After a beat, she draws her gun. "I'll cover you. Just don't expect me to die for you or anything like that."

It's the best I can hope for. I take a deep breath, filling my lungs all the way with oxygen before expelling it in a violent *whoosh*, as though if I exhale hard enough, I can rid myself of my fear.

It doesn't work.

So before my terror can freeze me stiff, I lunge out from behind the safety of the archway and sprint headfirst into the waiting darkness.

CHAPTER FORTY

The fog parts before me like a misty curtain to reveal the motionless form of the maverick lying facedown in the asphalt.

Even before I turn the body over, I know it is him.

His rumpled mav coat puddles around his body. The ground is already so dark and wet that I don't notice the blood soaking the ground by his head until I step in it. When I see where it's coming from, my stomach lurches into my throat. Piercing through the back of his helmet is a single round hole, smaller than a penny.

A bullet hole.

This was the work of a human.

As the shock kicks in, I shut down completely. I bite down on my knuckle to keep myself from screaming. Even when it starts to bleed, I feel nothing.

Stardust clumps around the wound, trying to heal the damage. It can repair even the most grievous injuries, so long as life pulses through your veins. But death . . . it cannot undo.

Suddenly, I am five years old again. Collapsed on the concrete, tears streaming down my face, frozen in terror as Mom shoots at the Deathling twisting Dad's head off his neck like a stubborn bottle cap. Until flesh and bone finally tear free and the monster swallows him all down in one gulp.

I see her turn to me, her brown eyes filled with rage and despair. *Run, Rei.* Her voice urges me now, too. *Run from those monsters before it's too late.*

And I want to.

I want to run away from this nightmare.

I want to run away from this world of senseless violence and unjust cruelty, where the people I care about *won't stop dying.*

I squeeze my eyes shut as I roll Kieran over. I can't bear to look at him, to imagine his unseeing eyes behind the silver wall of his visor. Though a bullet could fly out of the fog and end me at any second, I haven't forgotten what he asked me to do, what I denied him under the wishful belief that we would all make it to dawn. *If anything happens to me tonight, I need you to give a letter to Cassie.*

My hand feels along the edges of his coat for the inner pocket. I rummage around. A growl of frustration claws out of my throat. I can't find the damn thing. Gritting my teeth hard enough to split stone, I force my eyes open.

The first thing I notice is that the pocket is empty. The second thing is the locks of blond hair like finely spun gold escaping Kieran's helmet.

I clap a hand to my mouth to stifle a cry. Eventually, I unfasten the clasp and tug the helmet off.

Noëlle stares up at me, her blue eyes almost a muddy slate gray. Her teeth are clenched together like she couldn't escape fear even in death.

I brush my hand across her freezing cheek, which was warm and full of life no more than an hour ago as we embraced and I told her to count on her team. To count on me—her friend. I promised Noëlle she wouldn't have to fight alone any longer, and yet that's exactly how she died.

Then a worse feeling creeps in. *Relief.* That it's her, and not Kieran.

Guilt crashes down on me.

The static in my helmet wavers. Yuna's voice crackles in my ears. "Reynolds. Something's coming. Leave the body and get out of there."

I swallow. Gently, I reach up to Noëlle's face and slide her eyelids shut.

Slowly, I rise to my feet. "No," I reply. "Let them come. I'm done running away."

Years have passed since my parents were killed, but nothing has changed. As long as Deathlings still taint this city, as long as the blood of New Yorkers flows through the streets to empty into the gutters, then my vow to them stays unfulfilled.

"This isn't about running away. It's about surviving."

I draw my guns and dig my heels into the ground. "I refuse to leave Noëlle out here unguarded. I won't let them devour her body and fight over the scraps. I won't let anything touch her. Until dawn, no beast, human or otherwise, gets to her without getting through *me* first."

Silence answers me. At first, I assume Yuna has abandoned me, but then I hear three loud *bang*s. Sparks spatter across the ground as Yuna shoots three consecutive flares into the night. As I watch their brilliant comet tails spiral through the fog, painting smears of scarlet onto the sky, she dashes out from the cover of the archway, her footsteps light as raindrops, and joins my side.

Wherever Kieran may be, I can only pray that he—or any other maverick still alive—sees the flares. They're a plea for help. But they're also a declaration. A war cry.

Here we are, they tell the waiting darkness. *So come and get us.*

CHAPTER FORTY-ONE

S he must have the record for shortest time as a mav ever," says Yuna, her gaze lingering on Noëlle's bare face.

"You know what's the saddest part?" I murmur, recalling our final conversation. "She didn't even want to be one."

"How many of us do you think actually do?"

I blink. "What do you mean?"

Quickly, Yuna crouches down and touches Noëlle's forehead. "All I'm saying is that we all have our reasons, but for some people joining the Syndicate is just a means to an end." Before I can demand further explanation, she starts murmuring a short prayer under her breath.

And then she begins stripping off Noëlle's mav coat.

"What are you doing?" I exclaim, outraged. I might've understood if Yuna took Noëlle's helmet—despite the bullet hole in the back, the visor is still intact, so it'll provide better protection than the one she's currently wearing. But it feels wrong to take Noëlle's coat, the greatest and only trophy that she received for her hard-won achievements . . . and hard-fought sacrifice.

"Stop that!" Without it, she looks too exposed, almost naked. But Yuna plows on, wrestling one limp arm out of its sleeve, and then the other.

"Get a grip on your emotions, Reynolds. Can't you see how vulnerable we are right now? Whether you like it or not, Noëlle won't be needing her coat anytime soon. It's the perfect bait, and we need every edge we can get. So stop *gaping* and help me."

Yuna finishes peeling the bloodied coat off Noëlle in a rush and arranges the fabric upon the ground in a vaguely human-esque shape in the middle of the street. Together, we hoist Noëlle off the ground and carry her over to the park down the block. We've barely set her down in the grass under the cover of the trees when the smell hits. An all-too-familiar combination of waste and decay, and above all else, that signature eau d'rotten eggs.

But it's not the smell itself that hits so hard—it's the sheer *strength* of it. There's more than one coming.

We crouch behind the mighty trunk of an oak tree. I'm forced to breathe through my mouth to prevent myself from puking directly into my own helmet. "How many Deathlings is that?" Ten? Fifteen? More?

"I don't know. Just make sure you're fully loaded." Yuna checks her own guns, her movements as steady and methodical as a brain surgeon performing an operation. Her calmness unnerves me.

"You don't sound worried," I whisper.

"Should I be?"

"The prospect of fighting ten Deathlings at once would make any master sweat."

"I don't sweat."

I bite my tongue. The stench of the Deathlings grows so intense that I can taste it in the air. I can't tell if it's a blessing or a curse when the fog begins to visibly lighten, as if warded off by the imminent battle. Better for us to see by, but easier to be seen.

The nightfangs arrive first. A quartet of them, slinking from shadow to shadow as silent as the darkness itself. The largest one has too many fangs to fit into its own mouth, so they've begun to sprout out of its cheeks like wayward knitting needles. No less impressive are the barbed horns protruding from each of their skulls like crowns.

A sewer grate down the street explodes outward. Metal rattles and scrapes across the pavement. From within squeezes out the contorted form of a Deathling with rubbery gray skin that wobbles with every movement. Dribbles of saliva gleam on its chin, dripping off its whiskers. At the sight of the nightfangs, it freezes, and for a ludicrous second I think they'll tear each other apart.

But then I spot five, six, *seven* more of its rubbery kin wriggling out of the hole, thick reptilian tails and other wrinkled appendages dragging trails of slime and sewer water across the bike lanes.

Both parties convene around Noëlle's bloodied coat. They seem to be . . . *waiting*. For what, I haven't the faintest idea. I sense my own astonishment mirrored by Yuna. Other than to kill each other over territory disputes, nightfangs and other Deathlings never interact, plain and simple. They're not supposed to band together, to hunt in packs. In the war against them, it's one of the only advantages the Striker Division has been able to exploit, coordinating patrol routes throughout the city under the assumption that we'd only ever need to deal with one or two monsters at a time—if we were quick enough, of course.

But evidently, the enemy has evolved.

Frantically, I run through the logistics in my head. In the face of our weapons and training, the sewer Deathlings should be easy enough to take out from a distance. It's the four nightfangs that worry me, particularly since the last one I fought in the subway station all the way before the

Tournament seemed to have built up some kind of resistance against my bullets.

A surprise attack will be our best bet. I can't rely on Yuna since she doesn't have any real fighting experience in the field, but if she helps me take out the sewer Deathlings first, I might actually stand a chance—however inconceivable—against the nightfangs.

I signal to Yuna. She shakes her head fiercely and points in the opposite direction of the gathered Deathlings. My plan crumbles to dust before my eyes as the ground shudders and a horde of gigantic insectoid abominations flood down the street. There's one like a centipede, clinging to the facades of the buildings with hundreds of serrated forcipules. Another like a beetle, with only a gaping jaw for a head. There are a devastating six in total.

I clench my clammy palms into fists, scouring our surroundings for anything that can help us escape—anything that will quash the sudden, sickening awareness in my gut that we've got no way out of this. It would take the strength of a dozen mavericks to overcome this many Deathlings. My hand grips the bark of the mighty oak separating us from death.

I only have one idea left.

"I'll distract them," I tell Yuna.

Her head whips to me in surprise. "What?"

"It's my fault you're trapped here. But I can still buy you enough time to escape."

She doesn't react for a long second. Finally— "That's the worst plan ever."

I struggle to keep my voice down. "Look, there's no way we both get out of here alive. You don't deserve to die because of me."

"No, *you* look. I'll handle the distraction. You go right, I'll go left. Jump onto that building over there and shoot down as many Deathlings as you can."

She pulls out a fragment of white marble from her pocket in the vague shape of a crescent moon. I realize it must be her Artifact—I'd completely forgotten about using them, thanks to how utterly useless my own Artifact is.

But there's nothing useless about the Fourth Claw of Fortitude.

Before I can argue, Yuna murmurs to the claw in her palm and hurls it into the street as hard as she can. It bounces a few feet with a clatter. The nearby Deathlings stop nosing at Noëlle's coat and jerk to attention, snapping and growling at each other until they locate the foreign object. For a terrifying moment, nothing happens.

Then the claw springs to life, expanding rapidly into a slab that lengthens into a marble haunch, then swells into a massive mound of white stone, which continues to flourish until a thick, wild mane and majestic features begin to form. Four massive paws slam down, cracking the asphalt underfoot with a tremor that sends the Deathlings scattering. An immense marble lion rears up on its hind legs in the middle of Madison Avenue. Tossing its mane, it releases an explosive roar.

Fortitude, one of the magnificent twin statues guarding the entrance of the New York Public Library.

Although the big cat is hewn from stone, he doesn't seem to notice. He barrels headfirst into the congregation of Deathlings with the fury of a tsunami. Pouncing on the insectoid Deathlings, sinking his fangs deep into them with glee.

The sewer Deathlings ram their heads into Fortitude from all sides, knocking the lion back and forth like a punching bag. Fortitude spits out the beetle monster's leg and roars.

"What are you waiting for?" Yuna's voice erupts in my helmet. I jolt, realizing she's already in position. Amid the chaos, I manage to sprint across the street unnoticed. I lock my middle fingers to my thumbs. At my com-

mand, my exosuit boosters launch me thirty feet into the air. I twist my body midair and draw my guns to let the first bullets fly even before I land on the building closest to the fight. My bullets whiz past a snarling Fortitude and plow through the jaws of a sewer Deathling latched on to his mane. The other beasts reel away, but the earsplitting staccato of my gunfire and the *plink plink* of dropping shells never waver.

Their dying screams are the most beautiful song I've ever heard them sing.

By the time I've emptied both magazines, the ground is littered with Deathling corpses. I'm reloading my second gun when the largest nightfang raises its head. Two poison-black eyes zero in on me. The other three are quick to take notice. My heart hammers as they begin stalking toward me. When Fortitude moves to block their way, the big nightfang strikes, raking its talons across the lion's face. Off comes Fortitude's nose. The others follow suit, demolishing the lion piece by piece. Every time I shoot, they merely duck, using Fortitude's marble torso as a shield.

The lion lashes out at them with a roar. He lunges at the lead nightfang and grapples with it one-on-one underneath the traffic lights. When it tries to bite him, Fortitude bites back. With a heart of literal stone, he's fearless of its fangs. He swipes a paw at the nightfang's face, slashing right through a layer of its sable fur.

The Deathling lets out a howl and recoils.

Fortitude regards the monster, no less regal despite the absence of half his face.

Slowly, the nightfang bends its head in submission. Blood drips from the deep gouge slicing across the left half of its ugly face.

And then it rams its horns into the lion's chest. The marble fractures into a web of cracks.

The rest of the nightfangs descend upon Fortitude. My bullets do little to deter them from their brutal rampage. The lion thrashes desperately as they smash through his legs. Though he fights with the spirit of a thousand warriors, even stone crumbles with time. The next time he attempts to rise, he crashes back to the ground. He mewls mournfully at Yuna. It's the last I see of him before the nightfangs begin stomping all over his remains. When the dust clears, every last trace of the mighty king has been obliterated save for his fourth claw, which rests in a pool of Deathling blood.

The lead Deathling plucks it up between its teeth and scarfs it down.

Satisfied, the quartet of beasts settle themselves upon the curb in a neat row. They stare up at me in sinister silence, like four hideous, bloodthirsty vultures. Without breaking my own stare, I raise my gun and pull the trigger.

Out of nowhere, the centipede Deathling lurches in front of the nightfangs. Its wriggly, rubbery skin ripples outward as it absorbs the bullet's impact. Without hesitation, the creature leaps onto the side of the building I'm standing atop, using its forcipules like climbing picks to scale up to the roof.

It's all I can do to stand my ground as it clambers toward me with a triumphant gleam in its red eyes, like it's already imagining gorging itself upon my flesh. I open fire. It screams in pain as bullets tear through its body. Yet even as lumps of its body *squelch* onto the sidewalk below, it continues to ascend. Its head appears over the edge. I force myself to wait, backing away until it hauls its entire body laboriously onto the roof.

Only when I can see the back of its throat and feel its hot, noxious breath tickling the surface of my exosuit do I finally squeeze the trigger.

The bullet torpedoes directly down its gullet, finding home deep in its stomach. This time, when the bullet explodes, its entire body ruptures, bursting into a million chunks.

The remaining Deathlings are *not* pleased.

They rush at the building all at once, dragging themselves up brick by brick.

I curse, wiping grayish guts off my visor. "Park! Where the hell are you? I could use a little help over here!"

"Just stay focused on killing the lesser Deathlings. I'm counting on you."

"What? What are you—" My eyes widen. Down below, the nightfangs calmly observe the siege, unaware of the figure charging at them through the trees. Yuna brandishes her staff, the sound of her approach lost under the screams of monsters.

She's going to take them head-on.

I falter in horror for the briefest second. In that single heartbeat, one of the nightfangs' noses twitches. Lips curled back in a snarl, it whips around just as Yuna springs into the air.

The end of her staff erupts. Forks of lightning sever the night sky, lassoing the nightfang around the neck in ropes of electricity. It lets out an ungodly screech. The others flinch away from the lightning, ears pressed flat against their skulls. Even from here I can feel the heat of the hatred burning in their black eyes.

"Get out of there!" I holler down at her. I curse again. My hands are full with keeping the other Deathlings at bay. They attack me with fresh fervor, riled by the uproar below, scrambling on top of one another to get closer to the edge of the roof.

Another blast of lightning sunders the darkness. I manage to steal a glimpse of the pandemonium below. To my disbelief, Yuna's still standing. Not only standing, but fighting *four* nightfangs. *Single-handedly.*

She weaves between them like a tongue of flame, slipping through their grasps and striking where it hurts most. She leaps from one nightfang to the next, using their bodies as her personal launchpads, leaving a whirlwind of destruction in her wake. The stats from her file register at the back of my mind—*tae kwon do prodigy*. But however prodigious she may be, something doesn't add up. She treats her staff as an extension of her body, for attacks, for blocks, for righting her balance. Her every movement emanates confidence. She reminds me of the dancers at the Metropolitan ballet, every step limber and light. She flies through her choreography, fighting not with caution but intimacy.

She's done this before, I realize. No wonder she found my assumptions about her experience so amusing.

The scrape of nails yanks me out of my trance. I grit my teeth and turn my attention back to the sewer Deathlings seconds away from reaching the roof. My hand reaches for a new magazine, grazing too many empty pouches.

One Deathling makes it onto the roof. I kick it, but it grabs ahold of my foot. Instead of shaking it off, I hoist my leg higher, lifting it enough to aim my gun under my thigh right between its repulsive jaws. It staggers back at the impact of the bullet—*without letting me go*.

My heel slips on the grime of the rooftop. For a petrifying second I tip over the edge. Cold sweat pours down my back. With a snarl, I plant my boot against the midsection of the monster and press my thumbs and middle fingers together.

My exosuit rockets me backward, ripping me free from the Deathling's grasp. My back slams into a vent, knocking the air out of my lungs. I slide to the ground. Something explodes. Below, the shrill cries of Deathlings cut off with a tremendous, wet *THUD*.

I struggle back to my feet and dare to look over the edge.

A pile of monster corpses lies smoking on the sidewalk. The last bullet I shot must have been faulty—detonating late, yet at the perfect moment.

Another cry pierces the air. Human this time. Only one nightfang remains—the largest one. Head-to-head, Yuna somehow still manages to hold her own. Her strength has waned, but so has the nightfang's. Sluggishly, the beast swipes at her stomach. It's limping. She ducks easily and uses the opening to stab at its face. It barely dodges in time, retreating a few steps and circling her with a wary gaze, but she stays on the offensive, never letting it get too far.

With a growl, she raises her staff over her head to finish it.

I shout in warning as the nightfang bursts forward in a blast of speed. Too late I realize it's been feigning fatigue this entire time, herding her back toward one of the fallen nightfang corpses. My stomach plummets to my toes as she trips and hits the ground hard. She's already scrambling away, trying to get out of range as quickly as she can, only to find herself trapped by the limbs of the enormous corpse.

"*NO!*" I scream.

Yuna's eyes meet mine. They are filled with terror. Her lips move— two whispered syllables, almost too quiet for my helmet to pick up.

"*Find Jae.*"

Down come the nightfang's talons in a flash of silver.

SHHH-KLERUNCH.

Blood spritzes the air. The talons cleave clean through the soft part of her neck, but it's the snap of her bones that echoes louder than a gunshot.

I can't move. I can't breathe.

Her head rolls down the street. It bumps up gently against the curb.

My ears fill with static. The world goes fuzzy around the edges, like a signal too far away. It happened so fast.

The nightfang gives the bloody stump of her neck a sniff. After a moment of consideration, it grabs the stump in its jaws and tosses her corpse to the gutter. *Sploosh*. It lands right beside her severed head, splashing her face in brown filth and Deathling guts.

I rip off my helmet and vomit straight over the edge of the roof.

The nightfang turns its beady eyes upon me. It seems content to lick its wounds and wait now that it's got me backed into a corner.

I give one last heave. A horrible burning fills my chest. It festers through my veins, drowning out every other sensation.

Slowly, I wipe the bile from my mouth and lift my head.

Like wildfire, I let it consume me. Like storm, I let it swathe my bones with the promise of wrath.

I take a deep breath.

And then I step off the edge.

CHAPTER FORTY-TWO

My boots slam into the sidewalk. My heartbeat thuds dully in my ears—the steadfast, unstoppable beat of a war drum to which I march toward the enemy. I trudge over to Yuna's corpse and pry her staff from her fists. It purrs in my fingers, oblivious to the violent end met by its previous master.

All the fear, dread, and panic that flooded my system during the night has vanished. For the first time tonight, my mind truly empties of thought. As if I'm walking through a dream, everything fades away but for the weapon, solid and heavy in my palms, and the cold, seething fury in my heart.

The nightfang lumbers onto its feet. A low growl rumbles from its throat. I bare my teeth and growl right back. It crouches low, readying itself to pounce.

I don't let it. I slam the butt of the spear into the ground. Lightning surges forth. I swing my arm as far back as it goes, my shoulder protesting from the strain, and thrust the end of the rod at the Deathling's ugly snout. The lightning snaps around me like a whip and strikes the monster's flesh with an ear-popping *crack*. My eyes sting from the smoke, but I attack relentlessly, dancing out of range whenever it tries to swipe at me with its talons.

"What's the matter?" I shout, knocking the nightfang into the ground. It collapses onto its side, chest heaving, fighting with none of its earlier vigor. "What are you waiting for? Kill me!"

Again and again I strike it, until its entire body convulses with electricity and crimson-tinged froth spews out of its mouth.

"Did it satisfy you to kill those mavericks?" I scream. "Was it worth it?"

I make the mistake of looking into its spiteful eyes—except something's changed. Between one blink and the next, they remind me of another nightfang's eyes. Uncorrupted by evil. A tinge of . . . remorse, even.

The lightning fizzles out. Torture put on hold, the nightfang whimpers in relief.

And then it screeches as I stab the staff directly into its left eye and jack up the power to the absolute max. I count to ten, gritting my teeth and holding fast to keep it pinned down while it thrashes. I withdraw the blade. Then ram it through its other eye.

Long after its body stops twitching from the aftershocks, I keep the staff jammed into its skull, watching the smoke curling up from its incinerated fur. I can't bring myself to relinquish my grip. After a minute, the handle of the rod turns scalding to the touch. I merely drive it deeper into the nightfang's skull, crunching through cartilage and bone. A second later the shaft glows white hot, the only warning before it cracks straight down the middle, overloaded, erupting in a shower of splinters. Most bounce off the surface of my exosuit, but a few slice my exposed face.

I tug out a splinter embedded in my brow. Blood trickles down into my eye, tinting the world red.

My legs tremble.

The exhaustion doesn't so much creep over me as it body-slams me into the concrete. I stumble down the street and collapse against a bus stop sign.

The silence stretches out for miles. Now that it's all over, this city feels emptier to me than it ever has before.

Luminous white light glosses over the scales of my exosuit. The moon slips past the sliver of sky between two buildings overhead, inching toward the west like a furtive thief. I haven't slept in nearly twenty-four hours. Soon, dawn will . . . well, dawn.

I'm exhausted enough to curl up on the ground right beneath the bus sign and pass out for a thousand years. But morning is still a few hours away, and any number of Deathlings could round the corner at any moment. Meanwhile, I'm out of ammo, I wrecked Yuna's staff, and at this point I doubt I could lift anything heavier than a pebble to defend myself.

Grimly, I pick myself up and plod over to where Yuna lies. I cradle her head in my arms and carry it over to the patch of grass where Noëlle lies.

Afterward, I begin the grueling task of dragging the rest of her corpse across the street. I do my best to arrange the pieces of her in an appropriate manner and wipe the filth off her face.

Later, I loot their coats and uniforms for weapons. I only manage to find a used magazine on Yuna, and somehow Noëlle seems to have lost all her gear on the way here—including her Artifact. I consider sorting through the guts of the nightfang that killed Yuna to try to unearth the Fourth Claw of Fortitude, but there's no guarantee I'll succeed, and the queasy feeling in my gut informs me that I'm probably not up for the task anyway.

Click. I reload my gun with Yuna's magazine. Two measly bullets left. The nearest safehouse is blocks away. Until backup arrives, I'll have to make do.

I sink into the cool grass and prop myself up against the oak tree. My gun rests on my knee. I raise my eyes to the stars. Even before the Vanishing, before the curfew rules, I never saw them like this—a breathtaking expanse of dazzling light, like someone robbed all the diamonds on Earth and flung them straight into the night sky.

"The stars are beautiful tonight," I murmur to my fallen friends. "I wish you could see them."

A twig snaps somewhere in the park. I freeze, my gun already aimed at the darkness.

A young man emerges from behind a tree. Handsome face bloodied, mav coat torn.

My heart pounds against my rib cage. "Kieran?" I whisper hoarsely. The flood of hope and relief nearly overwhelms me to tears. "You're *alive*."

His face breaks into a flustered, awestruck smile. I'm alive, too. He nods, seemingly speechless in disbelief. Slowly, carefully, he begins approaching me, like I'm an injured animal he worries he'll spook off. When he catches sight of the two bodies resting beside me, sorrow flashes across his features. He holds his arms out to me.

I sway onto my feet and melt into Kieran's embrace. His lips brush my neck.

And then, without looking up, I blow a bullet through the side of his head.

He stiffens. His hold on me tightens to iron. Above, I glimpse the lower half of his face replaced by gaping jaws, teeth poised inches away from my jugular. I wriggle free just as the Deathling, reverted to its original form, plummets to the ground, bleating pathetically while the bullet dissolves its insides.

Before the monster's screeches have even fully faded, the sound of footsteps races toward me. I'm ready to shoot in case it's another monster, but then I hear a voice that knocks the wind from my lungs.

"Rei! Rei? Is that you?"

I shake my head, but I can't resist calling back. "Aunt . . . Aunt Minyi?"

A second figure rushes toward me from the other side of the park. I see her face, the worry reflected in her brown eyes, and I break. It can't be another Deathling—they can only replicate voices *or* appearances, not both.

Yet at the last second, before she can reach me, I grit my teeth and find the strength to holler, "Stop right there!"

She hesitates and holds her hands up.

"Sorry. I need . . . I need to know it's actually you. I heard you before I saw you. Say something to me now," I plead, tears welling in my eyes.

I'm so tired.

But when my aunt opens her mouth as if to speak, the shadows a few feet behind her shift, and another Deathling darts into the open. Jaws stretched wide, it launches itself straight for her neck.

BANG.

My final bullet embeds itself in the monster's throat. It screams and dies in a burst of rancid goo.

Aunt Minyi smiles proudly and continues advancing toward me, still unspeaking. My doubt instantly turns to dread.

"No. No, stop there," I exclaim. "Stop, or I'll shoot." I keep my gun pointed at her chest, but somehow the monster calls my bluff.

Once it's clear that I'm out of ammo, her smile widens into a wicked grin gleaming with razor-sharp teeth.

Hysteria seizes me. I shake my head in frantic denial. "How? How did you— I heard your voice. *I heard your voice!*" I yell.

My gaze lands on the corpses of the other two Deathlings I shot. I think of the ambush. A preposterous theory rises to my mind, but I don't even want to consider it as a possibility—since it would mean that for the first time since the origin of Deathlings, they're finally learning how to work together. And nothing that's happened tonight—*nothing*—compares to the sheer terror of that thought. Because if it's true?

Manhattan is well and veritably fucked.

Right before my eyes, Aunt Minyi's neck grows and grows, her skin deteriorating all the way to the bone as the Deathling sheds its disguise at last. Hungrily, it fixates on Noëlle and Yuna—easy prey that won't fight back.

"Don't even think about it," I hiss, but my arms are shaking. My hand claws at my bandolier, searching for any ammo I might have missed, then moves to the coat pockets I already know are empty. I have nothing to kill the Deathling with. I should have brought a staff, just in case. Now I'm screwed—

My fingers close around a tiny metal object, about the size of a dime. Recognition flickers through me. I pull out the old subway token.

My Artifact.

"Please," I whisper, pressing the token to my chest. "I still don't know what you do, but please do *something*."

The grass rustles. My eyes fly open as the Deathling charges, maw wide and teeth gleaming. I throw my arms out to the sides in a meaningless attempt to shield Noëlle's and Yuna's bodies.

My final act: to protect them.

Something in my chest throbs.

A scorching heat pulses through me, surging down my arms and legs to the tips of my fingers and toes.

A dome of gold light rippling with heat explodes forth, incinerating the Deathling in one fell swoop. The nearby trees buckle sideways from the force of the blast. Branches wither. Leaves crumble to dust.

The gold light pulsates outward and fades with a soft sigh.

In the aftermath of the explosion, my skin burns feverishly hot. I sway for a moment before my knees buckle and I crash to the ground. The Token ricochets out of my grasp, rolling through the grass. I don't see where it stops.

My head lolls against Noëlle's calf. Just as my vision blackens, I discern three shadowy silhouettes hovering over me. A badge glimmers on the chest of the one in the middle—a central gold star surrounded by ten smaller stars. Their mouths move, but their voices sound fuzzy, submerged underwater.

That's her? asks the first.

It would seem so, the one in the middle replies. A flicker of vague familiarity registers deep within the murk of my thoughts.

She's just a single girl, says the third dubiously. *Could she really be the key?*

Desperately, I cling to my consciousness. *Key to what?* I want to ask. But it's a losing fight. And after a night full of those, I have nothing left to give. So at long last, I surrender to the darkness.

CHAPTER FORTY-THREE

I didn't always believe that Deathlings deserved to die.

The winter break after I turned twelve, I read a book I just couldn't put down. Even when night fell, I simply opened the window, my eyes still glued to the pages, and stuck a glass jar outside to gather just enough glowing stardust to see by.

Tofu hopped onto the bed beside me, nuzzling sweetly into the crook of my arm before curling up for a nap.

Hours later, I startled awake to the shrill sound of barking. I peeled the half-finished book off my face and squinted into the gloom. "Tofu?"

My dog faced the window, his teeth bared in a vicious snarl like I'd never seen before. He must have smelled it first.

The reek of sewage.

Slowly, I lifted my eyes to the window itself.

The window I'd forgotten to close.

There was a Deathling trying to squeeze through the gap.

I lunged for the sash, slamming it down on the Deathling's wrinkled claws over and over again until it retreated. Panting hard, I locked the window and yanked the blinds shut. I snatched a sealed tin of coffee beans and scattered them around the window with trembling fingers. How could I have been so careless?

I hugged Tofu, burying my face in his soft fur until I stopped shaking. He licked my face and whimpered at me, his big round eyes full of concern. People said that dogs didn't understand emotions like humans, but sometimes I felt like Tofu understood me better than most humans I'd met.

Ten minutes later, I stood in front of Aunt Minyi's bedroom, staring awkwardly at her door. Tofu paced around me protectively, growling at every shadow. Although it was the dead of nightfall, she would have to get up in less than an hour for her shift. I cast a furtive glance out the kitchen windows across the apartment, but nothing disturbed the stardust save for the wind.

I decided to let it go.

A week later, I jolted upright in bed to a *crash* and the sound of growling. A framed picture of me and Maura lay facedown on the ground, the glass shattered. I staggered out of bed, struggling to catch Tofu as he ran rampant through my room. I knocked over a floor lamp and stubbed my toe on the edge of my bookshelf, painfully clumsy in the dark. I finally managed to grab him by the collar, but he strained against my grip, his whole body aimed like an arrow at the window.

Or rather, what waited beyond it.

I stared at the curtains blocking my view, my limbs stiff with fear for what I couldn't see beyond.

Tofu snarled.

I pointed at him and whispered firmly, "Stay, boy."

He swiveled his head at me, as if to say, *You've got to be kidding me right now.*

I gave him a stern look and released his collar. He let out a soft whine but grudgingly sat back on his haunches. I fetched the lamp on the floor. Gripping it upside down like a baseball bat, I crept toward the window.

With one hand, I whipped the curtains aside.

Four soulless black eyes stared through the glass less than an inch away from my face.

Except it wasn't me that they were fixated on—but my dog.

Tofu growled again, his floppy little ears pinned back. In response, the Deathling unhinged its jaws and produced a most peculiar sound from its throat.

It almost sounded like . . . a bark.

In the window's reflection, I saw Tofu freeze.

And then he lost his shit.

He leapt onto the windowsill, clawing at the panes, snapping his teeth at the monster, and foaming at the mouth. The Deathling darted off. I desperately tried to shush his piercing howls.

Too late—I heard Aunt Minyi's door bang open.

By the time my aunt burst into my room, I was cradling Tofu on the floor, stroking his fur and holding him down at the same time. Thankfully, he'd stopped barking, but his entire body still vibrated like an overheating engine.

"What's going on?" Aunt Minyi demanded, aiming her N.N. gun into the dark. Her eyes scanned the room for threats, sharp and alert as ever despite having been woken up seconds before.

I merely pointed out the window. "We had a visitor. It didn't get inside, though."

Tofu snarled again.

Aunt Minyi exhaled and lowered her gun. She approached the window and craned her neck to check outside. "They've been getting restless, these days." Drawing the curtains closed, she strode over and gave Tofu a scratch behind the ears. "I'll have someone install some reinforcement bars in the morning."

I ran my fingers through Tofu's soft fur. "Auntie?"

"Yes?"

"Do you think that Deathlings can make friends?"

She blinked at me for a second before letting out a laugh. She patted my head. "Of course not, my dear. They aren't like humans, or even animals for that matter. They're monstrosities."

I didn't respond. But long after she'd left, I thought of the Deathling trying to bark. And deep down, I couldn't help but think that monstrosities got lonely sometimes, too.

CHAPTER FORTY-FOUR

I gasp awake to the earsplitting screech of an alarm. I struggle upright, my body aching in places I didn't know could hurt. A threadbare blanket more like a sheet covers me. At first, I think I'm in the Sanctuary. But before I can swing out of bed, something clinks. I whip off the sheet, perplexed, and stare at the shackles locking my ankles to the rails.

Gooseflesh prickles my bare skin. My exosuit and mav coat are nowhere to be found. I'm naked but for a scratchy hospital gown. My hand shoots to my neck, groping frantically. I exhale in shaky relief as my fingers close around Mom's necklace. I could never forgive myself if I lost it.

The Token, on the other hand . . . vaguely, I recall it slipping out of my hand, disappearing into the grass. That burst of gold light, the searing heat. *It* must have caused that. If only I knew how.

My eyes dart around the tiny, dark cell, drinking in the low ceiling, the stark walls, and the spread of surgical tools gleaming on the cart beside the bed. On the opposite side of the cell stands a steel door. I can't tell whether it's designed to keep me in—or keep whatever might be waiting on the other side *out*.

I examine the lock on the cuffs fastened to my ankles. Whoever made the decision to leave my hands unbound should be fired immediately, but to me they're a goddamn saint. I scoot to the edge of the bed as far as the shackles will allow. Using the shackles as an anchor, I stretch sideways, half of my body suspended precariously over empty air. Fingertips straining, I just barely manage to brush the edge of the surgical cart. It rolls forward a millimeter. I tease it closer. I select my tools, simultaneously suppressing a shudder at the row of scalpels yet grateful for the variety, and set myself upon the task of tackling the locks.

The alarm screeches on. After the first few minutes, my head pounds from the sheer intensity of its ringing, like a jackhammer pulverizing the inside of my skull. But I have to focus. Someone could come through that door at any second. Brow furrowed in equal parts concentration and frustration, I feel a stab of relief when there's a satisfying *click*.

The other lock takes even longer than the first, and by the time I hear the second *click* and the shackles fall away, I'm at least reassured that whoever that atrocious alarm is for, it's not me.

The brutal chill of the rough stone floor stings my bare feet as I stagger toward the door. Weirdly enough, I detect faint outlines of spray paint on the walls. Evidently, someone did their best to scrub them within an inch of their life, but the unmistakable traces of graffiti still persist.

Where the hell am I?

To my dismay, there doesn't seem to be any way to open the door from the inside, which means I'll have to wait for someone to come in. I paste my back to the wall beside the door and arm myself, tucking one scalpel between each knuckle so that the blades point outward like nightfang talons.

My thoughts race while I wait. How long have I been unconscious? Who brought me here? Where are Yuna's and Noëlle's bodies? Is Kieran still alive? My gaze lingers on the scalpels. Why were they planning to cut into me? I try to remember the moments before I passed out, but they've already sunk into the muddy depths of my memories, growing hazier the harder I try to dredge them up.

The only thing I can recall is the familiarity of one of the voices that spoke before I blacked out.

A series of *beep*s on the other side of the wall jolts me to attention. I tighten my grip on the scalpels, poised to attack.

The steel entry grinds open. In slips a woman wearing a torn but familiar crimson sleeping robe, her black hair thrown into a hasty bun. I watch as she awkwardly kicks off an ill-fitting boot and wedges it into the door right before it grinds back shut.

Pivoting on her grimy, bare foot, she glances at the empty bed, then turns her stare directly at me. Her face is smudged with blood, but nothing about her hardened expression reveals any hint of whatever turmoil she might be facing inside.

My head spins with the rush of hope—and fear. But I can't take the risk.

I lunge at her with a guttural roar, slashing the scalpels straight at her throat. She reels back and grabs my wrist. With a hard upward twist, she wraps her own body around mine and drives her fingers into my shoulder. I let out a cry as my right hand goes completely numb. The scalpels clatter to the ground. I rip myself out of her grip, ignoring the scream of pain in my shoulder, and thrust the remaining scalpels into her stomach. At the last millisecond she manages to pivot a few inches to the side. The blades shred her robe into ribbons. Blood blossoms across the silk, but the pain doesn't even register on her face.

"Rei! Stop it!" Aunt Minyi exclaims. "It's me!"

"What do you want?" I sob. "Please . . . just—just stop stealing her face."

"Look at me," she implores. "Just look at me, Rei. It's me, I swear."

I shake my head. "I heard you speaking before, too, when you were a Deathling."

She pulls me into her arms and hugs me so tightly that my spine pops. "I'm sorry," she murmurs. "I don't know what happened to you, but I'm so sorry. I should have been there for you."

I draw back and force myself to stare at the woman who everyone—including me—feared to be dead. "If it's really you, tell me something that only you could know."

She doesn't hesitate. "On the fourth Mother's Day after I adopted you, you made me a charm bracelet with a little ramen bowl, a black cat, and a trophy with a #1."

My neck flushes. "You remember that?"

"Remember it? My dear, it's one of the most precious gifts I've ever received." She releases me. "Now, I know you must have a thousand questions, but I'm afraid they'll have to wait. I promise I'll answer every single one of them as soon as we make it out of here safely. But we have to hurry."

I can't help it. "So you really got kidnapped?"

"As did all the other masters." She reaches into her pocket and produces two keys. "Now you and I are going to get them out."

"I don't understand. At least tell me who kidnapped us," I insist. "Who we're up against."

My aunt pauses to consider her response. Finally, she says, "Individuals capable of both tremendous harm and good—one of whom gave me these."

Bile rises in my throat as she produces a plastic Ziploc filled with fluid. A pair of severed thumbs and eyeballs float within. She removes one of each, tucks them into her pocket, and hands me the Ziploc.

"You'll need them for the biometric scanners," she says grimly. She slips off her remaining boot. "Put this on. Take the other one out of the door when we leave."

"What about you?" I ask, lacing them up.

"I'll find myself another pair." She explains the rest of the plan to me. It's only at the end, when I catch her rubbing her wedding ring, that I realize just how well she's been concealing her nerves from me. In the last few days, it seems she's rubbed the ring so relentlessly that the skin around it is red and raw.

"So I can trust you to handle the cells down that left hallway while I handle the ones to the right?" asks my aunt. When I give her a firm nod, she takes my hand in her own. I'm astonished to discover tears gleaming in her eyes. "Rei, one more thing. It's been a privilege to have witnessed you grow into the strong, intelligent, brave young woman I've always known you to be. Your mom would be so, so very proud of you. I know I am."

I blink back my own tears and force down the lump in my throat. "I'm just lucky I had such an amazing role model to look up to."

Her smile fades. She pulls me into one last hug, hiding her face. I feel her take a deep breath against me and trap it in her chest. By the time she exhales and releases me, her expression has smoothed over completely. Mask back on, she nods. "Let's go."

We squeeze through the crack in the door and slink into the open. I tug out the boot blocking the door and lace it on as quickly as I can.

Outside my cell sprawls a series of narrow, dimly lit passageways. The bulbs overhead flash red in sync with the pulsing shrieks of the alarm, casting bloody silhouettes across the ground.

I keep my ears partly covered as we bolt down the hall. Unfortunately, the hospital gown doesn't come with pockets, so I have to carry my "keys" by hand. We pass a handful of passageways leading into the darkness, all equally deserted. Unsettled, I wait for the thunder of boots, shouted orders, the click of loading weapons—but nothing comes.

"Did you trip the alarm?" I ask.

"From what I can tell, the alarms get tripped more often than not. There seem to be a lot of catastrophes, but not enough people to deal with them. None of us have gotten a wink of sleep since we got here, except for Sasha. He sounds like a grizzly bear when he snores."

"Master Sasha?" I exclaim. "He's alive?"

The corner of her mouth twitches upward. "Of course. He'll be happy to see you, I'm sure."

We arrive at the fork where the passageway splits in two different directions. Aunt Minyi says, "I'll meet you at the exit as soon as I free the masters in this corridor. Remember what I told you—"

"Get them out, then run. They can take care of themselves."

"And?"

"And if you don't make it, I can't wait for you."

"Promise me, Rei."

"I promise."

She takes my face in her hands and touches her forehead to mine. We both freeze when the horrible alarm cuts off abruptly. Somehow, the silence it leaves in its wake is almost worse.

"Go," Aunt Minyi says firmly, releasing me.

"Wait," I blurt. "Promise me you won't get mad at me for asking this."

"No."

Great start. "You know about the Artifact that went missing?"

"Yes?"

"Do you have it?"

The way Aunt Minyi stares at me makes me instantly regret every life decision that has led me to this moment. "Why on earth would *I* have it?" When I fail to respond, she shoots me a glare. *"Go."*

I don't waste another second. Cursing Master Sasha in my head, I sprint away, the boots rubbing painfully against my bare ankles.

So. He was wrong.

For whatever reason, it doesn't bring me the sense of relief I was anticipating.

The first person I come across doesn't even see me coming. He rounds the corner, wearing a white lab coat with a clipboard in hand. I full-body tackle him to the ground. The clipboard rattles against the floor. I seize his throat with one hand, muffling his shouts. He thrashes underneath my weight, his eyes wide in panic. I tamp down my sympathy as he gags and wheezes. I should have knocked him out with a punch instead of this slow suffocation.

Earlier, Aunt Minyi warned me that I'd need to incapacitate anyone I ran into, yet I still wasn't prepared. I've been trained to hunt Deathlings. Not humans.

"I'm sorry," I tell him right before his body goes limp. I glance around for some convenient supply closet to drag him into, but no such luck. An idea strikes me. I wrestle him out of his lab coat and button it over my flimsy hospital gown. I move the eyeball and thumb bag Aunt Minyi gave me into the chest pocket. In the side pockets I find some markers, a timer, and a handful of zip ties.

His belt catches my eye, previously hidden by the lab coat. There's a holster clipped on to it. I flip it open and hold up the heaviest taser I've held in my life. The kind with multiple cartridges and enough voltage to kill a person.

What kind of scientist carries that kind of taser to work? Or any taser, for that matter?

Suddenly, a loud roar of pain nearly expels my soul from my body, echoing down the passageway like a train hurtling by. I poke my head around the corner from which the man appeared and spot a steel door identical to my cell door halfway down the hall. Unfortunately, I don't have the time to investigate, but I can't resist picking up the clipboard lying beside the man's head.

Scanning the mess of illegible handwritten notes and senseless data points, I flip through the pages, searching for anything coherent. I freeze on the final page. Attached to it is a single photo of a scowling young man, labeled SUBJECT XIX. At first, I'm certain I'm hallucinating. But there's no mistaking it.

"Tim?" I breathe. I flip over the page, searching for more notes, for an explanation, but the backside is blank. Unless Kieran's ex-teammate found himself a doppelgänger, it can't be anyone but him. Besides his scowl, he looks haggard but otherwise normal . . . except for one thing.

His eyes.

Wholly black from bottom rim to top lid, as though his pupils expanded to fill the entirety of his eyeballs.

I've seen eyes like these before—the woman from the Syndicate who came to scout our final combat education class. The one who wore sunglasses even when she was inside, with the bionic leg and the impeccable fashion taste.

On the ground, the man stirs. Panicking, I swing the clipboard as hard as I can and whack him across the head. He slumps back into unconsciousness.

I rip the final page with Tim's photo from the clipboard and stuff it into my pocket. Then I zip-tie the man's wrists and ankles and bolt off. Anyone could find him at any moment and sound the alarm, but there's not much I can do about it except run faster.

As I head for the cells, the photo of Tim won't stop plaguing me.

What did they do to him? How did he end up as some subject on a clipboard? Was he kidnapped as well? Could he be here now, somewhere in this creepy labyrinth of a base? I shudder, thinking about the cart of scalpels and hooks and forceps I woke up next to. If Aunt Minyi hadn't helped me escape, could it have been my dead-eyed photo tacked to a clipboard next?

That roar I heard earlier . . . I'd thought it belonged to a nightfang.

But now I'm not so sure.

CHAPTER FORTY-FIVE

I creep toward the end of the hallway and peer around the corner. Two guards. Both wear dark, mismatched uniforms. One leans against the wall, and the other straddles a chair flipped backward.

I burst into the open. "Put your hands in the air!" I shout, pointing the taser between the two of them. In his haste to get out of the chair, the second guard accidentally tips himself over.

The other guard, however, withdraws a wicked knife from her belt. "Who the hell are you?"

"I said put your—"

"Shut up," she snarls, leaping at me.

I swerve out of the way and yank up the guard on the ground by the scruff of his neck. He lets out a whimper as I dig the taser into his ribs. "Drop the knife," I tell the girl. "Or I'll tase him."

She grins. "Go for it. Pain builds character. He could use some of both."

I grit my teeth. Neither of them look older than Cassie. "Stay down or I'll make you regret it," I hiss into his ear. Without waiting for a reply, I shove him into the wall.

I whirl and dodge just in time for the girl's blade to slash the air inches away from my neck. Her knife slices through empty air again and again. She's a vicious fighter, but an amateur. Her movements are graceless. Every miss makes her angrier, and the more pissed she gets, the more desperate she grows.

The next time she tries to stab me, I twist the knife aside by the hilt and knock it straight out of her hand. She lets out a primal cry and launches herself at me. Nails scrape my face, just shy of my eyeballs. I hiss through my teeth. Instead of evading her, I drop my chin to my chest and grab her behind the neck, jerking her skull against mine. She topples to the ground, headbutted into oblivion.

"That's *my* champion," I hear a voice declare.

I turn around and face the cell behind me. Through the narrow grate, I meet a familiar blue gaze. "Master Sasha!"

Somehow, I manage to fish out the thumb and eyeball with only the slightest cringe. I try not to look at them as I hold them to the scanners. As soon as each cell unlocks, the doors open and the masters file out.

I move to zip-tie the two guards, but a tall woman touches my elbow with a smile. "I'll handle it from here, Miss Reynolds."

"Master Aaliyah," I stammer. I'm so starstruck that I almost forget how to speak, let alone look her in the eye without spontaneously combusting.

With her dark, striking eyes and her navy hijab, adorned with a pearl brooch, sweeping over her shoulder like a cascade of water, the Master of the Lower East Side looks even more regal in real life. Like the Phantom, she is one of the rare strikers with a signature Artifact: the Oyster. It can turn anything and anyone it touches besides its mistress to nacre—the hard, iridescent composite found on the inside of its shells. No one could get it to cooperate before Master Aaliyah, but after she presented the

Museum of Modern Art a sculpture collection of one hundred solidified Deathlings, she became henceforth known as the Mother of Pearl.

Her attention makes me flush all the way from my neck to the tips of my ears. The euphoria is dizzying. Master Eliza, who I met at breakfast before the first task of the Tournament, shoots me a wink. Master Jagdeep of Chelsea salutes me on his way by. I tell myself to play it cool—in truth, it's all I can do to keep from fainting or floating off into the ether.

It's only when Master Sasha's broad hands squeeze my shoulders that my soul returns to my body. "I knew you could do it," he tells me in a low voice as the other masters shepherd us down the passageway. "You will go down in history as the one who saved all."

"Master Minyi deserves the credit."

Master Sasha shakes his head impatiently. "I meant missing Artifact." When my face goes blank, his expression darkens. "Miss Reynolds. I heard guards babbling about what happened before you were captured. There was great burst of golden light, like bomb going off, that ravaged Deathling attacking you. You stole Artifact from Minyi's office, just as I instructed you."

I avert my gaze. "I didn't."

Master Sasha stares at me, all traces of his earlier pride gone. "Impossible. You must have been using missing Artifact. *You must have.*"

His rising anger captures the notice of the other masters. I shrink beneath the intensity of their attention. "I—I'm sorry. All I had was the Token, but—"

His mouth thins. "I shouldn't have put my faith in you. We could have ended all Deathlings today. *Ended* them. Do you understand?" He signals to the other masters and starts jogging off.

I scramble to keep up. "You were asking me to betray my own family! And my aunt would never just leave some object capable of mass destruction inside of her office, locked up or not."

His voice goes terrifyingly soft, barely audible over the thud of our boots. "And how can you be so sure?"

We round a corner. The walls slope inward, growing narrower and narrower until we have to run in a single file. "I asked her. Just now."

Master Sasha laughs. A slow, stone-cold laugh, hard and flat as a mortuary slab.

I clench my jaw to smother my irritation. "Was it something I said?"

"I was like you, once. Thoughtlessly loyal, never questioning the truths I was given. I worked for government back in my home country. My wife warned me of their ways, but it took seeing her mangled body parts strung up alongside my two sons like meats hung out to dry for me to finally wake up."

The air in the passageway takes on a sudden, deathly chill.

Master Sasha sees the look on my face and smiles without humor. "Never talked about that part in my autobiographies, did I?"

BOOOM!

I stagger forward, throwing my arms outward for balance as a thunderous explosion quakes the passageway. Up ahead, something clatters across the floor, too dark to discern. A hiss fills the air. Opaque purple smoke pours into the tunnel.

"Retreat!" yells Master Aaliyah, pulling the corner of her shirt over her face to protect her nose and mouth. But as we turn back, a hidden steel door rumbles out of the wall and seals the passageway shut, trapping us like rats in a maze.

While the other masters search for an alternative route, Master Sasha grabs me by the wrist. "You stay out of sight. Let the masters do the fighting. At very first opportunity, slip through the smoke and escape. If you can make it to the Manor, we still have chance to save this city."

I yank myself free. "I'm fighting with all of you. I'm a maverick now. I don't leave anyone behind."

"You forget who we are. *We* are not mavericks. We are the Masters of Manhattan. It is our duty to rise above rest. To fight, and to *win*. But we cannot guarantee your safety if you stay. So give us your trust. And also, that taser gun, since apparently you don't know how to use it."

"My job description is slaying Deathlings," I mutter, handing it to him. "I won't add humans to that list."

Through the din rises a guttural growling—and above it, the faint *click-clack* of stilettos.

Master Sasha flicks off the safety and exchanges a signal with the other three masters. "We'll see about that."

Before I can react, two snarling nightfangs surge out of the smoke. Master Sasha sweeps me behind him and punches the first in the face with his bare fist. He pulls the trigger on the second. Like spider silk, gossamer threads tipped with little nodes shoot out of the barrel and clamp on to the nightfang's body. It convulses violently and plummets to the floor, unmoving.

Clatters echo up and down the passageway. A metal canister bounces against my foot. Purple smoke gushes into the air. I cry out, my eyes burning, and jerk the collar of the lab coat over my nose and mouth. Lost in the chaos, I search for Master Sasha, but in seconds the smoke has transformed the world into a nightmare. My head throbs with the sound of my own frantic heartbeat, almost drowning out the impact of bodies hitting stone, the furious howls of both monsters and humans alike, a never-ending soundtrack of violence.

A hand shoots out of the purple haze and grabs my elbow. I'm about to twist away when a familiar voice swims out of the smoke. "This way," Master Sasha urges me. He drags me along with his head turned in the other direction. The knot of fear in my stomach loosens.

I stumble after him. The smoke plays tricks on my eyes as we race past shapes and shadows swirling behind the curtain of purple, twisting and warping like phantoms. Silhouettes of dark and light envelop me only to dissipate into thin air when passed through. Everything is a mirage but the solid grip around my wrist.

As Master Sasha leads me farther down the passageway, the clashes of battle fade away. Miraculously, we don't run into a single Deathling.

As the smoke thins, I pry off his grip with shaking hands. "I thought this was a base run by humans. Where the hell did those Deathlings come from?"

Master Sasha keeps walking. "Wrong question."

"You promised that you told me everything you knew, but you *lied*. You're hiding something from me. Something big. Something that will change everything. Who runs this base?"

"The only people in this city powerful enough to."

"The Syndicate would never work with"—I bite my cheek hard enough to draw blood and spit it at his feet—"*Deathlings*."

"Why not?"

"Because they're monsters! Even wild animals can be tamed, but Deathlings are uncontrollable. All they want is to devour people. They're the *furthest* thing from human. And nothing will ever change that."

Slowly, Master Sasha turns and approaches me, tilting his face to cast his features in total shadow. I freeze as he leans in close to whisper, "Are you sure about that?"

A startled cry escapes me as his hand locks around my throat and lifts my feet straight off the ground. For the first time, I actually meet his gaze and realize that his eyes are no longer piercing blue.

They are entirely engulfed in black.

With a ruthless smile, Master Sasha raises his other hand for me to see. My heart stutters as it begins to spasm. The tips of his fingers split open like a snake shedding its skin, peeling outward to make way for a set of wickedly sharp talons.

Nightfang talons.

I gasp for air, my legs dangling, clawing frantically against his inhumanly strong hold.

"You know," Master Sasha begins, his thick accent shifting into something more clipped, more local. He continues in this new, disjointed voice—a voice I recognize, but for all the wrong reasons. "I wasn't sure about this whole *Forsaken* thing at first." His lips stretch into a cruel grin. "But getting to kill *you* might be worth it."

Five talons whistle through the air, aimed straight for my chest. I jerk my face away, bracing for the pain.

Instead, another force collides into my body. I'm ripped free of the hand locked around my throat at the last second and sent crashing to the ground. My left shoulder takes the impact with an ominous *crack*. Pain explodes down my arm. Clutching it to my chest, I look up just in time to see Master Sasha deliver a jaw-shattering punch at . . .

Master Sasha?

Maybe I'm already dead, or delusional from the shock. My brain can't comprehend the sight of not one but *two* Master Sashas before me, identical in every way except for their eyes. And of course, the nightfang talons extending from the hand of the one that just tried to stab me.

"Rei!" bellows the blue-eyed Master Sasha. He thrusts his finger down the passageway while fighting off his impersonator at the same time. "Exit is that way! Get to the Ma—"

I scream as the impersonator plunges his talons into Master Sasha's stomach. They skewer right through his belly and out the back. Blood splatters wetly on the floor. A horrible, keening groan quivers from the true Master Sasha's lips.

Even as the Master of the Financial District dies, he manages to meet my eyes and gurgle out his final words.

"*Rise*, Rei."

My vision blurs. Somehow, as if possessed, my body finds the strength to move. My broken shoulder throbs and burns hot as the devil's fire, but I scream through my clenched teeth and haul myself upright. I have no weapons. All I know is that the impersonator stands between me and the exit, and I have to figure out a way to make it past him.

"Get out of my way," I growl with much more ferocity than I possess.

"Or what?" the impersonator jeers, readopting Master Sasha's accent just to taunt me. As he advances, he keeps his talons impaled in the true Master Sasha's body, dragging him upside down across the floor like a sack of dirt.

A flicker of movement catches my attention. The true Master Sasha lifts one limp, trembling arm. In his hand, the taser gun. He sends me a final nod.

Rise, *Rei.*

He pulls the trigger.

Electricity floods both of their bodies. I can do nothing but watch as their twin faces twist in soundless, grotesque agony. But even once Master Sasha has gone still and white, the impersonator's face *continues* to twist and contort. Until it begins to morph into another face entirely.

Just like in his headshot, Tim the Brute's eyes are wholly black. He bares his teeth at me and tries to grab me as I dart past him. The electric shock renders his limbs useless, but his talons strain for me. I duck. Pain slashes my cheek. I keep running.

Tim's momentum causes him to tip forward. Unable to catch himself, he smashes into the ground face-first with a resounding *thud*, where he lies twitching pathetically, slowly reverting to his human form.

Right before I make it to the exit, I cast a final glance over my shoulder. He raises one fist like a salute—and then extends his middle finger straight toward me.

✳

Somehow, I make it up the stairs leading out of the depths of that hellscape. I emerge into the sunshine and fall to my knees on the concrete.

A van idles at the curb. Its doors burst open. There's a flurry of commotion. Frantic voices. Strong, capable hands laying me down in the back seat, buckling me in. Holding me steady. The squeal of tires on pavement. The brush of a kiss on my brow.

Through the window, the shadows of Manhattan passing over my face. Then darkness.

CHAPTER FORTY-SIX

G hosts come and go from my bedside. Each whisper penetrates my skull like a power drill. There can't be anything left in my stomach, yet I can't rid myself of the urge to vomit. I feel the prickle of every individual fiber of the cool cloth draped over my forehead. I am too sensitive for this world.

Hours pass. Seconds. Years. I am caught in limbo, not quite conscious, not quite dead.

A hand caresses my hair, warm and featherlight as a sunbeam. The ghost of my sister kisses my forehead. I scream, begging her to stay, to not leave me, but all that comes out of my throat is a papery croak.

The next time I wake, I peel my eyes open to find myself lying alone in the dark. The taste in my mouth is appalling. But the pain has faded—physically, that is.

The pillow rustles beneath my head as I turn to the side. Half a dozen flower bouquets have been arranged on my bedside table. A huge squishy plush of a bubble tea with anime eyes and a sweet smile sits on my duvet, no doubt a gift from Zaza.

"Mother*truuuuuucker*," I groan at the ceiling. I'm in my room at the Manor. I reach up to rub my face, but something holds my hand down. With enormous difficulty, I crane my neck and squint into the darkness. A lump slouches on the edge of my bed: a head, a body, and two arms, one of which is propped up on the bed, the fingers at the end interlaced with my own. Their grip only tightens when I try to extract my hand.

I grab the bubble tea plush and hurl it at the lump as hard as I can. It bounces off. The lump shifts. Blinks awake.

"Rei," Kieran murmurs. He clears his throat and untangles his hand from mine. "How are you feeling?"

"Where the hell have you been?" I demand.

"Me?" Disbelief flashes across his face, followed by outrage. "Where the hell have *you* been?" he snarls.

Uh-oh.

"Valentine and I got held back by a swarm of Deathlings. By the time we arrived, all we could find were . . . Noëlle's and Yuna's remains. There was no sign of you. Then out of the blue we get some anonymous call to wait outside some random address, and you stumble out of one of the abandoned subway stations covered in blood and guts like you'd climbed fresh out of a grave. You wouldn't answer any of our questions. You wouldn't speak."

My voice is helplessly small. "I'm sorry."

The pent-up rage straining his expression drains away. "God, no. That's not how I meant it, Rei. I was just so scared. That you were dead, like the others. Whatever happened, we're all just grateful that you came back to us. Zaza, Declan, your sister, the other masters—"

My heart leaps. "They made it out? All of them? Besides—" My voice catches. "Besides Master Sasha, I mean."

He hesitates. "And Master Minyi. We kept another van waiting around until nightfall, but no one else showed up. We don't know if she's—we can't confirm anything. Did you see her?"

My voice comes out in a bare whisper. "She helped us escape." I shut my eyes, trying to recall the details. The alarm had never gone off again, and I hadn't noticed any surveillance cameras. How had we gotten cornered so quickly?

Unless it had all been a trap from the very start.

I shoot straight up. "The Token! I dropped it in the grass at the park. Did anyone find it?"

"Valentine sent a team to comb the area after we found the bodies. I heard they found the Fourth Claw, but they didn't say anything about your Artifact."

"Could you ask them? Or send someone to double-check?"

"Sure, but why? Isn't that thing useless until we figure out how to trigger it?" His eyebrows lift. "Unless you did."

"Not exactly," I admit. "It did *something*, though." More than something. It saved me from a nightfang's jaws. It saved me from death. What other Artifact has that kind of power?

"Do you remember seeing anyone else besides the masters and those guards before you escaped?"

My mind jumps to Tim. I can't shake off the image of his face half-morphing between Master Sasha's and his own.

You're hiding something from me. Something big. Something that will change everything.

I thought I'd said those words to the true Master Sasha, but it had been Tim all along. Grief stabs my heart. If the true Master Sasha hadn't shown up at the last second, I never would have guessed it was someone else disguised as him. I would have died believing he was a traitor. Yet in the end he sacrificed his own life to save mine.

Except I'm still missing the most important piece of the puzzle—how could a *human* harness Deathling powers, like shapeshifting?

Instead of responding, I heave myself from the bed, dragging the duvet with me, and trudge out of the room.

"Hello?" Kieran calls after me indignantly. "Where do you think you're going?"

I ignore him, trusting that he'll follow. I drape the duvet around my shoulders like a cloak and huddle into its warmth as I pad down the hallway and stop in front of Aunt Minyi's door. I try the knob. It's unlocked. I nudge my way inside, wincing hard against the bright midday sun streaming through her windows.

"How long was I out?" I ask as I cross the threshold and weave behind the desk.

Kieran appears in the doorway. Now that I can see him properly, I can officially attest that he looks like absolute shit. Dark bags underneath his bloodshot eyes, greasy hair . . . Then again, I probably look worse.

"Almost thirty hours," he replies. "The doctor said you snapped your collarbone in half. He drugged you up pretty hard to dull the pain. It was a while until nightfall when we could collect stardust to heal you up. God, look at them."

I glance up from Aunt Minyi's computer, fingers poised over the keyboard. "What?"

He gazes out the window, observing the bright little dots marching up and down the streets below. "Going about their days as if everything is completely normal."

"How inconsiderate."

"Do you ever wish you could be like them?" His face scrunches up. "Like . . . normal?"

"This *is* our normal, Kieran."

"Amen to that. Need the password?"

Grudgingly, I make way for him as he leans down and types in an unnervingly long and random combination of letters and numbers. "That's her password now?"

"Thanks to you, yes. Apparently she just opened up a blank document, grabbed a book from the shelf, smashed it on the keyboard, and then copied it all down. Don't you dare try to hack into her account again, I just finished memorizing it."

I merely smirk.

Kieran peers over my shoulder, close enough for my cheek to brush his jaw. "What are you hoping to find?"

I type in a name and hit enter. "Something good."

"*Storm, Sabrina,*" Kieran reads aloud. "*Ex-hellbringer.* That name sounds familiar."

"I've heard rumors about them," I say, thinking of hushed conversations I'd eavesdropped from my aunt. "They were some kind of undercover elite task force run by the Directors, but they got disbanded a few years ago. Something about an experiment gone wrong." I click on Agent Storm's file, but instead of opening, a box pops up on the screen asking for another password. "Classified," I mutter. "Maybe only masters have clearance. Try Aunt Minyi's log-in password again."

Kieran obliges. When he hits enter, the computer lets out an angry buzz. The box flashes. INCORRECT PASSWORD. 2 ATTEMPTS LEFT.

"You sure you're typing in that password correctly?" I ask.

"No," Kieran admits. "Let me try again."

He hits enter.

Bzzt. One attempt left.

His brow furrows. "Why would her entire file be classified from a master? They've got the second-highest clearance level after the Directors."

"Maybe there's something in it that the Directors don't want anyone to find out," I reply, searching my pockets. "Have you seen my phone?"

"Yeah, I plugged it in for you in your bedroom. I'll go and grab it."

While he's gone, I tap my fingers on my chin in thought. Exiting out of Agent Storm's file, I type in *Kieran Cross*. Mostly out of curiosity—so I'm all the more shocked when another access request box pops up. Why would *his* file be classified? He's just a recently graduated high school student, not a high-level striker like Storm. Is the system just glitched? Yet when I search up my own name, my file pops wide open.

NAME: REI REYNOLDS

AGE: 18

INSTITUTION: FINANCIAL DISTRICT PREPARATORY SCHOOL,

SYNDICATE PREPARATORY LEAGUE (GRADUATED)

NOTES: TOURNAMENT FINALIST. "WILD CARD." NOMINATED BY

SASHA SOKOLOV, MASTER OF THE FINANCIAL DISTRICT (DECEASED).

Deceased.

I close the file abruptly and bury my face in my hands.

The whoosh of air leaving his lungs. His blood splattering on the floor. His bright blue eyes meeting mine. A moment of clarity, then his final words—

Rise, *Rei.*

I scrub my eyes and release a shuddering breath.

The shock of Master Sasha's death still hasn't really set in. Nor Yuna's, or Noëlle's. Part of me still wants to believe that my first nightfall was all just a setup, like the trap I fell for at the Apollo Theater during the second Tournament task. But seeing it registered in the Syndicate's database like this, so officially and matter-of-factly . . . there's no denying it.

I feel numb. Completely, totally numb from the endless spiral of fear and doubt and grief that has plagued my every waking moment over the past few days. Yet as exhausted as I am, I dread sleep. I dread the possibility of reliving my real-life nightmares.

"Why do you have a picture of Nick Valentine as your phone wallpaper?"

I leap to my feet as Kieran strides back into the office, my cheeks burning. "Give me that!"

"I mean, I get it. He's handsome. He's charming. Everyone's got a bit of a crush on him. I'm just saying that especially since we're working with him now, you should probably consider changing it. In case he sees it and thinks you're a creep."

"Or he might be flattered by the attention. He's single, you know."

"Well, I'm sure you two will be very happy together," Kieran replies sarcastically. "He did come by to check on you earlier. He seemed very concerned about you. He even brought flowers. Expensive ones."

"Haha."

"No, I'm serious. They're in your room."

I try to hide my surprise. The Phantom paid me a visit? Certainly he has more important things to do.

"For the record, *I* didn't get you flowers because I was too busy watching over your snoring," he mutters. "I would've gone to the bakery anyway, since I know you'd pick banana pudding over a bunch of useless peonies any day."

I let out a dreamy sigh and twirl a lock of hair around my finger, pretending not to have heard him. "Oh, Kieran, do you think the Phantom finds me pretty?"

At Kieran's glower, I snicker to myself and snatch my phone out of his hands. I tap through my messages until I find the chat I'm looking for.

jie jie

i know this doesn't make up for me not being there in person, but i hope it helps. do NOT tell Mom!!!

ENCRYPTED FILE RECEIVED

I copy the hidden ciphertext into a different app to decrypt it. How she came by this password in the first place, I have no idea. All I know is that *not* knowing is the price I have to pay.

Sitting back down, I pull up Agent Storm's file once more. When the box pops up, I hesitate before typing. 1 ATTEMPT LEFT. If the password is wrong, it's game over.

I bite my lip and hit enter.

The file unlocks. My shoulders sag in relief—but not for long.

"What the hell?" I mutter, scanning Agent Storm's information. Or rather, the stunning lack of it. Besides her name and her role, her file is a blank slate. It doesn't even show her date of birth, let alone her work history at the Syndicate. Her description is bare but for one lone sentence.

"Head of Project Forsaken." There's a date next to it, when the project was founded six years ago.

I search up *Project Forsaken* in the database and get a single classified result. Even the master key doesn't work.

What kind of project could be so classified that even masters aren't allowed to know about it?

A playful knock at the door jerks me to attention. "Are you two making out in there or something?" calls a teasing voice.

I fly out of my chair, and I throw open the door to reveal Zaza standing outside, holding a fancy little package wrapped in gold ribbon.

I fling my arms around her. She kisses me on both cheeks and strokes my hair. "Good to see you too, hon. I'm on my lunch break so I can't stay long before I have to head back to the labs."

"Is that for me?" I say, gesturing at the gift.

"Yeah, but it's not from me." She passes it over. It's surprisingly light for its size. In fact, it feels almost empty. The tag attached to the ribbon has my name handwritten in beautiful, sloping cursive.

"Who's it from?"

"A secret admirer, maybe? Someone left it by the door for you."

Placing the box on the edge of Aunt Minyi's desk, I tug the ends of the bow until it comes free and tear through the gold paper to reveal the plain cardboard box beneath. Both Kieran and Zaza watch in rapt attention as I unfold the flaps to peer inside.

I clap a hand over my mouth to muffle my scream.

"What is it?" says Zaza, grabbing the box to see for herself. Her eyes widen. "Ooh, a severed ear. Looks pretty fresh, too. Maybe it's a declaration of love."

Kieran seizes the box from her, his expression twisted in disgust. "What a sick joke. Who brought this thing upstairs? I'm going to track them down."

"Is there a note?" Zaza asks.

Kieran pauses. "Yeah, actually." Nose wrinkled, he carefully lowers his hand into the box and extracts a small, bloodstained envelope.

I hold out my hand, grateful I haven't eaten yet. "Let me see."

"You sure?"

I nod. Reluctantly, he places it in my palm. I break the seal and slide out the note—heavy, unmarked cardstock, written in the same penmanship as the tag with my name on it.

Times Square. Midnight tonight.

*Be there, or your master returns
to the Manor in pieces, too.*

CHAPTER FORTY-SEVEN

I insert the note back into its envelope carefully.

"You're not actually thinking about going, right?" Kieran asks.

"Of course I'm going," I reply curtly, my hands oddly steady as I tuck the cardboard flaps back in place. A bizarre calm washes over me.

"Don't you realize it's a trap?"

"Obviously. But we don't have to let them catch us off guard. We'll be prepared this time."

"They almost killed you last time, Rei."

"Well, they failed."

His steely gaze pierces me. "They'll make sure that they won't fail again."

I return it, unwilling to back down. We're stuck at an impasse.

"Sorry to interrupt your steamy staring sesh," Zaza interjects, "but who are *they*? And why are they cutting off people's body parts? Is that actually Minyi's ear?"

I double-check. "No, she has piercings."

"Okay, but still, that's hella sus. And what did you mean about saving the masters? Did something happen to them?"

I falter, unsure how to answer. I almost never keep any secrets from my best friend—not even my illegal after-school escapades in the abandoned subway stations. However, this secret doesn't belong to me. It's much bigger . . . big enough to affect the future of the Syndicate. "Let's just say some of the masters are MIA. Also, we're not totally sure who *they* are. We just know they're planning something dangerous. Something Deathling-related."

Zaza gasps. "Oh god, that reminds me. Do you remember the last time you went hunting for Deathlings in the subway on the second to last day of school before the final exam? And I took that sample from you after you got maimed by that Deathling?"

Kieran whips his head around. "You got what?"

Zaza waves her hand. "Not my point. We never get nightfang samples because they're super hard to come by, so I was eager to get the results."

"But?" I prompt.

She hesitates. "Something really weird happened. And when I showed the sample to my boss, she told me to dispose of it immediately. When I tried to ask her why, she got really hostile and jumpy. She even threatened to report me for insubordination."

My eyebrows raise. "So you disposed of it?"

"Obviously not." Zaza casts a pointed glance at Kieran and tilts her head toward the door. He catches the hint and goes over to make sure it's locked. She lowers her voice to a hush. "I sequenced the nightfang DNA. Since I didn't have any other Deathling samples, I did a cross-check by aligning it to a couple of genomes across random species. There was only one match that worked almost perfectly, minus a few genes with some pretty wild mutations."

"A match?"

She walks over to Aunt Minyi's desk and perches on the edge, her brow furrowed in thought. "At first I wondered if it was a fluke, or if the sample I collected got contaminated by some haywire reaction your own body produced in light of your contact with the nightfang. Fortunately, nowadays I can just take a sample of your DNA and plug it into a fancy algorithm to essentially subtract it from the original sample—hence me asking for your hairbrush the other day to steal a few strands."

"I thought you said you were going to clone me."

"Maybe next time. Anyway, it didn't match up."

The sense of unease in my stomach only intensifies. Kieran remains utterly silent. I can't tell if it's because he's nervous or he doesn't understand a word coming out of my best friend's mouth.

"Except for those few crackpot genes I mentioned earlier," Zaza continues, "the only variants I observed are typical for a *human*."

Kieran's face goes slack. "No. That's impossible."

Zaza shakes her head with a flustered laugh. "I know. I must have messed something up. Maybe I shouldn't have told you guys. You have so many other things to deal with right now. The last thing you need on your mind are my ridiculous theories—"

I grab her hands in mine and squeeze them tight. "They might be ridiculous, but that doesn't mean they're wrong. You don't need me to tell you how brilliant you are. We're damn lucky to have you."

Kieran rubs his chin. "If we could get you the right samples, would you be able to run some more tests?"

Zaza nods slowly. "Though I have a feeling that my boss will be watching me more closely from now on. I want to get to the bottom of this as much as you, but I won't be of much use if I get fired."

"Why don't you use the labs here, at the Manor?" Kieran suggests. "If anyone asks, we can just say the order came directly from Master

Minyi's office. I mean, it's true. Technically."

I inhale sharply. "Could you both give me a minute? I'm going to the kitchen to get some water."

Kieran's gaze weighs on me. "Everything okay?"

I force a smile. "Just help Zaza figure out what else she might need to run her tests." Thankfully, he doesn't push any further as I unlock the door and slip out as quickly as I can before either of them can follow.

I shut the door behind me, muting their discussion, and head into the kitchen. It's a beautiful open space with marble counters and fancy cabinets full of crystal drinkware and china. And, of course, tea. My aunt is a tea fanatic, importing varieties from all over the world: sakura plum, cardamom and cloves, pu'er from old trees in far-off forests. My fingers brush one of the many teapots in her collection, its earth-colored ceramic surface smelling perpetually of rain and roasted rice. It's still full—she always brews a cup of tea before work. But she must never have gotten a chance to drink this one.

Zaza's words ring in my head.

Typical for a human.

Only one match that worked almost perfectly, minus a few genes with some pretty wild mutations.

I think of Tim, with his black eyes, his face morphing from Master Sasha's back to his own. His talons puncturing Master Sasha's flesh. His *nightfang* talons.

Somehow, somewhere in the depths of that base I barely escaped, Tim found a way to become one of the very monsters we all vowed to destroy. How many more of these hybrid abominations exist? How many of them were *created*?

I think of the nightfang that killed Yuna. The person on the roof who threw the grenade at her. Whoever shot Noëlle in the back of her head.

Were they all *one and the same*?

I think of my aunt, who told me that the "individuals" in the base were capable of both tremendous harm and good. Not people. Not humans. *Abominations.*

I yank open the cupboard, my shoulders heaving. I grab a glass and top it up in the sink. I guzzle it down gulp after gulp. When I'm done I do it all over again. I drink too fast and choke. I clutch my chest, coughing, gasping for air. The unfiltered water leaves a slightly metallic taste on my tongue. Almost bloodlike.

She knew.

She knew about them.

She must have.

She's lied to me before—countless times, as I told Master Sasha myself. But this. *This* is different.

This changes everything.

I don't mean to slam the glass back onto the counter quite as forcefully as I do. It shatters in my grip, shards flying. I curse and suck the droplets of scarlet welling from the tip of my thumb. Now my mouth really does taste like blood.

A hysterical bubble of laughter claws its way out of my throat. The guffaw that breaks the camel's back. I slump against the counter and slide to the floor, my entire body shaking silently. A steady stream of tears drips off my chin. I lie there, alone in the dark with Aunt Minyi's teapot collection, laughing hard enough to puke up my own intestines.

"Miss Reynolds! What in the world are you doing there?"

I crack open my puffy eyes to find a very alarmed-looking Declan hovering over me, carrying two paper bags bursting with groceries in each hand. When he tries to lower them to the ground, one of them gives a terrific *rrrrip!* and at least ten tubs of ice cream topple to the ground.

"Hell's bells!" Declan bends down, fumbling with a tub of mint chip. "So sorry. Is that glass? Oh, dear me—"

Sniffling, I help Declan gather up the rest of the tubs. No two flavors are the same, ranging from chocolate to caramel apple pie. "What are these for?"

"Well, we have guests coming in and out, and I figured everyone could use a little pick-me-up." He straightens and grabs a pair of tongs from the drawer, busying himself with packing the ice cream into the freezer—a domesticized cryotank that uses liquid nitrogen to keep things cool during nightfall when the electricity goes out. "I wasn't sure what flavors your friends would prefer, so I procured all of them." He digs through the second bag and presents me with a quart of chocolate chip cookie dough. "And of course, I couldn't forget your favorite."

I stare at his offering in silence. A beat passes.

"Miss Reynolds?" asks Declan softly. "Is everything quite all right?"

A lone tear trickles down my cheek.

Without another word, Declan sets the ice cream on the counter and pulls me into a hug. I hide my face in his chest, trying my best to suppress my sobs, but that just makes me cry even harder.

"There, there," he murmurs, rubbing my back. "It's okay to let it out. That's it. You've been putting up such a strong front, haven't you? Poor thing. I don't know how you've kept it together all this time."

"I couldn't save them," I sob. "And Tim . . . he . . . and Master Sasha . . . Zaza said . . . it's just that everything I've believed my whole life—"

"Breathe, Miss Reynolds. In and out. In and out. That's right, very good."

It takes a few tries, but I finally manage to choke it out. "I was right there, Declan, and I—I couldn't save any of them. Why? Why couldn't I do anything? Maybe it's . . ." My throat convulses. I can't even finish my goddamn sentence. "Maybe it's my fault. Just like the night Tofu died."

Declan goes still. Quietly, he says, "Don't say that."

But it's the truth. He knows it. And I can't forget that night.

The only night I ever missed curfew.

It was Christmas Eve. Well, Christmas Eve afternoon, anyway. I was almost thirteen, helping Declan decorate the apartment with crystal jars that we would fill with stardust when night fell. On the dining table, a feast awaited Aunt Minyi's return from Grand Central Headquarters. We originally set the table for four, until Maura had texted an hour before to let us know that she wasn't going to make it. It had been almost a year since I'd seen her last.

Tofu had caught a severe case of the zoomies. He wouldn't stop racing around the apartment at lightning speed, bouncing on and off the furniture like a loose firework. Declan all but begged me to take him out for a walk.

"But come back quickly," he shouted over the chime of the curfew bells as Tofu practically dragged me out of the apartment. "Just up and down the street. It will be nightfall before you know it."

On the elevator ride down, I zipped up my coat and realized I'd forgotten my mittens.

A menorah and Christmas tree shone in the lobby, decked with silver star ornaments and glowing fairy lights that would soon go dark. One of the guards on duty asked if I need an escort, but I promised to be back in a minute.

My breath fogged the bitter December air as I trekked down sidewalks lined with scummy brown lumps of sludge. Tofu snuffled his way through the snow, his tail wagging. Besides the vehicles parked into every available crevice and cranny, the streets were empty. I glanced up as a lone engine spluttered by—one last straggler anxiously navigating the icy roads home.

As Tofu chose a telephone pole at the end of the street to relieve himself, I tucked his leash under my arm and attempted to rub some warmth into my freezing hands. Yet even the subzero temperatures couldn't quite compare to the hollow chill of the disappointment seeping through me. I thought back to Maura's earlier text, desperately wondering if it was my fault—if I'd possibly said or done something to make her decide not to come home, even on Christmas Eve.

Zzzip.

A startled cry erupted from me as Tofu's leash slipped away from under my arm. He broke off in a wild sprint down 74th Street, his leash flying behind him like a kite tail. I slipped on a patch of ice and fell hard on my tailbone. I barely felt it as I scrambled back onto my feet. I sprinted after him, hollering his name, glad because there were no cars on the road.

Until the curfew bells went silent.

All at once, the nightfall warning sirens began to scream.

I covered my ears to block out their piercing wails and ran faster. Lungs burning, I slid and skidded across the slushy intersection to the southernmost tip of Riverside Park just as Tofu leapt over a low fence and disappeared through the trees.

Even with minutes left until nightfall, I didn't hesitate. I soared over the fence, plowing through a bank of nearly untouched, knee-high snow.

I was not going to lose my dog.

I caught up to him at last as he halted a few yards in front of a copse of evergreens.

"Tofu! C'mere!" I exclaimed, holding my arms out to him. He'd never run off like this before. In fact, he'd never run off, period. I cast a nervous look around the deserted park. "Come on, boy. We have to go, it's almost nightfall."

He growled at the trees.

I hissed. "Tofu, *please*—"

My voice died in my throat as the darkness between the trees liquefied and a hulking beast lumbered out into the open, its four eyes unblinking and black as sin. It was the same Deathling from outside my window.

Tofu stood his ground as the Deathling approached, his lips curled back in a snarl.

I calculated the distance between my dog and the monster. If I could grab him and use the trees as cover, then make a run for it . . .

But even at twelve years old, I knew that it was hopeless.

The final siren choked off, leaving a terrible silence.

The silence of dead things.

The Deathling came to a halt before us. I didn't dare move as it shook the snow off its tail. It regarded Tofu for a long minute before opening its maw.

From it came the sound of that strange bark it had made last time. A gravelly, rasping *ruff*, like an old man coughing. But this time, Tofu didn't go berserk. Instead, he cocked his head, puzzled.

Almost hesitantly, he barked back.

"*REI!*" a voice roared.

I whipped around. The stardust beginning to drift down illuminated the squad of mavericks charging through the snow-covered clearing, led by a tall man with slicked-back salt-and-pepper hair and a gun in each hand.

"Get back!" Declan shouted, cocking both guns and taking aim at the Deathling's head.

I threw out my arms. "Wait! Don't shoot."

Declan faltered. *"What?"*

"Don't shoot," I cried. "Look."

Neither Tofu nor the Deathling had moved since Declan's arrival. They simply observed one another. The Deathling took a hesitant step forward, its gnarled tusks carving trails through the snow.

"Rei," Declan warned in a low voice.

"Just trust me," I whispered without taking my eyes off the monster. My fists clenched in front of my chest, my heart full of hope. Yes, Deathlings slaughtered people all the time—my parents included. But what if they didn't have to? What if they could be befriended? Then people wouldn't need to patrol the streets at nightfall or fight Deathlings ever again.

No one else needed to die like Mom and Dad.

The Deathling slowly bent its enormous, withered head toward Tofu. *As if in submission,* I thought. I watched as the monster's jaws yawned wide open, revealing the rows of crooked, needle-sharp fangs within. For a moment, I wondered if was going to try to bark again.

Horror dawned on Declan's face. He saw what I could not and dove toward me, his arms outstretched.

Gunfire erupted through the park. Declan tackled me into the snow, enfolding me in his arms and doing his best to shield my eyes. He held me down even as I kicked his shins and screamed myself hoarse into his ears. And then when I had nothing left, he carried me, sobbing hysterically, all the way back to the Manor.

The mavericks blocked my view as we left the park. The only thing I saw was the snow, and the blossoms of red on white.

CHAPTER FORTY-EIGHT

For a long time, neither of us speak. We're both lost in the memories of the sweet little dog that used to nap under the table and gobble up scraps of food like a fluffy golden vacuum cleaner. I've lost count of how many times I've dreamed of waking to find Tofu curled up at the end of my bed or waiting patiently on the doorstep, tail wagging.

"For years, I've tried to block out that night," I whisper hoarsely. I've made a lot of mistakes, Declan. I've never forgiven myself for that one, but I was supposed to learn from it. So why haven't I? Why am I so completely, utterly useless?"

To my surprise, Declan lets out a rueful chuckle. "You know, the night-fall your parents were killed, your aunt said the same thing. When she failed to save them, she couldn't forgive herself, either. I still don't know if she has. She always believed herself to be responsible for every single citizen residing on the Upper West Side."

"Every single citizen?" I repeat skeptically. "That's nearly a hundred thousand people. She thinks she's responsible for protecting *all* of them? On her own?"

"Indeed."

"But that's ridiculous."

Declan sighs. "In her mind, she held a vision. A vision of her best self. Of perfection. She was always striving to attain it. Unsurprisingly, she failed more often than not." He grows somber. "I watched her descend into a destructive spiral. I wish I had noticed sooner, but she was so good at hiding it beneath that mask of hers."

I'm at a loss for words. I could have never imagined that Aunt Minyi—my patient, wise, compassionate aunt—could be that kind of person. In a small voice, I look up at him and ask, "What happened?"

Amazement kindles his tone like embers flickering to life. "*You* happened, Rei. You barged into her life like a ball of lightning. Unpredictable, ill-mannered, and so angry. Any other child in your place would have been crushed by the weight of such brutal trauma, but *you*." Just like when I was little, he crouches down to my eye level and grasps my shoulders. "You took all of your broken pieces and made them your weapons."

The air rushes out of my lungs.

"It wasn't easy for you in the beginning," Declan goes on. The corner of his mouth quirks upward. "I'll never forget your early days at FD Prep. Do you remember how you used to struggle in almost every class?"

"No."

Declan chuckles. "You used to hide your test scores in your pants so Master Minyi wouldn't see them. After your first day of combat education, I drove you home in tears."

"You're making that up."

He shakes his head, gazing down at me with equal parts exasperation and fondness. "You were *never* perfect, Rei. Yet you refused to give up. Because of you, your aunt came to realize that it wasn't being 'perfect' that mattered, nor achieving the godlike image that she had conceived for herself. It was accepting that we *can't* always be the person we want ourselves to be, and being brave enough to take our best crack at it nevertheless."

I stare at his wise, weathered face, the kindly crinkles around his eyes, and let his words sink in.

"Now, as it so happens, you have plenty enough to worry about already. Whatever Miss Alvarez told you, it can wait. Drink some tea. Have a bowl or two of ice cream. With all due respect, please take a shower. Smash some plates, if necessary—though preferably not the melamine ones, they're vintage."

I blow out a shaky breath and nod. He releases me to rifle through the drawers for an ice cream scooper. "Declan?"

He glances over his shoulder. "Yes?"

I rub my nose sheepishly. "I'm really sorry."

"What in heavens for?"

"I think I got snot all over your nice suit."

He blinks, then throws his head back in laughter. I grin despite myself as Zaza and Kieran emerge from my aunt's office. Before they can notice the mess, Declan offers them spoons. "Care for some ice cream, Miss Alvarez and Mister Cross?"

"There would be no greater honor," says Zaza, accepting her spoon with a dramatic bow.

"What flavors are there?" asks Kieran.

I grab a dustpan from the cupboard and tip my chin at the freezer. "Don't you want to see for yourself?"

When they peer inside, Zaza squeals and starts doing a little jig. Declan shoots me a wink as he hands me my own bowl of sugary goodness. I laugh as Zaza links arms and forces me and an only slightly begrudging Kieran into dancing like hooligans around the kitchen. It's a moment

I wish I could stay in forever, but just like the sweetness melting on my tongue, some things simply aren't meant to last.

But perhaps that's what makes them so precious.

Perhaps that's what makes them so worth fighting for.

CHAPTER FORTY-NINE

With less than ten hours until midnight, nightfall hurtles toward us at breakneck speed. After we call in the Phantom to inform him of the mysterious note, he promises to arrive by four o'clock. Zaza leaves for work, and Kieran claims the living room sofa for a much-needed nap.

Meanwhile, as right as Declan is about how badly I need a shower, there is one other thing I need to take care of before Valentine arrives.

I slink back into Aunt Minyi's office and lock the door behind me. I loiter at the threshold, guilt gnawing at my stomach, feeling like an unwelcome guest even though the office is deserted. My eyes dart from the bookshelf to the mantel behind her desk to the chairs by the window. I scrutinize the ceiling lamp, then the rugs at my feet.

If the Master of the Upper West Side had the equivalent of an atomic bomb somewhere in her office, where would she hide it?

I begin at her desk. Not only are the rest of the drawers unlocked but they're nearly empty, containing the bare minimum of office supplies and a half-eaten bag of peanut butter cups. I search the smooth wooden underside for secret compartments, then climb onto the table to check the inside of the lamp, which proves dusty but equally disappointing. I drag the potted plant out of the way to roll up the rugs, but they reveal no trapdoors, no floorboards loose enough to hide anything larger than dust bunnies. I lift the framed, wall-to-wall photo of Times Square, legs wobbling beneath its weight as I lower it to the ground, running my hands over the blank expanse and the backside of the frame.

Nothing.

I can't tell whether to be grateful or infuriated that her office is so uncluttered. It makes for an easy search, but I'm rapidly running out of possibilities.

In the end, I place all my bets on the bookshelf. As demonstrated by the library at the Sanctuary, there's something inherently badass about hiding things in bookshelves. Thus, a fitting choice for my aunt.

Thirty minutes later, I'm swamped in a sea of books strewn haphazardly across the floor. I've cleared every shelf and flipped through every page. I shove the last peanut butter cup from the bag in the drawer into my mouth and sink into a crouch, staring up at the empty shelves in despair.

With a loud groan, I haul myself back onto my feet to begin cleaning up the mess I've made. I heap books into my arms until they tower past my head, determined to make as few trips as possible. As I hurry toward the shelf, my foot catches on something. I go crashing to the floor. The books topple after me, thumping the back of my head.

Rubbing it sourly, I crane my neck to see what I knocked over. Aunt Minyi's potted plant lies on its side like a turtle stranded on its back. Cursing under my breath, I grab it by the stem to set it upright with a harsh tug, but the entire plant pops out, dirt and all.

I drag the heavy ceramic pot toward me and peer inside the shallow interior.

For a pot of this size, *too* shallow.

Carefully, I lower the pot onto its side again and flip it upside down. I peel away a thin outer layer on the bottom to expose a keyhole.

My excitement is smothered by the realization that I now have to find the key.

I cast a desperate look out the window, at the sun approaching the horizon. The Phantom could arrive at any minute.

With a grimace, I lug the pot over to Aunt Minyi's desk and hoist it up. It lands with a hollow *thunk*. Then I clamber up next to it. Like a champion weightlifter, I heave the pot high above my head, the rim nearly brushing the ceiling.

And then I hurl it to the floor with all my might.

With a ground-shaking *CRASH*, the pot smashes into a thousand smithereens. I jump off the table, my heart thundering. Amid the destruction rests a plain chest, about the size of a shoebox—dented, but otherwise intact. I brush away the detritus from the pot and hold the box up to the light.

Does it truly contain the missing Artifact? The one that Master Sasha believed could change the fate of Manhattan?

My stomach flutters as I pry off the lid and peer inside.

A ripple of confusion runs through me.

It's a load of junk.

I rummage through the mix of random items: a leather journal, a shriveled corsage, a small conch shell. A tiny silk pouch containing two tinier baby teeth. A broken watch. It's only when I pull out a familiar charm bracelet that these meaningless things suddenly make sense.

Tears well in my eyes. The little charms clink together—a bowl of ramen, a black cat, and the #1 trophy I decided to add at the last moment for the first Mother's Day gift I ever gave to Aunt Minyi. All these years, I never saw her wear it, so I assumed that she had just thrown it away.

The more carefully I look at the rest of the objects, the more I piece together where they might have come from. Engraved on the back of the broken watch, an *E* and an *R* for Elliot Reynolds, my uncle. The corsage contains blossoms that match my mom's wedding bouquet. The baby teeth could have been Maura's, or maybe mine.

Lastly, I take out the journal. My fingers stroke the soft, well-loved leather cover. I unwrap a long cord tying it closed. The spine crackles as I open it up to the first yellowed page and inhale a whiff of aged parchment and ink.

Property of Ru Chen.

I reread the first four words of my dad's journal, tracing my index finger along the letters of his name in silent reverence. I try to place the journal in my memory but fail. The paper whispers beneath my touch, beckoning me to turn the page.

Various sketches cover most of the surface, carefully continued across the middle seam. In the remaining space, immaculate paragraphs of Chinese characters I cannot decipher. Never have I felt my inadequacy in my parents' first language quite so acutely. The sketches, on the other hand, I do recognize. It's a rendering of a map.

Randel's Map.

A thrill ripples through me. The next pages I leaf through display a similar layout, with detailed sketches of Artifacts accompanied by more descriptions in Chinese characters, though not always complete. I flip past the Horn to the bronze bull sculpture on Wall Street, the Taxi Medallion, the Oyster . . .

In the early days following the Vanishing, Dad must have recorded all the Artifacts in this journal.

I hear someone stop in front of the door. "Rei, are you in there?" Kieran asks from the other side. "Valentine is on his way."

Hugging the journal to my chest with one arm, I scramble to my feet to straighten up the office. There's no way for me to tidy the broken pot shards by hand, so I opt to pull the thickest rug on top of them and pray no one will enter the room until Aunt Minyi returns. As for the chest, I'll hide it in my room until she comes back so I can give it to her—along with an apology—myself.

In the shower, I lather myself up with my favorite lemon-and-rose-scented shower gel, wash my hair, and pick out the blood and dirt caked beneath my nails. I crank the tap hotter until the water scalds my skin raw and pink, and thick white steam pours up to the tiled ceiling, watching the grime of the past few days all swirl down the drain until the reddish-brown-tinged water flows clear. It's probably too much to hope that the water will cleanse my mind as easily as it did the filth, but that doesn't stop me from trying.

By the time I emerge from the steam, I'm a changed woman. Well, maybe that's a stretch, but I *do* change into some fresh clothes. I pick out a pair of black joggers and a fluffy sweatshirt Zaza got me for my birthday with teddy-bear ears sewn onto the hood. I haven't found many (i.e., any) opportunities to wear it, but seeing as I could die tonight, it's probably now or never.

At four o'clock, I return to Master Minyi's office to find three figures already seated by the windows, eating ice cream and hot shawarmas wrapped in silver foil from the food carts down the street.

When Valentine sees my outfit, he chortles. "Wow."

Kieran's eyebrows shoot up. "You're not wearing pajamas to kill Death-lings, are you?"

The third figure turns to look. "I think she'd manage just fine."

I stop in my tracks and gape. "Everly?"

They shoot me a crooked grin. "Hey, Rei. Long time, no see."

"I—I wasn't expecting to see you here," I stammer out, because I'm not sure what else to say. *Glad you're not dead? Happy you chose not to fight by our sides and lived to see another day? Grateful you didn't end up like Noëlle and Yuna?*

Everly runs an awkward hand through their hair. "Yeah . . . I know. I haven't been able to stop thinking about all of you since the day I left, risking your lives while I was safe and snug in my bed." They avert their gaze. "Kieran told me what happened to Yuna and Noëlle."

I wrap my arms around myself. "Maybe it was the right call. If only the rest of us had possessed some of your wisdom, they might still be alive right now."

"But that's just it. If I'd been there, if maybe you and Noëlle hadn't been forced to split up . . ." Everly clenches their fists in their lap. "There's a certain kind of person I've taken pride in *not* being my whole life. The kind of person who steps aside and watches from the safety of the sidelines when they have the power to make change."

Valentine places his hand on Everly's shoulder. "We all have regrets. It's how we choose to move forward from our mistakes that determines who we really are."

"Easy for you to say," they point out. "You're the Phantom."

"The Phantom is just a title. It doesn't mean I'm any less human than any of you." At our skeptical silence, he exhales. "You think I haven't seen my fellow mavericks die? Or felt incredibly helpless when I could do nothing but watch?"

"Hire more, then," says Everly. "Surely greater numbers would increase everyone's chances of survival."

Valentine gives them a tired smile. "It's not so simple. Besides there being limited Artifacts and exosuits to go around, you can't just equip people with guns and expect them to turn into weapons. You already know that the Tournament pushes candidates to their limits. The tasks are designed to imitate the real challenges we face as mavericks—which is why you don't always have to win for the masters to see your true potential. But it's also the reason even some of the best enforcers in the Syndicate's history wouldn't last more than a single nightfall. Why throw a hundred people at a puzzle when you only need one to solve it?"

"The *right* one," I correct.

Valentine nods.

"So how do we know?" asks Everly. "If *we're* the right ones."

He clasps his hands together, his dark eyes gleaming with what might be regret. "Only dawn will tell."

CHAPTER FIFTY

Seven o'clock finds me perched on my bedroom windowsill with a cup of Aunt Minyi's favorite tea and Dad's journal. Next to me, a steady stream of sand tumbles through a custom hourglass Valentine gave to each of us in order to keep track of the time until midnight.

Zaza sits on the floor cross-legged, surrounded by charts and endless figures. She nibbles on her pencil and jots down a note, her brow creased in deep calculation. The stardust drifting outside casts a luminous golden glow through the curtains onto my bed. A bed I *should* be sleeping in right now.

If I were a true maverick, I could make myself sleep. Force myself to be still enough to fade away. With such erratic work hours, it's an invaluable skill. Even the most lethal striker can only pull so many all-nighters before exhaustion guides them straight into a Deathling's jaws.

Kieran, at least, does not share my plight. His snores rumble through the apartment walls like they're made of tissue paper.

"Find anything useful?" I ask Zaza.

She grumbles something unintelligible in response—so, no. Without looking up, she says, "You?"

"If I could suddenly read traditional Chinese characters, maybe." I rub my eyes. "Or simplified, for that matter."

Zaza tilts her head. "You've never learned them?"

"I can recognize maybe thirty words."

"That's not too bad!"

I laugh. "Yeah. Only, like, over eight thousand more to go. And that's just simplified Chinese. The same characters can look completely different when written traditionally. I tried scanning a page into a translation app on my phone, but I think he wrote in cursive or something, because let me tell you, it did *not* work."

Zaza brightens. "There's a guy in my lab who immigrated here after he graduated from one of the top schools in China. Maybe he could help you?"

I chew my lip, debating. It could take me years to translate everything myself. But can I entrust the Artifacts' secrets to someone else? Even— *especially*—if they're employed by the Syndicate? "There's a reason why my aunt kept this journal locked up for over a decade," I say finally. "Either she couldn't read it herself, or the information she learned was too dangerous. I have to be careful about whose hands it falls into."

"Well, there's got to be *some* solution." She pauses. "What about the Artifacts themselves? Is there one for translating things?"

"I wish," I sigh.

"Don't give up, hon. Maybe there's an Artifact out there just like your Token, waiting for you to figure it out. It's worth a visit to the Archives, at least."

"If I survive long enough, I'll go," I tell her.

I turn to an entry on the Phantom's Mask. Though I don't understand any of Dad's descriptions, his passion shines through the pages in every detailed stroke and lovingly rendered curve. I've studied the Artifacts for years, but it's like I'm seeing them through new eyes. His eyes.

The hairs on the back of my neck prickle. I glance up and nearly jump out of my skin. "Zaza!"

Her face looms inches away from mine. So immersed in the journal, I didn't even notice her creep up. In an oddly tight voice, she asks, "Will you?"

"Go to the Archives? I just said that—"

"No. Will you *survive*?"

I blink. "Gee, I sure hope so."

"Don't joke, Rei," she snaps. She takes a deep breath. "Just—just answer me."

I rest the journal on my knee and meet her gaze. "Zaza, you know the risks that mavs face."

"But aren't things different now? Nightfangs aren't just Deathlings. They're . . . part human. Somehow. Which means—"

I won't let her finish. "One sample isn't enough to come to a definitive conclusion."

"But—"

"No," I tell her firmly. "I watched one decapitate Yuna, and another butcher Master Sasha. Right before my eyes, without the slightest hesitation or iota of mercy. There's *nothing* human about them anymore. They're monsters, just like the rest."

She drops her gaze. "I guess."

I reach for her hand. "Come on, Zaza. I won't let them take me down without a fight."

She pulls away and heads for the door. Holding the knob, she turns to me. "I know how much the Syndicate means to you, Rei. All I'm saying is that the people who always told you to rise above the rest will never be the ones to warn you how far you might fall."

Before I can come up with a reply, the door clicks shut. I bite my lip and try to refocus on the journal.

When I turn to the next page, my heartbeat quickens.

There are only two sketches of the next Artifact. A front and back view of a perfect circle, inscribed on both sides. On the front, *New York City Transit Authority*, and on the back, *Good for One Fare*.

Three letters—*NYC*—fill the center of the all-too-familiar coin.

It's the Token.

Every sketch so far has represented the Artifacts in precise detail, and this one's no exception—from the spirographic design engraved on the outer rim of the coin to the various scratches and scuffs on its surface. Except unlike all the other entries, the Token's sketches seem to be unfinished. Plus, my dad screwed up one crucial detail—in real life, the Artifact bears an open Y-shaped notch in the center of the coin. But in both of Dad's sketches, the notch is filled, like it was never there to begin with.

At that moment, Zaza returns with two fresh cups of tea. The leaves have stained the water a mesmerizing, vivid blue of butterfly pea flowers. "Sorry for worrying."

I sit on the edge of the bed and pat the spot next to me. I take the cup she offers me. "Sorry for making you worried."

"Nothing I say will change your mind about going?"

Her imploring eyes tug at my heart, but I know what I have to do. When I don't respond, she merely sighs.

"Cheers," I say. "To saving Aunt Minyi."

"Cheers," she echoes.

I drain half my cup before the bitter aftertaste hits. I reel back, coughing. "Zaza, how much sugar did you add?"

Her face scrunches. "Ugh, sorry. I had no idea how to prepare it. The blue threw me off."

Discreetly, I spit a mouthful back into the cup. "You're lucky I love you so much."

She smiles, but it doesn't quite reach her eyes. "Love you, too."

"Look," I say, grabbing my dad's journal to show her the entry for the Token. "I think my dad drew this one wrong. The Y in the middle shouldn't be there."

Zaza rests her head against my shoulder. "Maybe it was there when your dad drew it."

"No way. Everyone would've known about that."

"Well, didn't you figure out how to use the Token when everyone else thought it was broken?"

"That's a bit of a stretch." I shake my head as a sudden wave of dizziness washes over me. "What if there was a missing piece? What if *I'm* the missing piece?"

"Last time I checked, you weren't shaped like a Y."

My bed looks more inviting than ever. When did it get so hard to keep my eyes open? Before I know it, I'm falling. I land with a soft *whump* on the covers and stick my arms out over my head. "I am now."

"Listen to you." Zaza strokes my cheek. I struggle to keep my eyes wide enough to see her lovely face swimming over me. "You must be exhausted. Just relax. Don't fight it."

Her command works like a magic spell. Before I can ask what exactly I'm supposed to stop fighting, I'm already fast asleep.

In my dream, it's Christmas morning. I wake up surrounded by presents wrapped in extravagant bows and glittery paper. A pair of bodiless hands set the first present in my lap. I tear it open with a grin. When I lift the lid, I find Aunt Minyi's severed head grinning back up at me.

I jolt awake, gasping for breath, my clothes damp from my own terror sweat. I'm tucked snug in bed, the bubble tea plush Zaza got for me propped up on the pillow beside my head. The *skritch skritch* of pen on paper breaks off suddenly as Zaza looks up from the floor.

Her face goes totally slack. "You're awake already?"

I lurch out of the bed, panting hard. "What time is it?"

"Rei—"

"*What time is it?*" I shout at her. I grab the hourglass and stare at it in disbelief. The sand has completely emptied into the bottom half. "Zaza," I whisper. "What the hell have you done?"

Tears flood her eyes. "I'm so sorry, Rei. He didn't want you to go. He made me do it, drugging you. He told me that you were going to get yourself killed. I could never have forgiven myself if I just let that happen. You weren't supposed to wake up until the morning after everything was over."

I freeze.

They almost killed you last time, Rei. They'll make sure that they won't fail again.

He didn't want you to go.

Don't you realize it's a trap?

He didn't want me to go.

Kieran.

CHAPTER FIFTY-ONE

I cuss all the way to the living room. Of course, the sofa lies empty. He's nowhere to be seen.

"Conniving, traitorous piece of shit," I hiss, shoving on a pair of combat boots and storming out the apartment door. Zaza calls after me, but I ignore her desperate pleas even though I know it's not her fault. He picked her because she would want to protect me. And that made her easy to manipulate.

It makes me hate him even more.

I burst into the Manor's stairway and thunder down to the tenth floor. Stardust flits past the windows in the corridor, lighting my way as I hurry to the vault where the Manor's stock of weapons and exosuits is stored. I yank the handle. Locked. Valentine gave Kieran the key this afternoon. We were supposed to gear up and head to Times Square together with Everly.

I'm such an idiot to have trusted him.

If he makes it to dawn alive, I promise myself that I will never let him be a part of my life again. And if he tries, I will make him regret it.

I kick the door hard enough to leave a thick black scuff mark and return to the apartment. I tell myself I can still make it to Times Square by midnight. But without an exosuit, my only choice will be to run thirty blocks by foot.

I find Zaza waiting anxiously in the foyer. "Rei, I'm so sorry—"

I grab her by the shoulders. "Zaza. It's okay. I understand. I probably would have done the same, if I were in your shoes. Nevertheless, I need you to *get the hell out of my way*."

She bites her lip and yields. I blow past her and ravage my closet for my combat education exosuit. I change into it in silence and zip the back myself.

"That's not a real exosuit, is it?" Zaza asks, her voice small.

Almost reflexively, I touch my fingers to my thumb. It's unnerving when I don't get any response. Same thing goes for my staff. Whereas the ones issued directly to mavs can feed off the energy produced by exosuits, this one only works during the day off a few hours' charge. If Kieran hadn't convinced Zaza to drug me, at least I would have been heading into a dangerous situation with the proper gear and protection. Now this is the best I've got.

"No," I reply. "But it sure beats pajamas."

From the closet in the foyer, I pull out a regular old trench coat— probably one of Aunt Minyi's. I strap my staff to my back. Right before I leave, I catch a glimpse of myself in the full-length mirror hanging by the door.

I don't look like a maverick. I look like a little girl playing dress-up.

I don't trust myself to speak, so the best I can do is give Zaza a terse, tight embrace and sweep out the door.

When I emerge from the stairs into the dark lobby of the Manor, I stride straight toward the double doors. It's only when my fingers close around the ornate handle that I hesitate for the first time. I stare out through the pane of glass into the desolate street. The shadows seem to take on new forms before my eyes, gloating, taunting, daring me to stumble into their depths.

Reality sucker-punches me in the gut. I lean my full weight against the door, suddenly light-headed. Even if I manage to make it thirty blocks in the middle of nightfall without running into any Deathlings, what am I going to do once I reach Times Square? Get on my knees and ask for whoever sent that severed ear to spare Aunt Minyi as nicely as I can?

I was stupid to trust Kieran, but I would be far more so if I didn't turn back now.

My hand falls to my side.

Yet as I take the first step away from the doors, Everly's voice echoes in my mind.

There's a certain kind of person I've taken pride in not being my whole life. The kind of person who steps aside and watches from the safety of the sidelines when they have the power to make change.

After we found Noëlle's body by the park, Yuna could have left me to fend for myself. She knew the Deathlings were coming—she could have chosen to escape to safety, but instead she chose to stay and fight by my side. A choice she ended up paying for with her life.

That day Roland showed up in the abandoned subway station, he didn't hesitate to put himself in danger for my sake. Roland was many things—arrogant, annoying, and self-entitled as hell—but he was never a coward.

The crisp nightfall air kisses my bare face as I forge downtown on Broadway. Before the Vanishing, nighttime was when this city truly came alive. Yet now I can hardly recognize the neighborhood I've passed thousands of times in the daylight.

I sprint through the smorgasbord of intersections right across from the plaza on 64th Street where the city features the finest of the performing arts. There's a huge fountain in the center that shoots breath-taking displays during the day, but the only showstopper tonight is the Deathling currently lounging in its waters.

I pick up my pace, praying it won't notice me.

But just before I round the corner, I hear a splash. The Deathling clambers out of the fountain, flinging water onto the sidewalk, and charges straight for me.

Without the extra speed from my exosuit, it catches up in no time. A claw scrapes my back. I dive behind a tree and roll out from the other side, staff up. I stab the end into the Deathling's sternum. It squawks and slashes wildly. Pain sears across my shoulder. My stomach lurches as I lose my balance off the edge of the curb. I slam the butt of the rod into the ground, clinging to the shaft to swing my body around, just out of the way of its next swipe. Before it can recover its footing, I let out a feral scream and spear it through the throat. I twist and slash all the way through, savoring the *thwack* of my blade cleaving through muscle and bone.

A mixture of stardust and the sweat dripping down my neck stings my healing shoulder and back wounds. I wipe my blade off the already-decaying corpse of the Deathling and glance up.

My heart leaps into my throat. Staff brandished, I scramble backward, away from the colossal mass of darkness and fur looming above me.

I stare.

A nightfang mere feet away bares its fangs at me. Not in threat, exactly. More like . . . excitement.

Slowly, I lower my staff.

Hardly daring to breathe, I whisper, "Boba?"

CHAPTER FIFTY-TWO

For a second, nothing happens.

Maybe I'm going to die after all.

But then my nightfang pup rolls onto his back, exposing his tummy, and gazes up adoringly at me with those luminous, starry black eyes.

My legs almost give out in sheer relief. I sheathe my staff and shower him with belly rubs. I don't even have to bend down anymore. "When did you grow so big? Huh?" When his tail beats the ground, the impact leaves cracks in the concrete.

Out of nowhere, he starts gagging. His entire body quakes with the force of his retching. In desperation, I scramble onto him and start thrusting my fists against his abdomen. I never imagined I'd be using my knowledge from my *Inhuman Anatomy IV* textbook like this, but a few seconds later my diligence pays off and a shiny object shoots out of Boba's maw. It jingles onto the sidewalk.

I slide off him and crouch down, squinting. I blink a few times, my mouth parted in stupefaction.

I reach for the object. It's covered in Deathling saliva and weird pink slime, but there's no mistaking it.

I hold up the Token and turn to Boba in awe. "How . . . ?"

He merely grins at me with all kajillion of his teeth.

A clatter echoes in the distance. Boba's ears flatten. A low growl rumbles from his throat. He rises onto his haunches and bends his neck down, looking at me expectantly. I don't understand until he begins head-butting me toward his side with increasing urgency. I grab a tuft of thick, surprisingly soft fur. I give it an experimental tug. When it doesn't seem to bother him, I hoist myself onto his back.

I've hardly sat down when Boba jumps onto his feet without warning and guns it down the street. I shriek, nearly flying off straight into the void.

By the time we hit Columbus Circle, I'm accustomed enough to the rhythm of his strides to loosen up slightly. But Boba himself slows at the inlet of the enormous traffic circle. He dances on his feet, head swinging to and fro, unsure of which street to take next.

I try squeezing my thighs, but his fur is so thick that he doesn't register the pressure at all. I pull on the tuft in my left hand. Immediately, he trots slightly to the left, ears perked up.

"Okay," I mutter. "I can work with this."

I guide him around the circle. Once we merge onto Broadway again, he launches back into full speed. The wind whips my hair into a frenzy as he barrels through the streets, his powerful muscles roiling beneath me like ocean waves.

I lean into him, spurring him faster. I notice with a start that he doesn't stink as strongly of sewage or sulfur as other Deathlings. He also smells like grass and mud. For the first time, I consider whether the signature scent of Deathlings belongs to Deathlings at all—rather than their subterranean habitats. I'd never questioned that fact.

Just like I hadn't questioned why Boba has never tried to hurt me.

An uncomfortable thought settles over me. What if Boba is just like Tim? A human turned nightfang? And even if not, if I were to kill him right here and right now . . . who would be the true monster?

It's not easy to cross the only line I have ever known how to follow. It's not easy to forget what I spent years learning at school, drilled into my brain by thousands of hours of study, nor to unravel a lifetime of disgust and hatred perpetuated by severe childhood trauma and a deep-seated desire for vengeance. Because if I'm to turn my back on everything I have ever believed about Deathlings, everything the Syndicate stands for, what will that mean for all the mavericks who died for this cause? For Master Sasha? For my parents?

As we pass a skyscraper built of reflective glass, I glimpse myself again, my staff slung on my back and my borrowed coat billowing behind me as I ride my magnificent creature of darkness.

I open my hand to stare down at the tiny unassuming coin resting in the cup of my palm, clenched so tightly in my fist that a little red welt imprints my skin in the shape of a Y. What if the Token really is missing a piece? And once it becomes whole again, what will it be capable of?

As we draw closer to Times Square, the colossal billboards and advertisements dominate the sky. Nightfall drains the vibrant colors of the electric screens to pure black. I feel tiny in comparison to their vast, flat emptiness. Such emptiness that soon each rectangle ceases to resemble a dead screen at all, but the windowless walls of a sinister fortress.

We pass the street I chased Cassie down after she stole my wallet. Not even a breeze graces these avenues.

Here, the city has come to a complete standstill.

At least that means Valentine and the other mavericks are doing the job they promised—to lure all the Deathlings in the vicinity away to prevent as many unwanted intrusions as possible.

Still, Kieran and Everly should have been here already, but there's no sign of them.

I tug Boba's fur until he slows to a halt. After I slip off his back, I reach up to stroke his neck. "Go on. No one can see you with me, it's too dangerous."

He whimpers, nuzzling his head into my shoulder.

I give him one last scratch behind the ears. "If I make it out of this alive, I promise to bring you enough cake to fill a bus. *Two* buses. And a taxicab full of banana pudding."

Even then, he doesn't budge until I push him away. Hard. Reluctantly, he sulks off around the corner, his head hung low. My chest aches to see him go, but I won't be able to live with myself if anyone got their hands on him—Syndicate or otherwise.

Right below where the New Year's Eve ball used to drop at the turn of midnight, I come to a halt. I search for signs of a fight, but the plaza lies unscathed.

"Well?" I declare to the darkness. I pull out the note that was delivered earlier today and hold it straight up in the air. "I'm here. Overslept a little, sorry."

Rotating in a full circle, I scan my surroundings.

Nothing.

"You were the one who wanted to see me," I call out. "So come out and play."

Just as I fear that I'm truly too late, I hear it.

Click-clack. Click-clack. Click-clack.

The same sound I heard echoing through the base where the masters and I had been held prisoner.

Heart hammering, I whirl around as the shadows shift and a figure emerges from the gloom beneath one of the screens. Like the first time we met, she wears sunglasses and stark white from head to toe, though tonight she's opted for a silk pantsuit tailored perfectly to her figure. Her platinum bob sways with each step, as celestial as the glowing stardust drifting between us. Even from afar, the steely glimmer of her prosthetic winks dangerously behind the bone-white cage of her stiletto straps.

She stops an arm's length away from me and speaks my name like she's savoring its taste. "Rei Reynolds."

I set my jaw. "Agent Storm. Or should I call you Sabrina?"

Her blood-rose lips curl into a serpentine smile. "If you wish."

"You can take off your sunglasses. There's no need to hide what you really are—not from me."

"And what am I *really*?" she says in a mocking tone as she obliges.

As her soulless black gaze drills into me, a shudder of horror convulses through my body. "Inhuman."

"Hm. I think I look perfectly human." She extends her arms and examines her manicured fingernails. "Though I suppose everyone is entitled to their own opinion."

"You're an abomination. And you know it."

Her smile sharpens. "Humans often are, darling."

My fists clench. "You're a traitor to your own kind. Part human, part Deathling."

At that, her smile vanishes. "It was my loyalty to my *own kind* that led to my current condition."

I snort. "What, an evil scientist injected your body with some Deathling mutation? Or maybe you were stupid enough to do it yourself?"

Agent Storm's hand shoots forward and latches around my neck. "Let me ask you something," she whispers, digging her nails into my pulse point. "Say I were to rip your throat apart, right here, right now. You have only one chance—one *way*—of surviving. Either you take it or die chok-ing on your own blood. Which do you choose?"

"I'd take it," I hiss, straining against her grip, "if only to rip *your* throat apart."

"Then we're in agreement." She smiles again, caressing my cheek with her knuckles as she releases me.

I touch the base of my throat, breathing hard. My fingers close around Mom's necklace, as if it will lend me strength. "I don't think we are."

"We'll see about that." She claps her hands together. "Anyway! What can I do for you, darling?"

My temper flares. "You're the one who summoned me here!"

"And *you're* the one who needs something from *me*. Desperately, I might add. So make your offer."

Patience, Rei. I hear Aunt Minyi's voice. I need time to gain the upper hand, so I take a deep breath and uncurl my fists. "What's your selling price?"

"I'm glad you asked," Storm purrs. On her whistle, two bodyguards materialize from within the nearest building, the Madame Tussauds wax museum. One carries a silver tray covered by a lid. The other carries a rolled-up napkin. Curiously, only one minion's eyes gleam black from lid to lid like molten obsidian. The other's eyes are brown and round as a fawn's, but still human.

"How much are they paying you?" I ask the brown-eyed minion.

In lieu of responding, he lifts the lid off the platter to reveal a slab of glistening, raw meat, topped with butter and garnished with sprigs of rosemary.

"Ta-da." Agent Storm leans close and murmurs into my ear. "Now eat it."

My brow furrows in annoyance. Of all the things I expected tonight, a dinner date with the enemy was the last. "What?"

"Eat it. That's my asking price. I'll give you back your aunt immediately. No strings attached."

I lift my chin. "How do I know you won't give her back to me dead? Or in pieces?"

"It wounds me that you think me capable of such cunning cruelty."

"You *did* send me a severed ear."

She waves me off. "It grew back quickly enough."

"Was it yours?"

"God, no." She sighs. "When I give an order, I expect my people to listen. One of the new recruits didn't, so . . ." She mimes a scissor motion. "His new ears are proving far more effective. But I digress. You'll get your aunt back, alive and whole."

"Tempting." But at least it means that Aunt Minyi must be somewhere nearby. I peer at the raw meat, struggling to keep my expression neutral under Storm's unsettling stare. "Is it poisoned?"

"Honestly, Rei, you insult me. It won't harm you—in fact, it will do the opposite."

My eyes narrow. "How so?"

She spreads her arms. "Imagine the power of an Artifact. Now imagine that power within *you*, not some object. The power of strength, the power of speed. The power to transform beyond your comprehension. To be one with the darkness."

A sickening suspicion festers in my gut. I don't dare let it show on my face. Instead, I lean forward, as if she's caught my attention—I'm no Master Minyi, but I've learned from her well enough—and say, "It can't be that simple, can it?"

She notes my spark of interest and smiles. The minion with the napkin unwraps it and hands me a fork and knife. "You know, Rei, I think you and I have more in common than you might think. I saw how you handled that Deathling in your combat education class. Together, we could make an extraordinary team."

I tear my gaze away from the platter. "And accomplish what?"

"Putting an end to the corrupt, evil ways of the Syndicate."

A bitter laugh of surprise escapes me. "By chopping off the ears of whoever doesn't listen to you?"

She clucks her tongue. "The Syndicate has brainwashed you into believing all Deathlings are evil."

"Deathlings delight in devouring human flesh. They killed my parents."

"No. They didn't."

"I watched them do it," I snap, my grip tightening around the fork and knife.

"The Deathlings weren't the ones who set your house on fire," Storm says quietly. My heart stutters. "The Deathlings weren't the ones who drove your family into the street. Into danger."

Eyes stinging from the fumes. Unbearable heat. Waves of it, simmering through the air. I close my eyes, struggling to stifle the memory. "How do you know about that?" I whisper.

"Who do you think caused the fire in the first place?"

"It was an accident."

"You know what the chances of a fire occurring during nightfall are?" says Storm. "Zero. Open flame? Banned. Electricity can't run, stoves don't work. So unless your parents smuggled firewood into your living room and lit a bonfire, it was no *accident*."

The world tilts askew. I was so young, and so focused on the actual murder of my parents that I'd never questioned the other details. "But . . . who would do that? Who would want my parents dead?"

"Good girl. Now you're asking the right questions."

I barely hear her over the thoughts raging through my head. "My mom was just an enforcer," I mutter. Unlike Aunt Minyi, she never achieved any high position of power. Dad, on the other hand, was the head curator of the Archives. I don't know enough about his work to guess who wanted him dead.

But Storm might.

I shake my head, playing ignorant. "And my dad just worked at the Archives."

"*Just* worked at the Archives? Darling, your father had one of the most important jobs in New York City. When the Artifacts first began to appear, he became the master of *all* of them."

The journal full of sketches flashes in my mind. "So?"

"He had unlimited access to them, as well as their powers. And then he stumbled across one that was powerful enough to blow this city to kingdom come."

"So he was silenced," I realize slowly, "because he was never supposed to find it."

"No," says Storm. "It was because he stole it."

CHAPTER FIFTY-THREE

I lunge for Storm, teeth bared, but her minions seize me by the arms and jerk me back. *"Bullshit,"* I snarl.

"Your father betrayed the Syndicate. He stole an Artifact from the Archives."

"Don't you dare talk about my father like that. My parents dedicated their lives to the Syndicate. They would never—"

"Then explain to me how you incinerated that nightfang."

I stop short. "What?"

"After your team was ambushed the other night."

I suddenly recall the three shadowy silhouettes hovering over me right before I passed out. The same Syndicate badge she wore before still glints on her chest now, taunting me. My skin goes cold. "You were there?"

"Oh, darling," she titters. "I arranged the whole affair. Your friends were all so heroic, splitting up in order to rescue that poor, delusional man in Koreatown. After that, it was just a matter of sending up those flares to separate you from your partner—that doll of a girl."

Blood rushes through my ears, consuming every other sound.

"Such a shame, what happened to her." Storm sends me a sympathetic smile. "I only ever kill out of necessity, you see. But she needed to die for you to realize what was at stake. For you to finally use the gift your father left you. Tell me exactly what it is and how you used it, and no one else needs to die."

"I don't know," I lie, only now realizing what a stroke of luck it was to lose the Token before Storm could get her hands on it.

Storm clasps her hands behind her back. "Perhaps I can help you remember. That night of the fire. Tell me how your parents perished . . . yet *you* managed to survive."

I falter.

She begins to circle me, her heels clicking with each unhurried, methodical step. "An unarmed, three-year-old girl versus a starving horde of Deathlings on a killing rampage. You think they just decided to spare you?"

Fingers scrabbling. The clink of metal.

I grit my teeth, struggling to shut out the memories flooding my mind. I press my palms into my temples and squeeze my eyes shut. "I don't remember—"

Mom's eyes, wide with fear but hard with determination, brown gone black in the night. "Wear this. Always. Never let it go. Never let them take it from you. Now run. RUN!"

Arms up, elbows locked, finger on the trigger.

BANG. BANG.

Storm's voice cuts through the crushing wave of anguish. "Something saved you. What was it?"

I don't see her anymore. I only see the Deathling reaching two of its many hands to grab Mom by the face, its claws raking down her cheeks as she thrashes and turns to me one last time. "Run, Rei!" Bloody tears stream down her face. "*RUN—*" she screams right before the *CRUNCH* of teeth cleaving through bone.

The other Deathlings, attracted by her screams of agony, prowl closer. But instead of her, their eyes lock on me.

"Think, Rei," Storm hisses. "What was it? What saved you? *Tell me.*"

My legs tremble. *Run, Rei.* I don't run. I can't. Mom's final wish, but my feet refuse to move as the Deathling gorges itself on her flesh. Once satisfied, it discards her remains on the concrete like an unwanted appetizer.

"Please," I whisper as the monsters advance. I clutch the necklace Mom gave me, unable to tear my gaze away from her mutilated corpse.

I don't want to be eaten.

When the monsters attack, I throw my arms out in front of my face, as if that will shield me from death. Mom's necklace dangles from my fist, glowing in the stardust, a single symbol hand-wrought in gold. *Shǎn:* 闪. *Flash. Lightning. To shine.* Except something's different. There's something attached to the other side of the talisman. Something round.

Good for One Fare.

As the Deathlings lunge, gold light crackles from my hands and obliterates the night.

My eyes fly open to find Storm's demonic pupils looming inches away. I scramble back from her with a yelp, still reeling from the flashback, but she grabs me by the shoulders, her gaze roving my face hungrily for answers.

"Well?" she demands.

The necklace suddenly seems to weigh a thousand tons around my neck. I choose my mask carefully. "I just remember the Deathlings tearing apart my mom. And then . . . darkness." My lip wobbles. "I must have fainted."

Storm's eyes narrow, trying to ferret out my lies. But apparently my half-truths are just convincing enough. With a disgruntled snort, she shoves me aside and spins off. She grabs the platter of meat from her minion and thrusts it toward me. "I'm sure we'll find a way to help you remember." She smiles. "Eat. Power awaits."

A moment of clarity sparks through me. It's not me she cares about, nor my allegiance to her cause. It's my connection to the Artifact. I may not really know how to use it, but she has even less of an idea.

I can't let that advantage go to waste.

"Bring out Master Minyi first," I tell her.

Storm considers me. With a sigh, she signals to her minions. They disappear beneath an awning across the street and return a minute later with a blindfolded woman in tow. Not only blindfolded—gagged. Her wrists and ankles bound, her ears muffled. She can't move except to shuffle inch by humiliating inch in whatever direction the minions prod her toward. Yet she still holds her head high as ever.

I start toward the plaza where my aunt stands, but Storm clicks her tongue and smirks.

"Not so fast. I held up my part of the deal. Now it's your turn."

I can't stall any longer. I bring my fork and knife up, trying not to examine the meat too closely. "Not that I'm a picky eater, but what is it?"

"You must have figured it out by now."

That sickening feeling in my gut returns full force. *The power of strength, the power of speed. The power to transform beyond your comprehension. To be one with the darkness.* I force out the words. "It's Deathling meat."

Amusement dances across Storm's features. "Freshly slain, just for you."

It's all I can do to restrain myself from stabbing her straight in the throat. But for Aunt Minyi's sake, I *have* to keep playing this game.

In the most pleasant voice I can muster, I say, "Just to clarify, this is how you became a nightfang? Some chef whipped up a Deathling steak and fed it to you on a silver platter?"

Her smug look wavers. "I told you I only had one chance to survive. While I was a hellbringer, the Directors sent me out on a last-minute assignment. It was nightfall. The master that had been assigned to escort me never showed. My destination turned out to be a Deathling nest. Mysteriously, my gun malfunctioned. I shot an emergency flare, but backup never arrived."

Movement darts across my peripheral vision. My stomach flips, but I keep my attention focused on Storm. "Coincidence?"

"More like convenience. I'd stumbled across some extremely sensitive information just days prior. The very same information that would come to save my life." She trails off, lost in thought. "I took out two Deathlings with my bare hands, but it cost me. When the third showed up while I bled out on the ground, I knew I was going to die. So I dragged my broken body over to the nearest corpse and took my chance." She takes the platter and holds it up to me with her own two hands. "Now it's your turn."

A shiver runs down my spine. I cast a furtive glance over to where Aunt Minyi stands between Storm's minions. The wind picks up. A low whistle rolls through the night.

"I'm sorry," I begin. "But my aunt told me to never accept food from strangers."

I slam my fist upward into the bottom of the platter. It bashes Storm in the face with a delightful *clang*. The Deathling meat slaps her across the forehead with a wet, even more delectable *splat*.

Gunfire erupts from a roof across the street. A figure in black showers bullets into the plaza. Storm's minions topple to the ground like puppets cut from their strings. I catch a glimpse of ash-brown hair and a swirling black coat as Kieran makes a dash for Aunt Minyi.

Storm growls and wipes away the bloody juices running down her cheeks. Before she can think of going after him, I drive the knife into her throat. Her hand shoots up just in time for the blade to pierce straight through her palm.

As Kieran manages to rip off Aunt Minyi's blindfold, Storm grabs ahold of the hilt, twists her hand with the knife still impaled in it, and wrenches it out of my grip. Blood squirts over both of us. With her other hand, she yanks the knife free.

"I would think twice about moving another inch, darling," she shouts at Kieran.

Both he and Aunt Minyi whip around. She starts struggling against her restraints, her fury smothered by the gag. I'm about to turn when cold, hard metal digs into my temple. I hear the click of the safety and freeze.

The color drains out of Kieran's face. "*Tim?* What the hell are you doing here?"

Tim's voice rumbles next to my ear. "Finishing what I started."

"Drop your weapons or she gets a bullet in her brain," Storm orders Kieran. "Your friend made it quite clear to me earlier how eager he is to pull that trigger, so I suggest you be quick about it."

"They turned you into a monster," says Kieran, horrified.

"We prefer the term *Halfling*," Storm replies. "Rolls right off the tongue, don't you think?"

Tim presses the barrel into my skull deep enough to bruise. "Can I kill her yet?"

My heart thunders. From across the plaza, I meet Kieran's pained gaze. With enormous reluctance, he opens his hand and lets his own gun clatter onto the street.

Storm nods at Kieran. She tells Tim, "Kill him."

Everything moves in slow motion. As Tim redirects his aim, I grab the

Token from my pocket and raise it upside down against my neck. Against Mom's necklace, the charm of the character *Shǎn*: 闪. Just like in the memory I tried so hard to repress, the central component of the character fits perfectly into the Y-shaped notch in the Token. They snap together with a satisfying *click*, two halves of a whole, reunited at last.

Tim pulls the trigger.

Otherworldly light explodes from my hands. A crackling dome of energy surges outward, obliterating the bullet, engulfing the sky to immerse the nearby skyscrapers in molten gold.

Warmth flurries over me. Cacophony fills my head: the rattle and screech of trains careening down the tracks; wind roaring through pitch-black tunnels; thousands of subway cars pulsing like blood through the underground arteries of the city, keeping it alive.

A miracle unfolds before my eyes.

As the golden dome continues expanding, Manhattan begins to stir. Color spills across the giant screens, dazzling the streets with ads for clothes and soda and Broadway shows. Car engines rev in the distance. Big band jazz blares from the speaker system of a nearby shop. The traffic lights flash from yellow to red to green like strobe lights. Times Square blazes so brightly that even the stars vanish from the sky.

For the first time in fifteen years, the city that never sleeps finally awakens from its deep slumber.

CHAPTER FIFTY-FOUR

How . . ." Storm breathes, gaping at the screens illuminating the streets as bright as day. The gun clatters to the concrete as Tim, equally thunderstruck, marvels at the stunning spectacle alongside Kieran and Aunt Minyi.

Exhilaration and terror alike rush through my veins. Times Square looks just like the huge picture framed in Aunt Minyi's office—alive in the darkness.

When I glance down, my entire body glows with the same gold light emanating from the Token.

But this power . . . it *burns*.

My awe shifts into discomfort. And soon into agony. I'm a phoenix ascending to full glory, only to discover that I can't endure the heat of my own flames. The Token levitates off my chest. Scorching waves ripple the air around it. My body begins vibrating so intensely that the concrete beneath my feet fractures. The web of fissures spreads across the stone. I scream, clutching my head, and fall to my knees.

Someone seizes me from behind. With a hard yank, the chain of

Mom's necklace snaps off against my throat. The Artifact's power evaporates from my body. I can only watch as Storm lifts the Token to the sky, her black eyes glittering with triumph and reverence.

"*Finally*," she croons.

At that moment, the dome of light flickers.

Storm glances up, her brow crinkling in confusion. Instead of continuing to expand outward, the dome begins to shrink. Her eyes widen in denial. "Wait. No. Stop!" She thrusts a finger at me. Tim hauls me to my feet. "How did you make it work? Tell me, or else I'll—"

A revving engine and the squeal of tires cut her off. A bright red Volkswagen Beetle drifts around the corner, burning black skid marks into the asphalt. Storm looks up just in time for the front of the car to ram into her and launch her twenty feet into the air.

The Token flies out of her grip. It bounces off the sidewalk, dangerously close to a gutter, before rolling to a stop on the yellow stripe painted down the middle of the street. Storm crashes through a cluster of safety pylons. Her skull smacks into a lamppost with a *clang*.

Everly rolls down the driver's window with a shit-eating grin, their sniper gear tossed on the dashboard. "Beep, beep, motherfucker!"

"Where'd you get that?" Kieran yells.

"Is that seriously what you're asking right now? Get in!"

He does his best to half carry, half drag Aunt Minyi toward the car. I stagger to my feet and sway toward the Token, but Tim gets there first.

He shoots me a savage grin and opens his mouth. He sticks the Artifact under his tongue. Then he crosses his arms over his face and curls over. His body swells, causing his expression to contort in a brief flash of pain. A crown of barbed horns spears through the skin on his forehead. His fingers lengthen into those grisly talons. His teeth sharpen, splitting in half, then multiplying, until hundreds of fangs protrude from his massive jaws. Only his eyes remain unchanged through the transformation, shimmering with hunger and hatred.

Grimly, I unsheathe my staff.

The size of Tim as a human is daunting enough. As a nightfang, he is unfathomable.

But I'm the only one standing between him and the others.

With an earth-quaking bellow, he charges at me. I plant myself in a defensive stance, even though I know it's futile. Everly yells something unintelligible. Out of the corner of my eye, I see Kieran lunge toward me, his arm outstretched and his face ashen in horror.

He won't make it in time.

A streak of darkness hurtles out of the sky like a falling meteorite. Fangs flash. I realize it's no cosmic rock.

It's another nightfang.

It squashes Tim flat into the ground, shredding bloody ribbons across his back with its talons. Chomping down on Tim's neck, it flings him from side to side like a dog playing with a chew toy.

At first I think it's Boba, but with its longer limbs and streamlined torso, this nightfang is built more like a panther than a bear. I stare, captivated. I've never seen two nightfangs brawling.

HONK! Everly blasts the horn at me. Kieran is still struggling to get Aunt Minyi into the car. With Tim distracted by the newcomer, I manage to skirt around the fight unnoticed. I sprint over to the car and help Kieran finally shove her into the back seat.

"Glad you decided to show up," he sneers at me.

My jaw drops. "*Decided* to show up? Like you gave me a goddamn choice, you absolute *dipshit*."

"Excuse me?"

"Go to hell. You didn't even have the balls to drug me yourself, so you forced Zaza to do it for you?"

Kieran's face goes totally slack. "What on earth are you talking about? You got *drugged?* When? How?"

His unequivocal shock and the concern in his voice make me falter. But before I can respond, the window of the passenger door in front of me shatters with a *BANG*. Everly screams. I leap back, ducking behind the car door as bullets whiz through the air. One zings right past my head, clipping my earlobe.

Storm crawls out of the rubble from across the street, battered and bloody but very much alive. The entire right side of her body hangs limp, one mangled arm bent completely the wrong way. Shards of bloody bone poke out of her blazer. Only her steel leg remains perfectly functional. Yet somehow it makes her no less terrifying—and certainly no less furious.

She manages to reload her gun with one hand. Already, the stardust is slowly mending her back together. "You're not going anywhere, Rei."

Kieran grabs my wrist. "Rei! What are you waiting for? Get in!"

"Hit the gas, Everly. Get Master Minyi out of here."

"We can't just leave you behind," they say.

"No. She's after *me*." For whatever reason, the Token refuses to work with her. She needs my help to use it, which means that despite her trigger-happiness, she needs me alive—for now. "She won't kill me yet, but she doesn't care about you three. I can't let her take the Token, and you'll just be in my way. Go, dammit, before she finishes healing!"

Kieran sees the look in Everly's eyes. "Everly, don't—"

I wrench away from Kieran and slam the passenger door shut. Everly nails their foot into the gas pedal. The little red punch buggy rockets away. Storm shoots at the tires, her aim improving with each round, but manages to ping only one bullet off the rim of the back tire. The car rounds the bend, out of sight.

A bellow of agony shakes the plaza. The unknown nightfang wallops Tim in the face, causing the Token to sail out of his parted jaws. With a tremendous heave, the beast hurls him into the grand entrance of Madame Tussauds. He smashes through the wax sculpture display of the original ten masters and topples into the red carpet, unmoving.

To my dismay, the Token bounces back across the street and clatters into the curb mere steps away from where Storm stands.

The other nightfang turns on me. Tim's blood drips from its maw.

Storm sees an opportunity and seizes it. "Whoever you are," she calls out, "bring that girl to me and you will be rewarded beyond your wildest dreams."

The nightfang tilts its head. Whatever hope I might have been clinging on to that this Halfling would be anything like Boba evaporates.

I whip my head back and forth between the two monsters on either side of me. I'm caught perfectly in the middle. My fingers clench around my staff.

Against the nightfang, the staff will probably be useless. Against Storm, however . . .

But if I kill her, nothing will stop the nightfang from devouring *me*. If I surrender now, if I hand over the Token, I can still survive.

This city cannot be saved, Aunt Minyi's voice reminds me gently. *Nor does it need or want to be.*

Find your way, Master Sasha's voice urges in my head. *I fear that fate of Manhattan may depend on it.*

Save yourself instead, says my aunt.

Save us all, Master Sasha insists.

Run, Rei, Mom begs.

Rise, *Rei*.

Storm leans forward in gleeful anticipation of the bloodbath. I cock my throwing arm in the direction of the nightfang. But at the last second, I pivot to one foot. The staff cuts through the air in a graceful arc, flying straight and true not at the Deathling, but at Storm.

A strange sense of calm washes over me. I will never fulfill my vow to my parents. I will die here, alone. But at least I can take one of this city's greatest monsters out with me.

Until Storm catches the rod by the shaft, halting the blade inches from her face.

"No," I whisper. "No way." No human could have reacted that fast—but then, she isn't one.

With a smirk, she brings the shaft down on her knee and snaps it in two. Part of my soul breaks with it. "I'm giving you one last chance," she warns me. "Teach me how to use the Artifact, and I'll let you live. You'll see that I can be quite merciful to those who serve me well."

"Take your mercy and shove it where the stars don't shine," I snarl back.

Storm sneers and raises her gun, but I'm already whirling toward the nightfang. If Storm managed to kill a Deathling or two with her bare hands, why can't I? Either I survive this moment or die trying. In a way, it feels like . . . liberation.

The nightfang charges. I rush forward to meet it in combat, but to my confusion, it leaps right over my head just as Storm pulls the trigger.

The hail of bullets strike its hide. It drops to the ground, howling in pain. Yet it doesn't waver, shielding me from the barrage with its own body. Then it shakes itself like a wet dog. Several bullets clatter onto the pavement. Not a single one detonates—instead glowing the same molten gold as the light from the Token. Could it be the Artifact's doing?

The gunfire ceases. In the time it takes Storm to reload, the nightfang snatches me by the collar of my coat. I thrash and holler, remembering how far it threw Tim. It tosses me up into the air. I land on its back with an *oomph*. I barely manage to recover quickly enough to seize a fistful of fur before it bolts off, away from Storm.

"Hey!" I holler, thumping my fist into its side. "I need my Artifact!"

Reluctantly, the nightfang circles around, but it's too late.

"You mean this?" Storm calls. With a smug smile, she steps off the curb and bends down to pick up the Token—

Only for it to whiz out of her reach like a leaf snatched by a gust of wind.

With a frown, she takes another step closer and reaches for it a second time. This time it surges into the air and darts right through her outstretched fingers. It hovers in front of her nose, winking playfully in the fading lights of Times Square. She growls and attempts to grab it again and again, but it evades her clutches with fluid ease. She curses. The Token zooms forward and jabs her between the eyes in retaliation. When she tries to trap it, she ends up striking herself in the face instead. She lets out a scream of frustration. It rolls down the bridge of her nose into the gloom.

With one final wink, the Token folds in on itself and vanishes into thin air.

I swear I can hear the wind laughing.

Storm's eyes land on me, two bottomless pits of blazing wrath. "You little *bitch*," she seethes, advancing.

"I think we've overstayed our welcome," I tell my new nightfang pal.

As the lights in Times Square flicker out one by one and Storm's enraged screams fade behind us, we flee into the night, swift as the absolute darkness sweeping over Manhattan once more.

✳

The nightfang carries me all the way to the west side of the city where the Hudson River laps against its banks and the wind moans between the boats in ghostly lament. My eyes dart nonstop between each shadow. The tight coil of paranoia in my chest refuses to loosen. After all, my only line of defense against any Deathlings is, in fact, another Deathling.

At last, when we reach the walkway, the nightfang slows and lowers itself to the ground, allowing me to disembark. But I don't budge. It swivels its head at me in confusion.

"Wait," I say. "Who are you?"

It snorts and tries to shake me off. I lock my legs around it and cling on to its fur. An annoyed growl rumbles deep out of its throat.

"You risked your life for me. Why?"

It bares its teeth at me, but when it doesn't attempt to bite my head off, my curiosity only fuels my determination. "Please. I thought Deathlings were monsters all my life. Prove me wrong."

At that, the nightfang stills. I stare at it expectantly. With an almost human-sounding sigh of exasperation, it paws the ground and shoots me a pointed look. I get the message and slide off its back.

With a final tentative glance, it turns to face the other way. The stardust drifting around it seems to halt midair. Then the glow begins to spiral, swirling faster and faster, forming a luminescent tornado that envelops the beast's entire body. I shield my eyes as buffeting winds push me backward. A hiss fills my ears. When the light dims and the wind dies, all that remains is a cloud of white fog vaporizing into the sky.

I startle and run over to the spot the nightfang occupied mere seconds ago. The disappointment leaves an acrid taste in my mouth. It's gone.

Then I feel a tap on my shoulder. I whip around.

A tall, slender girl stands before me, her beautiful brown skin and dark eyes kissed with the lingering golden shimmer of stardust.

My breath hitches.

"Hello, mèi mei," my sister says.

CHAPTER FIFTY-FIVE

"N o. No, it's impossible."

Maura bites her lip and steps closer to me. "I know it might be hard to—"

"*Stop*," I hiss, backing away. I search my sister's face, her eyes—not black, not like Storm's or Tim's. It's really her. "How? How could you be one of them?" A horrendous thought occurs to me. "You ate Deathling flesh?"

Maura holds her hands up. "Rei, please. I'm not like the other Halflings you met. I never ate anyone, I swear."

"Why the hell would I trust anything you say? You . . ." My voice trembles. My chest heaves. The world spins. "You're a *Deathling*."

"Look at my eyes," she urges me. "They're normal, right? That's how you can tell Halflings like me apart from the ones that are artificially created by eating Deathling flesh, like Sabrina Storm."

Her words barely register. My lip curls in disgust. "So this is the truth. This is why you never came home all these years. Because you turned yourself into an abomination."

Her expression twists into an ugly snarl. "Don't say that."

"Don't say what? That you turned yourself into a fucking Deathling?"

"I never chose this!"

I flinch. I can only stare at her in stunned silence. Like Aunt Minyi, Maura rarely loses her temper—and never with me.

Her shoulders slump. "I'm sorry. I didn't mean to . . . Please, just think about this for a second. The Vanishing. Hundreds of thousands of people disappeared into the fog, Rei, never to be seen again."

"What does that have to do with the fact that my own sister is a Deathling?"

"Everything!" Maura yells. "Don't you understand? Where do you think those people went? Haven't you ever wondered where Deathlings originated in the first place?"

The shock hits me with enough force to pummel the air straight out of my lungs.

"You're wrong," I whisper. My legs wobble. "Those people just died. They vanished. That's it. The end."

"I vanished, didn't I?" Maura says softly. I can feel her gauging my reaction. "But I didn't die. I became a Deathling."

I crouch down to the ground and bury my face in my hands. "So what you're saying is that every single human that disappeared during the Vanishing turned into a Deathling."

A beat of silence. "Yes."

"Which means . . . it was never just monsters that we were killing."

Maura averts her gaze. "It wasn't your fau—"

"No, shut up, Maura! Just shut up!" Years of pent-up resentment simmering beneath the surface finally erupt. I shoot back onto my feet and throw myself at her face. She catches me by the wrists, struggling to hold me back. "If you're really telling the truth, that means I've been killing humans all along!" A sob wrenches itself from my chest. I tear myself out of her grip. "*Humans*, Maura. New Yorkers. And you knew whose blood I was getting on my hands, but you never said a word!"

She winces. "I swore under threat of execution to keep that secret. You would have been killed just for knowing. I'm only telling you now because Storm already put you in danger by revealing the truth about Halflings."

"Thank liberty for that!"

"Look, none of this was my choice," Maura exclaims. "If it weren't for the Vanishing, I wouldn't have become a Deathling. If it weren't for Dad, I wouldn't have become a Halfling. And if it weren't for *you* running head-first into a fight with a bunch of Halflings practically unarmed, I wouldn't have been forced to jump in and save you, and we wouldn't even be having this argument right now!"

My eyes go wide with false, incredulous wonder. "If it weren't for *me*, huh? I bet it's also *my* fault that you're such a shitty sister."

Maura has the audacity to look hurt. "How could you say something so selfish?"

I bark out a laugh. "That's rich, coming from the person that just takes off for months at a time without the slightest explanation and then thinks it's perfectly okay to just pop back into other people's lives only to fuck off again for only god knows how long. You think that's been so easy for me? Constantly wondering and worrying about you while pretending I'm totally fine with how you fly in and out of my life like it's a goddamn airport just because I know you've been through a lot?"

"I—I didn't realize you felt that way. And I'm sorry. But what was I supposed to do?"

I hold myself, staring at her feet. "All I wanted was to see you more often. For you to be there for me. Like a sister is *supposed* to be."

"At least you had Mom," she replies with a touch of envy.

"Aunt Minyi is *your* mom," I say heavily, looking up. "Not mine."

Maura reels back as if slapped. It's not my intention to sound ungrateful, but of course I do anyway. For a minute, she doesn't respond. When she does, her voice is frigid. "Then by that definition, I'm not your sister, either."

Each word is a stab to my heart, and she knows it. Because even when we were just cousins, before my parents were killed and Aunt Minyi adopted me officially as her own daughter, Maura was always my jiě jie—my big sister. And I was always her mèi mei—her little sister. Those terms were never bound by blood. For us, they signified so much more—an unbreakable connection, a sisterly love and trust that transcended our many differences.

My voice cracks. "Why can't you just be part of my life like before? Is that so much to ask for?"

Maura rubs her forehead. "You don't get it. After the Vanishing, I couldn't be who you wanted me to be anymore. I *still* can't. Trust me—when I first came back, I hoped things would stay exactly the same as before, especially between us. Except when I saw you for the first time in two years, I realized that nothing could ever be the same again."

"But *why?*"

Her eyes shine with anguish. "Because *we* changed. Both of us."

I waver.

"I was . . . broken," Maura murmurs. "Traumatized by what little I could remember of my time as a Deathling. Meanwhile, your parents had been brutally slaughtered. You had become consumed by revenge. The first time we met up, I made the mistake of asking you how school was going. All I remember was the revulsion on your face when you talked about Deathlings—and the excitement in your eyes at the prospect of killing them."

Something leaden settles in my stomach. "So you thought that if I discovered your secret, I would hurt you. Me, your own sister."

She exhales. "How was I supposed to know, Rei? Maybe you would have turned me in to the Syndicate instead. Maybe not. But I couldn't risk it."

My lips twist into a bitter smile. "You mean you couldn't risk trusting me."

"Two years as a monster can radically change a person. I'm proof of that. Keeping you in the dark was for your safety as much as it was for mine. You know how many people would love to hunt me down if they knew my secret? They wouldn't hesitate to hurt or even kill those dear to me in order to get what they want." She touches my shoulder. "I was just trying to protect you."

"Protect me?" I shrug her off. "If you thought the best way to do that was to keep me in the dark, you shouldn't have bothered. As the last few years have demonstrated, I can take care of my goddamn self."

"That's not what it looked like when I showed up at the plaza. I shouldn't have been anywhere near that place to begin with. Mom made me promise to never venture out into the streets during nightfall, let alone crash Times Square in the middle of a gunfight. But I did it anyway. For *you*."

"Well, thanks a lot," I snap.

"You're welcome," she growls back.

A tense silence ensues, both of us caught in a standoff with neither willing to be the first one to concede. But even when we were kids, I was the one who could never sit still for longer than a minute.

So it's even more of a surprise when she hisses, "Say something, dammit."

I'm about to retort when I glimpse the tears glimmering in her eyes.

Suddenly, all the anger drains out of me. I can't remember the last time I saw Maura cry. I don't know if I ever have.

I turn my back on the river and sag against the railing. The salty, faintly pungent breeze ruffles my hair. I stare up wistfully at the stars. "I wish I could go back and unsay all those things. The ones that made you feel like you couldn't trust me anymore."

Maura leans against the railing next to me. "You have a perfectly valid reason to hate Deathlings. I never said I blamed you for any of it, so you shouldn't, either."

"Why did you leave? For months on end."

"I've been working undercover as one of Storm's advisors for Project Forsaken," Maura admits. "She doesn't know my true identity, human or otherwise. It's how I was able to help you and Mom escape from the research compound."

It takes me a second to realize what she's talking about. "The keys," I whisper. The Ziploc bag. "I asked Aunt Minyi what we were up against. She said *individuals capable of both tremendous harm and good*. She was talking about you."

"She was talking about all Halflings, mèi mei. So many of them are just ordinary people who were in the wrong place at the wrong time. Some of them did the wrong things for the right reasons—to protect their families. They deserve a future." She makes a face. "Well, almost all of them. But until we can figure out how to turn them back into humans, the priority is keeping Storm from using them to take over the city."

"At the compound, there were two kids guarding the masters' cell. Were they Halflings, too?" It's hard to imagine them taking over a corner deli, much less Manhattan. Had they been turned into Halflings like Tim against their will? During the Vanishing, or after?

Find Jae.

I shiver.

"Most likely," says Maura. "Though I suspect Storm positioned them there to provoke you more than anything. I tried to convince her otherwise, but she deduced that your dad had somehow planted the missing Artifact *inside* of you, and that you were the key to manifesting its power."

"She came to my combat ed class," I say suddenly. "She said she was a scout for the Syndicate, but by then she couldn't have been working for them anymore. Is that when she started tracking me?"

Maura's expression turns grim. "It's possible she began tracking you after your dad was killed. She probably never managed to verify your relationship to him until recently because Mom—Aunt Minyi—made so much effort to keep your family records secret. Maybe for that very reason. But I'm guessing Storm used your performance at the end of the first round of the Tournament as confirmation of her predictions."

The revelation makes me uneasy. "Were you really working for Storm all this time?"

"It was Mom's idea, and what little intel I did collect could make a big difference in the long run. She wasn't the Directors' favorite operative for nothing."

"No, I meant if that's why I never saw you anymore. Because you were always working."

She hesitates. "Well, yes and no."

"So you *were* avoiding me."

"Not for the reason you might think." My sister stares off into the distance. "As you grew up, I was afraid of what your hate would turn you into. That's what I told myself, anyway. But maybe that was just an excuse all along. I lost so many people to the Vanishing. All my friends. And Dad."

Uncle Elliot.

She lets out a shuddering exhale. The muscles in her throat work as she struggles to find the right words.

I wait. Patience still may not be my strong suit, but for this I can give my sister all the time she needs in the world.

"You and Mom were all I had left. Of course I wanted to tell you everything. But I never did because, well, I was scared of losing you, too. I had become the very monster you had vowed on your life to destroy." Her voice breaks. "I *am* what you hate, more than anything else in this world."

Tears well in my eyes. "Oh, Maura," I whisper.

For the first time, I see myself as she must have. I imagine how she would have felt every time I talked about Deathlings. *All I remember was the revulsion on your face when you talked about Deathlings—and the excitement in your eyes at the prospect of killing them.* How helpless I must have made her feel, to the point where she would rather bury her secret and let it consume her alive than share it with me.

I hold out my arms. She only resists a moment before allowing me to enfold her in a crushing hug. I rest my head against her chest as she cries. For a long time, we simply hold each other. Until her sobs quiet to hiccups and her breathing eventually evens into the same rhythm as my own.

"I missed you so much," I mumble against her shoulder. "When you stopped coming home, I actually wondered if it was because you hated *me*."

Maura draws back sharply. "I could never hate you, mèi mei."

I huff out a laugh. "Yeah, well, I could never hate you, either." I take a deep breath. "Maura, I love every part of you. Nothing else has ever mattered but the fact that you're *you*. At the end of the day, you'll always be my big sister."

She wipes her tears away. "You're everything to me, Rei. Never forget that. By the way, why are you wearing my coat?"

I glance down. "Oops. I thought it was Aunt Min's."

She smiles and straightens the lapels. "Keep it. It suits you."

We lean against the railing, watching the waves rippling across the Hudson in companionable silence. Exactly halfway down the middle lies the border between New York and New Jersey, where no stardust falls—only the lights glowing from the other city across the river. They brighten the windows of people's homes and illuminate the streets down below, just like they're supposed to.

The lights remind me of the Token and its incredible power. I've always thought of this city like a phoenix, dying with the fiery end of day and rising from the ashes come dawn. But within seconds, the Token somehow lit up all of Times Square and its neighboring blocks.

"What happened back there?" I ask. "When Storm tried to grab the Token?"

Maura nods. "That was some weird shit."

I stifle a laugh. I reach up to touch Mom's necklace, only to remember that it's gone. "Did you know that my dad stole the Token from the Archives?"

Maura's eyebrows skyrocket. "He *what*?"

"At least, Storm said he did. And I think she's right. He must have split it into two parts to obstruct the true extent of its power. He returned one half of it to the Archives. Then he brought the other half to a jeweler or something to turn it into a talisman, where it could stay hidden in plain sight. All along, the missing Artifact was never actually *missing*—it was incomplete." I bite my lip. "I just wish I knew where it went."

"Be glad that Storm couldn't get her hands on it."

I close my eyes, trying to sort out my thoughts. "Earlier you said that if it wasn't for Uncle Elliot, you wouldn't have become a Halfling. What did he have to do with it?"

She averts her eyes. "Only Mom knows about it, and I almost wish she didn't."

"Will you tell me?"

For a long minute, my sister goes very quiet.

"Those first two years felt like a never-ending nightmare," she murmurs at last. "Most of it has faded from my memory, but I still remember a few bits and pieces—like the nightfall before I came back. I remember emerging out in the street in front of our old apartment. You know, the old brownstone with the stained glass you lived in with my parents while I was gone, before Mom moved into the Manor permanently."

She takes a deep breath.

"I remember wandering the neighborhood during nightfall. I was so desperate. So hungry. Somehow, I found my way there. Home. And somehow, Dad . . . *recognized* me."

My chest tightens. "How?"

"To this day, I wish I knew. Like I said, I can't recall much else. Whatever it was, it was *human* enough to make him realize that I was his daughter." Each word she forces out sounds like a battle she's struggling not to lose. "I think I blacked out after that. When I woke up, I was covered in blood. Not mine. And I was no longer a Deathling. Dad was nowhere to be seen. It took me weeks to realize that it was because I had . . . had—"

My sister chokes on her grief, so raw that she can only be reliving the memory at this very moment.

"I devoured him."

I cover my mouth with one hand, not trusting myself to speak. But she's not done yet.

"You know what the strangest thing is, though? I'd devoured other humans before—whether I wanted to or not. It was the only way for me to survive. But none of them turned me back into a human."

I avoid envisioning the things my sister must have done as a Deathling. "What made that time different?"

"I'm not certain. But I have a theory. People who fall victim to Deathlings never want to be devoured, of course. Except that night when Dad found me, I was so weak and malnourished that I couldn't even stand anymore, much less attack him. He knew I was dying. And so he gave himself up to me. He sacrificed his own life so I could live." Her tears spatter onto the railing. The sorrow in her voice bites deep as a bullet into my chest. "I believe that it was his final act of humanity that ultimately restored my own."

Slowly, the gravity of her proclamation sinks in. I slip my arm around her and rest my head on her shoulder.

I don't know what else to do except be there for her.

But I feel her silent gratitude in the slight, sad smile on her lips. The way she leans into me and releases the breath from her lungs in one long sigh—like she's finally free.

"So what are you going to do now, mèi mei?" she asks me after a long while.

"I don't know," I admit.

"I didn't mean to make your life more complicated than it already is," she adds, sounding genuinely apologetic. "You've still got so much ahead of you. But you're allowed to take whatever time you need. To think, and to rest, too. You don't have to decide anything. Not yet. Not tonight."

I gaze out at the water's reflection of a city illuminated by stardust and simply allow myself to imagine what could be.

"Not tonight," I agree.

CHAPTER FIFTY-SIX

I spend the next day at Aunt Minyi's bedside, dozing in and out of slumber myself as I wait for her to wake up. If only stardust could do the work for her, but the one medicine it cannot replace is rest.

While I'd stay next to her for as long as it takes for her to recover fully, when Zaza shows up at the door with her mouth set in a familiar hard line of determination, I know better than to put up a fight.

One hour later, I'm sucking tapioca pearls out of my extra-large mango milk tea and flipping through a stack of handcrafted leather notebooks. Sunlight streams through the windows of Chelsea's indoor market, the maze of stalls bustling with the typical lunchtime rush.

"Oh, this is too cute," Zaza exclaims, plucking a necklace from the jewelry rack and holding it up for me to see. I pause my search and wander across the walkway of the market to see the long gold chain in her hand. A strawberry shortcake charm adorns the end.

I smile, thinking inevitably of Boba. "Definitely cute. Just not really my style."

"Oh, come on. Babe, what do you think?"

Bomani's head pops up over a rack of vintage jeans at the vendor to the left. He grins and flashes us a thumbs-up. "It's perfect for you, babe," he calls back.

Zaza rolls her eyes. "For Rei."

"Oh." He eyes my outfit up and down. Black turtleneck, black distressed jeans, black chunky military boots, and Maura's trench coat. I haven't gotten a replacement for my mav coat yet, but during the day this one does the job just fine.

Besides, drawing attention to my identity is the last thing I want to do with Storm still on the loose. For all I know, she still thinks I have the Token. I may be under the Syndicate's protection, but I still have to resist the urge to listen every few seconds for the telltale click of her heels.

Necklace in hand, I strike a pose for Bomani. "Well?"

"Uh, no comment."

"Excuse me," a voice pipes up from behind me. "You're Rei Reynolds, right?"

I turn to find a young boy with curly brown hair staring up at me with a napkin and pen in hand. His mother hovers nearby, smiling pleasantly.

"I watched you in the Tournament. You were *so* cool, especially on the obstacle course! Could I please get your autograph?"

"Of course," I say, flattered by his bright-eyed enthusiasm.

When I hand him back the napkin, he grabs my arm and leans forward to whisper. "Is it true?"

I'm too startled to react. "What?"

The gleam in his eyes turns fanatical. "The rumors. That you brought back the light at nightfall. That you're going to bring the light back to all of us and break nightfall for good. That's what they call you," he whispers. *"Nightbreaker."*

A shiver passes through me. "I don't—"

"Whoa, whoa," interrupts a loud voice. Bomani takes the kid by the wrists and pries him off me. "Give her some space."

Zaza appears by my side. She puts her arms around my shoulders and guides me to the exit. I hear the boy calling after me, demanding, but I'm too shaken to answer. Other people stare as we pass.

"My brother lives near Times Square," one woman murmurs to her friend. "He told me he saw the light, too."

"Well?" her friend says, casting me a look. "Is it true or not?"

"As if one girl has the power to change the entire city."

"Why shouldn't she?"

"Just keep walking," Zaza mutters into my ear.

We escape the market and burst out into the sunshine, only to be confronted by a parade of protesters marching down the middle of the street. My first instinct is to dismiss them as the usual crowd of disbelievers, but something is different this time.

I read the closest signs aloud. "*We the People want the Truth. Transparency or Tyranny? Your move, Syndicate.* What the hell is that supposed to mean?"

"I think some people were upset when the Syndicate canceled the Tournament without any explanation," Zaza replies. "The funding comes from our tax dollars and donations, after all. Don't take it personally."

Once Bomani catches up to us, we take a detour through an alleyway. Still troubled by the protesters, I don't even hear Zaza's question until she elbows me in the side. "Huh?"

"I said," she repeats in an overly casual tone. "Any word from Kieran yet?"

My eye twitches. "Nope. Which is totally fine."

At that moment, my back pocket buzzes. I fumble with my bubble tea, nearly dropping it in my haste to withdraw my phone. I scan the screen.

Big Italy Pizza

Get 10% off any SAUSAGE PIZZA

this Tuesday at Big Italy Pizza!

I flush and hide my phone from Zaza, but she sees anyway.

"His phone is probably just dead or something," she reassures me. "Or broken. Or lost. Or maybe he's just sleeping in."

"I said it's fine. I really couldn't care less."

My phone buzzes again. I purposely make a big show of checking it as unhurriedly as possible.

asshat

Hey. We need to talk.

My stomach flips. "It's Kieran."

"What? Let me see!" Zaza headbutts her way in front of my phone screen as another message pops up.

Are you available tomorrow?

Zaza practically vibrates with excitement. "See? I told you he was thinking about you. Say yes. You know you want to."

I bite my lip and type out my answer.

I could be.

Could I take you out to lunch? On me, of course.

I made a 1pm reservation at Remy's.

"Oh my god," Zaza squeals. "He's taking you to *Remy's*? That place is like, the hottest restaurant in the city."

"And the most expensive," I say with a frown. Back when we were dating, we never really went to fancy restaurants, and certainly nothing near Remy's caliber. "He must have gotten paid in diamonds during his internship with Aunt Minyi."

"Well, what are you going to tell him?" Zaza demands.

"I don't know," I mutter, slightly nauseous from the tumult of emotions swirling inside my stomach. We haven't seen or spoken a word to each other since I told him to go to hell and he drove off with Everly and left me in Times Square to deal with Storm. I want to ask Zaza for an exact rundown of last night's events, but I have no doubt that she'll try to cast him in a better light—both because she wants us to get back together and because she's just nice like that. I don't want her to have to make any excuses or apologies on his behalf. I want to hear them from his own mouth.

Zaza brushes my arm. "Give him a shot. He still cares about you."

"I don't know," I say again.

My best friend only smiles sadly and squeezes my hand.

"Even the best of us make mistakes, Rei. As my abuela used to say, our world is filled with too much hate to push away those brave enough to ask us for one more chance. And besides, he's not asking for your forgiveness, only lunch. At a very, very nice restaurant."

"And he's paying," Bomani chimes in helpfully.

I sigh through my nose and look back at my screen.

Fine. See you then.

Wonderful. It's a date.

✴

At five minutes to one, Declan pulls the car up to the curb of Remy's. He opens the passenger door as I check my lipstick in a pocket mirror one last time. No amount of concealer can erase the dark circles beneath my eyes. I step onto the sidewalk in my stilettos and straighten out my dress beneath my coat.

"You look ravishing, Miss Reynolds."

I snort. "You're too kind, Declan."

"Have a lovely lunch. Don't forget what I said about that boy."

"That you would—and I quote—beat the living shitsticks out of him if he tried anything funny? Not to worry. I have you on speed dial."

"Very good. And I've already taken care of that mysterious delivery of ten gallons of banana pudding to Rector Street station."

I give him a peck on the cheek. "Thank you, Declan. For always being there for me, especially when you didn't have to be."

He bows, the picture of gentlemanly grace, the mischief in his eyes twinkling as brightly as ever. "It has and always will be my privilege, Miss Reynolds."

Bundled up against the chill, I hurry into the gleaming silver chrome foyer of the restaurant. Sculptures and art fixtures deck the entrance area, crafted entirely from metal like a luxurious junkyard. Beyond a screen of platinum filigree drift the quiet murmur of overlapping conversation and live classical piano.

My heels clack against the spotless marble floor as I'm led past the main dining area to a private room. The host slides the door open to reveal the crimson, candlelit interior. Streaks of blue and purple branch out along the velour walls, mimicking the veins inside the chamber of a heart.

The door *snicks* shut behind me. The outside chatter and music cut off abruptly, plunging the room into silence. I'm left to frown at the two empty chairs.

Kieran is nowhere to be seen.

However, it's not his absence that confuses me—it's the open bottle of champagne. And the half-filled flute abandoned on the far side of the table beside two untouched menus. Figuring that he must be using the restroom, I take the seat with the empty glass and start rehearsing how I plan to greet him when he returns.

A flicker of movement in my peripheral vision catches my attention. I glance up across the table.

I freeze.

The bottle is levitating midair.

"Champagne?" asks a disembodied voice.

I forget how to do anything but gape.

The bottle floats across the table to my glass and tips over anyway. Bubbly golden liquid froths to the top. As the bottle floats back down, the air across the table shimmers like a mirage in the desert.

The darkness ripples outward. From it, in the chair opposite to me, materializes a man dressed in an exquisite navy tuxedo. The top two buttons of his silk dress shirt are undone, revealing an artful hint of collarbone. Coupled with the flickering candlelight, his earthen skin drinks in the reflection of the red walls like the fiery glow of charcoal smoldering in flames.

The Phantom places the ivory half mask in his lap. "So glad you could join me today, Miss Reynolds."

"What are you doing here?" I exclaim, breathless in bewilderment.

His smile could soften even the stoniest of hearts. "I just wanted to check in. To see how you've been faring."

My eyebrows raise. "Me? I . . . Where's Kieran?"

"Ouch," he says, clutching his heart with a wounded expression. "Do you so despise my company, my lady?"

I roll my eyes. "It's just that Kieran texted me earlier asking me to lunch. He never said anything about you being here."

"I won't take up too much of your valuable time," he promises. "I was hoping to have a word with you, that's all. Would that be admissible?"

"You didn't have to go to the trouble of coming all this way. You could have just called me or popped by the Manor."

"The Manor is full of ears and eyes and, most of all, mouths that like to talk. I didn't want to risk it," Valentine replies, swirling the contents of his glass. "Besides," he adds with a playful glint in his eye, "phones are much too easy to hijack these days. In any case, I understand that you made contact with Sabrina Storm the other night."

A vague sense of unease settles into my stomach. "How'd you know? I haven't turned in my report to the masters yet. Did Kieran tell you?"

He tops up his glass. "I was in the area, naturally."

A loaded silence stretches out between us. I stare at him, then the bottle of champagne, then his mask resting on the table.

Then it strikes me.

"Wait a second," I say. "When Storm tried to grab the Token and it floated away . . . that was *you*! She thought I was the one messing with her, but it was you riling her up all along!"

He shrugs. "I certainly wasn't about to let her get her filthy claws on such a treasured New York City heirloom. No doubt she would have used its power to cause irreversible damage and harm to our dear city. I imagine she didn't mention any of that, of course."

"She just talked about putting an end to the corrupt, evil ways of the Syndicate."

Valentine throws his head back with an uproarious laugh. It's the kind of delighted, infectious sound that leaves you helplessly chuckling along with him without quite knowing why. He shakes his head and shoots me a boyish grin. "I bet she really sold it to you."

I fake a sip of champagne. "Absolutely. So it's true that she's a hell-bringer?"

"Not anymore."

"She told me a wild story from about six years ago. You know what I'm talking about, don't you? The one where her gear malfunctioned when she was ambushed by nightfangs."

Valentine leans back in his chair. "So I've heard."

"And then after she miraculously survived even though she should've been torn to pieces, the Directors put her in charge of Project Forsaken. Was that before or after they realized what had happened to her?"

"After, of course." It takes him a second to realize his mistake and backtrack. "Storm was always a devoted and valuable asset to the Directors. They were already searching for someone to lead the project—"

"And who better to fill the position than an actual Halfling?" I smile and raise my glass. "Sure, the Directors' attempt to neutralize her after she uncovered some sensitive intel didn't go exactly to plan, but they ended up with one of their best strikers becoming a Halfling herself. Serendipity is a marvelous thing, don't you agree?"

He hesitates before raising his in turn. "Indeed."

"Honestly, I don't blame the Directors. It makes perfect sense to make one of your best and most loyal strikers the head of a project so classified that not even masters were permitted to know about it. How could they have guessed she would go rogue? It's not their fault that she discovered their plot to assassinate her." And by then, it was too late to stop her. She had already taken full control of the project.

"Right," he says, regarding me warily. "So you agree with their methods?"

"I never said that." I set my glass down. "Nick—I can call you Nick, right? The Directors already knew that Deathlings were once New Yorkers. But they sent us out to kill them anyway."

Nick goes silent. He refuses to meet my gaze.

"Why?" I ask, clenching my fists in my lap. "Why didn't they just tell us?"

"I don't know," he admits quietly. "But now that you do know this terrible secret, what do you plan to do the next time a Deathling attacks you? Surely you don't intend to lie on the ground and let it devour you out of righteousness. Wouldn't it be kinder to put it out of its misery?"

"You told us we should be working to protect. Not to kill. If Deathlings were once people, we can't say we're protecting humanity by killing them, either."

Valentine folds his hands on the table and gazes at me. "Then what do you say we ought to do, Miss Reynolds?"

I waver. I think of Bea, and every other citizen who has fallen victim to rules—or lack thereof—that I can't even begin to imagine how to reform. I know it's not simple. Like so many others, I wasn't trained to govern, but to kill.

"Well, every striker deserves to know the truth," I say at last. "And scholar, too."

"The Directors have forbidden it."

"But what if we could figure out a way to turn Deathlings back into humans? We could eliminate their existence without any bloodshed," I argue. "Our scholars should be working around the clock on *that*, not more efficient ways to hunt Deathlings. Isn't that why the Directors created Project Forsaken in the first place?"

"Between you and me, Miss Reynolds, there are secrets restricted even from myself. But here's something we both know perfectly well: *nobody* defies the word of the Directors."

I look him dead in the eye. "And if I decide to anyway?"

He smiles, but there is nothing charming about it this time. "Then it might be the last thing you ever do."

The flatness of his tone makes the hairs on the back of my neck stand on end. I fake another sip. "Death threats. Classy."

"Please don't take it personally. I'm merely trying to give you the best advice."

"Which is to keep my trap shut."

"Exactly. I would just hate for you to end up like the late Miss Park."

I freeze.

"I know it all seems quite grim and worrisome," Nick says with a comforting smile, "but you should trust the Directors. They know what they're doing."

"I'd like my Token back," I grit out.

"I don't have it anymore."

"You mean you already gave it up to the Directors."

He drains the rest of his champagne and pushes himself away from the table. "I know it may not seem like it right now, but I'm on your side. Trust me."

"If you were on my side," I growl, struggling to resist the overwhelming temptation to throw my champagne flute straight in his face, "you wouldn't have taken the Token from me in the first place."

"It's not like I had much of a choice," he says. "If you hadn't figured out half of it was missing and assembled the two pieces, it would still be yours."

"My bad. I guess I shouldn't have gone to Times Square either to *save Master Minyi.*"

Valentine rises to his feet and casts me a sideways look. "To be fair, I did try to stop you. Or rather, your friend did."

My blood runs cold. "What did you just say?"

"We suspected it was Storm who had written the note to you," he explains, "but we had no idea what her endgame might be. Especially in case she tried to turn you into a Deathling—which she did—I was assigned to stop you from going."

Zaza's tear-filled voice fills my head. *I'm so sorry, Rei. He didn't want you to go. He made me do it, drugging you. You weren't supposed to wake up until the morning after everything was over.*

"Kieran wasn't the one who drugged me," I whisper. "It was you."

Valentine heads for the door. "She was very sweet, very understanding of the whole situation. I hope you won't hold on to any resentment toward her. Of course, you went to Times Square anyway, but it all worked out well enough in the end. Most importantly, the Directors took notice of you. Overall, they were very pleased with how you handled the situation." He shoots me a wink over his shoulder. "Play your cards right, Miss Reynolds, and you'll be a master in no time. The Financial District needs a new one, after all."

Everything else fades—the table, the lights, even the Phantom himself. All I can see are the walls, red as rage.

I stand up suddenly. "Hey, Nick? I've changed my mind."

He pauses mid-step upon the threshold, one hand on the door handle. He glances at me over his shoulder, one eyebrow raised in expectation.

"I know I said that we should stop hunting Deathlings for the sake of killing them, but in case you ever become a Halfling . . ." I send him my sweetest smile. "I promise I'll be the one to put a bullet through your skull."

His dark, unforgiving eyes regard me for a long moment, his mask dangling at his side. Although it was originally a theater prop meant to hide a grotesque, physical deformity onstage, it seems the Mask has been concealing something far more monstrous all along.

"A word to the wise, Miss Reynolds. Wear your heart in the open, and your enemies will know exactly how to rip it out. You never run out of enemies in a profession like this, but your heart? You've only got one, so keep it close."

He steps out of the door, only to pop his head back inside a moment later, his expression all dimples and cheer. "By the way, feel free to order whatever you'd like from the menu. The bill's already been taken care of . . . courtesy of the Directors."

The door slides shut, leaving his words hanging forebodingly in his wake. I reach for my champagne flute, hating how my fingers quiver ever so slightly. Gripping the stem until my knuckles go white, I lift it to my lips and drain it dry.

Perhaps I should feel dread. The Directors have their eyes on my back. My Artifact is gone. Storm could be waiting for me around any corner.

And I can't stop hunting Deathlings without others suspecting I have a secret that could topple the Syndicate forever.

A secret that I don't want to keep.

But maybe there's another way. After all, if Storm managed to hijack Project Forsaken right beneath the Directors' noses, who knows what someone with a little power could get away with?

Or someone with a lot of power—like a master.

The Financial District needs a new one, after all. The Phantom's words haunt me.

The door opens yet again. Thinking Valentine is back, I snap. "What do you wa—"

My voice falters.

"Sorry I'm late," says Kieran as he breezes into the room. He unbuttons his mav coat with one hand while pulling out the chair Valentine occupied minutes ago with the other. He runs a hand through his carefully styled hair and sends me an oblivious, almost shy smile. "The bus driver was like ninety-nine years old."

"What the hell?"

"I know, right? I mean, good on her, but is that legal?"

"No, I meant . . ." I'd arrived at the conclusion that lunch with Kieran had just been a ruse set up by Valentine all along. "Honestly, I wasn't expecting you to actually show up."

Kieran looks taken aback. "I was only a few minutes late. Your text said one thirty, didn't it?"

"*My* text?"

He raises an eyebrow at me. "Yeah, the one you sent me this morning inviting me to lunch? I was about to ask if we could meet up, but you beat me to it." For the first time, he notices the half-empty bottle of champagne on the table. He gapes. "Holy—you didn't drink this all on your own, did you?"

My mind reels. I recall the playful glint in Valentine's eye. *Phones are much too easy to hijack these days.*

He duped both of us. I grind my teeth. A true master—or should I say maverick—of deception, through and through.

"Rei?" Kieran prompts after a beat. "You good? What were you talking about in Times Square about getting drugged?"

"It was just a misunderstanding," I say distantly. I glance up to find him frowning deeply at me. "Sorry, I just have a lot on my mind. I'm fine now. Really."

"I can only imagine. But hey, I'm here for you whenever you need me." He shoots me a crooked smile. "Even if that means never."

Something stirs in my chest. He has his secrets—but now I have mine. They're ours to tell. Maybe, in time, we will. If I can't trust anyone completely anymore—not even him—at least I can trust that he'll always have my back. Besides, if competing against Kieran in the Tournament taught me anything, it was that we're better off as a team after all.

And for once, I think I'm going to need one.

I pick up one of the menus. "Hey, Kieran."

"Yeah?"

"You hungry?"

"Starving, actually." He glances at the menu and winces. "Uh, on second thought—"

"What do you say we order absolutely everything off this menu?" I send him a wicked little grin. "This one's on me."

ACKNOWLEDGMENTS

Nightbreaker is my love letter to Manhattan. Here is my love letter to the people who made it possible:

My everlasting thanks to my team at Viking and Penguin Teen—my production editors, Krista Ahlberg and Sola Akinlana; managing editor Gaby Corzo; Kristin Boyle and Anabeth Bostrup for cover and interior design; Felicity Vallence, Shannon Spann, and James Akinaka at digital marketing; my publicist, Lizzie Goodell; and Tamar Brazis. To AZ Hackett, Sarah Liu, and Maddy Newquist, and especially my ingenious editor, Jenny Bak, for not only championing this book but also whipping it into Tournament-ready shape.

Holly Root, my literary agent and real-life superhero. How? How do you do everything? And so good?! Like, damn. And Alyssa—I bow down to you both.

Sophie Zixia Licostie. Justin Hsieh. Emma Meinrenken. Ariel. Jade. My eagle-eyed beta readers, thank you for your incredibly insightful suggestions and detailed critiques that would make Master Minyi proud. Thanks especially to Madison, for never failing to be first in line to read my work even in its most incoherent state, and for making me the happiest author every time you blow up my phone at 2:00 a.m. with your enthusiastic/enraged Google Docs comments. You're a real one.

My deep appreciation to artist Uliks Gryka, the real-life creator of the Sisyphus Stones, for giving me permission to use your work as my muse and for being an extremely cool dude in general. And to Billy Mitchell at the Apollo for patiently and generously answering all of my weirdly specific questions about the lighting booth and staging an ambush inside the theater. Cheers for not calling the cops on me.

I am honored to have the guidance and support of the true masters of my world: Holly Black for always being there to give me the wisest of wisdoms and for believing in this book even when it was a single messy chapter. V. E. Schwab for your unwavering encouragement and passion. My momma, Nic Stone, for being my #1 and my motivation to get shit done. My 姐姐, Amélie Wen Zhao, for loving Nightbreaker long before it had a title. Jackie Parker for hyping me up since the day I had the privilege of meeting you. Manny Ax for always having faith in and enthusiasm for my writing and piano career. Peter Oundjian and Nadine Eliane for ALL of your love and for buying way more copies of my book than you needed to on my launch day—I'll never forget that! And to Rebecca Kuang, Chloe Gong, Xiran Jay Zhao, Axie Oh, Samantha Shannon, and Naomi Novik for supporting me during the final push to the finish line.

To my professor Derek Green. You taught me how to write. So. Much. Better. Without you, Kieran and Rei would never have been exes. Can you imagine?!

To Jags, my dear friend and dealer (of rare and UK special book editions). Eternally grateful for your kindness and care.

Thank you to Cristi Balenescu for your artistry and for bringing both the world of Nightbreaker and Rei to life on this cover.

Yuen Ning, Laura, Alice, and Jona, my ride or dies. Tony, Cam, Hanah, Duncan, Ryan, Juan (my inspo for Zaza), and Emma (again). I love you guys more than Deathlings love cake. Possibly more than even I love cake, which is really saying a lot. Thanks to Jacob for the cookies. And huge, huge props to David Stanley for the last-minute photo shoot!

Mum and Dad, I'm indebted to you for moving us to NYC so I could study piano at Juilliard. You may not have known about my secret escapades and late-night shenanigans outside the practice rooms, but this book would have been tremendously boring without them, so we'll call it a win?

To my boys: Kevin and my son, Potato (the puppy. That's right y'all, I FINALLY GOT A DOG). Po, even when you climb all over my keyboard with your tiny paws and accidentally/purposely delete all my documents, your cuteness is unparalleled. Kevin, I guess you're pretty cute, too. Thanks for sticking by me through it all. I love you both very nearly almost equally.

And finally, my readers . . . whether you have no idea who I am or you've been on this journey with me from the Shadow Frost trilogy, this one is very much for you. I hope it was fun. With all my heart, thank you for every single thing that you do. Until next time . . . AKA the SEQUEL (distant evil laughter).